MW01129619

End of Summer

Seasons of Man
Book one

S.M. Anderson

This book is a work of fiction. Names, characters, places and incidents are either the product of the author's imagination or are used fictitiously.

End of Summer
Seasons of Man: Book one

First Edition

Other Books by S.M Anderson

The Eden Chronicles:
Book 1 - A Bright Shore
Book 2 - Come and Take It
Book 3 - forthcoming

Seasons of Man:
Book 1 - End of Summer
Book 2 - forthcoming

Chapter 1

"These little shits are going to end up killing us."

Dr. Janine Folkman had worked long enough with her colleague and friend, Dr. Seth Maygood, to know that the six-foot-three PhD across the counter from her was not referring to the deadly strands of viral DNA he was looking at on his monitor. A portion of the 4K screen was visible to her as well, and showed the output of the electron scanning microscope in the next room.

"They aren't that bad, Seth." Though, when she stopped to think about it, she suspected this year's crop of interns probably were. They were all PhD candidates, and no doubt as a group, less than amused, delighted, or entertained with the fact that they'd been assigned to one Dr. Seth Maygood for the summer.

In this day and age, every high-tech industry involved in R&D, inside and out of government, had to fight for the best candidates with a breadbasket of amusement, delight, and entertainment. The Virologic Research Center, housed in a level 4 containment facility, 150 feet below the surface of Aberdeen Proving Grounds in rural Maryland had very little to offer in the way of benefits this current generation of students held as basic human rights.

Under Seth's mentorship, she knew there would be zero amusement, and even less entertainment for his interns. Any delight the PhD. Candidates experienced, had best result from having learned something from the legend himself, or simply by working another day with the world's most dangerous pathogens and living to come back the next day.

"The hell they aren't." Seth grumbled and sat back in his chair and swiveled his stool to face her directly.

"You know the skinny surfer kid? from Berkeley? Max? The one with section of PVC pipe in his ear lobe, with the two last names?

"Yes," she nodded, doing her best not to laugh. "Dodson-Kerry." She wasn't a fan of the young man either, but she had always figured the crusty old farts that had mentored her through her field work had probably thought she'd been a pain in the ass as well.

"I lit into him this morning." Seth held up a massive hand and waggled it back and forth, "hard."

"What he'd do?"

"He was complaining the suit gloves made his hands all sweaty and wrinkled. I said something to the effect that it went with the job, and he came back with suggesting this new lotion and how he had some and could bring it in for us to try."

"He said *that*? To you?"

Seth grinned back at her, a hint of an apology playing on his face. He could have played professional football coming out of the University of Washington, but science and biology had been his calling. Seth, in his late fifties, still looked as if he could dead-lift a house.

"Yep," Seth laughed. "I'd credit his guts, but I think he's too stupid to realize what he was saying. He just wanted to argue about it."

"And you counseled him?"

Seth had a smile playing at the corners of his mouth, "I did."

"Seth? I'm going to hear about it anyway."

Seth rubbed his face and looked back at her. "I printed up a copy of the safety protocols, specifically the one that has three signature blocks at the bottom for acceptance, understanding, and agreement. I held the thing up in front of his face and quoted the section on the prohibition of foreign substances introduced to the containment suits, particularly gloves. I then went over each of the three signature blocks and very politely asked which one he ignored or did not understand. I may have raised my voice a little."

Seth paused a moment and shrugged in what may have been an apology. "Sooo, when Burkett tells you to counsel me... you can tell him we've already had a chat."

Unbelievable, she thought. Lotion inside the gloves? They should let the kid go. The young man had already demonstrated that he thought the sanitization procedures coming out of the autoclave between the clean room and the containment area was in his own words... "overkill." She silently wondered if they even *could* let him go. Berkeley had supplied a good number of interns over the years and that particular source pool of interns would disappear overnight if they dismissed Maxwell something-something.

"He get the message?"

Seth grinned a little. "Oh yeah, he got the message. Said he felt threatened." Seth folded his hands in his lap and smiled like a little kid who'd just found where his Mom had been hiding the cookies. "He said, he'd report me for workplace harassment... if I wasn't African American."

Janine, sucked in a breath and pulled her hands in front of her face. "Wait a minute! You're black?"

Seth looked down at his own hands and smiled up at her over the tops of his reading glasses. "Evidence would seem to indicate that I am. I'd appreciate it, if you'd keep it between us."

"And you reacted to this in your usual calm demeanor?"

"Actually, Janine, it calmed me down. I was trying not to laugh. I did take a moment to read him and the rest of the 'me generation' in on the fact that the bugs we work with absolutely do not give a shit that my ancestors came from Africa. What they do like are suit gloves that have been potentially compromised by a petroleum-based hand lotion."

"Wait," her hand shot out between them. "Had he actually used the lotion? Or..."

"Said he hadn't, and I watched them all scrub down in the outflow locker room."

"I'm going to talk to Burkett in the am," she shook her head. "We need to let him go, set an example."

"You have my vote," Seth shook his head, "but we won't. You know we won't. It would kill our pipeline."

Three days later...

The problem with lotions used in a confined space of high heat and humidity, for example, inside a pair of latex gloves, was that small molecules of talcum intrinsic to the gloves themselves could become sheathed in a shell of long-chain carbon molecules, aka petroleum by-product. This made the enwrapped molecules heavier, and more to the point, 'stickier' in the chemical sense of the word. The fact that the lotion was unscented, therefore making its user, Max something-something, comfortable in thinking he wouldn't get caught, did not affect the basic chemistry involved.

Max had not in fact carried out any pathogens on his gloves. One of his boots though had picked up several molecules of the now sheathed talcum powder. The molecules, some of which had fallen to the floor in the prep room had been walked on. The pneumatic pressures created by simply walking, had pulled up a small sample, deep into the treads of the boot's sole. At the end of the day, the boots weren't incinerated like everything else, but they were sprayed down with an alcohol-based solution and then bathed in UV light for the night until they were ready for use the next day. The alcohol wash missed a couple of the sheathed molecules in question, and the UV light did nothing but partially dry out the lotion derived carbon shell.

Max from Berkeley was wearing the same boots, with the 'sticky' molecules still in the tread the next day, when his colleague, Brittany from University of Wisconsin removed a test tube holding something very nasty from a centrifuge. When she removed the rubber stopper, unseen by anyone, a small droplet flew through the air and came to rest on the floor of the lab next to Max's boot. It was nearly a minute later before the droplet was stepped on and its fluid was hydro-dynamically pushed up into the treads of his boot.

Infused with the suspension liquid, the long chain carbon shield around the now 'infected' talcum molecules became whole once more, cocooning a mutated version of CBR-1d safely within its carbon-based shell.

Still, all could have been well had Max something-something not had such an aversion to the cold tile floors of the wash-down locker room. He kept his boots on till the last possible moment, having already removed his gloves. The gloves were for him, the worst part of the job; besides Dr. Mayhew that is. The guy may have been a legend in the virology community, but he needed to chill. He pulled the boots off, sitting and crossing his foot on his opposite knee. His hands didn't pick up the passenger molecules, but the handwoven friendship bracelet his girlfriend had made for him, did.

The mood inside the locker room once they were all dressed was nearly euphoric. It was 1:45 pm on a Friday, and they were getting out early. Monday was Labor Day, and they were all excited about the three-day weekend.

"Anybody up for Starbucks?" Max almost shouted, "before we hit the beach?"

"Gaawd yes," Brittany breathed. "You'd think they'd have a decent Keurig or something other than that antique brewer thing in the break room, "but nooooo..."

The Ocean City beaches weren't that far away, and it promised to be a killer weekend before they all had to be back here on Tuesday. It was the end of summer.

*

Thursday, September 9

The news commentator on the wall of his office's flat screen was far too happy with himself for Seth's taste. The useful idiot with the quaffed hair was just doing his job, but Seth couldn't get past the fact he knew this 'breaking story' was a final chapter.

"We are still actively tracking the reports that have been forthcoming from local hospitals on the east coast and from government officials at the CDC regarding the serious illness that some are calling the Chesapeake Flu. We now have reports of several cases in Europe and Latin America to go along with the nearly three dozen cases reported in the

US. In all reported cases, the sick remain in serious condition and we have unsubstantiated reports of several deaths.

The CDC, whose director will be giving a press conference in a few minutes, has so far reported that the illness is not the dreaded bird flu, but that it has similarities to the pneumonic plague that reared its head in Madagascar and parts of south east Africa in the last few years. That 2018 outbreak in Africa resulted in the deaths of nearly a thousand people before burning itself out, so we are of course watching this story closely. We'll have an update following the CDC press conference. Stay tuned to CNB for all the latest."

Seth held up the bottle of Talisker and waggled it in question at Janine's almost empty glass. They'd both already had one. Given the number of hours it had been since they'd slept, the scotch was either a very good idea or like most things Seth could think of right now, it just didn't matter. Nothing did.

Janine shook her head. "There's got to be something ..."

"There isn't," he said as he refilled his own glass, "and you know it." He held his glass up to the light coming through his office window. For a moment, one of the ice cubes and the side of the glass worked in prismatic concert to send a rainbow through the amber liquor. A small miracle of the type that had gotten him so interested in science as a kid, right up there with the tadpoles he'd caught in the local stream and observed in a bowl his mother had made him keep in the bathroom. More of the type of shit that just didn't matter anymore.

"This mutation is airborne, with a slow symptomatic presentation, as much as a week or ten days. There are millions, if not tens of millions of infected right now.

Janine looked at him for a moment like she wanted to argue the point. Hell, he prayed that someone would prove them wrong. Instead, she gave a short nod of acceptance and tossed back the remainder of her scotch.

"Do you think Paul will be honest with them?" Janine asked.

He shook his head. Paul Simone, a friend to both of them was head of the CDC and chair holder at the United Nation's World Health Organization (WHO). He was a man of high character and would no doubt want to be honest with people, but he'd be under strict orders just like the two of them were. The two-armed men in dark suits, flanking his doorway in the hallway, emphasized that.

"He can't, the panic would..."

Would what? End up killing some of the perhaps five percent of the lucky, or were they unlucky? bastards that would prove to be naturally immune in another one of those neat little evolutionary tricks that nature so loved.

"It won't burn itself out..." Janine had just unknowingly agreed with him.

This particular mutation of the pneumonic plague, known in their circles as CBR-2a, had hit the lottery in its humanity killing permutation. Often times the most virulent viruses killed quickly. Quick enough to effectively stop the spread of the outbreak, which if luck held, would not be airborne but spread through liquids; saliva, sweat, tears, or sex.

Right now, they were faced with a bug that did indeed kill quickly, but only after the symptoms manifested themselves, which seemed to be taking somewhere between a week and ten days post infection. In that intervening period, the infected felt no symptoms. They did what people do; they traveled, went to work. They touched, they kissed, they coughed, sneezed, breathed, and laughed; their literal presence killing their fellow man in an invisible daisy chain.

"No, it won't." He agreed.

"What are you going to do?" Seth barely heard the question; he was wondering that himself.

"Seth? Why don't you come over for dinner tonight, it's just Jim and I. The kids won't get home until tomorrow."

He looked up at one his best friends. Janine and her husband had been there for him when his Carmen had gotten sick, through the chemo, through the quiet days that followed.

"Thanks, Janine," he shook his head. "All I can think about right now is the mountains I grew up around. I want to see the mountains again, before…"

… before the lining of my arteries and blood vessels are eaten away by a virus that escaped under my watch.

"Seth?"

"I'm fine, Janine," he stood and went around his desk to give her a hug. "Go home and see to your family. Give my best to Jim."

"You going to be all right?"

He wanted to laugh; the gallows humor was there walking the knife's edge. The other side of it was grief, pain, and guilt.

"No worse than anyone else," he laughed.

She smiled, wiped a tear off his cheek and then leaned in to kiss him in the same place.

He didn't envy her and the peace of her family as she walked out of his office. He was thankful he didn't have to go home and explain to Carmen that they were all going to die.

Chapter 2

"This doesn't sound good." Samantha's voice snapped him out of his thoughts. The television was on, the news channels had quickly fallen into the familiar pattern of just repeating the reports from other channels. They all knew they were at the frenzied edge of a big story, and didn't know shit. One thing was clear; they were all scared.

Jason's chin jerked once to the side. "It doesn't." Anything they were saying on television wasn't half as scary to him as the fact that the government had already announced that it was going to shutter its doors tomorrow, excepting essential personnel. Every public announcement hammered away at the need to minimize public contact and stay inside. Whatever it was, the bug was airborne and the government was doing its part in shutting its doors and keeping its people at home.

He was essential personnel. His whole office in the DoD was deemed essential. The war on terror wasn't going to take a break, bad flu-bug or not. He'd already scheduled leave for tomorrow so he could accompany Sam to her three-month prenatal appointment. The doctor's office had left an automated call earlier, canceling the appointment. No doubt, they were closed as well.

"You already took leave, don't go in tomorrow." Sam didn't make it sound like a suggestion.

"I won't." He'd already decided that much.

The news program switched over to a briefing room, an empty podium in front of a plain black curtain emblazoned with the initials CDC. The US flag stood off to the side, next to a group of three or four people awaiting the speaker. Jason recognized the form of theater. The group standing behind the speaker would add authority and gravitas to whatever the speaker said. The camera backed off for a moment as it refocused to catch the speaker approaching the podium. As it did, it showed the press room two-thirds empty. Jason's blood ran cold. They'd been promising this briefing since the night before, it was all any of the channels were talking about, and the room was nearly empty of reporters. Something was very wrong.

"I'm Paul Simone, Director of the CDC, and I come to you tonight in that capacity, as well as my position as the co-chair for the UN's Infectious Disease Center. In the interest of time and accuracy, I'm only going to report what we have confirmed at this time. My colleagues and associates around the world are of the unanimous opinion that we are facing a mutated version of the Ebola virus. At this time, we believe with a high degree of certainty that the virus is air borne, sharing communicability pathways more in line with the common cold, as opposed to previous versions of the virus which spread only through bodily fluids. To repeat, and to state this information as clearly as possible, this is a highly infectious, air born virus.

"Unfortunately, this particular mutation also has characteristics of some of the more common pneumonic versions of certain flu virus, in that it appears to have an extraordinary long incubation period. This means that any opportunity of containing the spread via quarantine procedures has most likely passed us by. In short, for the last week and a half, infected individuals who have felt fine, shown no symptoms, have travelled through international gateway airports, gone to work and lived their lives while carrying the virus.

The virus itself; what has been reported previously and what we are continuing to see are initial flu-like symptoms which quickly evolve into a secondary symptomatic track wherein it attacks the lining of blood vessels and arteries resulting in the internal hemorrhaging that we see with Ebola."

The speaker paused glancing at his notes. Jason could tell the CDC Director didn't like what he saw there.

"This is a pandemic level event. We are facing a prolonged incubation period, which means, given modern travel patterns, the virus is truly global at this point. Cases have been reported in every major city across the globe and many points in between.

"The health care system at the national level and medical care facilities at the local level are overwhelmed or soon will be. If you or your loved ones become ill, do not travel to a facility that in all likelihood will be unable to provide assistance. Minimize all contact with the infected and the public. The safest place for everyone right now is in your own home.

"We are working diligently towards a solution, a vaccination protocol, but at this moment those solutions have not yet been successful. There is no miracle cure that is being withheld or used selectively."

The CDC director paused in his speech and shuffled his notes, and wiped at his eyes.

"My... my own wife has contracted the virus. If there was something to be done for her right now, I would be doing it. Rest assured, the best minds on the planet are working this issue. I have time for a very few questions."

"Where does this virus come from? Do you have a name for it?"

"Nature produced it; we know that. Viruses mutate all the time, rarely does this have any affect, let alone a mutation so virulent as what we are seeing here. The first reported cases had all spent time at the Maryland or Delaware beaches. The name, Chesapeake Flu seems to have stuck."

"Is there any credence to earlier reports that this is an engineered virus and that it's part of a biological attack?"

"No, none whatsoever. This virus, minus its long incubation period, has been catalogued in the past. There are perhaps three national level labs in the world theoretically capable of doing what you are suggesting. I would add that all those countries, including our own, have reported breakouts in their urban centers. Any motive for something like this is frankly ludicrous."

"What sort of lethality are we potentially looking at here? And what kind of prognosis do those that have contracted it have?"

The CDC Director nodded at the question; he'd clearly been expecting it. "We have reports of over 3000 deaths from the early diagnosed, that's a global number. Many others remain in critical condition. As is usually the case with viral outbreaks, the elderly and the young are at particular risk. We are continuing to monitor the situation - we just don't have enough data at the moment to put out a credible statement of a prognosis. That said, this is an extremely virulent strain, and the precautions I laid out earlier should be taken to heart. Stay in your homes, minimize all contact with the public."

There were more raised hands but the CDC Director collected his notes. "That's all I've got time for at the moment. I'm scheduled for a conference call with colleagues in Europe and Asia. We will be back the moment we know more."

"You see that?" Samantha pointed at the television from her nest on the couch. "He's lying through his teeth."

Jason had seen it. He didn't have to have to be clinical psychologist like his wife to see the man's change in demeanor.

"This isn't good," he sat down on the couch, grabbing the one cushion that wasn't already being used. Sam's feet snaked into his lap immediately.

Samantha snorted to herself. "Dagman must be loving this."

Howard Dagman lived four houses down. Howard was a self-described prepper. Debbie, the man's wife, went along with the description with a smile and a good-natured roll of the eyes. Something like this; a global pandemic probably had the man crowing 'I told you so' from his rooftop.

"No doubt," he agreed, already wondering how many days of food they had on hand. It sure didn't sound like a trip to the store was good idea. Northern Virginia grocery stores were famous for the shelf emptying runs that would occur with even a hint of snow. Something like this? He imagined traffic jams, just trying to get into the parking lot at the shopping center.

The former Army Ranger in him was already thinking in terms of contingency planning. He'd always been friendly with Dagman, even if the guy did strike him as a little bit too gung-ho. Dagman had served in the Navy, as a Master Chief back around the first Gulf War, almost 30 years ago. Upon leaving the Navy soon after, he'd founded a company that had built some sort of fleet maintenance software. He wasn't sure what the company was, how big it had become, but one of the neighbors had told Sam that Howard had sold it for nearly a hundred million about five years ago. That had been long before he and Sam had moved into the upscale neighborhood when her medical practice took off.

Their neighborhood block parties, were usually replete with high level corporate types, doctors, lawyers, CFOs and the like. Jason as a former soldier, and current government contractor, didn't really fit in. They sure as hell wouldn't be living in this neighborhood if hadn't been for Sam's Doctor salary. Howard had latched onto him at those occasional gatherings like a long-lost friend. It had been clear from their first meeting that Howard Dagman was a couple of points off center, with far too much time and money on his hands.

Jason liked the guy, but nothing beyond neighborly hellos and the cursory wave through the windshield when they passed each other in the neighborhood. Howard had tried to get him into prepping and US Civil War reenactments. Howard would joke that they could play at civil war while they got ready for the next one. Prepping sounded like a waste of time and money to him. His own work at the Pentagon, and his familiarity with contingency plans related to counter-terrorism which was his account, gave him enough insight to realize no one within 35 miles

Washington, DC would live through the first few tenths of a second of an all-out nuclear exchange with Russia or China. The myriad of other natural disasters had always seemed over hyped to him. That said, he knew how disruptive even a snow storm could be in the Washington metro area and he and Sam had enough food to get them through any short-term event. Now though? He wasn't so sure. They had a new issue to contend with as well.

"I'm just askin here," he tried to be as nonchalant as possible. "How are you set for all those prenatal vitamins and stuff?"

"Probably enough for the next three kids... Costco."

"Three more?"

"Mmm hmmm," Samantha waved at the muted television. "You think it's that bad?"

He shrugged, "I think it's worse than they're saying, yeah. You're the doctor in the family."

"That part about the incubation period is the scary part," she shook her head. "He's right, the time for containing it is long gone, but it's only half the story. What they pointedly didn't address was the recovery rate, lethality, or symptomatic vectors which is a little weird, right?"

He nodded in agreement. "Unless it's bad on all those counts, then they'd be looking at social order issues which could kill as many as the disease, think nationwide riots."

"You're thinking like a soldier, hon." Sam's head shook sadly. "Think of the Black Plague in Europe. There were times when there weren't enough healthy people to have a town meeting or bury the dead, let alone a riot. Immunologically speaking, we are way over-due for something nasty, and there are bugs out there that laugh at our antibiotics."

"You're a ray of sunshine, Doc."

"I'm just sayin..." Sam squirmed deeper into the cushions of the couch. "Well since tomorrow is Friday, and you're not going into work... you've got three days to finish painting the baby's room, right?"

"Medically speaking, how long does this nesting thing last?"

Her heel dug into his ribs. "Watch it, mister."

*

Saturday, September 13

The President of the United States, Eugene Huffman, was amazed at how quiet the White House was. Not very long ago, he had fantasized about a moment like this.

His Chief of Staff dropped two pages on his desk, he could past her, out the door from the Oval Office. It was quiet out there as well. No line of people waiting to bend his ear, every one of them, with a pet project or an axe to grind.

"Bad?" He nodded at the document.

"Bad." Pauline Dirksen had been with him since he'd been a Lt. Governor in Colorado and had never been one to sugar-coat or spin bad news.

"The Post's advance copy for tomorrow morning and it's close to the truth, so yeah, it's bad." She dropped into the extra chair behind his desk. His own chair was some rare piece of Amazonian hardwood, a gift from the government of Brazil a hundred years ago. Like his famous desk, he wondered how long it would take before the survivors burned it for firewood.

"They are going to print that we are looking at 70% potential lethality. AP, UPI, and the global outlets will run with the story, within minutes of it dropping here. All electronic media, no one's been able to print anything for two days."

He caught himself nodding; *that* made sense to him. It took people to produce something, people that were at the moment huddling in their homes or beginning to take to the streets in anger. They could wish for 70%.

"The Pentagon is still advising that I kill the internet, didn't know we could do that." After a moment of staring at the typed pages on his desk, he nodded in acceptance. "Have them cook me up a speech, the truth, we aren't buying anything by shielding people at this point."

"Sir? The result..."

"Will be horrific, I know. I've given this some thought. Those few that are going to live through this need as much heads up as we can give them." He looked closely at Pauline. She was sick as well, and she knew it. He could see the fear in her eyes. What the hell was she doing here?

"An extinction level event, I thought that term was something cooked up by Hollywood..." He waived at the pile of binders on his desk; stacks of DoD and think-tank contingency plans that he'd been reading for the last week. It was truly amazing the amount of money and effort that had gone into US government planning for natural disasters and war-related events that killed 50% of the US population. It was all a holdover from the Cold War mindset and a result of the policy of mutually assured destruction that had kept the US and Soviet Union from killing the planet.

He could remember the drills at school, in his childhood, crouching under a desk in a laughable attempt to survive Armageddon. There was no dodging this virus. Most of the contingency plans he'd read, had been updated to the age of cyber and bio-terrorism. Every one of the blueprints for the rebuilding of civilization assumed there would be some kernel of surviving command authority or military command structure from which to begin.

Not one of the multimillion-dollar studies envisioned an event that wouldn't leave enough people alive globally to warrant the term 'civilization'. He'd suffered through endless briefings from scientists and soldiers for the last week. He was now well aware that mankind had been reduced to perhaps 40,000 people during some past ice age, and this current culling would leave millions alive globally, even if the worst-case scenarios of 97 or 98% lethality came to pass.

'A much better starting point, than we've survived in the past' one of the scientists had proclaimed. Somehow, he didn't think that would matter to the billions of people who were already in the process of dying. People like him.

"Sir, let the press break the news."

He snorted in laughter, maybe it was derision. "Pauline, most of humanity, you and me included, will be dead within a week, if not far sooner. What's the point of trying to spin this?"

She just looked at him in confusion. He looked closer now, and could see she was numb with shock, running on autopilot. He knew what she was thinking. He'd seen the same look in the first lady's eyes a day ago.

"You think there's someplace safe to go? Maybe a vaccination we've kept secret?"

He saw the answer to that in her eyes.

"If such a place existed, Pauline, you'd be coming with... it doesn't. I'm in the same boat as everyone else."

She nodded numbly, in what he prayed was understanding.

"Scratch the speech writers. I'll do this myself; I need to..." He shook his head and looked out the window across the gardens surrounding the back of the White House. "Send everyone home, security staff as well, if they'll go."

"They won't," she wiped at her eyes. "Neither will I."

"Then I'm making it an order, at least for you. Go home. If I thought the Secret Service would let me, I'd steal one of the Tahoes and see if Mary and I could get down to The Keys."

She had nowhere to go, no one to go home to. That much was clear on her face. She'd sacrificed an entire life to her career. To his career, he corrected himself, knowing that should somehow mean something. Right now, all he could think about was his own family. He reached into his drawer and pulled out a foil packet of pills that the Secret Service Doctor had given him.

"I'm told its quick and painless," he held it out to her. "It certainly beats the alternative."

She shook her head in defiance, but after a moment, reached out and took the pills. "Are you?"

He shook his head. "Mary will. I think the least I can do, is go out like everyone else."

He got up and hugged her goodbye and walked her to the office door. From the look on her face he didn't think she'd delay in taking the pill. He hoped she wouldn't, she looked ashen, the corners of her eyes were already bloodshot.

He shut the door to the Oval Office and went back to his desk. On the side table was a computer terminal. He brought it to life and entered the password, and held still as the biometric camera authenticated his face and irises. He added a thumb print when queried and waited until the monitor resolved to show an empty office cubicle, eight thousand miles away in Antarctica.

The camera at the other end of the connection shook for a moment as a man dropped into the chair, wearing a heavy green, military style sweater and a faded Chicago Cubs knit cap.

"Mr. President." The man's deep voice, full of gravel, somehow seemed at odds with the runner's build, and bookish glasses. He'd been assured that that this was the man who could do what was needed; part of a long-standing program straight out of one of the Cold War era binders on his desk.

"Colonel Skirjanek," he nodded. He'd had several conversations with the man over the last few days, this would be the last. "What's your status?"

"We're still virus free at McMurdo, Sir. The joint Brit/Aussie station has reported infection, as have the Argentines. They'd both just had a resupply flight from the mainland, so that was probably the delivery vector. There's been no communication with the Chileans. We had a plane up for an hour this morning and saw a lot of smoke from their site, it looked like a complete loss. There's been nothing from the French, and the same flight revealed their supply tender had left the harbor. I think they are running for the mainland. It's just us, and the Russians at this point."

"How's that relationship holding at your local level?" he asked.

"Good, so far. Their President has sent the same message as you did. We'll both hold out for as long as supplies last, and then rendezvous together with one of the boomers, ours or theirs."

"President Medleniyov was less than confident that his subs could stay down that long and/or make the trip. If that comes to pass, and they're free of infection. Make every effort to get them a ride home as well."

"Understood, Sir."

"How long will your supplies hold?"

The Colonel shook his head. "Canceling our resupply couldn't have come at a worse time, with respect to food. Three months at half rations, fuel for heat will be an issue before that, but we'll hold out as long as we can. We've had several suicides over the last two days, and I doubt that will stop anytime soon. Our food estimate... may get stretched out. The biggest problem I have right now is personnel security. Some people don't want to go out alone. I can only imagine that's what happened at the Chilean base."

He couldn't imagine what it would be like to know he had a chance at survival on that barren, frozen wasteland while everyone he knew back home, was dying. Colonel Skirjanek delivered the report without the accusatory tone he felt he deserved. For his own part, there was nothing comforting he could say. There were no words that wouldn't have tasted like bullshit in his own mouth.

"Sir, has there been any report on the status of the personnel we sent home on the on the *Odyssey*? My volunteers here have a lot of friends, some have family on that ship."

"I understand, Colonel," he replied. "It's up to you whether you want to share the news, but we had reports of infection on board last night. Apparently, the crew brought it with them, they had made a port call in Auckland before heading down to you."

The Colonel's gray eyes seemed to grow harder. "Understood, Sir."

"Your certain you minimized contact with the ship, Colonel?"

"Yes," Skirjanek nodded, looking as if shouldn't have needed to explain something like this to the president.

"The ship didn't dock. It stayed down wind of us. The people we sent out, transferred by small boat – they were picked up miles down the shore. We didn't recover the boats used."

It was part small talk on his part, part anxiety. If any part of America was going to survive this, it would probably come down to Colonel Skirjanek surviving. He couldn't help himself, there had to be more that he could do even as he knew there wasn't.

"Colonel, the eggheads tell me your best hope is that the virus burns itself out after killing us all." He felt himself smile with gallows humor.

"In the simplest of terms; the longer you wait, the better your odds." He looked at the notes on the side table. "I'm assured that the dead, their bodies will not constitute a threat to you beyond the hazards you would expect." My God, there would be bodies beyond count. At least he would be spared that. This man and his people, if they survived, would have to live in a world carpeted with the dead.

"That's comforting, Sir."

He caught himself smiling at the Colonel's sarcasm. The man would need that to survive, to keep his humanity. For himself, it was the only thing keeping him sane.

"I doubt that", he replied.

"Forgive me, Sir."

"There's no need for that, Colonel. At least on your part."

Skirjanek just calmly stared off camera for a moment, reining in emotions that he'd dealt with himself for the last week. The frustration, the anger, the realization that humanity had figured out how to kill itself and there was fuck all he could do about it.

"Any confirmation from the Navy, Sir?"

"Yes," he grabbed up his notes. "The missile boats Missouri and Ohio will be on station, near you, within a week. They won't surface and pop their lids until they have to start fishing to stay alive. They'll be joined by an attack sub, the Boise. Everything else has been compromised, and I'm told the Boise is already on its last legs, in terms of supplies and maintenance. It will be on the surface, fishing for food in less than two weeks, staying well north of you. If they remain virus free for a month after popping the hatches, they'll move south and join the other two boats. The timing for your retrieval is entirely up to you."

"Copy that, Sir."

"One last thing, Major." He typed another command, "I've just sent you a file containing kill commands for the submarines." Since gaining office, and being read in, he'd known the codes existed for the last line of insurance against a rogue submarine that had more fire power than all weapons ever used in the history of war. He'd never thought he'd be giving them to someone else. "If the code's entered when you're in communication with them, the process is hardwired in the sub."

The process? Billions were dying and he was calmly discussing how to kill another 200 souls. But it was insurance that the subs wouldn't abandon the people at the Antarctic base.

"Your command authority has been transmitted to the sub's commanders, and acknowledged, so hopefully that won't be needed. I've also dead-lined all the warheads in our inventory. The Russians say they've done the same, and I actually believe them this time. The Chinese aren't talking to anybody, but they're dying too."

"Understood, Sir," the Colonel nodded.

"Your family, Colonel?"

Skirjanek looked away from the camera for a moment. "I spoke to my daughter this morning on Skype. She and my wife are both symptomatic."

Symptomatic? He could see the struggle for control on the Colonel's face.

"The First Lady is as well," he nodded. "And..." he pulled down the collar of his shirt where the beginnings of what looked like nasty bruise was showing at his neck line. "It's quick Colonel, people don't linger. There's that."

The Colonel just stared back at him, a human statue. Control and rage in a precarious balance.

"God be with you Colonel Skirjanek."

"And you, Mr. President."

*

Chapter 3

Sunday, September 14

Jason came awake with a start, from a sleep that had been anything but restful. Sam wasn't in bed, but he immediately saw the light from underneath the bathroom door. The girl had always had a bladder like a golf ball, and it was only going to get worse as the pregnancy progressed. If it progressed, he reminded himself. The President's address had hit them like a fast-moving train. The leader of the free world, sitting behind his desk, sweating, clearly already sick himself, telling them that perhaps 90% of world's population was at risk. Sam had cried herself to sleep, he was numb with worry and exhaustion. They hadn't left the house in a week, praying they were going to miss it. One out of ten were not good odds.

He waited for Sam but didn't hear anything outside of the occasional gunshot in the distance. Gunfire had been a constant reminder the last two days of how bad things were getting. He'd been sleeping with his .45 next to him. He padded to the bathroom door, "You ok?"

He caught the sound of a sniff, before her voice scratched back.

"Stay away! I'm sick."

The door was locked, but the door jamb shattered easily with the shoulder he put in to it.

Sam lay in the bathtub, in her robe. Her dark hair was plastered to her face and forehead with sweat. She was shaking her head, "Don't..."

He picked her up and carried her back to the bed. He could feel the heat coming off her body in waves. The heavy cloth of her robe felt like an electric blanket cranked up to max.

She reached out and grabbed his hand, "The baby..." She got no further before bursting into silent tears, too weak for anything else.

He felt an icy chill run through his body, he couldn't breathe. This couldn't be happening. In the light spilling from the bathroom, he could see the rosetta flush of broken capillaries in her cheeks, turning to dark blue at her neck and chest. He folded her up in his arms and held her close. There had to be something he could do. The despair in knowing that there wasn't, felt like the floor dropping out from under him. A fall through empty space that wasn't going to end.

"I love you, Sam."

She shifted against him. "And I love you. It won't be long." It was the doctor speaking, not his wife.

"I won't be far behind you."

"Yes... you... will," she shivered.

He knew she was wrong. One way or another, she was wrong.

"You are going to live." She stared at him with eyes that seemed to fill with blood as he watched. She squeezed him hard and quick. "Promise me... if you don't get sick, you'll stay alive. You have to stay alive."

Why? He wanted to ask. He just hugged her back and held her in silence.

She pulled her head away from his, staring at him. "People will need you, there'll be kids out there. You are going to live... promise me." She said it with such belief that he had a growing worry in his gut that she was making it so through pure will.

"I promise."

She held his gaze for a moment and then nodded in acceptance. She folded herself against him and shivered in what he thought were fever chills. "You promised," he heard her whisper.

"It hurts!" she cried out a few minutes later when her stillness was broken with another round of shivering.

"Hang on," he remembered he still had the six pills of oxy he'd gotten from the dentist after having two wisdom teeth out last year, he hadn't needed them.

He came back with the bottle and gave it a shake.

"What are they?"

"Oxy from the dentist."

She nodded, "I'm already gone, Jason. God will understand."

He hesitated as the realization of what she was saying hit him. Her body went rigid as she keened like a wounded animal in pain. It passed and left her breathing in gasps.

He held her head as he helped her take the pills. God damn him, all of them.

She hugged him tight, her mouth on his cheek, she kissed him. "Live..."

The pills took affect quickly and she was soon asleep. He watched her chest rise and fall feebly, growing shallower with time, until it didn't. He held her tight, willing himself to start shivering with fever. He prayed for a head or body ache, the chills, some sign that he was going to follow her. At some point during the night, he gave up with a sickening feeling in his stomach that Sam had more pull in this matter than he did. He held her until the sky outside the window began to lighten, shaded in red from a world that was burning.

He dressed her in one of her Sunday dresses that she'd complained was one of the only ones that still fit her. He laid her out on the bed, amid the echo of gunfire in the distance and the near continuous peal of car horns. He watched over her body, thinking that he'd lay down next to her, and sleep that final rest as soon as he got sick.

Around noon, he tried to call Sam's parents but the phone just rang until the machine picked up. Sam hadn't been able to get a hold of them the day before either. He called her brother Will, who lived in San Jose, with his wife Rose and two kids.

The phone picked up almost immediately. Rose's voice sounded odd to him after the quiet of the house.

"Rose? This is Jason... is Will there."

"I'm the only one left," Rose sounded like she was in shock, emotionless.

"They died two days ago, Jason. I've tried calling to make arrangements, and I've left messages. No one's called back! Jason, I don't know what to do. They're... they're still here, and now I'm sick. Somebody has to do something!"

"Rose?"

"I don't know what to do Jason, I can't get out of bed. Can you and Sam come out here?"

He almost delivered the news he'd meant to.

"We'll try Rose, ok?"

"Ok," Rose said, sounding a little more hopeful. "I'll tell Will... when he wakes up."

Rose hung up on him.

He dialed his own parents, dreading the answering machine.

"Jason?"

"Mom?"

"It's Kate," his sister's voice had always sounded like their mother's.

"Sam's gone, Kate."

"Oh, Jason," his sister tried to comfort him. He could barely hear her. There was growing sense of dread in the conversation as it went on with no mention of their parents and he could tell Kate was just barely hanging on.

"Kate?"

"It's just me, Jason. I tried calling, but the lines were all busy. They went within a couple of hours of each other."

Somehow, he'd known they were gone from the tone of her voice. "How are you doing?" he asked.

"Waiting..." she sniffed. "To either get sick or shot. The south side of town is burning, been rioting since yesterday. Everyone's dying or going nuts."

He knew it would be the same everywhere. He'd seen war up close, a lot of it. None of it compared to what people could do when they were scared, angry, with nothing to lose.

"You've got Dad's guns, don't hesitate using them. Call me tomorrow, ok?"

"I'll try, be safe."

"You too, love you, Sis."

Kate called, just as she'd promised to do. She was sick, and resigned to what followed. They reminisced about the past, even laughed a little at long-forgotten memories until Kate broke down in tears. Their final goodbye had a sense of the inevitable. They said the words, both expecting to see each other again, soon. And then he was alone, sitting on his living room couch, the smell of smoke in the air and the sound of sporadic gunfire in the distance. So very alone.

As much as he wanted to deny it, smoke wasn't the only smell in the house. Knowing what he had to do and doing it were two very different things and he sat there for another hour, willing himself to get sick. The power flickered off and then back on as he walked into the garage from the kitchen. It was only a matter of time. They had a name for it; cascading systematic failure. He was surprised the power had lasted this long. Civilization, like the species that had created it, was living its final moments.

He stood in the garage holding a shovel, wondering where he should bury his wife. He was self-aware enough to know he was in shock and wasn't thinking clearly. Where to bury Sam? Front yard? Back? He was hit with a sense of horrified astonishment that this was happening. He'd just painted the baby's room. Sam's friends were going to throw her a shower and had been secretly reaching out to him to figure out what she wanted or needed. This couldn't be happening... he had to wake up.

Leaning against the shovel handle, dimly aware of his distorted reflection in the side of Sam's car he slammed his forehead into the shovel's handle, again, then again, pushing the handle away from himself and pulling it in as he headbutted the solid wood until he saw flashes behind his eyes.

He went out the side door of the garage, dragging the shovel behind him like a piece of luggage and stood there as he blinked the tears out if his eyes. He was looking at the sycamore tree they'd planted three years ago when they moved into the home where they thought they'd raise a family. He had just gotten back from Afghanistan, his last and final, ever, deployment. Sam had made him promise that, too. She had envisioned a rope swing off the tree, a place for their kids to climb and play. The nursery up the road had been correct, the tree had grown quickly, faster than their family had... or would. Still dizzy, and aware of a trickle of blood running down his nose, he dragged the shovel to the tree. He'd dig a big hole, big enough for two. He nodded and mumbled in agreement with the voice in his head and started digging. Big enough for two.

The autumn sun, bright and empty, was almost setting by the time he finished. He noted the blood red sunset from all the smoke. Fires were burning all around him. If there had been winged serpents in the air, the sunset as seen from his yard would have looked like the book cover to Dante's Inferno. Back inside the house, he was on the stairs when he realized he hadn't eaten since dinner, a day and a half ago, the last dinner with Sam who had said she wasn't hungry.

He felt at the knot on his forehead and looked at down at his hands, crusted in thick Virginia clay, raw sores of torn blisters standing out, hurting now that he'd noticed them. He wasn't going to touch Sam until he washed up. Back down the stairs, a slow step at a time, untrusting of his legs, he made it to the kitchen and cleaned up. He inhaled three protein bars and guzzled down a Gatorade. Sam had always joked that the sugar in the stuff was going to kill him.

He could feel the energy from the food course through him. He was reminded of the end of hell week in the Ranger Qual Course. They'd been forced to exist on maybe 500 calories a day, while burning something like eight thousand. Their bodies had all begun cannibalizing themselves. The first real meal after it was over had pulled back the fogginess, the confusion that draped over everything like a wet blanket with a rapidity that had been like an electric shock to the system. Physically, right now, the calories hit his system the same way. The emotional fog, the numbness, stayed.

He took another look at the open sores on his hands left from the shovel. Red ellipses, oozing with clear pus. He wondered if they'd increase his odds of contracting the virus. He hoped so.

In a half daze, knowing he needed sleep as much as he'd needed to eat, he made his way upstairs and wrapped Sam up tight in the sheets of their bed, swaddling her tightly before carrying her outside under a rising moon the color of blood. The horizon was burning worse than it had the night before. A single gunshot broke the momentary silence. In the distance, someone was laying on a car horn.

He laid her out in the bottom of the grave and said a prayer. He asked, begged, tried to explain that he'd dug the grave for two. He remembered why he'd come out here with his .45 tucked into the back of his pants. He could feel the weight of it pressed against his lower back. It would be so simple, over in an instant. They'd be together again... big enough for two.

"*Already two...*" a voice in his head whispered. The heavy 1911 was in his hand when he looked back down at Sam's shroud wrapped body. Their unborn baby was there as well. She'd have company. *You promised.*

Tears streaming down his face, sobbing in uncontrolled gasps he screamed in defiance at the dead world around him. His chest heaved, the only sound he could hear was the pounding of his own heart, the blood rushing in his ears. He looked up at the tree, the obscured moon and the few stars he could see through the hanging smoke. Their indifference pissed him off in a way he couldn't explain. They'd go on. The tree oblivious to what it shaded beneath its limbs in the summers to come. It wasn't right; the world was supposed to burn at the end in a nuclear fire, crack apart from an asteroid or bury itself in an unending ice age – it wasn't supposed to die bleeding in bed.

He stood slowly, and began filling in the grave running on auto-pilot. He knew, how he couldn't have said; he was going to live. He'd never been angrier or more terrified in his life. How was he going to honor the promise he'd made Sam? Tomorrow, he'd make a marker tomorrow.

He woke slowly, becoming aware, remembering in pieces of why he was on the living room couch. Why his hands smelled like dirt, why they hurt. Why he was alone. The sky outside was lightening and the air tasted like smoke. Not the forest fire smell he was familiar with from his childhood, but a dirty, melted plastic, public incinerator stench. The quiet of the house struck him. He could hear only the slightest tick... tick... tick from the small clock hung on the wall in the kitchen. No hum from the refrigerator, no sounds of traffic from Rt. 7, a mile away, no air being moved by the HVAC system. The power was out, and it wouldn't be coming back on. For the moment, he didn't hear any sirens, or gunfire. He had a dim memory of collapsing the night before on the couch, the sound of a firefight raging in the distance.

"What now?" he wondered out loud, knowing there would be no answer. His voice reverberated off the walls, sounding strange to him as the world was suddenly a very big, very empty auditorium.

The power must have just failed, the ice in the freezer was still hard. He dug out his ice chests, and the gallon jugs of ice he'd prepped last week when the virus story first broke. Their basement freezer was well stocked and he quickly transferred the meat to the ice chests. The gas was still on so he had his cook tops, but their ovens were electric and there was no way he'd be able to eat all of the meat before it went bad. He decided to cook all of it while he could. He'd dry the meat out, smoke it, if he could figure out a way to do it on his barbeque. He had a smoker he used to make jerky out of his yearly deer, but it was electric and as useless as almost everything else they owned.

They hadn't gone to the store for over a week and a half and he was down to some pasta, oatmeal and assorted boxes and bags of rice, crackers and cookies mixed in with a few cans of tuna and chili. He wasn't going to starve but his diet was definitely looking at an incoming curveball. He stood in the kitchen chewing on a protein bar, listing out his priorities in his head. Water, food, shelter... survivors, security got added immediately. His first step was to find out how many people like him were left, and where the authorities were holding firm. In the back of his mind he was aware that he lived in one of the wealthiest areas of the country, and the supplies he needed were probably all around him surrounded by dead people and others looking to survive as well.

He spent the next hour filling every thermos, and large pot he could find with water. The water pressure was way down, but for the moment it still flowed. He filled the bath tub upstairs and covered the top of it with a brand-new shower curtain he found under the sink. He'd drank out of mud puddles before, but the experience had left him a firm believer in clean water.

He got the barbeque going on the deck, studiously avoiding looking at the disturbed ground under the sycamore tree. *I'm going to try Sam.* He ended up cooking most of the day, overcooking everything, slowly, in an attempt to dry it out. He used the hickory chips that he'd smoked meat with in the past and jury-rigged a tinfoil smoke bag inside the barbeque. The resultant jerky ended up being less smoked and more cooked, but it'd serve. He had a distinct feeling that *'it'll serve'* was the new bar.

Howard Dagman... the thought of his neighbor crossed his mind. He pictured Howard and Debbie sitting at their kitchen table, playing scrabble in their HAZMAT suits. The crazy bastard would probably shoot first and ask questions never. But he needed to figure out who was left, where the authorities were running their relief efforts from. If the declining gunfire over the last couple of days was any indication, they were getting a handle on the situation. It was still there occasionally, some of it a lot closer than the distant echoes he knew were miles away, but it had definitely become less frequent.

One of the last reports they had seen on TV, nearly a week earlier, had been focused on the institution of martial law. They'd already been shooting looters and trouble makers on sight for days before that. He only heard a dozen or so shots during the day, most seeming to come from Tysons or Reston, as their neighborhood was located roughly half way between the two urban centers.

He got ready to go, a surreal experience as he pocketed an extra magazine, checked the action on his .45 and reloaded its magazine, putting a round in battery, before attaching the clip-on holster to his belt - in his living room. He done this before, in Afghanistan and Iraq, wearing body armor and carrying an assault rifle; this was Northern Virginia for God's sake. He'd considered taking his 30.06 as well, but the scope on it was worse than useless at night. He had thought about taking a hacksaw to his 12-gauge's barrel, but figured he might need it for hunting later. Besides the shotgun was bulky, so was its ammo, and he wanted to have his hands free.

He looked outside at the darkness, no street lamps, no houselights, no distant hum of traffic from the always busy Rt. 7 which lay to the west of their neighborhood. For a split second he meant to check the time and then snorted to himself. Not a lot of need for a watch, not anymore. The big egg timer in the sky would probably be the only clock he would ever need again. *It'll serve...*

Deciding to be back by dawn, he set out, armed and in the dark. It bothered him how fast his tactical mindset reasserted itself; this was his neighborhood, for God's sake.

He had about a half a mile of large *Mc-mansions* sitting on two acre lots to get through before making it to the main road. He never thought he'd live in a place like this, but he'd fallen in love with, and married a doctor. The area was known as Great Falls, and the big expensive lots held a dirty secret. The entire area wasn't tied into Fairfax County's sewer system, and each house needed a big drain field to contain the individual septic systems. Big houses needed big drain fields, which made for big lots, nice neighborhoods and astronomical real estate values.

The joke had always run that Great Falls smelled like shit and money. Looking at the darkened houses around him as he made his way down the side of the road, staying under the overhanging branches, the whole area now smelled of death, rot and decay. It wasn't overpowering out on the road, but it was persistent. Money hadn't saved his neighbors.

By the time he made it to the neighborhood's entrance he was starting to lose his shit. There hadn't been a single flicker of a candle, or of a flashlight. Nothing to convince him he wasn't the only person on the planet. The main road beckoned at the entrance to his neighborhood. It connected to Rt. 7 in either direction, left towards Tysons, right towards Reston. He went right, staying on the side of the road, always aware of where the closest cover was; the next tree trunk or the concrete drain culvert off the side of the road, or an abandoned car which were everywhere. Old training and hard-won experience were reasserting themselves like old acquaintants he never expected to see again.

The chill in his mind grew, as the next road he came to was the entrance to a neighboring subdivision. The first house he could see had a body in the front yard just a few yards from the road. There was enough light from the moon that he could make out a patch of darkened earth next to the body, a grave. He moved to the bottom of the yard and hesitated a moment before climbing the shallow sloping hill. The woman was dead, and had been for two or three days. Her eyes were gone, the turkey vultures and crows had already been at work.

He made his way up to the house and went through the open door, immediately cursing his stupidity for not bringing a flashlight. The moonlight outside was reduced to just a faint glow of light at each of the windows. He stood in the entranceway listening, hoping. Nothing.

"Hello?" he shouted. His own voice gave him a start. He shivered for a moment aware of the goosebumps that had broken out on his arms.

"Anybody home?" he yelled and walked further in. There wasn't the smell that was so evident outside. He figured the house was empty; at least of bodies. He noted the empty couches in a living room and reached the staircase going up as quietly as he could. He entered each room after a polite knock that echoed through the silence and mocked his caution. The master bedroom was a mess, but next to the bed was a 9mm and a box of ammo. He collected both, dropping them into the book bag he'd brought with him.

For all the good it did them, everyone had probably armed themselves as best as they were able to over the last week and a half before they got sick. The last of the news reports had seemed to focus more on the riots and the military's response than on the fact that humanity was dying. Somebody had probably thought that story would sell better.

The house was empty. He found a large jug cooler in the garage and filled it up from the sink. The water pressure here wasn't as strong as it had been at his house, but he managed to fill it and left it on the counter. He could collect it later. He went through the kitchen cupboards and dropped everything canned or boxed, anything that would keep, into a large duffle bag he'd found and then left it on the front stoop. He could grab it tomorrow.

The Costco sized box of pepperoni sticks was too good to pass up. He ate one, and stuffed the rest into his backpack and headed off on a quicker pace to Rt. 7, which he hit five minutes later. He still hadn't heard or seen another person until a rifle shot sounded in the distance off to the west towards Reston. An M-4, his mind clicked instantly. He'd know that sound anywhere for the rest of his life. It gave him a direction, somebody was alive. He moved back to the side of the road under the trees. Whoever they were, they were a lot better armed than he was.

Once he'd reached the divided four lanes of Rt. 7, it was all the abandoned cars that he couldn't figure out. Every thirty or forty yards there'd be a vehicle pulled off to the side of the road. Occasionally there'd be two or three parked on the side, bumper to bumper. They were all, on both sides of the highway, headed west, towards Leesburg. The direction of travel made some sense, given the riots. What he couldn't figure out, was the 'where' all these people thought they could go to outrun the end of the world.

He left the shoulder of the road at the next car he came to, a Subaru wagon. Looking in through the window, the keys were on the seat and the car was empty. He opened the door and sat behind the wheel. He tried the engine and it cranked over immediately but didn't start, the gas gauge told him why. Had all these people just ran out of gas? He leaned over and clicked open the jockey box. The car's windshield blew inward with a thump, cobwebbing instantly along with the rifle's report.

Jason hugged the seat and pulled the keys out of ignition, he drew his gun and smashed out the dome light. Expecting another shot, feeling someone else's gun sights on his back, he crawled out of the car backwards doing his best to stay below the dashboard. He judged the distance to the next car and sprinted forward in a crouched run. Another shot rang out in his direction just as he reached cover. His whole body flinched at the report, but the shot didn't seem to hit anything close.

"Dumbass!" He mumbled. The car's interior light had lit him up like a Christmas tree. He sat back against the rear bumper of the old Volvo he'd run to, and waited for his night vision to return, shaking his head in disgust at the rookie mistake. It had been something a green recruit right out of basic would have done. He'd been behind a desk for too long. This isn't Fallujah, he reminded himself. In an instant he realized, it was worse. Missions, deployments, they ended, you went home. This was home.

He waited a few more minutes before raising himself up against the back of the Volvo looking forward through the back and front windows of the car. He saw a brief flash and ducked back down slowly, at least the muscle memory was returning. Quick movements got you dead, the human eye was attuned to them. Raising back up he looked again, two vehicles ahead was a pickup, with someone in the back, sitting in a lawn chair. It was easy enough to locate now that he knew where to look. The shooter held a weak flashlight that seemed to wobble all over the place. Jason caught the outline of a rifle laid across the front of the lawn chair in the light beam's wandering.

He crabbed back to the right-hand shoulder of the road, went belly down, and waited a few minutes before beginning a slow crawl, forward to the next car. He moved slowly, as he'd been taught, one limb at a time, slow but constant forward movement. He was out of shape, something like this wouldn't have registered on him when he'd been active duty. His shoulders and arms burned with the effort of the crawl and a cramping twinge in his lower back told him he wasn't twenty-five any more, or even thirty he realized. That had come and gone a few years back.

He paused; he smelled the body before he saw it. Laid down in the leaf filled ditch was a woman in a Virginia State trooper's uniform. She was on her back, her empty eyes sockets and pecked at face staring sightlessly up at a sky too smoky to see the stars. Jason wondered briefly if she'd succumbed to the virus or been a victim of the lawlessness. He did his best to crawl past her without altering his pace, but failed miserably. The ditch was deep enough here, his target couldn't see him unless he came up on his knees. He moved as quick as he dared, trying for quiet instead of quiet and slow until he had left the trooper behind him.

Thankful for the darkness the lack of street lights provided, he crawled up the slight slope back onto the road behind a small SUV parked directly behind the F-150 that held the shooter. He knelt at the back of the vehicle, staring at a bumper sticker commemorating an honor student at Thomas Jefferson H.S., knowing the proud parents and student were in all likelihood dead.

Then he heard it. It was a woman talking to herself, sobbing. He risked a look around the bumper and crawled up the side of his vehicle until he could see the woman sitting in a lawn chair facing in his direction. She held the flashlight in her lap, the outline of her rifle again visible as the weak beam hit the road side bed of the truck. The woman would gasp in a large breath and moan, talk to herself and cry. It was a pattern he picked up on, as he began to worry less about getting shot than being relieved. He wasn't the only person alive; although, there something very wrong here.

She was delirious, maybe drunk; he couldn't tell. Either one could get him shot. He slowly unzipped his backpack and pulled out a couple of the packaged pepperoni sticks he'd liberated earlier. He threw one over his head, grenade style out into the middle of the road and coiled himself. It landed with far less noise than he wanted, but it was enough.

"Who's that!? Who's there!" the woman gasped.

Jason waited until the flashlight's beam came up out of the bed of the pickup and shot out into the road, away from him, before springing forward and vaulting into the truck's bed. The woman was still focused on the middle of the road, trying to get her rifle up by the time he landed with his .45 drawn with one hand, the other pulling the rifle away from her with an ease that surprised him.

He was struck by the smell of alcohol, barely concealing the scent of shit and blood. Then he saw the pillow of blood-soaked bandages around the woman's midsection. At a second glance, he realized it was a sleeping bag tied around her midsection. How was she still alive?

She seemed to notice his presence with a drunken, surprised smile.

"You real?"

"I am."

She wiped away the tears and snot from her face with her sleeve and then leaned forward slowly, the movement clearly causing her pain, until her forehead made contact with the barrel of his gun that he'd almost forgotten.

"Please..."

He laid her out in the bed of the truck, which was well stocked with sleeping bags, a tent and assorted camping gear. If the truck was hers, someone had left her behind. There was a lot of gear, too much for one person, and too much to have been carried on foot when the vehicle had run out of gas.

Unwrapping the blood-soaked sleeping bag from her midsection, there was no mystery surrounding her gunshot wound. Experience he'd just as soon forget, told him it had been a shotgun, up-close, right in the gut. She shouldn't be alive. The woman herself held no illusion that he could fix her.

"They killed me this morning, said I was too old."

"Who?"

"Tysons crowd," she grimaced. "Fucking whack jobs, bunch of," she paused and tensed in pain. "Bunch of bullies."

She'd been facing in the direction of Tysons in her lawn chair. Maybe she had planned to take one with her if they came back.

"Please, it hurts so much..." Her eyes were slammed shut in pain.

She didn't have much time left and he almost gave her what she wanted. In the end he couldn't, as much as he wanted to.

"I can't," he shook his head. "You're the first... person I've seen, alive."

She cursed him until the pain made her stop.

Holding her head up, he gave her more of the whiskey she'd been drinking. She coughed on it, but wiped her lips with a jacket sleeve blackened with dried blood.

"Don't be sorry," she said. "I couldn't do it either."

"Where were you headed?"

"Away... from them. We got out, killed a guard, but they caught up to us."

"Tysons?"

She nodded, "They were supposed to help, but...."

"Where, where in Tysons?"

"FEMA center at the Ritz," she smiled and started coughing until it turned into a mewling silent scream.

He gave her some more whiskey.

"Will you stay? Until...?"

"I'll stay." He nodded back at her pleading look. *And watch you die, it's what I do.*

Whether it was from blood loss or the septic shock hitting her system, she went quiet and passed out for the last time a few minutes later. Within an hour, he was alone again.

For the briefest of moments, he wondered if he could find a shovel and bury her, but after a moment's consideration realized the lunacy of the thought. It was a world owned by the dead. What was he going to do? Bury them all? Screw Johnny Appleseed, he could be Gordon Gravedigger, the man that buried the human race.

Ashamed at the realization he hadn't even asked her name, he wrapped her in a sleeping bag from the truck and moved her to the shoulder of the road.

Reston would have to wait. Whatever was going on in Tysons was close enough that he needed to know. First though, it was time to go see if Howard had made it.

Heading east on Rt. 7, back the way he had come, he took the time to look through the windows of the abandoned cars. They were all stocked with camping supplies, pillow cases of canned goods, bottled water, abandoned for the most part. People had either left on foot with what they could carry or been caught by whoever was operating out of Tysons. He heard the even paced staccato pop, pop, pop of an M-4 somewhere down Baron Cameron towards Reston. Steady firing; clearly not a fight. Somebody deciding to get in a little target practice at the end of the world.

Every lifeless body he saw, young and old alike, had a backpack, book bag, suitcase or duffle bag stuffed with canned food, water bottles, liquor and the requisite family photos and stuffed animals. It was the latter he couldn't ignore; it explained the smaller forms lying next to their parents that would swim into his vision as he marched along. Slowly, he began to construct a story in his head about what had happened. Whole families driving out, or walking, had stopped when a family member got sick, or when they ran out of gas. The rest had waited to get sick and die. It was clear that many people hadn't waited. The virus killed quick but it didn't put holes in heads.

He passed the road he'd used coming out of his neighborhood earlier, and decided to stick with the highway. Heading down the big sloping hill to the cross road at the old Difficult Run Mill, he had a strange thought; the revolutionary era corn mill, turned tourist attraction, had definitively outlasted the people that had built it.

Even though the Dagman's lived just five houses down from their own on the same road, he had already decided to work his way back home through the back entrance to the neighborhood, via the bike trail along the Difficult Run green space. He'd get a look at a large section of the subdivision that he hadn't seen since he and Sam had holed up ten days earlier. In the back of his mind, he also knew Rt. 7 or Leesburg Pike was a straight shot into Tysons Corner, and this route would take him that much closer to whatever was going on there. He picked up his pace, moving from car to car along the left shoulder of the road.

The sound of an engine running at the edge of his hearing pulled him up short. It wasn't a car, it sounded like a big lawnmower. Generator... he thought immediately. Crossing Rt. 7, he shook his head when he realized he had looked both ways for traffic. He almost smiled at the ingrained habit. Traffic wasn't likely to be a problem, ever again. Entering a subdivision on the opposite side of Rt. 7 from his own, he followed the road sharply downhill.

The heavily forested, hills on either side of him were so dark, the dim glow of electric light emanating from deeper within the neighborhood stood out. The road bent sharply down to his right into a cul-de-sac, the noise of the generator suddenly distinct, and much too loud in a world that had suddenly gone quiet. Rounding a corner, the house stood out like a beacon of technology in a sea of darkness. Welcoming light spilled from the windows on both floors.

Someone had to be fueling the generator he thought immediately. He crossed the narrow neighborhood street and sat with his back against a tree and watched the house from the shadows... and waited. It couldn't have been much past 10 pm, 11 at the latest, and with all the lights on, he doubted if they were asleep. If they were alive. After five minutes without seeing any movement, not even shadows from behind the shades, he crossed the street and headed up the pipe-stem driveway.

Halfway to the house, he was hit by a wall of necrotic stench that stopped him in his tracks. Not the underlying sweet smell of rot that permeated the very air; this was a concentrated, physical barrier. Memories of Fallujah, of a house that had been an enemy bunker, and then subsequently, a pile of rubble in the summer heat. His unit had spent two days in the compound on the other side of a narrow street, having to bear the stench of rot. He pulled his bandana over his face and went forward, breathing as shallow as possible.

A large bay window let him see directly into the living room. There were at least a dozen bodies laid out on the floor, in chairs and on couches; all were clearly dead from the virus. Blackened faces stared at nothing. Maybe this neighborhood had lost power earlier than he had. People, neighbors probably, had gathered here.... and died. The one house in the neighborhood with a backup generator, the flame for the moths.

The sound from the generator was a physical pulse he could almost feel as he followed the noise around the side of the house. It was a large grey box sitting on a concrete slab. There was enough light coming from the window above it that he could make out the simple ball and cock valve six inches above the ground. It was plumbed directly into the house's gas line.

Passing the generator, he walked around to the back of the house and stepped up onto a cedar patio. A large sliding glass door lit up the expanse of wood that shined with a sun bleached white against the surrounding darkness. Walking up to the glass door, he saw yet more bodies, laid out in makeshift beds or on sleeping bags along the floor. One body, lying on the floor next to an overturned kitchen table chair caught his attention. A teenage boy, dead, his legs a torn mess of carnage, bones showing white.

He was still wondering what he was looking at when a gray blur slammed up against the window from the inside. Some large doodle mix of a dog was barking furiously at him. Startled, it took him a moment to see the dog's muzzle was stained dark red. The story clicked into place. His gun came up of its own accord and he shot the dog twice through the glass. Numb, he walked back around to the generator and closed the gas valve. The engine coughed once and sputtered to a stop a few seconds later. The house and the world around him went dark. If he'd had a gallon of gas with him, he would have burned the house down.

He retreated slowly back across the street to where he had waited earlier. He sat against the trunk of the same tree while he chewed on a pepperoni stick and drank a bottle of water, waiting for his eyes to readjust. He wondered if his gun shots would attract any attention. He half hoped they would. He felt like a fight. Against what or who, he wasn't sure he cared, but this wasn't fair. Humanity hadn't had a chance to fight. They'd just died, to be eaten by their own pets.

What had started out as a foraging trip had resulted in the sad discovery that he was surrounded by the cast-off detritus and dropped supplies of the world's richest country. Food, at least for the shelf life of canned goods, wasn't going to be a problem. The dead though - he hadn't been prepared for the numbers.

At the end, when the severity of the pandemic couldn't be hidden, the government had made an announcement that had claimed a worst-case infection rate that approached 90%, with a lethality rate approaching 50%. He now knew that for the absolute bullshit it clearly had been. Whatever the actual number was, it was a lot higher than that. The government's last lie, he thought. There wasn't anybody left to fact check this one. He was alone, or as near as, and if the woman in the truck had been telling the truth; at least some of the other survivors had already gone Mad Max.

Sam's face, as he had held her that last night echoed behind his closed eyes... "Promise me you'll live."

He'd said 'yes.' Right now, those words were all he had to hold on to. Water, Food, Weapons – he clicked off in his head. Howard Dagman; he wondered if the paranoid former navy chief had survived, and how dangerous it would be to check.   *

Chapter 4

The Dagman's large house was dark, except for the slightest sliver of light escaping from what he knew was their kitchen window facing out towards their massive stand-alone garage. The partial moon was now high enough in the sky that he could make out the blackout shades covering every window. He was directly across the street in the Schaffer's yard, prone on the Astroturf putting green that no one in the neighborhood had ever seen anyone use.

The Dagmans had a big front yard, sloping up from the tree-lined street. The yard itself was just an expanse of grass with a single large tree, leaves already shed, standing in the center of it. Knowing who lived in the house, he couldn't think of the yard as anything other than a free fire zone. He could almost picture the old goat having emplaced some jury-rigged landmines for good measure. Howard would have referred to them as solicitor repellent devices or some other euphemism. The house sat on a large three-acre lot, with a big backyard that backed up against the green space that bracketed Difficult Run.

The small stream was paralleled by a section of the Fairfax Cross County Trail that he and Sam had jogged and biked along since they'd moved in. He wondered for a moment why he hadn't approached the house from the back, from the trail. Just as fast, he dismissed the idea. If Howard was alive and saw somebody sneaking up, he'd be dead before he hit the ground. He'd gone to the range with Howard once. The guy may have had a little wannabe warrior in him, but he had been a very good shot and had brought a duffel bag of guns with him that he hadn't seen since his last deployment.

He sat up, left his backpack on the putting green and moved his clip-on holster around to the small of his back. Straight up, he thought; right up the driveway was the only way. Friendly neighbor, no reason to sneak. He went down the embankment to the street, crossed and started up the sloping driveway.

He stopped at the turnaround area in front of the large garage and held both hands out, fingers splayed out as wide as he could get them. His active duty was firmly in the past, but he could remember how hard it had been to see whether or not someone was carrying a weapon in the dark.

"Howard!? Debbie!?" he called out. "It's Jason Larsen – you alive?"

A fierce barking erupted in the house. Damn, he'd forgotten about Dagman's new dog. The last time he'd spoken to Howard, the man had been walking a hyper lab on a leash, very much still a puppy in energy if not size. But that had been early in the summer, several months past.

Thor? Loki? He tried to remember the dog's name. Loki sounded right.

"Loki! It's a friend!"

The dog's barking stopped abruptly and then started up again.

Shit... He didn't want to kill another dog. There was no movement that he could sense within the house, no Krieg lights snapped on, no laser dot from a tactical sight dancing across his chest. He started up the sidewalk paving stones, moving slow, hands still up and out. He rang the doorbell and wasn't surprised at all to hear the chimes within. He waited a good ten seconds, hit the bell again and was about to try the door latch when a dog's deep throated warning growl froze him in place.

He turned around very slowly. The black lab was just a shiny shadow in the moonlight, its teeth showed much more clearly. Loki had grown since he'd seen the puppy in the summer. It was clear the dog had some growth left in him, but he was still staring at close to a hundred pounds of overly protective muscle.

He showed the dog his empty hands.

"Good Loki..." He did his best to take the tension out of his voice, and add some praise.

"You're quite the stalker, boy. Good Loki." He meant every word of that. He hadn't heard a thing behind him until the warning growl.

The dog's ears twitched at his name, but he growled again almost immediately.

"Loki, good boy! You're a good boy, good dog!" he took half a step forward and kneeled down, holding a hand out.

The dog growled, whimpered in confusion, growled again and added a short-lived tail wag at the praise.

"You must have a doggie door out back, don't you? Don't you boy? Good boy!"

The dog held his ground, the tail wagged and then stopped. Loki whimpered again; head tilted to the side. He kept his hand out and steady, a peace offering.

"Come here, boy! You want your belly scratched?"

The dog took a tentative step forward. Jason smiled. "Good boy, I'm a friend. You lonely? Come on, come here, come here, boy."

The lab bowed his head once and took a closer sniff of his hand and then barreled into him, all tongue and excitement. He'd grown up with dogs, and gave Loki a sound belly rub and scratched all those hard to reach places that had the big puppy almost paralyzed in pleasure. Pulling out a pepperoni stick, he took a bite and gave the other half to Loki, a couple of pieces at a time.

"Don't suppose you have a key?" he asked the dog, who just sat there licking his chops after inhaling the treats.

It wasn't needed, the front door was unlocked. Considering who lived here, he felt he knew what that meant. The smell in the house confirmed it. He glanced down at the dog who was wagging his tail in expectation, and wondered how Loki looked so well fed.

"Where's Howard, boy? Take me to Howard..."

Loki barked once and tore past him through the door, almost taking him out at the knees in the process. The beast hurtled itself across hardwood floors like an out of control Zamboni. Loki almost tumbled as he negotiated a corner. The dog's claws striving for purchase with an excited clatter as he disappeared into what he knew was the kitchen.

Jason followed, noting the heavy silence of the house. There was dry dog food everywhere. Three 50-pound bags had been cut open and left to spill their contents. He breathed a sigh of relief at the dog feed. He then realized Loki wasn't in the kitchen. He heard a bark from outside and went out onto the back deck through the kitchen door. Howard had cut out the bottom panel of the door and hung a remnant of carpet with nails to act as the doggy door. It looked like something that he'd done recently. Loki was running around the backyard with his nose to the ground in excitement, but he could see the mound of disturbed soil. Sorry Loki, I can't bring him back.

There was a dark hole next to the filled in grave, a white cross planted at its head. Somebody hadn't made it to their grave. The injustice of people having to dig their own graves struck him, and he could feel his anger building again.

"Come on, boy!" he yelled, relieved that Loki obeyed him, making for the deck stairs like a blurred shadow.

He found Debbie upstairs in bed. She was in what looked like a Sunday dress, her face almost purple with bruising, but she was whole. Loki wouldn't enter the room. He sat in the hallway at the room's doorway watching, expecting that somehow the nice man with meat snacks could bring his family back.

He found the note next to Debbie's head, pinned to the pillow. It was written in old school, flowing cursive with big loops. The note would have been from the past in any age.

To whomever finds this, I praise the Lord that you're alive, that someone survived this plague. We were well prepared for everything, except something that just didn't fight fair. You may have and use whatever we have. My Howard believed in being prepared and prayed that we'd survive to help the many who would need us. The Lord had other plans. The lock on the basement door is 3560#. I turned the alarm off, but there's instructions down there so you can alarm it if you want - though I don't think the police would come and help. There's a lot down there and more besides at Wolf Gap, our farm out west. There are directions to it down stairs. I only ask that you bury me next to my Howard in the backyard. I couldn't bring myself to lay down in that hole and wait, as much as I tried. God bless you and keep you. His kingdom awaits.

Sincerely, The Dagmans

P.S. – Please look after our Loki, he's still a baby. Howard insisted he was the smartest dog he'd ever seen. I'm not so sure about that. He thinks he's a lap dog, but he's got a big heart.

"You've got a solid reference here, Loki," he managed, wiping away a tear. Reading the letter, he couldn't help but imagine Sam outliving him and what a horror that would have been for her. Another husband and wife going out together – just like he'd planned for himself and Sam.

He found a sleeping bag in the garage, which was a spotless, well ordered three door behemoth. The garage was deep enough that the Dagmans could have parked six cars bumper to bumper. The space not taken up by their two BMWs, a coupe, an SUV, and Howard's restored 1970's Land Cruiser, was given over to a shop, complete with a table saw, welding cart, a squat rack and more outdoor gear than an REI store. It was a man-cave extraordinaire and he doubted if Howard had ever used half the stuff.

The sun was coming up as he finished burying Debbie. Loki laying on the grass, watching him a few yards away. In the growing light, he noticed for the first time the two big rows of solar panels; sixteen of them stretched across the roof facing the backyard. That explained the house's power being on.

"Ok Loki, let's check out the basement."

Loki came to his feet quickly and barked once in expectation of some great adventure.

The door to the basement was heavy steel, set in a steel frame. It had a push button simplex lock, no different than what he'd used countless times before getting into SCIFs at the Pentagon. A Secure Compartmented Information

Facility was designed to control access to sensitive information within. What the hell was Dagman protecting?

He pulled the note from his pocket and entered the code. The door swung outward heavily, and revealed an enclosed stairway. He hit the light switch at the top which must have been Loki's signal to proceed, as the dog barreled past him and went down the rubber treaded stairs and disappeared out of sight, around the corner. He couldn't see any of the basement until he reached the bottom landing.

He pulled up short, looking around... "Holy Shit," he managed.

Loki let out a single bark in agreement from somewhere unseen in the back, behind the row after row of shelving and gun racks. His eyes were immediately drawn to the vertical gun racks of M-4s, AKs, and assorted rifles and shotguns. He walked up and thumbed the tag on one of the AKs, it was brand new, produced by a reputable American manufacturer under license. From each trigger guard hung a price tag. He walked to the next aisle over and noted the cans and crates of ammo, barrel after barrel of dry goods, boxes of MREs and miscellaneous tactical gear ranging from slings, to optics, to boxed up porta potties.

A large American flag hung from the center of the room, its bottom half laid out on the top shelf holding boxes of water purifying life straws and larger percolation systems. One wall at the end of an aisle was taken up by a bank of massive deep-cycle batteries, above which hung a heavy peg board. The house's fuse box took center stage amidst a neatly laid out pattern of heavy wiring. Each piece of hardware had a 3x5 index card taped to it. He saw something labeled charge controller and it read 96%. Labels

61

for the solar panel inputs, another labeled generator and one for inverter.

He took a moment to look at the layout and read the cards, noting the generator wouldn't kick in unless the batteries fell below 30%. Jason could hardly tell what he was looking at, he didn't have a clue how this stuff worked. He didn't have to; everything was labeled, detailed instructions for maintenance laminated and attached to the peg board.

Howard had gotten sick first, he realized. Maybe he'd just acted on the chance that he would. He'd wanted his wife to be able to survive without him, that had to explain the detailed instructions he was looking at.

A slow walk around the perimeter brought him to what looked like a sales counter made up of a waist high desk with two hand-built counters extending outward from either end. The wall behind the counter held yet more guns, these had price tags on them as well. Under the glass topped desk, facing the prospective customer were four Federal Firearms Licenses from the ATF. Licenses #1, 3, 7, and 8 were prominently displayed just as the codicil at the top of each license said it must be.

That explained the guns and ammo; Howard had been an FFL licensed gun dealer. Jason wasn't fooled for a second. Howard may have sold the occasional gun or prepper supply but what he was looking at was a well-heeled, hardcore prepper that had gone the legal route to cover his obsession. He noticed Loki laying behind the counter on a big dog pillow worrying a rawhide bone watching him as if all was right in the world. The basement was huge, bigger than the footprint of the actual house, running under the foundation of the garage. A good one half of the space's heavy-duty shelves held six-gallon plastic buckets of vacuum sealed dry goods, and smaller #12 cans of dehydrated fruits and vegetables.

"Howard... you crazy, paranoid SOB... Thank you." He walked around the perimeter until he came to another locked door. He tried the same combo and wasn't surprised when it worked. It was a smaller room, maybe eight feet wide and twice as deep. The House's HVAC system sat against the back wall. Between the door and the electric furnace unit were four heavy gun safes, the doors hanging open. Each safe door had an index card with the safe's combo taped to its mechanical spin lock.

He walked around the open door of the first safe and saw suppressors of several makes for different calibers, still in their manufacturer's packaging. The next safe held a dozen M-4s and AKs, labeled "automatic" in Howard's straight-line script printing. He shook his head and moved on. The next safe may have been worth protecting a month ago, but was now worthless. It had stacks of gold coins, bags of old silver coins, a baseball card and stamp collection and well as a shelf of labeled personal documents.

The final safe had three shelves of labeled, thick, white three ring binders. There were house records, FFL license applications, training course material, bug-out plan, hole-up plan, firearm and ammo inventories and the list went on and on. A clearer picture of Howard was forming itself. His neighbor hadn't been only a licensed gun dealer and a prepper; he'd also had a serious case of OCD.

Thank you, Howard, he thought quietly.

He'd been dreading going back home since leaving the night before. His neighbor had just given him the out he needed. He'd go back, get some memories and clothes but he'd known he wouldn't be living there when he'd left.

Loki had followed him in to the safe room and was looking at him in expectation.

"Loki... when you're right, you're right. I'm moving in. You ok with that, buddy?"

Loki snuffled a bark and wagged his tail.

"Going to take that as a yes."   *

Chapter 5

Pro had slept on the couch by the front door again; just as he had every night since his little sister Rose, and his Mom had died hours apart in his parents' bed. He'd lost track of how many days ago that had been, four, maybe five, but the smell in the apartment was getting bad and he was hungry. He'd eaten everything he could find in the kitchen, and since the power had gone out three days ago, he hadn't even been able to boil the water for the oatmeal and rice. He'd eaten it uncooked and now it was gone too. His mom had told him to keep the water jugs full of water, and he'd listened. Now, they were almost empty too, and the faucet hadn't worked in three days.

His Dad wasn't coming home. It had been too long. The thought that he might had kept him here, afraid to leave. He had listened for the rumble of the big delivery truck, because he knew his dad wouldn't bother to go to the warehouse to get his pickup. He'd sometimes show up in the truck if his delivery route finished close to home. His dad knew what was going on with everybody dying, that's why he'd taken the job to deliver medical supplies to Philadelphia. His bosses had offered him triple time to make the trip. 'An important delivery working for the Army,' he'd said, except he hadn't come home. He'd left ten days ago and was supposed to have been back later that same night.

Thinking back, his mom had waited up with him. Both of them had been watching the news, flipping between the channels, from story after story of riots. Philadelphia had been one of the places that had burned. They'd shown a large crowd charging over the barricades towards a thin line of police and soldiers before switching over to a car commercial with no warning. His mother had gone to bed right then, crying. He'd stayed up, and waited, flinching every time he heard a siren or the gunshots that seemed to be ringing out all directions. His mother had known, even then, his dad wasn't coming home. Almost two weeks later, he needed to do the same.

Their apartment complex sat in a wooded area just off the Dulles toll road in Herndon, Virginia. The road noise from the busy thoroughfare was continuous, or had been. He hadn't heard or seen a car moving in two days, hadn't heard anything except the shouting of a crazy guy somewhere deeper in the complex and gun fire. That sound he knew well; it wasn't something that could be confused. There'd been a lot of it a week ago. Now, though, it seemed like the shots came by themselves, a couple every hour. Sometimes all at once, and then nothing for a few hours.

His aching stomach reminded him he had to leave and find some food. The gun shots scared him, though. So did the screeching of the crazy guy. For protection, he didn't have anything more dangerous than his pocket knife and whatever he could find in the kitchen.

He turned around from his perch atop the back of the couch where he had a better view of the apartment building's parking lot and the high walls that lined the toll road in the distance. From the hill their building sat on, he could just see over the concrete walls. The empty lanes and abandoned cars scared him too. It looked like something out of the "Walking Dead," but he knew his mom and Rose were just dead behind the bedroom door. They weren't going anywhere.

He looked back at the cardboard barrel of oatmeal. He'd eaten the last of it an hour ago and it had done little to stop the growling in his stomach. Mama had always teased him that his ears would freeze off, as he was always looking for something to eat in the fridge. That wasn't going to happen, the last time he'd opened the door just to be certain he hadn't missed anything, the smell had been unbearable. Different from the smell coming out of his parents' bedroom.

He wanted to do the grown-up thing. He should bury his mom and Rose; but where? The nearest grass was the apartment complex's playground and it was on the other side of the building. His last trip outside had taken him past the place where his sister had spent so much time playing. There hadn't been any grassy space left, even the sandbox for the little kids had held graves. It had been so important to him to stay by the front door. He'd wanted to stop his dad from seeing what was in the back room. That would be a grown-up thing to do too. Then, they could leave together, and go find some food and water... and a place to sleep where the bodies of his family didn't lay on the other side of a door.

He knew those were things *he* needed to do - now. His dad was dead. He needed to stop pretending he was going to come home. He'd cried days ago; cried in fear and anger until he had nothing left. At the moment, looking out the window at the quiet world, he began to realize, he'd die too if he didn't leave. He held out hope that Pete was still alive, but he knew his best friend, and his parents, and his little brother were probably dead too. Pete was the only kid in school who wasn't afraid of his fastball. When they'd both made the Herndon 13-14-year-old All-Star team this last summer, they'd imagined that they were going to play in the major leagues someday.

Pete and his family were gringos but they didn't care where Pro's family had come from. Pro's father had always insisted that if anybody asked, he was to say he was born in Arizona. He wasn't sure he'd ever been to Arizona. He couldn't remember living anywhere other than Virginia. Pete's family was cool about it, they never asked. And they were rich. They had their own house with a garage. Pete even had his own bedroom and only had to share a bathroom with his little brother. He knew what he'd probably find, but he still had to check. Pete would do the same for him.

The book bag with his last water bottles was as heavy as it had been with the books he'd carried to school. He took the biggest knife he could find out of the kitchen and put it into the bag as well. That, with his Swiss Army knife in his pocket, made him feel a little safer as he shut the apartment door and blinked in the harsh autumn sunlight. The smell of smoke was strong, like someone had been burning trash. He glanced back at the apartment door, taking a deep breath. After the apartment, the welcome taste of the acrid air outside felt like betrayal. He wiped away tears as he turned to walk away, promising himself he'd be back to bury his mom and Rose.

His bike was still chained to the apartment complex's staircase where it emptied out into the parking lot. With all the riots and crazy people, especially last week, he was surprised it was still there. He gave the tires a pinch, and straddled the seat wondering where he was going. The empty hollowness in his gut made the decision. Find some food, then check on Pete. A moment later, he dug out the Swiss Army knife, opened the main blade up and curled it into his hand against the handle bar's grip.

Armed, he was riding out on to the main road a few seconds after. He'd be back, he told himself, but he knew that was a lie. He didn't think he could ever go into that apartment again. He'd said his goodbye days ago, while they were alive. He'd cried himself to sleep for two days. It was enough, he could hear his dad's voice; it was time to grow up.

The shopping center; the one named for the clock tower, was a mile down the road, almost all downhill. He coasted most of the way, moving slowly, keeping constant pressure on the brake, listening for anything, anyone. He heard two gunshots way off to the west, maybe at the airport. There had to be rich people there, people with the money to fly away from this.

He'd ridden halfway to the grocery store when he realized the smell from the apartment was still there. It wasn't his sweatshirt. He confirmed that by pulling the collar up over the bottom half of his face and giving it a good whiff. In fact, the Redskins sweatshirt was clean and still smelled like the soap his mom used in the laundry. It blocked whatever was stinking which seemed to get worse the closer he got to the shopping center.

He saw them as he came around a corner and slammed on his brakes leaving a mark of rubber on the sidewalk. He could see down into and across the shopping center's parking lot. Bodies, hundreds of them, maybe thousands, were piled up in the middle of the parking lot. The pile was almost as high as the big dump truck parked next to them. Orange parking cones were set up around the edges of the pile. He stared at the cones, confused for a moment. Who would have put the cones in a parking lot? Did people need the cones, so they didn't park next to the bodies? Or did the bodies have to go inside the cones? It wasn't right.

Where had they all come from? Who had put them there? He realized the pile was moving. His ears started working again. Giant black birds looking like vultures covered the pile, fighting each other and smaller birds for whatever piece they were eating. There were rats moving on the asphalt between the pile of bodies and the grocery store that looked as big as cats. The only other time he'd even seen a rat, was during a weekend delivery trip to New York that his dad had brought him along on.

He swallowed hard as his stomach rebelled at the sight and he pulled up his collar again to try and block the smell. The front of the grocery store was in ruins. All the windows were broken out, and it looked like the store next door, a pharmacy had been burned. The bodies were piled right in front of the store. There was no way he was going anywhere close to that. He rode past the shopping center slowly, trying to make sense of what he was seeing. Someone had hung a bedsheet on the Starbucks in the middle of the shopping center's parking lot. *"The End."* Was it? Was everyone else dead? He couldn't be the only one left, could he?

Pro put his head down and pedaled as fast as he could past the shopping center, turning right, he rode towards Herndon's city center. There was another grocery store there, the one with the good bakery. When he'd been a little kid, and gone with his mom, she'd always let him get a doughnut. He told himself it was the wind in his face making his eyes water.

He left the squawking pile of dead bodies behind, his legs pumped with the energy of having been locked in his apartment for two weeks. He was scared, alone and surrounded by dead bodies. Everywhere he looked there were dark storefronts with broken windows, cars abandoned in the middle of the road, or driven half way into a store and then left as a reminder of the driver's last action. And everywhere... bodies. In and out of cars, some shot, many just laying peacefully, all purple black with disease and rot.

His mom hadn't allowed them to open the windows after the news had told everyone to stay at home. It hadn't helped, they'd still died. These people, who'd left their houses, had died too. It hadn't mattered what people did. Why was he alive? The man on the TV had said some people would be immune. He only knew it meant you wouldn't get sick. It wasn't fair to be immune and then have to live alone.

The parking lot of the Safeway Center had another pile of bodies, not as big as the first, and not directly in front of the storefront. That didn't matter, the grocery store had been gutted by a fire, its roof had collapsed and looked like big flat soup bowl. He stopped his bike at the edge of the parking lot, willing a fireman or a cop to walk out from behind one of the quiet firetrucks or climb out of the police cars. Somebody he could ask for help, but there was no one.

The only sound was the squawking birds and the squeak of the rats if he listened hard enough. He looked across the street at the 7-11, whose windows were all missing. It was dark inside as well, but there was enough sun that he could make out the back of the store even from across the road. At one end of the small building, where the ice freezers had lined the sidewalk, a pick-up truck had driven its nose into the store. The ice boxes now sat in the middle of the store along with the front half of the truck.

He pedaled across the street, and leaned his bike up against the half-buried truck. He could still hear the birds across the street as he stood in the doorway listening as hard as he could for the sound of rats or people. The store seemed as quiet as everything else as he stepped inside, thinking it looked like a bomb had gone off. There were two bodies lying on the floor at the end of the counter in front of where the pizza slices and chicken wings used to be. His stomach growled in protest with the memory of the spicy chicken wings his dad would bring home for dinner sometimes.

The bodies on the floor hadn't died of the sickness. He could recognize the gunshot wounds that had killed them. The top of one woman's head was missing and he could see the missing parts on the wall above the soda machine. He'd watched the Walking Dead at Pete's house when he'd spent the night. His family had all those streaming channels. He half expected the bodies to get up and start coming after him as he took another step into the store.

He couldn't be scared, he knew that. If everyone was dead, he was going to have to get used to dead bodies. Zombies weren't real. Besides, he knew he was fast enough to outrun any clumsy zombie, but only if they weren't the crazy fast zombies that never got tired, like in that one movie.

Thoughts of zombies and his fear were forgotten when he saw a Snickers bar on the floor, still wrapped. He'd unwrapped and eaten the bar in four large bites before he realized it. His confidence growing, he used his feet to rummage through the store. The shelves were pretty much empty, or tipped over, everything was on the floor. He found a small plastic jar of peanut butter. It wasn't the extra crunchy kind he liked, but extra creamy. It still went really well with the jerky he found in a plastic jar behind the counter. The jar looked like it had been shot a dozen times with a bb gun, but the lid still worked. He scooped out the peanut butter with the thick slices of Jerky.

Several of the glass cooler display cases had been shot at, and the floor got sticky when he got close, but he found a bottle of Gatorade, something called Pom and a can of beer. Brushing off the ants which seemed to cover the floor, he polished off the Gatorade in several long pulls and then cracked the top of the warm beer can. It smelled like the beer his dad would sometimes drink when he was watching football. He sipped at it, and spit it out almost immediately. Pete had said his dad let him taste it one time, like it was a big deal. It was awful, and it was already something he was going to scratch off the 'look for' list. Out of habit he looked for a garbage can and a second later tossed the can onto the pile of broken shelving in the middle of the store.

He loaded his backpack with some crackers, a bunch of Vienna sausages, and more candy bars. A box of granola bars under a shelf was the real find, and he only eyed the cans of cat food. He'd never be that desperate. There was bound to be lots of cat food, the man on TV had said cats got the same disease that was killing everyone and died too. Not as many as with people, but a lot of them. He added a small flashlight to his collection. It was the kind you hooked to a key chain, but it was more than he had at the moment. He headed back outside, the weight of the book bag pulling on his shoulders felt good. He figured he had enough to not show up empty-handed at Pete's house.

The throaty roar of a truck growing closer didn't even register as he stood there, blinking in the bright sunlight. He didn't react until a panel truck followed by an Army jeep drove by on the road directly in front of him. The squeal of brakes snapped him out of his surprise. He ran forward ducking down between his bike and the pickup truck whose front end was parked inside the 7-11. Leaning against the cracked rear window of the truck was the head of the driver, twisted backwards, facing the wrong way, his milky eyes seemed to be seemed to be looking right at him.

Dropping to his knees, then his stomach, he crawled underneath the truck, its front end was propped up on the window sill of the store and he had plenty of room. He belly crawled towards the back where there was just enough space to see out across the street into the grocery store's parking lot where the truck and jeep had turned into. Three men got out of the jeep, and another from the delivery truck. All of them were dressed like soldiers, sort of. They didn't have helmets; a couple even wore baseball hats. Only one of them had army pants. They all carried rifles, which looked like the M-4s he recognized from his video games.

He watched the strange group as they walked over to the police cars in the parking lot. Pro jolted in surprise and hit his head on the underside of the truck when they shot at the police car's window.

They took another gun from the cop car, and some more stuff from its trunk and then repeated the process on the other car. Why hadn't he thought of that? Of course, the police cars had guns in them. He watched as the men spread out and checked the stores in the shopping center. One of them came out with a plastic barrel of something from the fast food chicken place next to the store. The two that went into the Safeway with flashlights, emerged a few seconds later, with a chopping sign at their throats. Empty. He could have told them that.

He watched them as they loaded the guns into the big jeep-looking vehicle, a *Hum* something he knew. The man carried the barrel of whatever he'd taken from the restaurant to the back of the panel van, where he waited for the other three to join him. They pounded on the door, and waited a second before unlocking it and rolling up the back door. They sat the bucket up into the truck, and were talking to somebody he couldn't see in the back. After a moment, Pro watched as someone came forward from the interior of the truck and grabbed the bucket before disappearing out of sight again.

The men with the guns seemed to be discussing something and then pointed into the back of the truck. That's when the screaming started. One man came out into sight, sat down on the back edge and stepped down out of the truck. He was an old man, and he moved slow. One of the soldiers kept a gun pointed at him. There was more shouting, this time from the soldiers pointing their guns into the back of the truck. He saw four people, three of them dragging and pushing a woman between them to the back edge of the truck. One of the soldiers handed his rifle to one of his buddies, reached up and roughly pulled the woman out of the truck dropping her at the feet of the old man who had crawled out on his own.

The other soldiers pointed their rifles back at the people in the truck, as one of the soldiers stepped up on the bumper and pulled the door down and relocked it. They dragged the woman, Pro could see she was older too, to her feet. They prodded the two elderly prisoners forward towards the pile of bodies in the center of the parking lot. The old man walked ahead and Pro saw him flip the bird over his shoulder to the men with guns behind him. He could hear the soldiers laughing. He knew what was going to happen. He didn't want to watch, but couldn't look away. The woman started screaming again, Pro could hear her across the street. "You bastards!"

They shot her before they got to the pile, laughing as they walked past her body. Two, maybe three of the soldiers shot the old man in the back as he reached the pile of bodies.

Pro stayed underneath the truck until the sun was starting to go down, long after the soldiers had departed. His head on a swivel, he rode his bike the three miles or so to Pete's house which was as dark and quiet as the rest of the nice neighborhood. The house was unlocked and empty, and didn't smell like the apartment he'd left. He hadn't realized how tired he was, until he sat down on Pete's living room couch and wondered where Pete and his family had gone. The sleep that caught up to and enveloped him didn't even register.

In the morning, he found them, out back behind the garage where Pete's mom used to have a garden. Two graves already lay with markers. One for Pete, and one for Pete's mom. He looked at the dates on Pete's cross, born Oct 1, 2005. Pete would have had a birthday soon; maybe that was already past. Pete's dad lay in a shallow, open grave, next to Seth, Pete's little brother. Mr. Dobson was still holding the gun that he'd used to kill himself as he'd lain down, the mark of the sickness across his purple face and down his arms. He took the gun as carefully as he could, recognizing it as one of the guns that Pete's dad had let them fire at the range. He covered Seth and Mr. Dobson up with the shovel stuck into the pile of dirt, waiting for him or somebody else to come along. He wished he could have done that for his mom and sister and promised himself, again, that he would.

Over the next month, he ate everything he could find to eat in the Dobson's home. He slept upstairs on the extra bed in Pete's room. The same place he'd slept when he'd spent the night, underneath the life size poster of Aaron Rodgers. He used to complain to Pete about that. A die-hard Vikings fan, it had somehow felt like he was betraying a trust, sleeping under Aaron Rogers. Now though, it didn't bother him. He imagined all the football players were dead too. Sometimes he caught himself wondering if anyone would ever play football or baseball again. His dream of someday pitching in the big leagues was gone like everything else.

Chapter 6

Pro had learned his lesson from the grocery parking lot. He rarely left the house during the day. He'd explore the houses in Pete's neighborhood at night, with a bandana around his face, sprayed with Mrs. Dobson's perfume. It didn't block all the stench, but it helped him breathe as he collected food in a duffle bag, stocking up for the winter. He wondered if he was being clever or just scared, but he never used a flashlight until he was inside a house. Even then, he taped a dark sock around the front of the lens, giving him just enough light to look through cupboards, closets and drawers for something he could use. The soldiers couldn't catch him if they didn't know about him, didn't see him.

He wasn't sure how long he'd been there when his luck changed. The days were shorter than they had been, and ran together. He'd stopped counting weeks ago, marking the days on a piece of paper on the kitchen table when he'd reached thirty. It had snowed a little bit, twice in the last week, leaving the bodies lying outside covered in a thin shell of frosting the animals and birds had no problem penetrating.

He hadn't left the house since the snow, and he wasn't going to until it melted enough that he could be sure he wasn't going to leave footprints leading back here. He could see that the coyotes and wild dogs were leaving tracks everywhere and they seemed to be around all the time. The coyotes mostly kept their distance, the packs of wild dogs didn't. The soldiers weren't the only thing Pro was hiding from. He'd already had to shoot one of the dogs in a pack that had started following him.

He'd collected quite an arsenal from just the 84 houses he had explored so far. He kept a list in a small notebook of the streets and house numbers he'd searched. After a while they all started to look the same, especially in the dark. He now had a shotgun, that he cut the barrel off of like he'd seen the Punisher do. It was a 12 gauge, and most of the shotgun shells that he'd found, fit the gun. He'd also found several .22 rifles, one of which he'd used to shoot the dog with. He could still hear the snarling hunger of the rest of the pack, when they'd forgotten him and torn into their injured pack mate.

He'd occasionally practice shooting the .22 or one of the 9 mms when he was in a basement of a house he was searching through. Never more than a few shots at a time. If the soldiers came, he wasn't going to let them put him in the back of truck. He needed to be ready. Which was why, looking out his bedroom window that morning, his hand went to the gun on his hip.

Down the middle of the snow-covered street in front of his house were tire tracks. Wide tracks, like from a truck or one of the big jeeps the soldiers used. He hadn't heard a thing while he'd slept. He crept out of his room, down the hall to Pete's parents' bedroom. He'd stacked boxes and boxes of collected food and bottled drinks up in every room, but had left the space in front of the windows open so the house wouldn't look any different from the outside. The window he went to overlooked the front yard and the street corner the house's lot sat on. The tire tracks only went one-way, down Monroe St., the neighborhood's main road, and he thought it looked like it had been headed towards Reston. It was hard to tell without going outside through the snow, to look at the treads, and he wasn't about to add his own tracks.

Auburn Street's surface of snow was clean and unbroken, except for the pile of frozen red and black flesh that he knew was the body of the big fat guy who had died with a Redskins hoodie on. The animals had been at the body through the dusting of snow covering it. From a distance it looked like a big, jagged edged, red and black speedbump in a blanket of white.

He checked his gun. It had taken him a while to figure out how it worked, and he'd tried everything he could without bullets until he was sure what made the trigger click and what didn't. He dropped the bullet holder out, and then worked the slide on the Glock, ejecting the round. He tried catching it like he'd seen on TV but the bullet spun out over his shoulder before he could grab it. He picked it up, wiped it against his sweat pants and put it back into the stack of bullets - which was always the hardest part for him. The bullet holder was almost full, minus the one round he held, and it was all he could do to push down hard enough to get the final round in. He shook his head wondering why it should be so hard to load. But he had several of the stacks loaded and he'd made sure they all worked.

Over the next three days, he spotted a Hummer, two different ones because one of them had a pirate flag bumper sticker using the same road. He saw a panel van, from some bakery with the Hummer, and then once again, by itself. He didn't think for a second that the van was carrying fresh bread.

It hadn't snowed again and most of the ground cover had melted or blown away. Working at night, Pro started moving supplies to a house two blocks away. He thought it would be a good idea to have another hideout deeper within the network of neighborhood roads away from Monroe. The road in front of Pete's house was getting too busy for his liking. It was a few hours before the sun would be up, and he'd already made two round trips. He was tired, but at least the two duffle bags were empty as he was almost back to Pete's house, his house, for the last load.

It was quiet that night, no dog howls, no possums or squirrels making noises in the bushes, nothing but a little bit of cold wind that stirred the top branches of the bare trees and made them creak. It was later that he realized those sounds, the absence of them, meant something. By then it was too late. He was across his back yard, up on the stone patio headed for the backdoor when he heard an electronic beep and something that sounded like the empty static that he could hear on the battery powered radios he'd found. It was coming from inside the house. He froze in place and then took a couple of steps backward until he was even with the back corner of the garage.

He slid backwards around the corner, his eyes focused on the back door to the house, when a strong arm slid around his neck. A strong gloved hand clamped down over his mouth and jaw, stopping his scream before it started.

"Relax kid," the voice whispered in his ear. "There's some very bad people in your house. I'm not with them."

Pro struggled and the grip just tightened. "If you make a sound, I'm out of here and you're on your own with these assholes. You understand what I'm saying?"

The words registered, as the backdoor swung open. Two soldiers came out, turned away and walked down the driveway towards the street.

"Call for a truck and get this stuff collected," one of the voices said clearly. "Set a team up across the street. Whoever it is, they're a scrounger, worth snatching up."

"I think it's a kid," the other voice said. "No booze inside."

"Even better," the voice first voice said. "I'm outta here, get that stuff back to the mall tonight."

They kept talking but their voices faded out as they moved further down the driveway away from them.

"Did you hear that?" the voice in Pro's ear whispered.

Pro did his best to nod.

"You going to keep your shit together? If I let you go? If you run, they will find you."

Pro weighed his options. The guy who held him was as strong as shit and he clearly wasn't with the soldiers. But that didn't mean he wasn't a perv or something.

"Give me a nod if you're good," the voice whispered. "I'll let you go. You can run if you want. If you're that stupid, you're on your own."

Pro nodded and the pressure on his neck and jaw released. He fell to the frozen ground over legs that wouldn't quite work. He looked up and saw a black suited figure in front of him backing away a few steps, hands held out. The man's face was blacked out like soldiers he'd seen on TV. He wore what looked like a solid black bicycle helmet, but rounder. The helmet had what looked like a pair of binoculars strapped to its front. There was an army gun, the same type carried by the soldiers hanging free on some sort of sling. One hand held a small pistol with a really long barrel, the other was empty.

"I'm leaving now," the voice said. "You should come with me, it's not safe for you here."

"Where?" Pro asked in his own whisper.

"It's safe. I promise."

"Nowhere is safe," Pro replied shaking his head. They could still hear the two soldiers talking, just fragments of mumbles, out on the driveway, around the other side of the garage.

He saw the man's teeth in what might have been a smile. "Not out here on your own, it isn't. Especially with these guys around."

"You a soldier?"

The man took a while to answer. "I used to be. Not like these pretend assholes that are looking to grab you up."

"They kill people."

"I know," the man said after a moment. "Not when I can help it. We need to go..." The dark suited soldier holstered his funny looking hand gun with the long barrel and took half a step forward holding a hand out to help him up.

Pro crab-walked backwards, away from the offer of help, unaware that he popped back out around the corner of the garage. The sound of shattering glass exploded from the second story of the house overlooking the patio and backyard.

"Snyder! Kid's out back!!" A man shouted from the window above him.

The soldier next to him grabbed his jacket sleeve and pulled him back around the corner of the garage, turned him towards the back fence of the yard by his shoulders.

"Run."

Pro ran for all he was worth, hearing a strange sounding cough from the behind him. He vaulted the short wooden fence that had been put there by Pete's dad to keep Trouble in. Trouble had been their family's beagle. The fence proved no barrier and he could hear the crunching of booted feet on frozen grass behind him.

"Kid, stop!" one of them yelled. He turned just enough to see the two soldiers raising their guns towards him. He was frozen in fear. He saw a shadow move behind the garage. Two flashes at the end of the shadow's arm accompanied by a strange sounding *phuut... phuut,* and both soldiers collapsed in a pile making more noise than the dark suited soldier's gun had.

The soldier looked up at him and saw him watching, and waved him on frantically. He heard the back door of the house slam open, the soldier in the house was joining the chase "He's running south!" he heard a voice yell.

Pro turned and ran, the roar of one of the Army jeeps coming down Monroe had his name on it, every bit as much as the pack of wild dogs had. He crossed the alley into another backyard and went left, and was through three more back yards before he knew it. He turned right, and hugged the edge of a house, his cheek coming in contact with the cold aluminum siding. He crept up towards the front of the house and dropped to his knees between two big shrubs. He peeked out at the road in front of him. This was his neighborhood. He'd scavenged these homes weeks ago, and knew there was another narrow alleyway behind the line of houses across the street.

He did his best to listen over the sound of his heart hammering in his ears and chest. He could hear at least one, maybe two of the Army jeeps moving behind him back towards his house. Occasionally he could hear men shouting but they were too far behind him for him to tell what they were saying. He sat there for at least five minutes wondering if the soldiers had killed the stranger behind the garage, of if he'd managed to kill all of them. But then he'd hear a revving engine, a car door, or a shout that carried through the night. There were more of them in the area than he'd thought. The voices were not happy, that was very clear.

He'd waited long enough. Jumping up, he sprinted across the road, and shot between two houses, across a backyard, and through a gate that opened up on an alley. Pro hugged the fence and peaked out in both directions down the frozen muddy track riddled with mud puddles edged in ice. He didn't like alleys. They were usually lined on both sides with tall solid wooden fences. There was no way to go, but forward or back, and half the gates leading into backyards, always next to the big garbage cans, had locks on them. He had worried about getting into an alley and being chased by a pack of dogs that would catch him before he could get to the next open gate.

He ran from one gate opening to the next, staying out of the middle of the alley and hugging the fence line on his right. There wasn't much moonlight, but what there was shone on the other side. At each gate he stopped at, he'd step out of the alley into the small alcove and listen. He could hear more vehicles than he'd heard at any point since everybody died. At one point he saw one fly past the alley opening ahead of him, but it was going far too fast to be looking for him in the alley. He jumped out and ran on, past two openings and was aiming for a third, when the angry revving of an engine behind froze him in place.

Powerful lamps atop the army jeep came on and he was bathed in light. They almost blinded him when he glanced behind and could see the headlights bounce through the potholes as the Jeep screamed down the alley towards him.

Snapping out of it, in his mind's eye he could see the pack of slobbering dogs running him down and he sprinted to the next gate opening.

A dark form stepped out of an alcove to his left as Pro dove for the possible safety of the one in front of him on his right.

He thought he was going to get shot in the back, as the soldier's rifle opened up, firing like a machine gun. Pro could feel the pounding of the shots with his whole body. Ears ringing, he turned back around and saw the man firing back down the alley at the soldier's jeep. It was the soldier from the backyard, he realized. Frozen in shock, he watched as the stranger stopped firing and stepped back into the shadows of his own alcove, dropped a box out of his gun, replaced it with another in a smooth motion, and leaned out of his hiding spot and fired again before rolling back behind cover.

"You ok?" The man yelled at him.

Pro nodded, "Yeah."

"That gate behind you unlocked?"

Pro turned and saw the heavy chain looped around the gate post, he pulled on the chain pulling the lock through to his side. He shook it in frustration.

The man fired another dozen shots down the alley. Pro heard shots coming back, whistling, cutting through the air between them, several bullets kicked up the frozen mud of the alley.

"If they catch you, you tell them I tried to shoot you."

Pro just looked at the man in confusion.

"Get down, I'll shoot the gate. Go to the park. Get to the baseball diamond, hide in the dugout, I'll get there if I can."

Pro didn't know what to say.

"Down!!" The man yelled and raised his gun, Pro kissed the cold concrete pad that held two garbage cans. The shots fired in his direction, impacted the gate behind and above him. He was paralyzed with terror and couldn't move; his ears were ringing. He could barely hear the strange soldier yelling, "Go! Go!"

Another blast of machine gun fire ripped out from behind him, spurring him to move. He was through the remnants of the gate and had crossed the yard, the next street, another two yards and the final street at the edge of the small park before he'd realized it. He drew up behind one of the massive trees that lined the neighborhood park. He was breathing hard and could feel his heartbeat in his face and at the ends of his fingers. The sounds of more gunfire reached him, coming from where he'd run. It sounded like a lot more guns than it had before. He felt bad for the strange soldier, figuring that he was going to get himself killed.

He could see the two small baseball diamonds, their outfields backing onto one another. Only one of little-league fields had dugouts. He waited until there was another blast of gunfire and sprinted for the nearest dugout along the third base line.

The concrete dugout still held a half inch of snow sprinkled over two or three feet of fallen leaves that had blown in during the fall. No one had bothered collecting the leaves out the park while the world had died. Pro almost felt like he was swimming in the dugout, every movement accompanied by the crack and rustle of freeze-dried leaves that reached above his knees. He sat up on the lowest concrete step, buried up to his neck in leaves and watched out past left field in the direction of the alley for any sign of pursuit.

The black suited soldier couldn't have survived. There were too many of the others out there. He could hear their jeeps roaring around the neighborhoods surrounding the park, looking for someone. He couldn't imagine why they'd want to catch him; he was just a kid.

The thought that the soldier might still be alive made the guilty feeling that had been beginning to gnaw at him, go away. The hope that he was, made him feel bad for not trusting the guy. Just as quickly, he realized he didn't know anything about him. Probably just another crazy dude that liked killing people. He shook his head at the memory how quick, and easy the soldier had killed the two men in the back yard. Two shots to their heads, with that strange sounding gun. The guy could have killed him had he wanted to. He knew that. Probably could have snapped my neck or cut my throat behind the garage and the soldiers never would have known he was there. But he hadn't.

He waited for what seemed liked twenty minutes, trying to decide if he would be better off alone, or with some stranger. The flicker of lights across the road at the edge of the park grabbed his attention.

Two men using flashlights had walked out from the neighborhood between the park and the alley he'd escaped from. They were walking together and shining the flashlights into the bushes along the houses on either side of the street. Were they still looking for him? Or the soldier? He imagined they had to be a lot madder at the other soldier than with him, but he still didn't want to be caught. Which was starting to look more and more likely as the two men crossed the road into the park, their flashlights inspecting the playground equipment out beyond left field.

Pro pulled his Glock from his holster and slowly made his way to the other end of the dugout by walking along the aluminum bench bolted to the wall. He hopped over to the steps leading up to the batter's circle, and crouched down for a moment looking behind him. He couldn't see the flashlights so he left the baseball diamond, going around the back stop, and behind the far bleachers. He bolted for the dark open area of the park, running for all he was worth. He tried to follow a line of tree trunks that led to the far edge of the park. There, another row of houses promised safety. He had to find a house to hide in before the sun came up.

He was out of the park, and in the middle of the road when a big jeep, hidden behind a bank of bright lights froze him in place as it came around the corner to his left. It jumped the curb and came directly across the corner lot's lawn before bouncing back into the road and coming to a brake squealing stop in front of him. He was about to run, when another jeep roared up the street behind him, the glow of its lights pinning him place as it came to a stop twenty feet back.

"Drop your gun," an angry voice yelled from the first jeep. "Get on your knees." The voice, a different one, yelled. Hidden behind the glare of the headlights that surrounded him, he could hear doors opening and closing.

He fell to his knees, and realized he still had the gun in his hand just before something hit him on the back of the head. He saw the road coming up to meet his face, but the descending darkness was complete before it got there.

*

89

"Dammit, Lonny," Jason heard one of the dark shadows backlit by the Hummer's headlights yell. "He's just a kid, don't kill him."

Jason knelt behind the bumper of a VW Jetta, its tires flat, three houses away from where the Humvees had corralled the boy. He'd watched with his night vision (NODS) as the kid had made a run for it from the dugout. He'd tried to circle around and intercept him, but he'd been too far away at the start and the kid could flat out fly. He was now looking at six hostiles, with one of the Hummers being a surplus Army vehicle sporting an M-60 mounted on a roof spindle. It wasn't a fight he was going to risk with the kid in the middle. Especially with the spray and pray fire control he'd seen these clowns display over the last half hour.

He watched as two of them dragged the kid to the civilian Hummer and lifted him into the back seat. Gun thugs; they were no different from those he'd come across in Afghanistan, Somalia or Mindanao. He couldn't think of them as anything else; not since he'd discovered their propensity to kill anyone too young or too old to be of use to them. Not just a few psychos, they were a cohesive group, systematically culling the survivors.

The goons, all loaded back into their vehicles, amid laughter and self-congratulatory slaps on the back at having captured a scared teenager. The Hummers jumped the curb and roared off directly across the park. Their headlights lighting up the flat featureless expanse and backlighting the trees. He watched their brake lights pop as they dropped back onto a side road on the far side of the baseball fields and followed them until they disappeared up a side street headed back towards Monroe.

"Well... shit," he muttered. He'd caught himself doing that a lot when Loki wasn't with him. This hadn't gone down like he'd imagined. He'd intercepted the thugs' radios that morning. They had been onto somebody hiding out in Herndon, and he'd thought it would be a great opportunity to hunt a few of them down. In that, he'd been successful. Besides the three goons at the house, he thought he might have at hit another one in the alley. He hadn't counted on the kid.

Whoever he was, he was smart. The kid had survived on his own these past months, and he'd overheard the thugs talking about the treasure trove of gear and food that had been squirreled away in the house. Fast as hell too, he thought as he glanced back across the park where he had followed the kid's sprint. The teenager might have gotten away on his own had he not interfered. He stood up and flipped the NODS back down over his eyes, and started moving. He knew where they were going.

*

Chapter 7

Pro came awake as the jeep jumped a curb, crossed a median, then dropped back down into the roadway. He started to move, when he realized he was pinched in between two men in the back seat. A strong grip pinned his left arm to his own leg,

"Easy, kid." The voice from the man holding his arm, to his left, came from a pale, pock-marked face, whose smile sent a chill down his spine.

The man in the front passenger seat turned around to face him.

"You're safe now. We saved you from that lunatic out there tonight." The man had a crew cut and looked like he belonged in the Army. He was big, almost fat, but more solid looking. He glanced up to his left. The man pinning his arm had long blonde hair and bright blue eyes that regarded him with a scary looking smirk. Even seated, he could tell the man was tall and skinny.

The hand holding squeezed his arm a little harder. "This is where... you say, 'thank you.'"

"Ease up, Lonny." The man's voice in the front seat sounded like he was used to telling people what to do. The pressure on his arm slacked off a little bit.

Pro glanced at the other soldier in the back, on his right. He was shorter, with dark hair, and he seemed to be interested in the passing darkness outside the window. The driver was an Asian man who seemed to be focused on the road in front of them.

"You ok, kid?" the soldier-looking one in the front asked. "You speak English?"

Pro nodded.

92

"Good," the man nodded back and smiled a little as if that explained everything.

"We're taking you somewhere safe. Lots of folks like you, tired of living by themselves, scrounging for food and trying to stay warm. Have you been living on your own since the suck?"

The suck? Was that what they called everyone dying? "Yeah," he answered.

"How does a hot meal and a warm shower sound?"

He was scared enough that neither one sounded very good.

They got off the toll road at Rt. 7. Pro was reminded of going to Tysons Mall with his parents. They'd last taken him there to see the new Star Wars movie. Pete had come with him, and they'd stayed at the theater all afternoon going from one cinema to another. It seemed like a long time ago, but he knew it had only been a month or so before everyone died. He only had to look out the window, riding through an empty wasteland of abandoned buildings and vehicles to remember where he was, even if what he saw was a different world.

"That man tonight?" the one in the front who he thought of as the leader, turned back around at him as they made a turn between dark office towers looming above them. "How long have you known him?"

Pro shook his head. "I don't know him. He tried to shoot me." How had the soldier known these men would ask? "He just showed up."

"In the alley?"

Pro almost said yes, but remembered the men at the house on their radios. They had said something on the radio about him being there.

"No, at my house. He just showed up when I was sneaking back. He asked where I was taking my food. When the people in my house started shooting, he shot back. I just ran."

The man just stared back at him for a moment before nodding. "So, you never saw him before tonight?"

Pro shook his head, "No."

"You're lucky, that's for certain. He killed four of our guys tonight, could have been you. You'll be safe with us."

"Can you just take me back?" Pro asked, hope winning out over the growing feeling of dread.

"No can do, kid." The leader didn't bother to turn back and look at him. "We're just about the only authority left. We can't leave kids out there alone to be eaten by wild dogs, now can we?"

Pro almost replied that the dogs were doing fine eating the people they'd killed, but he kept his mouth shut.

The leader turned around and looked at him again in challenge. "Can we?"

"I guess not."

The jeep turned again, going through what felt like a canyon of tall office buildings and came out onto a wide six lane road. They shot across the road without slowing, into the parking lot of the Galleria Mall. There were two malls in Tysons; the big one and the nice one. The Galleria was the nice one, and its power was on.

The soldier in the front passenger seat smiled at the look of surprise on his face.

"The Ritz Hotel here got turned into a FEMA site during the suck. The feds kicked out all them Arab princes that stayed there and nationalized the place," the leader grinned.

94

"Of course, they were dying like everyone else, so no biggie. They set us up real nice, we got power and a well for water."

"Ever stayed at the Ritz, kid?" The driver laughed, speaking for the first time.

"Kid's never seen the inside of a hotel," the skinny one to his left snickered. Lonny; he wasn't about to forget that name.

A part of him wanted to tell them all to eat shit. His All-Star team had stayed at a hotel in Richmond last summer, for a whole week during a tournament.

The vehicle pulled to a stop along a line of other jeeps and trucks parked neatly in front of the entrance. Pro could see three guys walking around the parking lot with rifles. They looked like guards and he wondered if they were keeping people in or out.

"Who wants to go tell Bauman we missed him again?" The leader asked with a grunt as he opened his door and stepped out.

"I'll get the kid sorted out," Lonny said, keeping a tight grip on his arm.

The leader glanced back through the cab of the hummer at Lonny and then looked at Pro for a moment.

"No, you get the loaders ready. The kid's supplies will be coming behind us."

"Sure thing, boss." The look of disappointment on Lonny's face was real enough it scared him.

"Sleepy, you take the kid. Get him squared away."

"Right." The dark-haired soldier, the quiet one, that had been on his right in the back seat, waved at him to follow as he headed towards the mall's entrance.

The mall's entrance was between a restaurant and a deli of some sort with a long Italian name. Both of the businesses were dark inside, except for the reddish glow of exit lights and a few emergency floor lights. There was enough light to see inside the mall itself. Every forty yards or so there was a weak pillar of light falling to the floor from the ceiling far above them. The presence of power, the fact that at least some lights were on, took him a moment to adjust to. He'd lived the past months by candle-light and when he could find batteries that worked, flashlights. The mall's storefronts, minus the emergency lighting, were all dark and empty.

They went past a Starbucks, its tables and chairs all set up for business and looking empty and lonely in the dim light. Then the soldier, with nothing more than a glance back towards him, led him up a frozen escalator. It was nothing more than shiny set of metal stairs without power. A reminder that lights, or not, the power here had a limit.

At the top of the climb, he could see into one of the big department stores. The lights were on inside and there were half a dozen people inside moving boxes. They even had a boom box playing. The music sounded old, like the stuff Coach Dunleavy would play in his car when driving a load of them to a game.

The soldier, Sleepy, caught him watching the others inside the store. "Storage in the mall, we live in the hotel."

Pro nodded, amazed at all the stuff they had, most of the stores he could see from the top of the escalator were packed with storage bins, boxes and barrels.

"Why do they call you Sleepy?"

"I don't know." The man didn't bother to turn around to address him, he just waved a hand over his shoulder beckoning him to follow.

The elevator entrance from the mall to the Ritz was working. Pro tried to conceal his surprise when the doors parted with a quiet chime. He had thought elevators were part of that very long list of things that would never work again, like heat that came from a thermostat on the wall, television, air conditioning, jet planes, and his little sister's laugh.

They rode down a few floors in silence. He was starting to form his own opinion of why they called this guy Sleepy. The doors opened up in a dark alcove, of wood paneled walls and deep red carpet. He followed the soldier around the corner into the main lobby, and was shocked to see at least a dozen people going in different directions. It was more people than he'd imagined he'd ever see again.

They all looked busy. Many had rifles, some of them carried big hand guns strapped to their legs with thigh holsters that he had always wished he could find, but never had. How many people lived here? With all the soldiers he'd seen and the people inside the mall, there must be dozens of them.

Sleepy prodded him into motion with a tap to the shoulder and pointed at the big wall of polished dark wood, with a long, chest high counter in front of it. Sleepy led him over to the counter under a shiny brass sign that said 'Front Desk.' The woman behind the desk nodded at Sleepy, as she typed away on a working computer.

"Give me just a second, hon."

Pro watched as Sleepy just nodded, and saw his eyes just glaze over into that faraway look he'd seen inside the jeep. Pro glanced around the lobby, at the people working or conversing with others. He noticed right away the dozen or so people without guns, looked a lot busier than those with.

He imagined they were the ones who kept the brass sign over his head polished.

The woman behind the counter finished typing and after a disapproving glance in his direction, smiled up at Sleepy. She looked like a teacher to Pro. She had dark hair streaked with gray in a bun on the top her head, and he noticed right away that she was kind of heavy set. At least the people here weren't starving. Of course, if they stole food from everyone they rescued, like they had with him, how could they be?

"A new foundling?" She greeted him just like a teacher, with a well-practiced fake smile of someone who felt a lot different than they let on.

Sleepy pulled a map book from inside his army vest with a dozen pockets and straps. As the soldier leafed through the map, Pro noticed the look of frustration on the lady's face until he found the page he was looking for. He put a finger on a spot in the page and turned it around to show the woman.

"Hmmm," she made a few notes on a pad of paper. "Page 26, Herndon/Reston, grid C-6?"

Sleepy nodded in agreement. "Yeah, residence was at the corner of Monroe and Auburn Street, house number 420. He'd cleared out everything for about a four-block radius, three trucks worth."

"Somebody's been a busy little beaver," the woman beamed at him. "So, what's your name, sweetie?"

"Pro," he answered, and glanced up at Sleepy who didn't look to be listening as he leafed through the map book.

"Pro?" The woman almost squealed. "What kind of name is that?" He couldn't figure out why she was so happy.

"It's short for Prudencio," he said. "Prudencio Guerra."

"How do you spell that?"

"It's just, Pro," he said. "P-R-O."

He could tell the woman wanted to say something more, but after a shake of Sleepy's head, she let the issue drop.

"Ok. P-R-O," she breathed out as she typed his name into the computer.

"And 420 Auburn Street? Was that your home or were you squatting?"

"Squatting." Sleepy answered for him.

Pro hoped that wasn't illegal or something. He wasn't sure what the word meant.

"Where was your real home, sweetie?" She smiled that fake teacher smile. The kind they all used when there was a parent visiting the classroom or the principal was in the back of the room observing.

"Why?" he asked. "My family is dead."

"I'm sorry about your family, but we'd just like to know what areas you passed through or have seen, before you got to Auburn St."

"It was my friend Pete's house," he turned and explained to Sleepy. He couldn't imagine he'd get into trouble for staying there. Didn't this lady realize everyone was dead? There weren't any rules, not anymore.

"Your friend from before?" Sleepy asked.

"Yeah, he was my best friend."

Sleepy nodded, "Ok, where did you live? Close by?"

"The Hillview Apartments in Herndon, behind the clock tower shopping center. I stayed there, until I ran out of food." He hoped they weren't going to ask about his mom or Rose.

"You speak English really good," the woman said, "but, what was the address, sweetie?" the woman persisted.

"We're good," Sleepy interrupted and showed the lady a spot in the map book.

Pro wanted to correct her; *speak really well*, but he knew he was just wanting to be a smart ass.

"Ok," the lady finished her notes. "For now, you go with Sleepy. We'll have a few more questions for you, nothing serious. Then you see the doctor. Just because the flu didn't get you, doesn't mean you don't have the creeping crud, right?"

Pro just looked back at her. He knew he wasn't sick, and he'd kept himself clean, even if it been with paper towels and hand sanitizer.

"Here's your room key, number 512. It's yours until there's a problem with you or your work." She raised her eyebrows at him, as if she knew there would be a problem. He managed to keep his mouth shut and just stared back at her. He knew the type; she was hoping he'd say something that would land him in trouble.

"If there's a problem with either, you'll be sleeping in the ballroom with the other layabouts." She waved a finger at a group of people coming in the lobby door carrying boxes as she said it. Maybe it wasn't him, maybe she didn't like anybody.

He pocketed the key which looked like a credit card. Sleepy tapped him on the arm and jerked his head at him to follow.

"Thank you," Pro said, knowing he should.

"You're so welcome," she said, flashing the fake teacher smile again.

He let Sleepy lead him through the lobby. He noticed a lot of the other soldiers, those with guns, nodded at Sleepy as he passed. Most of those without guns seemed to try to not be noticed, but he saw several of them looking at him in curiosity.

They went down a hallway, through a pair of heavy swinging wooden doors, the brass plaque on the outside said 'Business Operations.' Down the carpeted, dead-end hallway, they passed darkened offices on either side until they reached an office with its lights on. There was a large empty desk with nothing on it except a computer monitor in one corner. A small leather couch lay against the opposite wall and there were two leather chairs in between, facing the desk. Sleepy took the chair closest to the door and pointed at the other in silence.

Pro sat and noticed the big stereo looking radio on a counter behind the desk. It had power too, with lit up dials and digital displays that seemed like they came from a different world. He watched Sleepy unhook his rifle from the sling across the front of his chest. He put the business end of the rifle on the floor, its back sticking up between his knees. Pro watched the soldier for almost ten minutes, gently slapping the rifle back and forth between his knees, until he couldn't take it any longer.

"What is this place?"

He didn't think Sleepy was going to answer him, but the man looked up and regarded him closely for a moment.

"You stay away from Lonny, you hear me?"

Pro nodded. He wanted to say, *no shit,* but he didn't know if he could curse here or not.

"You understand what I'm saying?" Sleepy tilted his head, "He's... not right."

Pro nodded again. He knew.

A minute later a short stocky guy came into the room. He didn't look like an Army officer, but he noticed the light in

Sleepy's eyes come on as the quiet soldier sat up a little straighter. The newcomer wore blue jeans and cowboy boots with a shiny gold colored metal toes that matched the badge pinned to his white shirt. The guy wasn't just stocky, he was thick in a way that was a little scary as he leaned forward and crossed his massive forearms on the desk in front of him. He didn't look happy and Pro felt himself sitting up a little straighter as well.

The man regarded him for just a moment before rubbing his face and turning to Sleepy.

"I was listening in on the radio," the man said.

Sleepy just nodded. "It was him."

Pro realized they weren't talking about him, but the other soldier that had been there.

"Kid," the man's eyes moved over to him. They were cold, hard eyes, almost empty. Not crazy empty like Lonny's had been, but like a little league coach who was just way too serious about the game. The kind of coach the parents would get together and have removed halfway through the season because the kids weren't having any fun.

"That man you ran into killed four of our people tonight. Which makes nine in the last three weeks..."

The man leaned forward with his elbows on the desk. "You are the only person we know, who has ever spoken to him... who didn't wind up dead. How did that happen?"

Pro felt like he'd just been trapped in a lie that he hadn't told. The man with the badge didn't look like he would believe anything he said.

"I'm told you speak English?"

His mouth felt dry. "I never saw him before tonight." He shifted under the man's glare and glanced over at Sleepy who seemed to have found something interesting on the far wall to stare at.

"All right," the man relented after a moment. "What happened? What exactly did he say to you?"

"I was sneaking back to my house, for another load to move. I heard a radio inside the house, voices. I went behind the garage to hide and he was already there, behind me in the shadows. He grabbed me and choked me until I fell down. He wanted to know if I was with you guys. I told him I wasn't."

"What did you say?"

Pro shook his head. "I didn't know who he was talking about. I haven't seen hardly anybody. He let me go after I promised to be quiet. I was scared and took a step backwards, that's when somebody upstairs in the house saw me. They broke out the window, and started shooting."

"At you?" Sleepy asked.

"I'm not sure," Pro shrugged, realizing it was the truth.

"What happened then?"

"The soldier pulled me back behind the garage, and he started shooting with a funny gun that was really quiet. Your guys started shooting your rifles. I was behind the man, so I just took off, while he was shooting at the house."

"I ran." He was desperately trying to remember what he'd told the guys in the jeep. "Through some yards, then I hid for a few minutes while I could hear all the shooting behind me. I was just trying to get away. I thought I was safe, until one of the Army jeeps started chasing me down an alley. Then the soldier was there again. He just jumped out, and started shooting at the jeep. I ducked behind some garbage cans, and went into a backyard next to the alley.

He paused and shook his head as remembered what the soldier had told him.

"I think he shot at me as I was going through the gate. I just kept running until you guys caught up to me on the other side of the park."

"Smart..." the man said just looking at him. Pro wasn't sure what he said was smart, or what he'd said he had done was smart.

"And lucky," the man said after a moment. He turned back towards Sleepy.

"All that track?"

"As far as we could tell. Combs, Larabie, and Snyder were all dead at the house. It's not like we can ask them. Combs definitely knocked out a top floor window looking over the backyard, he shot from there."

The man behind the desk looked back at him and then pointed at Sleepy. "This soldier guy? His gun in the alley? Did it look like Sleepy's?"

Sleepy pulled his gun up against his shoulder and pointed it out the doorway into the hall.

Pro nodded. "It had a different thing on top, but I think it's the same kind of gun."

Sleepy nodded, "It sounded like a five-five-six."

"Did the man seem angry? Excited? Maybe scared?"

"No." Pro answered truthfully after a second's thought, and wondered if he answered too quickly. The man with policeman's badge almost flinched at the answer.

"He seemed really calm, it was kind of scary."

The policeman didn't like that answer either, he could tell.

"Ok, kid, what do we call you, besides Lucky?"

"Pro," he answered. "It's short for Prudencio."

"It certainly is," the man said with a smile that was as empty as his eyes. "You go with Mr. Sleepy here and get some warm food and some sleep. Day after, we'll put you on one of the foraging teams. From what I've heard, they could all learn from you. Work hard, and we'll have you carrying a gun next to Sleepy here. You're almost old enough."

"What is this place?"

"Son," the man leaned back in his chair, "it's what goes for civilization these days. I'm the last survivor of a team of local law enforcement that got deputized under the Feds... the government. I used to be a deputy sheriff in Arlington." The Sheriff paused and blinked his dead eyes.

"That was a long time ago. This is now home. We are all that's left, and this," the man spread his massive arms wide, "is how we start to rebuild."

"Can I just go home? Back to my house, or a different one? I don't care. You can keep all the supplies and food that I collected. I'm sorry if I wasn't supposed to do that."

The man smiled; Pro could tell it was a hard thing for the man to do. Like he had forgotten how.

"I appreciate the offer of your food, son. I do. But understand, I'm the authority that's left. I'm it. You are a lot safer with us, than out there on your own."

The Sheriff stopped what he was about to say with a wave of his hand...

"Look, I know you're a tough kid. Tougher than half the adults we've found to tell you the truth. You're a survivor. We need survivors, people who know what it takes out there in order to help other people and put things back the way they were. And you, Pro," the Sheriff stuck a thick finger out towards him. The smile was gone. "You are going to help me do that."

105

When the dismissal came, the Sheriff looked at Sleepy, and waved at the door.

They were down the hall, almost to the swinging door when he tugged at Sleepy's jacket. "Who was that?"

"Sheriff Bauman," Sleepy answered. "He's in charge here."

There'd been a quick visit to the doctor before breakfast. The elderly hippy answered to Doc Adams. Sleepy had shouted for him at the door to his office, which was out in the mall under a sign that said Lens Crafters. The doctor hadn't looked or acted like any doctor he'd ever seen. The old man had to be at least 70 years old. He reeked, as did his whole office, of pot. He recognized the smell right away. There had been an apartment in his complex where clouds of the stuff, would come out every time they opened the door.

"S'up my man, Sleepy?"

Doc Adams had long hair gray hair, braided into a rope that reached halfway down his back. The first thing besides the smell of pot that Pro noticed were the glazed over eyes of the old man.

"You squared away enough to check out a new arrival?"

Pro could tell Sleepy didn't think much of the doctor.

"Just a kid," the old man pronounced after staring at him vacantly for a moment that seemed to stretch far too long.

"No shit. Can you do your thing or not?"

"In my sleep," the skeletal figure pushed the door open further and waved them in. Pro could have sworn there was a layer of blue smoke hanging just below the ceiling.

Doc Adams was the first person over maybe 60 years old that he'd seen so far at the mall. He figured they probably needed a doctor really bad, or else they'd have shot him too. The whole examination took less than five minutes. The old stoner took a tiny bit of blood from a prick on his thumb, and sucked it up into a tiny clear tube of some sort. The Doctor listened to his heart for a long time. Pro was starting to wonder if the man was still awake with his head bowed and eyes closed.

The old man pulled back and patted him on the shoulder. "You got one, it's working." He checked in his ears, looked down his throat and tapped his knees with the little rubber hammer all doctors seemed to have. Pro said a silent thank you when he didn't have to drop his pants and do the "turn your head and cough thing."

"He's a kid, Sleepy. Hell of a lot healthier, than most of us."

"Great," Sleepy yawned. "Give me the blood type for the file, and you can get back to whatever you were doing."

The Doc smiled as he checked something on the counter. "He's A positive, and if you want some, my greenhouse is finally turning out some decent pain killer."

"Is that what you're calling it?"

"Must be checked for quality on a regular basis." The Doc nodded seriously to himself, pleased with his answer.

Sleepy paused as they were leaving and stuck his head back in. "Sheriff catches you baked? When he needs you..."

"Noted, my good man." The crazy old man seemed to hum the words and was smiling as he shut the door.

One of the hotel's ballrooms was set up with a bunch of dining tables. It was now well into the morning and Sleepy ate next to him in silence in the near empty room. Pro was starting to think it was better to be lonely, than with somebody that never spoke. It was less awkward.

The food though, he thought, as he shoveled it in, was awesome. Scrambled eggs - even if they were the fake kind, roasted potatoes, a patty of some sort of fried meat, all of it warm and a box of fruit juice. There was toast with fresh bread too, but he hadn't even touched it, as he shoveled in the rest, eyeing the plastic cup of diced fruit.

"Packed in syrup" the label said. He tore the label off and tilted the cup back and drank the syrup before shaking the contents into his mouth. Sleepy just watched him and may have even smiled a little, before handing over his cup of fruit.

Sleepy had shown him how to get through the food line with his room key. They tracked who ate and when, he'd explained. That seemed strange to him, because what if somebody wasn't hungry? Though, he couldn't imagine ever being 'not hungry'.

One of the women who had been serving the breakfast came over to their table when they were just about finished and handed Sleepy a cup a coffee.

"Pro," Sleepy perked up. "This is Ms. Long; she's going to show you to your room."

"It's Michelle," she smiled and stuck out her hand, shaking her head at Sleepy. Pro had the thought that Sleepy and Michelle were more than just friends.

"Pro? Short for Prudencio?" she guessed.

Pro nodded enthusiastically, "Yeah."

"Have you been out there on your own, this whole time?"

He nodded and Michelle pulled out one of the chairs and sat down. Her eyes he thought, were pretty. In fact, she could have been beautiful but she looked tired and worn down in a way that had nothing to do with missing sleep.

"What's it like out there? Have you been out to Ashburn?" She seemed excited that he might have some good news for her.

"I was in Herndon," he answered with a shake of his head, "at the edge of Reston."

"Michelle…" Sleepy warned her under his breath, with his cup of coffee poised for a sip.

"How many other survivors have you seen?"

"Just a couple," Pro admitted, and that included the soldier last night.

Sleepy put a hand on the table between them. "This doesn't help anybody." He stood up and regarded Michelle with a shake of his head.

"Pro," Sleepy was all business again. "This was breakfast, even if we were a little late. Lunch is at one, dinner is at seven. Breakfast tomorrow is at seven. Don't miss meals, they'll just come looking for you. I'll find you here tomorrow morning after you eat and get you situated. You can rest today."

"Daniel…?" Michelle almost whispered to Sleepy's retreating back.

"Is that his real name?"

She just nodded, as she came to her feet.

"Are you ok?"

"I'm fine," she smiled. "Come on."

The fifth floor was reserved for kids and women only, Michelle had explained during the long walk up the bare concrete stairwell that couldn't have been more different from the rest of the fancy hotel. When he'd asked the obvious question of why they hadn't used the elevator, she'd just shook her head.

"Only the soldiers can use the elevator, the rest of us use the stairs."

She stopped at the landing for the fifth floor and looked him up and down.

"You're big for your age, you probably won't be here with us for long."

"How many people live here?" He could hear some younger children shouting from the other side of the door.

Michelle glanced over her shoulder at him as she pulled the heavy door open and led him down the hallway.

"We aren't supposed to ask, or to know," she pointed at the ceiling and he noticed her wedding ring for the first time. "But I cook for everybody, so I know. Four hundred and eleven."

They reached the door labeled 512, she stopped with a grin. "But after last night, we are down to 407, plus you – 408. So, hey... progress."

Pro realized she was referring to the soldiers that had been killed last night... and wondered why she seemed so happy about it. He almost asked her why they shot old people, but he didn't think that would do him any favors.

Once they were inside the room, she showed him how the swinging dead bolt worked. She made him promise to use it whenever he was in the room. She explained that the hotel's house phones still worked, and that he had to answer if somebody called him. Which they sometimes would, when they needed another pair of hands for something downstairs. But he could only use the phone if it was an emergency.

"Who's they?"

One corner of her mouth smirked upward. "Anybody they let carry a gun."

"Michelle?" he asked as she looked out his window on the expanse of forested office parks stretching off into the distance. "What'd you mean I won't be here for long? What are they going to do to me?"

She smiled at him as she turned around. It was sad smile, the kind his mom had used when she'd gotten sick.

"You're a tough kid, Pro. You'd have to be, to have survived out there. How old are you? Sixteen?

He had to think for a moment, his birthday was in November, so he knew he'd had one, but hadn't even thought about it until now. Maybe people weren't going to have birthdays anymore.

"I just turned fifteen."

"Wow," she pulled her head back in shock. "You *are* big for your age."

She looked angry all of a sudden.

"They'll be moving you to soldier for them as soon as they make sure you can be trusted. After that, you'll be moved off this floor. If you don't want to soldier, you'll go to the labor pool and sleep on a roll away bed in the ballroom."

"Where do the soldiers sleep?" he asked.

Michelle's eyes looked away from his. "Wherever the hell they want."

She walked past him, giving his arm a friendly squeeze on the way out. He'd been alone for so long, the sensation of physical contact almost shocked him.

"Sleep," she said, from the door. "You look like you need it. I'll swing by and get you before dinner."

He'd nodded, not quite sure why her eyes were tearing up. The door clicked shut behind her, and he locked himself in with the swinging deadbolt. He hadn't been rescued. He'd been caught.

*

Chapter 8

"Wanna see how they caught you?"

It was the first words that Ben had said to him after being introduced that morning. Ten of them had loaded up in to the back of a panel truck, just like the one that he'd seen in the Safeway parking lot that had delivered the old people to be killed. No one else seemed to be scared. In fact, everyone on his *team* seemed to be happy for a chance to get away from the mall. The guy driving had told them they were going into Arlington. Hid knowledge of the area was built on the locations of community baseball diamonds and school gyms from AAU basketball. He knew Arlington was "inside" the beltway, toward DC, a long way from Herndon and areas he knew well.

Ben, or Benjamin as some of the others called him, backed away from the kitchen cabinet he was shining his flashlight into. "Take a look and tell me what you see."

It was the second house he and Ben had scavenged, or had tried to. There was nothing here worth taking. The cupboard that Ben was referring to was completely empty except for an empty plastic spice rack.

"Picked clean," Pro said. "Like the first house. Somebody else around here beat us to it."

Ben nodded at him with a knowing smile. "I was part of the first team that combed your neighborhood. We knew right off there was a survivor close by, and that you were a kid."

"How'd you know I was a kid?"

Ben reached into his pocket, and pulled out a glass pint bottle of whiskey and gave it a shake.

"You left the booze behind. I guess you haven't developed a taste for it yet, have you?" Ben held the bottle out to him.

Pro shook his head. He'd tried it early on, something called gin. He hadn't liked it all.

"Good. Stuff'll kill you." Ben had a warm laugh.

"How'd you know what house I was in?" He tried to bring the conversation back to the part he was interested in.

"The snow on the roofs, with no heat," Ben took a slug of the amber liquid and smacked his lips with a smile. "It stays a lot longer. But even a warm body sleeping in the same room, maybe cooking in it, with candles or whatever, it'll melt the snow on the roof above just a little bit quicker, sure as shit."

Pro nodded in understanding. He wouldn't make that mistake again.

"Come on," Ben waived his flashlight. "Let's check the basement for gear, no food here."

He followed Ben down the carpeted stairs at a distance, already wondering if the basement had another exit.

"Biggest adjustment you need to make in your scavenging, is size. You see something like a big generator, solar panels or a welding cart, you'd never have tried to take it before. Well, we can use that shit."

Ben kept up a running commentary on the likelihood of finding various gear in different types of houses, standalone vs. townhouse vs. apartments as they wandered around the large basement.

"Same goes for things like motor oil, construction material, stuff the Sheriff can use down the road." Pro began to wonder if he'd been put with Ben for reason. Much of the one-sided conversation had a ring of repetition to it.

114

Ben switched his flashlight to its lantern setting and sat it on the edge of a big pool table that dominated the largest room in the basement.

"You know how to play?"

Pro shook his head.

"I'll rack em." Ben was grinning as he moved around the table pulling pool balls out of the pockets. "We'll have to be quick about it. Can't have them think Benjamin has lost his edge scavenging."

Pro followed Ben's lead and pulled a pool stick off the rack on the wall. "I thought I was being careful not leaving my house. I mean during the snow."

Ben was bent over the edge of the table lining up his shot. His friendly face looked up from the pool table and regarded him for a moment.

"Well there's careful, and then there's shit you just don't think of." Pro wasn't sure if Ben was still talking about him getting caught. Ben shattered the pyramid of pool balls with a loud crack that made Pro jump. One of the balls went in. "Guess I'm stripes."

Ben moved around the table like he was a cat. Old guy or not, Pro guessed the tall, thin, thirty-something black man was just as quick on his feet as he was.

"Like me," Ben continued after a moment. "I was waving my flashlight around outside, that's how they found me. I hadn't realized you could see that shit from a mile away these days, no street lights. I just didn't think about it, ya know?"

Pro wanted to say that he had figured that part out early on, but didn't think Ben's good humor would go that far.

"Your turn, amigo."

Pro tried to mimic what he'd seen Ben do with the cue ball, but just barely made contact.

"I thought you was gaming me; you've never played before?"

"Nope."

Ben saw him eyeing the pistol on his belt. "That's my hush puppy." He smiled, giving it a pat. "It's for the wild dogs, get it? Hush puppy... bam!"

Pro nodded, he got it.

"A little .22 like this ain't gonna start any shit. They don't even give me a clip for it, and I have exactly one bullet. That ways, if I find some ammo the soldiers missed, I can't load up."

"The soldiers have already been through here?"

"Sure, they ain't gonna let the sheep into an area they haven't picked clean for guns and ammo." Ben reached into his pocket and pulled out his pint bottle of whiskey and gave it a shake, "or the good stuff."

"Once they've marked off an area that's clear, they send a foraging team in. We grab up the food and gear. The soldiers always take the best shit. First come, first served, eh?"

So, the scavengers were like him; prisoners, working for the soldiers. Ben had called them sheep.

"Makes sense," Pro agreed. "So, they don't trust us, foragers?"

Ben looked up at him for a moment from where was leaning over into his next shot. "Ain't like that. You see, most soldiers started as scavengers. If you ain't willing to fight to protect what we have, you're a sheep, and you're going to be a second-class citizen."

The words sounded different than the rest of Ben's conversation, like he was repeating something that he'd been told, or had heard someone else say a hundred times.

"So, we can't leave if we want? Go live on our own?" Pro asked.

"Why would you want to?" Ben shook his head like the idea was crazy. "I was out there on my own. Now, I don't worry where my next meal is coming from. I can close my eyes, actually sleep without worrying someone's gonna steal my shit or slit my throat." Ben missed a shot after sinking two balls in a row.

"And I ain't by myself. I didn't like being alone. You?"

"I didn't mind so much," Pro shook his head, lying through his teeth. "But I miss my family." Pro concentrated on his next shot and actually got a ball to go in.

"That was one of mine," Ben laughed. "But you go ahead, take another shot."

"We all miss our families," the older man said after a moment leaning his face into his pool cue. For a second it almost looked like the pool stick was holding him up.

"You don't want to do a runner, kid. We'd find you, and bring you back. The Sheriff would make an example out of you."

"An example?"

Ben nodded, "Yeah. The Sheriff's a good guy, but he definitely don't take kindly to anybody that don't appreciate what he's trying to do. Man's got a serious temper."

"You never thought of running away?"

"Hell, no," Ben shook his head. "I was running west when they found me. They fed me, gave me a place to sleep, they trust me. The best part is, they ain't trying to eat me."

Pro felt the blood drain from his face.

"I came out of Springfield, there's a big group down in Alexandria that's just plain crazy. Like a pack of wild dogs, hopped up on God knows what, gone cannibal just for show. You know that word?"

Pro nodded, he knew the word. "Why would they do that? There's plenty of food."

Ben shook his head looking at the remaining balls on the table. "Because they can."

Ben glanced at him as he walked around to his next shot. "Like that ninja soldier you got tangled up with. Why's he going around killing our folks? Because he can. I think the suck just really did a number on some people." Ben tapped his forehead with his stick, "in the head."

"I guess," Pro shrugged. "That guy was crazy scary, people shooting at him and he was just... chill. I was scared to death." Pro no longer thought Ben was a forager, he was a soldier. They were trying to get him to say something different from what he already had.

Ben looked at him quietly, like he could hear Pro's thoughts, but he relaxed after a moment and motioned at the table for him to take his shot. "You were lucky," Ben agreed.

"I guess, so." Pro tried to line up his shot.

"You think he was from your neighborhood?" Ben asked.

How stupid did they think he was? Just because he was kid, they didn't think he'd be able to hear the Sheriff's words coming out of Ben's mouth.

"I don't think so. The only other person in my neighborhood was a woman I saw a couple of times in her window. But then, I stopped seeing her. When I checked on her, she'd..."

"Killed herself?"

"Yeah," Pro nodded, remembering the empty bottles of aspirin on the floor next to the couch where he'd found her swollen body. She'd had an unopened box of frosted cherry Pop Tarts in her cupboards that had almost made him forget the body he had to walk around to get back out of her house.

"Just the woman, then?"

"I saw some old people in Herndon, in the beginning. But they were just walking. I didn't see them again." He knew Ben hadn't been among the soldiers in the Safeway parking lot, they'd all been white, except for one, who may have been Hispanic.

Pro concentrated on his shot. That way he didn't have to look at Ben who was suddenly watching him more closely. "If he'd been in my neighborhood, I would have gone somewhere else."

His shot went in and he looked up with a forced smile. "This is fun. Do we get to go out like this every day?"

"Nice shot," Ben answered absently, before turning to look at him. "Most days. You think you'll try to be a soldier? Or do you want to make a career out of digging through dead people's kitchens."

"Am I old enough?"

Ben waffled his hand back and forth. "Maybe not quite. Give it a bit, work hard, don't give them any reason not to trust you."

"I won't," Pro shook his head. "I don't like the sound of cannibals." He could tell from the look on Ben's face, it was what the man had wanted to hear.

By the middle of the afternoon, he'd lost count of how many houses they checked. He got enough glimpses at the map that the truck's driver had, to know his team was working a three by three block square of single-family homes. It was at one of those he found a knife in a tool box, under a shelf in a tiny garage that had a rotted backboard hanging lopsided. He'd asked if they needed more tools.

Ben had just grunted back at him, his back turned. "Hell, no. What we need is people who can use the ones we have."

Over the course of his first day of scavenging, Pro watched Ben become less and less committed to pretending he was a forager, or a sheep. Pro only needed to see the way the other people on the team avoided looking at him, to sense he was somehow in charge. Even the driver, who yelled at everybody else for moving too slow, or for collecting the wrong stuff, never even questioned Ben or by extension him.

Pro had taken the knife. A simple short blade, the kind that didn't fold up and had an old leather sheath stained with what looked like oil. He stuffed it inside his sock, praying that it wasn't too heavy and wouldn't flop out. One rule for the foragers had been made crystal clear to him. Everything went into the bags; nothing was kept back for personal use. The truck they'd come in was nearly full by the middle of the afternoon and they were left sitting on the side of the road, trying to stay warm inside abandoned cars. A soldier, armed with a rifle, as bored as they were, watched them from the steps of a house.

By then, Ben had given up pretending. He'd hitched a ride back to the mall with the supplies. The rest of them waited for another truck to come and get them. He'd been worn out, and was thinking he was done for the day. One of the other foragers, who seemed to complain about everything, had kicked his leg when he started to nod off sitting in the back seat of the old minivan.

"Don't get too comfortable, kid. We'll have to unload the truck when we get back home."

Pro had just nodded in acceptance. *Home?* No way, was this ever going to be his home.

Chapter 9

By the end of the first week, he had added four scavenged energy bars to his secret stash in his room, hidden inside a slit he had made in his mattress. He was ready to run. There was nothing for him here. Nothing beyond working as a slave for the soldiers, until he was asked to become one.

He couldn't imagine forcing himself on the women that the soldiers "collected." He couldn't imagine Michelle looking at him in fear or disgust as she did the others when Sleepy wasn't around. The Sheriff acted as if his 'Community of Survivors' were the last chance of civilization. Pro didn't care about that, he just knew if people were going to live together, they shouldn't be terrified of or used like slaves by the ones with the guns.

Today would be the day. He made his way through the ground floor of the mall's concourse along with the rest of his team. He'd strapped the energy bars to his waist with some duct tape he'd found. The cold weather, and the layers of clothes he had to wear, would hide the lumps of the bars and he had the knife and scabbard taped to his ankle inside his sock. They meandered through the darkened ground floor of the Macy's until they reached store's loading dock, where they always left from. Several of his team were placing bets on whether the trucks could get out in this weather.

"What do you mean?" He asked Marjorie, their assigned leader. Marjorie really liked being the leader.

"Been snowing hard for the last three hours, where have you been?"

Inside, eating everything extra that Michelle could sneak him, he wanted to say. He just looked away in silence.

Marjorie didn't like anybody to challenge her. And he knew some questions were better off staying unanswered.

They popped out the emergency exit door onto the loading dock, and were greeted by a quiet blanket of white, under a frozen, heavy dark sky. There were already a couple of inches on the ground and it was snowing so hard that Pro couldn't see farther into the parking lot than forty or fifty yards. The first row of light poles in the parking lot were just barely visible. Beyond that, it was a dense fog of windblown snow.

"Cold as hell," the soldier on the loading dock said to Marjorie, who nodded in agreement.

"You guys get us there, we'll fill a truck," Marjorie said, sucking up to the soldiers like she always did. Pro saw a couple of the others on his team roll their eyes behind her back.

Five minutes later there was still no truck and most of the team had gone back inside the door to get out of the biting wind. Pro stared at the parking lot stretching out in front of him and could almost see the footprints he'd leave behind him if he made a break for it today. He wasn't worried about anybody on his collection team, he could out run any of them on one leg, but Marjorie had a radio. The truck's driver would have one too, and the soldiers at the mall would welcome the excitement of hunting him down. The snow though, he thought, it would slow them down too.

It wouldn't work he told himself. Making a run for it; depended on getting on the truck, and getting into a neighborhood away from the mall. By the time the soldier's radio squelched, it was just him and Marjorie left on the loading dock. They heard the Sheriff's voice. No collection teams were going out today.

The storm looked to be a big one.

"Down day," Marjorie sounded disappointed.

"Not so fast," the guard blew on his hands. "Take your team up to the third floor and clear out that bookstore. We need more space up there. Johnny's team is already up there, you can help him."

The walk back through the mall was quiet. No one was happy with the idea of carrying heavy books all day. At the top of the first escalator climb, on the second-floor landing, Pro paused, and snagged Marjorie's jacket. "I don't feel so hot, I need to go to the bathroom."

Marjorie shook her head in disgust. "Hurry up, none of us want you to shit your pants."

Pro nodded, "I'll be right there. I promise."

"See that you are," she said and turned the corner to go up the next flight of escalator.

Pro continued off down the concourse, towards the mall's internal entrance to the hotel, breathing a sigh of relief. He had to get rid of the protein bars, because they'd all be down to t-shirts after a few minutes of emptying out the bookstore and the bulges would show and they'd know he was going to run. As he climbed the stairs to the fifth floor, all he could do was wonder how long the snow would take to melt. How long before he could get away from this place? Could he keep pretending for a week? Two?

Once in his room, he unstrapped the protein bars with a silent grimace as he ripped the tape off. He stuffed the now squishy packages back inside the mattress with the ball of duct tape. He used the bathroom; for all he knew they checked. They were all allowed one flush a day, and a shower every other day. Supposedly, the water tanks on the roof of the hotel filled slowly from the well the FEMA people had drilled.

He was about to head back down to his crew when there was a knock on the door. Marjorie didn't trust him at all. He glanced back at the bed to make sure the slit was hidden under the mattress cover and pulled open the door.

"Room check..."

Lonny stood there with that creepy grin on his face.

"I was just headed back down," he said, as he tried to get past the man.

Lonny put a hand on his chest and pushed him back into the room, following him in. The door swung shut on its own with a loud bang.

"You were trying to get out of your work detail," Lonny smiled. "I tried to counsel you." The soldier took a step towards him, tried and failed to rub the smile off his face. "You fought me. You needed to be shown some respect."

"I just..."

"Sshhh..." Lonny waved his hands. "I just told you what is going to happen. Sleepy and his bitch ain't here to help you."

Pro feinted to his left, went right and tried to get to the door. Lonny body-slammed him into the wall and he went down seeing stars from where his head hit the bathroom's metal door frame.

"That's the spirit!" Lonny was laughing, as he hauled him to his feet by his hair. Lonny turned him around and backhanded him hard enough that he was spun back to the floor, landing by the side of his bed. He could taste blood in his mouth and he shook his head to try and stop the ringing in his ears.

He looked up, seeing double. He could still see Lonny unclipping his rifle from its sling and leaning it against the wall by the door. The soldier's smile changed from amusement to something scarier. The soldier his belt that held his side arm and a big knife to the floor. Lonny took a moment to look at him, before he kicked his belt into the corner, next to the gun.

"You get up... I'm just going to put you down again," Lonny's eyes looked excited but he stayed where he was.

Pro curled into a fetal position, and pulled the bed cover down off the bed over where he lay on the floor. He had to reach the knife while he had the blanket over him.

"Oh, come on," Lonny complained, licking his lips. "People keep telling me how tough you are. Here you are... going all sheep on me."

Pro focused on Lonny's face, willing his blurred vision to settle on seeing just the one of him. He tried to gather his feet underneath him and surged up to his feet as Lonny took a step closer. He held the bed cover out in front of him with his left hand as he rushed the soldier, the right hand holding his small knife down low out of sight.

"Slow learner," Lonny said excitedly, as he stiff armed the blanket, but Pro added his right hand to the push and stabbed through the blanket into the man's hand.

Lonny screamed like he'd been bit, and his hands pulled in close. Pro's momentum carried him in tight up against the man and he swung his knife up and around, as high and as hard as he could. His grip on the blade's small handle was tight enough that he felt his knuckles pop. He felt the knife go into something soft, and he ripped it out with a slash and heard another scream from Lonny from the other side of the blanket.

Lonny grabbed him by the sweatshirt through the blanket and they both went down in a tangle. Pro stabbed, and stabbed through the blanket. He ignored the fist beating against the side of his head, knowing at an instinctual level, if he stopped, or let up, he was dead. Lonny wasn't screaming anymore and Pro could see the right sleeve of his own sweatshirt soaked in blood. He was able to roll to his knees, and pushed as hard as he could. The soldier's body gave and he ended up straddling Lonny's blanket covered torso. He hammered the knife into the man's chest more times than he could count.

Lonny finally quit moving and he pulled the blanket off the man's face. The soldier looked pale, as blood squirted out of the jagged rip in his neck, out on to the carpet and up against the side of his jaw. Lonny was looking up at him in panic, trying to say something. He heard himself scream and pounded the knife into the man's chest until the blade snapped. He looked at this blood covered hand and the remnants of the knife before looking up at Lonny's face. The crazy light had gone out of those eyes.

Pro rolled off, and looked at down at his arm. Blood was dripping from his sweatshirt. His stomach rebelled, and he was on all fours retching until he was sure his stomach was empty. His head was pounding in pain and his hands were shaking. He knew he had to move, and now. Marjorie would send someone to check on him, if she hadn't already. He lost the sweatshirt, dropping it over Lonny's face and put another one on. He ran into the bathroom and almost threw up again, when he saw his blood-spattered face in the mirror. Faces... his left eye was having trouble focusing.

He wiped away the blood, and realized some of it was his. His lip was split, his left ear torn and his eye on that side of his face was already starting to swell shut.

He cleaned up as fast as could, and grabbed his coat. He stopped to retrieve Lonny's belt and holster with the .45 and a real knife. It took him a moment to get it adjusted so it was tight and he made sure his coat covered it all, except for the knife. He unsnapped its scabbard from the belt and fed it up his coat sleeve. He looked at the rifle. Sleepy had told him it was an M-4, and he briefly considered it. As much as he wanted to, he couldn't take it. Sheep didn't carry guns; they'd stop him on sight.

Leaving the rifle behind, he was out the room, down the hall and pulling the stairwell door open when Michelle and another woman reached the interior landing coming up.

"Pro!"

He stood there in shock. The look on Michelle's face went from surprise to anger in half a second.

"What happened?"

"Nothing," he managed, as he bulled his way past the two women, taking the stairs down two at a time.

"That bastard! I'll kill him." He heard Michelle on the stairs above him.

Pro wasn't thinking as he ran through the mall's concourse. On the second level, he entered the Neiman Marcus without having seen anyone and ran past boxes of supplies stacked throughout the dark interior. He came to the store's interior escalator, and went down to the bottom level. They used the Neiman Marcus loading dock to unload the supply trucks when they returned, but there would be no trucks today. He paused, just inside the heavy strips of plastic that served as the door when the panels were up as they were now. He couldn't see a guard.

Peering out between the strips of plastic, the snow was falling fast. The mall's lower road in front of the loading bay was completely covered by a solid four inches or so, the curbs were almost buried. Directly across the narrow road was the bottom level of the parking garage, its dark interior pitch black, but free of snow.

He didn't hesitate, parting the panels of sheeting and squeezing through enough to make certain there wasn't a soldier posted to either side of the loading door, out of sight. It was snowing so hard he couldn't see very far up the road, and he thought the sooner he went, the more time the snow would have to cover his tracks. He jumped down off the platform into the strip of mulch up against the foundation of the mall, and ran about fifty yards along the edge of the building until the loading dock behind him was hidden by the storm. He crossed the road straightaway, sprinting to the far back wall of the dark interior of the parking garage. Once there, he went right until he came to a set of concrete stairs that led up to the garage's street level.

He knew he had to be careful. The soldiers would sometimes post a guard along the outer perimeter of the parking lot. His foot had just touched the first concrete step when the PA system inside the mall blared to life. To him it was just a muffled echo of noise. He didn't have to guess at what it was saying. Reaching the top of the stairs, he breathed a sigh of relief as he couldn't see a guard in either direction. The near white-out meant there could have been one or several close by and he'd never know it.

Sprinting across the big road in front of the mall, 'International' they called it, he kept going into an office park of several office towers. He ran right up to the entrance of the office building, and then along its dark glass and steel front, staying under the overhang of the building trying his best to get as far away from the mall as he could with the fewest number of footprints.

He made it to the back side of the tower complex and hit a chain link fence. The parking lot on the other side, was a sea of white indistinguishable humps of snow with wheels. He knew it was the back lot of a big car dealership where the soldiers got a lot of their cars, and it stretched all the way down to Rt. 7. He needed to get across the big highway to make his way to the neighborhoods in Vienna. He needed a residential area he could hide in. They'd never find him as long as the snow covered his tracks.

Sooner or later, they'd give up, or figure he froze to death. The last thought caught him up, as he realized in his panic, for the first time, how cold it was. And he was out here with no hat, or gloves. Just blue jeans, his week-old Timberland boots from the mall, and his heavy coat. He imagined his mother telling him he was going to get sick. She would have been right; his ears, face and hands were already burning from the cold.

He paused at the chain link fence, which was almost clogged solid with snow. If he climbed it, they'd see where he knocked the snow loose. He ran along the edge of the fence towards Rt. 7, careful not to brush up against the chain link. He went through the first gate in the fence-line he came to, and disappeared amid a sea of cars that would never be sold.

Hunched over, staying between the lines of vehicles, he made his way to the front edge of the lot that faced out onto Rt. 7. The tell-tale sound, a rolling crunch of tires on fresh snow caused him to freeze behind the final line of cars before the edge of the road.

A Humvee, materialized out of the storm, its high beams and roof mounted rack lights on. It moved towards him at a creep, down the middle of Rt. 7 from the direction of the toll road. He hoped they were looking for his tracks because he hadn't made any out there yet. His heart stopped as the Humvee did the same. It just sat in the intersection of Rt. 7 and the road that ran along the car dealership's fence line.

He'd entered the car lot far enough back up the road that there was no way they'd see be able to see his foot prints. What were they doing just sitting there? Another set of headlights, came down Rt 7 from the opposite direction and stopped in the intersection, on the other side of the median. The radio! He should have grabbed Lonny's radio, he could be listening to them talk right now. If his head wasn't already hurting, he'd have pounded his forehead.

The quiet of the storm was nearly complete, the occasional gust of wind which would shift the snow to the horizontal was all he could hear. The idling Humvees may as well have been on the other side of the moon. He could just barely see the headlights of the farthest vehicle, and the one on his side of the road would have to be looking behind them to see him. Still Rt. 7 was a big road, especially here in Tyson's Corner. The median alone was fifty yards wide by itself. It had to be, because of the Metro tracks that ran down the length of the road, supported by the massive concrete pillars that held it sixty feet off the ground.

Pro looked up at the elevated tracks, hidden behind high walls of concrete lining the suspended trough of concrete and steel. The metro station was directly in front of him, off the ground, accessible by a covered staircase. If he could get to the staircase, he could be hidden above the roads they'd be checking, and the tracks ran all the way out to the airport, right through Reston and Herndon that he knew like the back of his hand.

He was about to risk breaking out from behind the cars when he heard the crunch of snow again out on the road. The Humvees were rolling away from each other, moving slowly. Dropping back down behind the SUV he'd been hiding behind, he waited until he couldn't hear anything. He peeked out and could just see the tail lights of one of the Humvees before they too were swallowed by the storm. He sprinted for the staircase, thankful he didn't have to leave his prints on Rt. 7. He was leaving prints on the sidewalk, but they wouldn't be seen from the road unless the soldiers actually got out and looked.

He made it up into the above street station, and dropped down into the graveled bottom next to the train tracks. He was under the massive transparent curved roof of the station, but it was entirely blanketed by snow, casting the station into a dark shadow. A hundred yards in either direction the track bed became an unbroken ribbon of white, with high walls on either side shielding him from the worst of the wind and more importantly, from anybody on the street looking up.

Taking off at a run, he knew he had about six or seven miles to the next stop in Reston. There, he'd be surrounded by neighborhoods that they could never find him in. Knowing how they found people, he knew that unless people wanted to be found or were stupid, they could stay hidden. Safe. He was never going to be stupid again.

Except, he realized, for leaving his room without a hat, gloves or Lonny's radio. He ran on at a steady pace, and his thoughts drifted to Michelle and Sleepy. Was Sleepy out there now, hunting him with the others? What would Michelle think of him after what he'd done to Lonny?

The headache got worse the further he ran, until each footfall began to send jarring flashes of pain and light behind his eyes. His face, ears, and hands were numb with cold. Between thoughts of what he was going to do, of maybe finding the ninja soldier again, he wondered why his head hurt so bad. He'd never had a headache that felt like this before. He'd gone about a half mile when the raised tracks began to gently slope back down to ground level over the length of a gradual curve to the west. Too soon for his liking, he was back at ground level; the rail bed now stood between the two sides of the empty toll road.

The cement walls to either side were gone, replaced by a snow clogged chain link fence on either side of him. The fence was topped with barbed wire sloping outward to stop people from getting onto the tracks, but they worked just as well to keep him inside. The fence was packed with snow. He could barely see through it on either side, but if the soldiers drove down the toll road he might be seen unless he could he drop down before they saw him. He stayed to the natural trough between the two tracks and checked behind him as often as he could.

More than an hour later, he had no idea how far he'd gone, only that he couldn't go much further. The storm had gotten worse. It was getting colder and his lungs burned from sucking in the frigid air. His head was pounding, his hands were frozen and his ears hurt, especially the one that had bled where Lonny had punched him. He dropped out of his jog, and walked a few steps catching his breath before he turned around to check behind him.

There were headlights coming towards him from Tysons, and they included the familiar, roof lights, that some of the Humvees had. He crashed to his stomach in the shallow depression between the tracks and waited for the spot light most of them carried to highlight him. He'd played with one in the foraging trucks once and he knew how bright they were. Or maybe they'd just shoot first. Somehow, he knew they wouldn't. He could remember Ben's warning of what happened to those who were caught running away. He didn't want to be an example, not for the Sheriff.

He lifted his head enough that he could see the roof and equipment rack of the Humvee roll past, sticking up above the concrete dividers that lined the toll road. *Lazy*, he thought. They should be on foot. They were never going to see him in the storm from inside their vehicles. Of course, they weren't going to freeze to death either. The thought almost made him laugh. He was starting to worry that he was going to, as he climbed to his feet and brushed the snow from his jeans with hands he couldn't feel.

He started running again, faster now, following the tail lights that had disappeared ahead of him in the swirling snow. He had to get out of the storm. Wiehle Station, in Reston couldn't be that much further ahead, could it? He focused on that, knowing each step brought him a little closer to someplace he could find shelter from the snow and wind.

*

Michelle knew she was in trouble. She was doing her best, trying to convince herself she was beyond caring. The man behind the desk staring at her was broken. She could imagine that Arlington County Deputy Sheriff Kent Bauman had been a good man. Before, in quieter times. She knew he'd been a family man. The framed picture of him standing with his wife and three children next to a fountain at Disney World sat on the shelf behind his desk. The man in that picture looked nothing like the one staring back at her.

"You saw him, knew something was wrong and didn't bother stopping him. Didn't alert the duty desk immediately. Why?"

She knew why, or she had guessed right. Her key card gave her access to the whole fifth floor and she'd gone straight to Pro's room. The door shut behind her, she had seen Lonny's body, the blood seeping out from under Pro's sweatshirt and the bed cover. The whole room smelling of rusty nails.

"He was running from his room, I thought I'd check there first. Lonny was still breathing. Much as I hated that sick bastard, I tried to help him." She'd even gone as far as getting blood on her hands and the knees of her jeans to help prove the point. She left out the part where she'd spit in his empty, lifeless face.

Bauman just stared at her for a moment. "He looked like he'd been attacked by a mountain lion, I seriously doubt he was alive."

"He was breathing," she answered. "I did what I could."

Bauman just nodded. "Lonny was one of my best soldiers, my number three. Sleepy will step up now." He paused looking at her and shook his head. "And that is the only reason I'm going to believe you, at least officially. To keep Sleepy content. Our soldiers are all that's keeping your sweet ass safe from what's out there. Without that, you'd be back down in the ballroom, servicing firstcomers."

Bauman got up slowly and came around his desk. Standing too close to her, he leaned in, almost whispering. "You remember that, don't you?"

She bit her lip and nodded, ashamed of her fear. She knew it was what he wanted.

He leaned a little closer, his heavy hand going around the back of her neck.

"If I find out you and Sleepy, or you by your lonesome helped that little wetback in any way, I'll make an example out of you that our little community here will whisper about in the dark a decade from now."

She jerked her head once up and back down. It was with great effort she forced herself to take a breath.

"You do know Lonny was trying to rape him? The kid was just defending himself." She half expected to get hit. Bauman liked to hit his women. She remembered that too.

She took strength from the fact the blow didn't come. "Pro wouldn't have been the first, not by a long shot. Maybe this community would work a little better if all of us not carrying a gun didn't have to live in fear."

"I'm not debating this with you." Bauman didn't yell. She'd never seen him yell. They had all watched him beat a soldier to death in the cafeteria who had been caught sleeping on guard duty. Even then, he'd been calm. He'd pounded the man's face to a pulp and then stomped on the guard's head with his boots, for far longer than he'd needed to. When he was done, Bauman had just stood over the guard's lifeless body and looked over the crowd that he'd ordered to gather. "Rules will be followed," was all he'd said before walking out.

He just stood there now, next to her, the same empty look in his eyes. She could feel his gaze as she focused on a glass

136

ornament on the shelf behind his desk. *Best Hospitality Staff – 2015*, it said. A meaningless message from a world that no longer existed. Sleepy was always telling her to live in the here and now, to forget what had happened. She couldn't and she knew it was driving her crazy.

"Do you have anything else to add? Or can I get back to hunting this little shit down?"

She shook her head.

"Then walk out of here while you can."

*

Chapter 10

Jason woke up on the couch in the living room. It may not technically have been his house, but it was *his* couch, no matter how often Loki would try to assert his ownership privilege and try to 'share' the cushions during the night. The small bell he'd attached to the dog's flap door had awoken him. For a short moment he thought he'd left the lights on, but a quick glance out the front window gave him his answer. The world outside was in a complete whiteout of blowing snow, coming down hard.

He closed his eyes for a moment, grateful he had an excuse to stop the work he'd been focused on for the last few days. Taking a page from the kid's playbook, he'd been moving a bunch of his supplies to another house. A backup plan; Howard Dagman would have approved. His chosen location was across Difficult Run, a different neighborhood completely as far as road access was concerned, but only a quarter of a mile away, across the creek and through the surrounding woods. From where his backyard met the greenspace it was downhill to the small creek, across a large fallen tree that made a great bridge, and uphill into the adjacent neighborhood.

Still, he'd carried the gear and supplies by hand, multiple trips, Loki providing executive level supervision. By the end of the day yesterday, when Loki looked tired, he had realized that he was exhausted. He'd been too tired to fix anything for dinner and just inhaled the best part of an MRE and crashed.

Loki padded up to him, coming through the dining room from the kitchen, his dark coat wet with melted snow.

"Breakfast?"

Loki barked once in agreement.

"Great… coffee, couple of eggs, some bacon and hash browns, please."

The dog just looked at him, wagging his thick tail, waiting in expectation.

He closed his eyes a moment. He heard the quick pad of feet just before the bundle of canine enthusiasm landed on his stomach.

Loki couldn't decide what to do first, lick him in the face or walk across his gut and crotch trying to find a comfortable spot to settle in. He knew the dog was getting close to a hundred lbs., and would probably be close to 120 before he stopped filling out.

"OK, I'm getting up."

Sitting up and giving the dog a morning rub behind the ears, he looked out the window and half wondered what the Ritz gang would be doing right now. Hunkering down he'd bet. The temperature had gotten down into the teens last night before he'd crashed. This storm didn't have the feel of a quick moving flurry, but rather a full nor'easter. The sky, what little he could see of it out the window looked heavy. A closer look revealed it was snowing so hard he could just barely make out the road at the bottom of the front yard.

He had turned the heat off in the house last night because it had felt like snow. He knew there was still a lot of warmth inside, compared to the outside, but he'd cracked all the upstairs windows in all the bedrooms to make sure the roof of his house wouldn't look any different from others in the neighborhood. This wasn't just snow, it was a storm, and he could hear the wind outside buffeting the trees. Hopefully that would keep a lot of roofs clear.

He walked into the kitchen and turned the scanner on. He'd taken radios from two of the Ritz thugs he'd killed, and so far, their concept of communications security revolved around switching channels on their unencrypted radios. It usually took Howard's high-end receiver less than a minute to locate the thug's chosen frequency of the day.

The Ritz was never far from his mind, they were too close to forget about. He'd been lucky so far that their foraging efforts had focused on high density neighborhoods. That was good sense on their part. Sooner or later though, they'd come this way. After they'd taken the kid, he'd spent two days scouting through Tysons and watching them from the office towers across the street from the mall. He'd even spotted the kid once, being loaded up into a delivery truck that they used to forage for supplies. They seemed to rely entirely on vehicles to move around, which so far, he had used sparingly. He had only driven at night, without headlights, using his NODs to see by.

What he gave up in mobility, he gained in stealth, but it meant he hadn't been able to follow the kid's foraging group. From what he could tell, they'd work an area for several days at time before moving on. That's how he'd first got to them in Reston. Too late to stop them killing a group of survivors that had tried to fight back.

But he'd gotten a couple of them, and then two more a day later. When the captured radios had led him out to Herndon, he'd found the kid, killed three - maybe four more, but he'd lost the kid to them in the process. Without relying on ground transport, he needed time to get somewhere he could intercept the kid's foraging team. A week past, he'd thought he'd gotten lucky, but the team that had broadcast their location on the radio had turned out to be a different one. He'd watched them for hours without any sign of the teenager. It had meant a twelve-mile round trip over two wasted days, only moving at night.

He wasn't going to give up. Sooner or later, he'd figure out their schedule and which team the kid was working. He glanced at the whiteboard on the kitchen wall above where he had listed all the names and call-signs he'd been able to identify, as well as hashmarks for the thugs he'd managed to service. Which was exactly how he thought of it. There was doing what it took it to survive, and then there were the actions of the Tyson's gang. A gang. That was exactly what they were. They had a protection scheme going, slave labor in exchange for food and shelter and he'd seen enough of their selection criteria to be sickened to his core.

He boiled water for the coffee press, and rehydrated some eggs. He was wolfing down his breakfast, almost seeing his breath inside the house when the scanner started going apeshit. There was a lot of chatter about "finding Pro," which meant nothing to him. Maybe somebody else took one of the goons out during the night. He started in on the delicious microwaveable bacon that the Dagmans' had stocked in one of the freezers downstairs. Four slices for him, one for Loki. They had their system and Jason was pretty sure it was the highlight of the day for both of them.

"All teams, this is the Sheriff. Snow day is officially cancelled. He took out Lonny. I want that little spic bastard alive... all teams search west, he'll be trying to get home. I repeat. I want him alive."

Jason paused, a strip of bacon in front of his face. It had been dark, but the kid could have easily been Latino. Remembering back, he was confronted with the fact the teenager might never have been caught if it hadn't been for him. He owed him, whoever he was. *'Pro?'*... that had to be short for something.

He looked at Loki whose attention was firmly focused on the slice of bacon still in his hand. He bit the strip in half and tossed the rest to the dog.

"Could be our boy," he said out loud and sipped at his coffee. Watching the storm through the kitchen's window overlooking the back yard he couldn't help but think it was either a very good day to run or a very bad one. They were probably going to find him in the next hour or so and he was trying to think of something he could do about that, but kept coming up empty. There were just too many of them for him to assault directly. He could get in unseen, but getting out would be next to impossible once the shooting started.

He fixed some more breakfast, and loaded up Loki as well with one of the cans of dog food. As always, he was amazed how fast the dog could inhale food. He eyed his bug out bag leaning against the back wall of the kitchen next to the door, mentally going over everything he had in the bag, and thinking of what he would add due to the blizzard. An hour later, 'Pro' still hadn't been found; and it had to be the kid. They referred to him as *the kid* themselves on the radio, but the kicker had been the Sheriff's voice directing a team out to Herndon "where they'd found him."

The voices on the radio, especially Bauman's, were growing more frustrated. Their target had disappeared, they hadn't found any tracks, which wasn't surprising given how fast the snow was coming down. He listened as the orders came down to turn the mall and the hotel upside down.

Another hour passed and they still hadn't found him, and he listened as the thugs expanded their search grid westward. Jason glanced out the kitchen's back window, the clock shaped thermostat read 13 degrees, and he could hear the wind from inside the house. The snow piled up on the patio furniture had to be close to six inches deep and it was easily coming down at a rate of an inch or two an hour. He hoped the kid had thought this through. Knowing from the radio that the whole incident had been kicked off by him killing a soldier, he doubted if the teenager had been given much time to prepare.

"I want constant patrols on Rt. 7, the Toll Road, and Dolly Madison and switch to the tactical channel now."

Jason stood up, that decided it. He may not know how to help the kid, at least yet. He could still hunt those who were looking for him. Geared up, he waited long enough for the scanner to locate the new channel they were using.

By midday he was cutting cross country, following Difficult Run on a general southwest heading. He walked along the banks of the small stream, beneath the frozen dirt edge of the creek's flood channel. Loki was in his element, scouting ahead and bounding through the snow. He worried a little about that, Loki's coat was jet black and stood out against the snow. Their tracks wouldn't last long, and for the moment they were well hidden from the nearby roads by all the scrub brush and small trees that grew in the stream's flood plain.

For most of his planned route, he didn't even have to worry about roads. The stream was flanked on either side by neighborhoods. The water level was low enough, with frozen banks that he was able to utilize the stream's concrete underpass as it flowed under Rt. 7 and then several hours later, he passed beneath the Toll Road. As it was getting dark, he left the stream's green belt near Hunter Mill Road, south of the Toll Road, adjacent to the W.O.&D trail in Reston. The old train line had been turned into a paved bike path that ran from Washington, DC all the way out to Purcellville, beyond Leesburg to the west.

He followed the W.O.&D path until he found what he was looking for. An older house with an enclosed earth basement. He got in, and dropped his heavy pack, fed and watered both he and Loki and listened to his radio. He found himself rooting for the kid, who still hadn't been found. He prayed the teenager was dressed for the storm. The wind chill outside was brutal and could kill just as easily as the thugs hunting him.

He'd come far enough for now; he was cold and tired himself. His pack was heavy, and he'd come nearly six miles through snow pack and hard ground. He looked over at Loki, who had already claimed the only couch in the basement. The dog was curled up with his head resting on his paws, looking up at him, daring him to make him move. The little bit of light coming through the single door's window at the bottom of the service entry was enough to see by, but he reminded himself to stuff a mattress against it before using any light after dark.

He sat in the recliner facing a dead flat screen TV, and leaned back, listening to the radio chatter in the dark. The reception wasn't as good as it had been outside, but it would do. The storm was playing hell with the radios. He knew it was the static load in the atmosphere from the snow storm and it would be affecting his prey as much as it was him. It seemed like they were all coming his way or were already at points further west through Reston and Herndon. He could afford to warm up a little, rest and wait for the sun to go down. He smiled at the thought. 'We own the night,' the words had been a near mantra during his time in the Rangers. The words were never truer than now.

*

Pro's legs were heavy and cramping with fatigue. It was all he could do to jump and pull himself out of the track bed onto the cold concrete platform of the covered Wiehle Metro station. The effort left him blinking watered eyes due to the pain behind his left eye. It was a relief to get out of the wind, the open-air station was a roofed tunnel, open at both ends but it blocked the worst of the wind. Pro looked out to where he'd come from and shook his head at the tracks in the snow. From here, they were as plain as day. Out above his tracks, Wiehle Ave crossed the Toll Road. If anybody got out on the overpass and looked down, they'd know in a second that he'd come this way.

The best he could manage through the station was a shuffling fast walk after struggling to make it up the frozen escalator. Still, he was thankful to be moving without trudging through a foot of snow. He paused at the main level of the station, he could go north or south. Either direction was served by a covered sky bridge crossing the toll road. The parking garage to the north, whose outline he could just make out through the storm, was a lot closer than the residential areas to the south. Knowing he was going to freeze if he didn't get warm quick, the garage was an easy decision. He should be able to find a car to rest in.

Then he would find a house; hopefully one with a pair of gloves and a hat, but there was still too much light to safely move around in. He went north through the elevated walkway, across an open area between buildings where the wind swirled and cut through him. He was nearly bent over double against the cutting wind before he found the stairwell to the parking garage. He probed downward in the dark interior stairs by feel alone, counting the number of landings he descended past. The stairs ended at the fourth story underground and ran out into a pitch-black garage. He wondered how far underground he was. It was at least twenty degrees warmer inside, with no wind, and it felt good enough that he almost collapsed where he was. He should find a car, he thought, one with a big back seat.

He tried the back door on the first car he bumped into in the dark. It blasted to life, lights flashing, alarm blaring. His heart skipped a beat in frozen terror. His legs were running the moment his feet touched back down in the strobing of the car's lights. The car alarm went on for what felt like an eternity as he crouched behind a car further down the aisle watching the dark entrance to the stair case, expecting a soldier to pop out behind one of the flashlights they all had on their rifles.

The alarm and strobing lights stopped with a suddenness that he didn't trust. He could still hear the car horn in his head, right along with the pounding of his heart. Breathing again, and in total darkness, he moved by feel alone, a light touch on trunks and bumpers until he found the staircase. He sat down on the bottom steps and leaned against the concrete wall. He almost fell asleep before he remembered his remaining energy bar. His fingers were numb. He gave up trying to grip the slick foil with fingers he could barely feel and used his teeth to rip the package open. He chewed slowly, the worry of how far the sound of the car alarm would have carried moving farther and farther away as he struggled to stay awake.

By the time he'd finished the snack bar, he knew he was in bad shape. The pain behind his left eye flared every time he moved and there was a duller headache that seemed to pulse with his heat beat. He couldn't believe how sleepy he was. Worn out, that made sense to him. But he felt sleepy and sick, like he was about to throw up. Something was very wrong and he knew it. He'd rest here, for just a bit. He'd feel better when he woke up.

*

Ben was tired of driving around looking for the kid. It sucked out here, it was too damn cold. He should be back at the Ritz riding out the storm with one of the new chicks they'd rounded up. Either the kid had gone to ground somewhere close to the mall or he was frozen dead in the woods; somewhere the wild dogs would find him when the snow melted. He hoped it was the latter. He'd liked Pro well enough, and as far as he was concerned, he'd been justified in draining Lonny. At any rate, it was better to freeze to death than get what he had coming to him back at the mall. Pro was just a kid, too young to be beat to death by the Sheriff. But, on that note, so am I, he thought. So am I. That was why he still out here looking.

They'd spent the afternoon driving in the snow, retracing every road through Tysons. A couple of hours ago they'd been directed out Rt. 7. He was driving, Charlie Liu was riding shotgun wielding a spotlight out his window looking for tracks. Fatboy was in the back, pretending to be doing the same out the driver's side. They hadn't seen shit until they found tracks, plain as day on the side of the road going west on Baron Cameron. They followed the foot prints in the snow, all the way into a neighborhood next to the entrance to Lake Fairfax. The trail went right up a drive way and sidewalk, disappearing at the front door of a brick house.

They'd found 'Steve' boiling water on a Coleman stove inside his kitchen, or somebody else's; things like that didn't matter anymore. The dumb shit had just looked surprised and asked them if they'd like some tea. He was an old man who had reached for his gun a moment later, before they'd had a chance to ask if he was a Doctor or an electrician, somebody worth a shit. Charlie had made the decision for all of them and cut the man in half with his sawed off 12 gauge. They'd called it in, and made the report of the location but it looked like the stupid old man had been a nomad. There hadn't been anything worth taking, no hoard of supplies. He'd been angry that Charlie couldn't have waited to take the man up on his offer of some hot tea.

Back out on Baron Cameron, they'd turned south on Wiehle Avenue and headed back down toward the Toll Road. Just more unbroken snow, although in places it was being cleared away and blowing into drifts against anything that would block the wind. Ben glanced at the thermostat on his dash, it read 11 degrees and was still dropping as the sun had gone down.

This was bullshit. If Charlie hadn't been assigned to this rig, he would have long ago turned off into a neighborhood and caught a nap in the warm car. It wasn't like Fatboy would have complained. Charlie was here though, and he was an ambitious, brown-nosing SOB who acted like he had the Sheriff's ear. Which was why he stayed on point. Bauman had made it very clear that no one was coming back until they needed gas or had found the kid.

"Where in the hell, did that little shit go?" Charlie asked no one in particular.

Ben smiled to himself, wanting to point out that the kid was bigger than he was, but thought better of it.

"He's smart," he said. "A bottle of whiskey, we find him in one of the office buildings next to the mall."

"Or in the mall," Fatboy offered up from behind him. "Million places for a kid to hide in there."

Charlie turned around in his seat to glare at Fatboy. "You sound like you've given it some thought."

"Don't think I'd fit," Fatboy snorted.

Even Charlie laughed at that. Fatboy had been Fatboy since they'd found him living in a Costco. The idiot probably would have eaten himself to death if they hadn't brought him back to the mall along with the food he and his group hadn't consumed.

"He sure as hell hasn't used any of these roads," Fatboy added as they began crawling up onto the overpass that crossed over the Toll Road. There was a car blocking the middle of the road, looking like an igloo at this point except for the roof which had been scoured clean by the wind. Ben drove around to the left, glancing out his window, his eyes following the bouncing shaft of light from Fatboy's spotlight. One of them had to.

He slammed on the brakes and slid to a stop.

"You see that?" he shouted, backing up quickly, "Shine your light down at the tracks!"

"The tracks?"

"The train tracks!" Charlie ordered, already hopping out of his door.

They stood at the railing in the middle of the overpass looking down at the Metro tracks.

"Son of a bitch," Fatboy said just loud enough to be heard. "He walked all the way out here and never touched a road."

Charlie was already on his radio reporting it in. Ben shook his head; he could just imagine that ass-kissing conversation.

"Not exactly fresh," Ben noticed the footprints were almost filled in, "It could be some other loser."

"Load up," Charlie ordered. "Let's check the far side of the station."

"Yep," Ben nodded. That's one tough kid, he thought. Stupid as hell to run, and it was going to end ugly. He had to give him his due, though. Tough as nails.

*

Chapter 11

He was back in the hotel room with Lonny towering above him. The soldier's smile, the look on his face, scaring him worse than anything that came out of his mouth. Lonny unfastened his belt and tossed it to the floor, took a step towards him...

Pro jolted awake in complete darkness, panicked, thinking he was blind until he remembered where he was, how he'd gotten here, and what he'd done. The lingering shadow of his nightmare had him spooked. What had been a safe place to rest, out of the storm, suddenly became a dark tomb full of dead things.

He was slow getting to his feet, fighting the feeling that he was going to throw up. His throbbing headache was now a constant pain behind his left eye and that whole side of his head. On his feet, and dizzy; he took a moment leaning against the concrete of the wall and realized he was incredibly thirsty. He started up the stairs, moving slow, keeping his hand on the rail and counting the landings he passed. His legs felt weak and tight at the same time, like thin ropes stretched till they were about to snap.

He'd passed two landings in the pitch black of the stairwell when he felt the chill in the air begin to grow sharper with each step upward toward the surface. He couldn't go back out there, he thought. He'd freeze. But they'd find him if he didn't find some place safe. A house, with blankets and some food. He realized he'd stopped moving up the stairwell. He was leaning against the wall, eyes slammed shut in the darkness holding back what he knew were tears.

Have to get somewhere safe. If you stay here, you're dead. Reaching the surface level of the garage, he stepped out of the stairwell to be met with a blast of frozen wind that cut right through him. He hadn't thought it could get any colder, but it had. It was so dark outside, with no moon, that he couldn't tell if it was still snowing until he stepped out from under the garage. It was, and the wind was driving the flakes sideways into his face.

Kneeling in the snow he melted several handfuls of snow in his mouth. The process caused the pain in his head to blossom further, and left him shivering, still thirsty. He looked across the expanse of the roads leading out to Wiehle Avenue and momentarily weighed North Reston versus South. He knew South Reston a lot better. His baseball team had practiced on South Lakes High School's field a few times and he remembered it being surrounded by neighborhoods. Homes that he could disappear into. Hopefully he could find some warm, dry clothes and some food. At the moment, he'd settle for a blanket or towel to wrap around his head and face.

South then. He skirted the edge of the building's courtyard working his way in a big circle back to the elevated walkway leading out to the metro station sitting between the two halves of the toll road. The wind pushed him from behind telling him to hurry up, but it was behind him. South had been a good choice. He reached the entrance to the sky bridge and went across after looking for headlights on the toll road beneath him. He felt like he was going to throw up again and knew, if he stopped moving, he would. Forcing himself to keep moving took a strength of will he hadn't realized he possessed.

The swirling wind that met him within the open sided sky bridge almost turned him around as he ducked his head and plowed forward. He made the temporary refuge of the station situated high above the toll road's median, and almost collapsed. The far side of the sky walk looked impossibly long and he paused to glance back towards the relative warmth of the garage which he could no longer see. This was a bad idea, the voice in his head spoke alongside the pain that wouldn't let go. Another voice screamed that he had to keep moving. He focused on putting one foot in front of the other.

He turned east as soon as he reached the open-air parking lot on the far side and skirted between buildings, staying close to the structures themselves as they helped block the worst of wind. He noticed the wind had blown some patches of road and sidewalks bare, but they were just patches. He did his best to stay in the landscaped mulch beds, close up against the buildings themselves, relying on the shrubs to hide his path through the snow.

There was a T intersection where Wiehle dead-ended into Sunrise Valley Avenue. He crossed Wiehle, jumping from tire track to tire track. Wide, fresh tracks that he knew had been made by the soldiers hunting him. He didn't wonder if they knew he was in the area, he just assumed they did. Stupid! He should have tried to go into Vienna. It would have been a lot closer to the mall. He'd be warm by now, hiding in some strange bed, under covers.

The other voice in his head yelled at him. The same voice that had told him to keep stabbing Lonny. *They would have found you, dummy. You tricked them with the train tracks, don't go crying now. You need to be grown up. Keep going.*

The cold was unbearable, and the shivering made his head hurt even worse. *Keep walking. You stop, you die.* He told himself that he wasn't going to let them take him without a fight. It took him far longer than it should have to draw the half-forgotten gun from its holster. His hands wouldn't work right, but after a struggle he managed to rack the slide. He ignored the previously chambered round that fell to the ground and disappeared in the snow. He felt the teeth of the zipper on his coat pocket cut into the back of his hand as he forced his fist and the gun inside. It didn't hurt the way he thought it should. It was strange, the warm blood he could sense on the back of his hand felt good. This was better than the holster he thought, he could shoot through his coat if he had to.

He continued east on Sunrise, back the same way he'd walked on the tracks, paralleling the toll road through an office park next to Sunrise Valley that he knew would take him to South Lakes and the neighborhood around the high school. He used to be embarrassed that he had to ride his bike to baseball practice on those days when Pete's parents hadn't been able to give him a ride. Everybody else's parents, or in some cases, their foreign nannies had driven them. But at least he knew the roads. South Lakes was up ahead; it wasn't far. He just had to keep going.

He caught himself standing motionless, staring at the side of an office building made of dark glass. He didn't remember having stopped. How long had he been standing there? He could go inside and sleep. He was so tired. He couldn't put his feet in motion.

The side of the building flared with light. For a moment he just stared at it, thinking the sun was coming up. Then he

154

heard the engine behind him, felt the sound of the tires sliding to a stop in the snow behind him. He turned around slowly into the glare of the blinding lights and heard the unseen car doors pop open. He was mesmerized by the snow he could see falling at an angle through the light of the high-beams. He hadn't realized it was still snowing.

A gunshot pierced the cold air causing him to jump in surprise as his mind worked to wake up.

"Show us your hands, Shit Stick!"

He couldn't feel the gun he knew was in his hand, he couldn't feel his hand. He hoped they'd let him sleep.

*

Jason left the back door open. Loki stood half-in, half-out of the doorway looking at him expectantly, head cocked to the side in confusion.

"No, you stay," he repeated. "Stay inside."

The dog whimpered in complaint, but went back in the house. Jason propped the door open with a clay pot holding a long dead, freeze dried plant. If something happened to him, Loki wouldn't be trapped in the house.

He made sure one last time, that his stolen Motorola radio had its mic muted; he'd heard of the talk button getting pushed by mistake, either out of habit, or more likely by a belt or another piece of gear. He could hardly believe that they still didn't seem to realize he could be listening in. It was a situation that he wasn't going to spoil out of carelessness.

He made sure the wired ear piece was fit tight under his watch cap and set out at a slow jog until he warmed up. The radio had gone spastic a few minutes ago. They still hadn't found the kid but they'd found his tracks on the metro line, several hours old. The gun thugs had a general area to focus on now. There were already two units in the area of Wiehle Ave., going up and down Sunset and Sunrise Avenues on either side of the toll road hunting the kid. Another unit was coming back in from Herndon to help out. He had to give the kid credit. No one, himself included, had thought of the Metro track line.

The kid, Pro, he corrected himself. The kid had a name; had to have planned some of this in advance. At least for clothing he thought, as a blast of wind cut through him and the trees above creaked and moaned in protest. If he hadn't, he'd be holed up or dead from exposure by now.

He cut through the neighborhood he was in, climbing the gentle hillside that led up from the creek, through half a dozen backyards working his way straight north from his hideout to the W.O.&D bike path. He and Sam had jogged or biked along its length on weekends over the last couple of years and he knew he was less than two miles from Wiehle Ave. It was surreal to be jogging down the edge of the same path, in the middle of the night, carrying a suppressed M-4, with the hopes of finding somebody to kill.

He didn't think of it in those terms, he never had. There was only the mission, and right now, the mission was to find the kid or help him get away. Period. He knew what that would entail, and it bothered him not at all. He only wished the Sheriff, whose voice he'd come to know well over the course of the day, was out here conducting the search himself.

As cold as the wind was, he was thankful for it, even the gusts which sand blasted and stung his face. He could see it was scouring clear open areas, in the roads, and on the bike path. Deep drifts were piling up to the sides. Anything that helped him not leave a trail was good in his book. He picked up his pace into a steady jog, which he knew was stupid. It dropped his situational awareness. Worse, was the fact that he'd be risking much more if he worked up a hard sweat in these temperatures. Then he remembered the kid had been out here all day, running. He ran a little harder.

He jumped into the tree line as the bike path came up on Sunrise Ave. He had just heard one of the mobile search teams report they were "going back down Sunrise again." From the trees he could see the fresh, wide tire tracks of a Humvee, they had clearly already been up and down this road several times. There was another unit reporting in from across the toll road, on Sunset, and a third one going up and down Reston Ave. a mile and a half further west. He closed his eyes and built a map of the pursuit in his head. They clearly thought he'd left the tracks at the Wiehle station, or they'd all be further west.

He tried to put himself in the kid's shoes. Where would I go if I was a scared and being hunted by the local militia? He kept coming back to Herndon, the same reasoning of familiarity that had been driving the gun thugs all day.

But the kid hadn't made it that far west, so he'd jumped off the tracks in Reston. Jason looked around at the neighborhoods he'd just run through. I'm cold, I'm hungry, I'm looking for something familiar. Something residential...

He dashed across the lanes of Sunrise Ave into the open cut of the bike path where it crossed the expanse of the road and disappeared into the darkness and a gentle curve of trees backing a neighborhood. It would lead him up to Reston's business center, and the Reston Town Center. This side of the toll road was much more residential.

He'd just decided to leave the bike path and cut west along Sunrise, when a glow of headlights grew ahead of him in the direction of Wiehle, coming towards him. He stepped back into the trees and waited, watching the vehicle roll slowly towards him. A spotlight was dancing out the passenger side window. It continued on, rolling past his position, heavy metal music blaring from within the vehicle.

He mentally shook his head... idiots. Once the glare of the headlights was past, he stepped out from behind his tree and could see the profiles of two occupants. He waited until the tail lights disappeared, ran down to the road and jumped out into the tire tracks and took off running west down the middle of Sunrise. He knew from their radio chatter that the Humvee he'd just seen and the other unit already in the area were opposite from one another running a loop between Wiehle and Hunter Mill, checking the side streets as they went. He had a clear path and a gap to exploit for the next few minutes as long as there wasn't another team out there that was staying off the radio. So far, they all seemed anxious to convince the Sheriff that they were working hard.

The radio transmitter atop the hotel was a target that he'd have to address in the future. He didn't know how the Ritz had come to have a radio base station, or the acres of solar panels on the top of the mall, that drove the water well that had been dug in front of the hotel. He doubted if the assholes living there now had anything to do with it, beyond taking or inheriting the infrastructure from someone else. But for now, it was nice being able to listen in on what they were doing.

He kept up his steady jog, careful to keep his footfalls within one of the meandering tire tracks. He kept a look out for other footprints as well. If he could think of the trick, the kid might have been able to do the same. He pulled up as his eyes focused on a glow of light off to his right. He saw it again, there was a vehicle in the office park, somewhere down below the road he was on. He could see the glare of its lights casting a sliding glow off the sides of buildings. He left the road and jumped into the line of trees separating the office park from the road. He ran to the back of a building and hugged the side of it as he crept around the corner until he was facing the front parking lot. Headlights were coming his direction via the road in front of the office building.

"We've got fresh tracks!"

The voice on the radio was the same one that had found the boy's footprints on the train track.

He had no way of knowing if he was listening to the same vehicle that he could now hear less than a hundred yards away and rapidly growing closer. He was almost to the front corner of the building when he heard a gunshot followed by a voice shouting something that was lost to the wind.

He peeked around the corner. The building had a single line of parking spaces in front, then a line of shrubs separating the lot from the road where the Humvee sat. The vehicle's headlights clearly outlined another figure, frozen still in the middle of the road, head bowed against the glare from the high beams.

"What's your location?" The Ritz came back on the radio.

The query went unanswered and Jason watched the front two doors and one of the back doors open and unload its occupants. He brought his rifle up as they surged forward towards their prey, but the angle was wrong. The last thing he wanted was a hostage situation. He needed to wait.

They tackled the figure to the ground, and Jason couldn't help but notice their target had just stood there looking into the headlights as they came at him, seemingly too stunned or cold to move.

He surged forward himself and crossed the narrow parking lot in a low crouch, coming up against the line of evergreen shrubs that separated him from the road. He moved forward until he was opposite the Humvee. He was watching the scene unfold between two shrubs in time to see one of the thugs punch the kid hard in the head until his body went slack. He was close enough to hear their laughter, and see their faces. In the light cast by the headlights, he could see it was Pro, now laying on his back in the snow, not moving. The same kid who might have never been captured if it hadn't been for him

It took every bit of control he had, to hold back from taking them out as they stood laughing over the unconscious form of the teenager. He thumbed the M-4's selector to full auto and waited. He had to wait to have a chance of doing this and getting Pro and himself somewhere safe.

He watched them through the shrubs, seething in anger from fifteen feet away as two them dragged the limp form by the shoulders back to the Humvee and threw him in across the floor of the back seat. Jason felt his hand tighten on the stock and he consciously focused on keeping his right index finger out of the trigger guard. He had to wait.

One of the thugs, who looked to be built like an offensive guard, as wide as he was tall, sat in the back. Before he pulled his door shut, he propped his feet up on the kid's frame on the floor. The other two hopped in the front and slammed their doors. He watched as they gave each other a high five. He tensed, picturing his movement through the gap in the shrubs, two strides across the mulch bed, down a step, off the snow buried curb into the road and he'd be outside the passenger's side window, half a foot away from the thug who'd just knocked out the kid. He was almost trembling in anticipation, concentrating on breathing deep. He waited... they'd have to call it in.

*

Ben was almost shocked at Charlie's gesture of the high five. The asshole was smiling. No doubt he'd get the lion's share of credit, but that was a hell of a lot better than having Charlie spin the story to have the blame fall on him and Fatboy for having failed.

"Yes!" Charlie yelled as he dug around in his seat for the radio.

"You think we have a reward coming?" Fatboy laughed from the back seat.

"Yeah," Charlie answered. "I won't leave your fat ass out here to freeze."

"And you," Charlie smiled across the front seat at him, "you owe me a bottle of whiskey."

"Was that a bet?" Ben felt himself smiling. They could get back to the hotel now

"It is now," Charlie laughed, and brought the radio up.

"Control, this is Charlie, we got him. He's a popsicle, in rough shape, but he's alive. On our way back."

Ben sat behind the wheel watching Charlie, it would all depend on the Sheriff's mood, like everything did.

"Straight back, Charlie." The Sheriff's voice sounded friendlier than it had all day. "And he better be alive when you get here, good job."

"Copy that, on our way, out."

Charlie tossed the radio up onto the dash board. "You heard the man, straight back."

"Let's warm the kid up," Ben fumbled with the climate control, this civilian version Hummer was a lot nicer than the couple of military versions they had, but the dashboard controls were as confusing as hell. Satisfied he had the heater on max, he put his hand down on the gear shift and looked over at Charlie.

There was another face just on the other side of Charlie's half fogged window. The man was smiling.

"What the..."

*

Jason sent a wall of .556 through the front of the Humvee, through the passenger side window and out the driver side. The contents of the two heads in the way went with it. He let up on the trigger, adjusted his aim between the passenger seat headrest and the window frame, and sent two three round bursts into the tub of lard in the back.

Moving fast, he pulled their bodies out of the vehicle and left them in the snow in the middle of the road before checking on Pro. He was out cold, but breathing with a pulse that seemed weak. The kid was half frozen. He ran through several competing plans in his head, all of which needed the kid moving, on his own two feet. He shut the doors and crawled in behind the wheel, dimly aware of what he was sitting in, what covered the steering wheel, dashboard, and a good portion of the inside of the windshield.

He confirmed the heater was set to max and took off through the parking lot. He went through the office park and fishtailed going left on Sunrise, following the route the Humvee that had passed him on the way in had taken. He figured he had a good twenty minutes, maybe thirty in these road conditions before the thugs would be expected back at the Ritz.

He could go anywhere there were already tracks in the road, or he could leave new tracks as long as they didn't lead to where he'd left Loki. He had supplies there and a place to warm the kid the up. He sped east along Sunrise as fast as he dared, relieved that there were tire tracks already on Hunter Mill. He followed those tracks, heading south towards Vienna. His long-term survivability and maybe the kid's as well, depended on keeping the Great Falls location secret. Let them think he was operating out of Vienna, southwest of the mall, instead of northwest.

He knew with having to carry the kid, and with the weather, he was limited to how far away he could go from where he'd stashed Loki and his gear. He was willing to push it as far as he could. He passed the W.O.&D where it crossed Hunter Mill, and continued south for another mile, clamping his jaws against the frozen wind blasting through the shattered windows but thankful it was clearing some of the dry snow from the roads. He was aware that every minute he drove, would mean more time outside in the environment, time the kid may not have. It also wouldn't do either of them any good unless they could truly hole up, once he got somewhere safe.

He thought he'd gone far enough to sell the southerly direction of travel. Staying inside an existing track of packed snow, he stopped the Hummer on the side of the road, and jumped out into another track of packed snow. Staying in the track he walked around to the front of the vehicle and put four rounds into the front grill until he was rewarded with a billowing cloud of steam.

He immediately fired two shots into the driver's side tire and climbed back into the vehicle and eyed the temperature gauge as it ticked upward.

He drove another quarter of a half a mile before pulling the jeep over. He left the engine running, opened the back door and checked on his cargo.

He felt like a real asshole doing it, but he slapped the unconscious kid a couple of times on the cheek and on the back of the hand. He breathed a sigh of relief when his eye lids fluttered open. The kid tried to push away from him, weakly.

"Easy there, Pro," he held the kid's hands down against his chest. "I'm a friend. I wasn't going to let you get taken by them again."

His patient just stared at him with the one eye that wasn't swollen shut.

"You understanding me?" He spoke loud, half wondering if he was getting through at all and not just talking to himself.

"It's you, the ninja..."

He tried to smile. He'd heard the name they'd given him on the radio.

"Not hardly. But yeah, it's me."

"What happened?" The kid seemed to focus on his surroundings for a moment before looking at him again.

"They caught you," he explained. "I caught them and stole their ride. Right now, we need to walk, can you walk?"

"Just want... sleep," the kid slurred sounding like he was drunk. To his credit, he also tried to sit up.

Jason pulled him upright to where he sat on the back floor, between the seats, his feet hanging out the door. He took a closer look at what the kid was wearing, he had on good boots and a heavy coat, but no hat or gloves. He kicked himself knowing he could have taken either from the Humvees owners.

He pulled off his own watch cap, and pulled it down over the kid's ears and pulled his gloves off, and held them out. "Can you get these on?"

Pro tried to wriggle his fingers, but ended up shaking his head in defeat.

Jason spent far too much time, getting his gloves fitted on Pro's hands and jamming hand warmer packets down inside. The kid's fingers were almost unresponsive. He activated the remaining two boot warmers he had on him and stuffed them into the kid's jean's front pockets. It wasn't much, but he figured every little bit might help.

"OK, we need to walk out of here, to get somewhere safe and warm." Jason held Pro's face between his hands and spoke slowly. "We aren't going to stop. You walk as far as you can, then I'll carry you. You ready?"

Pro's one functioning eye seemed to focus on him, and he was rewarded with a weak nod.

Feeling like a total prick, he half lifted, half dragged the kid back outside, but they didn't have an option. He was walking a knife's edge of timing and risk with this plan. If Pro survived and they made it, they'd be able to hole up until the kid was healthy, they wouldn't have to move again in a few hours. He didn't need to be a doctor to know Pro was in serious need of the kind of shelter and rest that would be impossible to get on the run.

His respect for the young man went up a notch as he looked over to see Pro trudging along, slowly putting one foot in front of the other.

"You're doing great," he egged him on. He worried how short Pro's second wind was going to be. The kid could barely lift his feet.

"Stay in the tire tracks, that's it." They were headed north, back towards Reston, in the same direction they'd just come from. Jason had made sure to drive right up against the right shoulder of the road on his way here, weaving in and out of the old tire tracks. His new tracks looked like he'd been having trouble keeping the Humvee on the road. Lord knew there was enough carnage and blood in the cab of the Humvee to give some credence to the idea that he'd been wounded as well.

They made it somewhat less than a mile in the thirty minutes he'd mentally allowed himself to use the road. Now it was going to get hard. His ears were already hurting in the cold wind and he was amazed the kid was still upright. He'd been out in this storm all day.

"Just a little further," he tried to encourage the teenager. "Then you can ride for a bit." He wasn't certain the kid even heard him, or knew he was there with him.

He looked back to see the firm set of determination on the young face as well as a streak of frozen tears. Whether they were from the cold or something else, Jason was just as determined that the animals at the Ritz were going to pay for what they'd done to the kid. What they'd made him do.

By the time they reached the bottomland surrounding Difficult Run, Pro was at his end. Jason did a double check on the location, there was a large meadow, part riding rings for horses, part flood plain. This was the spot. He stopped and waited for Pro to take another three steps catching up to him, at which point the kid just bumped into him, running on auto pilot.

"How much do you weigh?"

The young face just looked back at him in numb, confused silence.

"Doesn't matter," Jason tried to smile. This was going to suck, for both of them. But he was wearing the right boots for it, and the kid wasn't. Besides, nobody was going to suspect that they would use the creek in these temps, but from here, upstream, the creek ran to the bottom of the hill, behind the house where he'd left Loki. He only had a quarter of a mile to go, wading through ice cold water.

He tightened the straps on his M4, pulling it in tight to his chest.

"Going to pick you up now." He shook his head, "This is gonna hurt, but I promise, it's not far. Then you get to warm up." He waited for a response, the kid may have nodded, maybe not.

Jason bent down in front of Pro, reached up and pulled him down and across the back of his shoulders by the front of his coat. Pro managed a *whooof* of air in response and Jason stepped out of the tire track he'd left on the road's shoulder, his foot up against the base of a small tree. He repeated the process, using the base of trees to keep from sliding. His ankles protesting with each stride as he made his way down the shallow embankment to the stream.

Their combined weight; Jason figured he was about 215 these days, and the kid was at least 140 lbs., plus their clothing, boots and weapons crashed through the shelf of ice on the stream's edge. Which was what he'd expected. These tracks would break, melt or be washed away as soon as the snow melted. The water came up over the tops of his boots and he could feel the shock of pain as it ran down filling them. That he hadn't expected. *You knew it was going to suck.*

He charged ahead, his lungs bellowing like a steam engine, sweating hard inside his jacket, his feet numb from the cold. He forced his knees to keep pumping. Three hundred yards through the water, going upstream, he climbed the bank at a shallow point, knowing within a day of some warmer temps these tracks would be washed out by rising melt water. He powered on along the streams edge, until he stopped, suddenly worried that he may have come too far.

He set Pro's feet on the ground and propped him up against a tree.

"You still with me?"

Pro blinked at him. "You're... crazy."

He managed to smile, ignoring the fire in his lower back as he straightened up. "Crazy keeps you alive," he nodded. "Not like I've been doing this all day, like somebody else I know." He got his bearings; a hundred and fifty yards uphill, through two back yards and they could rest.

"You ready?"

Pro's eyes were closed again, but he managed a slow nod

*

Chapter 12

"And?" Bauman, behind his desk had been listening to him deliver the report. With Lonny and now Charlie dead, Sleepy was now firmly in the number two slot. Deputy to the crazy SOB sitting across from him.

Sleepy had already delivered his report on the results of the search for Pro. Bauman liked his after-action reports, almost as if he wanted justification for tearing someone's head off when things went sideways. Sleepy knew his report, at best, was full of holes. Those who knew what happened; starting with Lonny and ending with Charlie, were dead. There'd been no sign of Pro.

His own team had been concentrating on Herndon itself when Charlie's team had found Pro. Charlie's report of success over the radio had raised mixed emotions in him. He'd been at once thankful the kid was alive, he'd survived whatever Lonny had tried to do him, and the storm hadn't killed him. He'd weighed that against the fact that Bauman had planned on making an example out of Pro. He could remember the shame he had felt, wishing Pro's body had been found in the snow.

When he and his own team had reached the Ritz in Tysons before Charlie, they'd all realized something had gone wrong. Every team they had available was sent back out to Reston. It had taken them nearly an hour to find the bodies; Charlie had never reported where they'd found their runaway. It had taken almost another hour until they found the shot up and abandoned Hummer half way to Vienna. Between the strengthening wind at the tail end of the snowstorm and the dry snow, they hadn't been able to find any tracks. The three bodies in the office park left no doubt, Pro had had help.

That had started a two-day hunt for whoever had intercepted Charlie. They all knew who they were looking for, if not where. For his part, Sleepy hadn't wanted to look that hard. He was glad the kid was gone. Besides, teams that ran into this ninja character never seemed to come back. Not that he would ever use that word in front of Bauman. No one would; not after he'd kicked the shit out of one of the teams that had come back empty-handed that night. That team's driver, Carson, after seeing the scene left in Reston, had commented off hand, that the 'ninja character was the real deal.' He'd made the mistake of being overheard by Bauman. Carson would be laid up for a week, and might lose an eye.

Bauman gave the appearance of being in control, never raising his voice, always calm. But Sleepy knew the man was paranoid and wired so tight that it took precious little to set him off.

"That's it," Sleepy shook his head. "For now. We're still combing the area, concentrating on areas south of Lawyers Road, the Vienna side, they were clearly headed that direction. He drove that Humvee till it died, and it was shot up enough that unless he was an idiot, he knew it was going to die. I think he was running south.

"Do you?" Bauman's voice dropped an octave as those dead eyes looked at him in accusation.

"Yeah, I do." He knew the fastest way to get in trouble with Bauman was to give the man a reason to think you were hiding something. He half suspected, perhaps hoped, Bauman wanted somebody he could confide in, someone to share the load with. Charlie had come closest to that, until he'd had his head blown off.

"So, we hunt him south? Southwest? Vienna? Oakton? How far do we go?"

Sleepy decided to gamble. "If you're asking my opinion, we don't. We've got enough worries with all the new folks we caught up during the snowstorm, almost a hundred plus new mouths to feed. Every time he runs into us, it's an ambush, he's clearly listening in on our radios. It's a morale hit. Whoever, whatever he is, he's already the boogeyman to a lot of the guys. Let's bide our time, train up some more guns, keep growing."

"And just let it go?" Bauman's voice raised in pitch.

Sleepy shook his head. "If recent history is a judge, he'll find us again. We need to be ready. Get him reacting to us, instead of" he almost said something that would probably set Bauman off, "the other way around."

Bauman stared back at him, silent, for long enough that Sleepy didn't think for a second he was weighing the option he'd laid out. The bastard was considering something else.

"You came out of this smelling like a rose." Bauman's meaty index finger pointed at him, making a small circle. "Between Lonny, who I know you didn't like and Charlie who was a good deputy, you've just moved up in quick order. For all I know, you helped plan this."

Sleepy shook his head, he had to level set the crazy bastard right now, and try not to get moved to the shit list in the process. Michelle too; he knew Bauman thought of them as a pair.

"You got me, Chief."

Bauman's whole head twitched. "I'm not trying to be funny."

Which *was* funny, because if Bauman had ever had a sense of humor, it had died along with the rest of the world.

Sleepy leaned back in his chair. "Yeah boss, I convinced Lonny to try to sodomize the kid like he had others. I planned with the kid to kill Lonny. The tough part was arranging the snow storm, and of course I've been in secret communication with this psycho nut job out there as well. I would have had to vector Ben and Charlie into the kid as well, in order to complete the ambush, even though none of us knew where exactly they grabbed the kid up, they never said. All the while, I was with my own team out in Herndon and on the radio with you back here. I'm a criminal genius."

"Don't be an asshole, Sleepy." The man's eyes flicked towards his own in a feeble attempt at understanding. "As long as it's just the two of us in here, fine. But, don't push it."

He sat up a little more and leaned forward. "I get it, and you know I won't. But you need help running this circus. If you want my help, I need to be able to speak the truth as I see it, with you, in private. If you want another ass kissing yes man or psychopath, there's plenty here to choose from. I guarantee you; Wayne is out there right now complaining that it's not him in here"

Sleepy saw the flurry of emotion flick across Bauman's face. Facets of the former sheriff's personality at war with the others. He was certain at least one of them almost got him shot right there.

"I'll salute and follow orders, but some shit has to change, or the next time one of the sheep decide to fight back, it may not be a single, fourteen-year-old kid."

Bauman's jaw twitched, and his hands were white knuckled against the arm rest of his chair. Sleepy did his best not to notice.

"Your woman said the same thing to me."

"She wasn't wrong, Boss. I don't need to remind you that we just took in a dozen or so able fighters. Some of them have strong attachments with women or children that were found with them. We can't break them up." Sleepy knew how thin the ice was that he was walking, but Bauman was still listening.

"That won't be popular with the men."

"The men will follow orders." He said it with an assurance he didn't feel. Wayne was getting tired of following orders, and the man was developing his own powerbase among the soldiers. "So will I."

Bauman looked at him for a moment and shook his head. "I'll consider it, I will." He sat back, "Lord knows I'm overdue for a little feel good. The people have been working hard. They believe in what we're doing here. I might be able to afford easing up, a bit."

Sleepy didn't say anything just nodded in feigned understanding. Bauman's switch had flipped from paranoia and anger to full bore delusional justification in half a second. The only reason he hadn't killed the asshole is that he knew he had zero chance of controlling Wayne and the three dozen or so hard cases that liked things the way they were. Bauman may not be able to either.

*

Pro had a moment of panic as he slowly came awake. He was dreaming that he was sleeping next to his mom and sister, warm in bed during those few days before they'd gotten sick. His family morphed into Lonny, but in the feather-light control he had of the dream he remembered that Lonny was dead. He had killed him. It was the ninja; he was a perv too! Aware of somebody breathing next to him, weight pressed up against him, his eyes shot open.

The dog's head came up from where it had been resting on his chest. The warm tongue, nearly the width of his face started at his chin and slathered upward until he could feel it catch his eyebrows.

"Ugh..." he managed, and pushed the dog's head back.

Laughter from the couch on the other side of the dimly lit basement surprised him. He remembered the man's name, Jason. The *ninja*, and the dog, Loki. The last few days, he wasn't sure how long it had been, had passed in a sleepy blur. He remembered the man waking him up, always with a bottle of water, aspirin and something warm to eat. He remembered the dog keeping him warm.

"Better you than me," the man said. "I usually get the slobbery tongue in the morning."

"Is it morning?"

"No, it's past noon, but don't worry about it. We aren't in any hurry."

The man got up and came over, and put the back of his hand against his forehead. It was all he could not to flinch, and he felt guilty about it. The man noticed his reaction but didn't pull back.

"Fever's way down, and you look a lot better. How do you feel?"

"Good, a little sore. Hungry, I guess."

The man nodded at him. "That's as good a sign as anything. I am too."

174

The ninja man stood and stepped back. "You feel like getting up?" He held his palms out. "There's no rush, I'm just concerned."

He rubbed the dog's ears, and nodded. "I think so." The dog clearly thought he was ready.

He unzipped the sleeping bag and was confused to see two soft plastic bags down in the bag next to him.

"I found a couple of hot water bottles upstairs. You were damn near frozen."

Pro noticed he was wearing sweat pants, and a long-sleeved t-shirt that was way too big for him. Did the man dress him?

"Pro," the man was pulling a gun out from a pile of gear near the couch he'd been sitting on. It was Lonny's gun, the .45.

He took two steps towards him, and Pro couldn't help but flinch. He wouldn't be able to fight this man.

Jason took a knee and held the gun out to him. "You know how to use this?"

Pro nodded.

"Keep it. I understand you earned it. I don't know what kind of asshole you took it from, but it needed cleaned in a bad way. But, it's a good gun, and loaded."

Pro took the gun and sat up in his sleeping bag. He set the gun down on the floor next to him, breathing a sigh of relief. The man, Jason? What was he supposed to call him? Jason knew what he he'd done to Lonny, maybe knew why. Pro could see it in the man's eyes. Jason knew he was scared. Giving him his gun back, was the man's way of telling him he didn't have to be.

"Ok, you may know how to use it, but you need to learn some basic rules."

Pro wasn't sure what the man was talking about.

The man withdrew his own hand gun and placed it next to his own on the floor.

"Hand me my gun," the man smiled at him.

He did so, careful not to point the barrel at either of them, Sleepy had shown him that.

"Someone hands you a gun, you always....," Jason paused and looked at him intensely, "always, check its status."

He watched as Jason pulled back the slide and looked down into the gun from the topside. "Visually inspect to see if there is a round in battery, if you don't see one, you can do one of two things, confirm with your finger, or," Jason looked away, and then back down at the gun, "check visually twice." The gun ratcheted closed, "I always keep a round in battery."

"Even if we are right next to each other, and you see me unload a gun. If I hand it to you, you do your own check."

Pro nodded, it made sense.

"Now, let me see you check your gun."

Pro did just as he'd seen the soldier do. His didn't have a round ready to shoot, or in battery, as Jason had called it. But he could see the stack of rounds beneath. He pulled the rack back all the way then let it slap forward.

"Ok, now you're ready to fire," Jason said, as he reached out and tilted Pro's gun sideways and checking where he had his trigger finger.

"Good, where you'd learn to keep your finger away like that?"

"Sleepy taught me," he answered.

"One of the guys at the Ritz?"

He nodded. "He was a friend, I think."

The ninja looked at him doubtfully, he was reminded that this man had killed a lot of the soldiers. "Ok, your hammer is back on the gun, do you want to carry it like that?"

"No," Pro shook his head. "This part makes me nervous."

The man just nodded. "It should."

Pro pointed the gun at the floor and gently pulled the trigger, with one thumb holding back the hammer, the other in between where it snapped forward.

The man stood up slowly with a groan and rubbed his knees. "Keep it with you. I'll see if I can get us something going food wise."

"Umm??? Sir?"

The man shook his head. "Not sir, not ninja, just Jason. Ok?"

"Ok," Pro nodded. "Where are my clothes, Jason?"

Jason laughed at him. "Drying out next to the stove I rigged up in the garage. Your clothes were soaked through, you were freezing to death." The man looked at him and shook his head with a sad smile. "You're not my type, kid. I think you did right with that asshole at the hotel."

"How'd you know?"

"Some I heard on the radio, and you've kind of been mumbling in your sleep. I can guess what happened. It's not your fault. You did right, don't ever doubt that."

"It didn't happen," he answered. "But it was going to. He didn't know I'd found a knife."

The man nodded at him as if that explained it all. "Don't give it a second thought, he got what he deserved." Jason headed for the stairs leading out of the basement. He stopped halfway up, and looked back down at him. "I've got bad news, we're down to Chicken a la King or chicken in white gravy, they are both god-awful, you have a preference?"

"Anything," Pro laughed. His stomach rumbled at the mention of food.

Loki barked once, adding his two cents. "You'll get what you get," Pro heard the man complain from the top of the stairs. He looked across the room, at the gear piled up. The M-4 leaning against the couch. Jason trusted him enough to leave him here with the guns. As far his recent experience went, that went a long way towards making him trustworthy in turn.

Jason warmed the MRE pouches in a pan of almost boiling water atop the jury-rigged coffee can stove in the garage, half wondering if the kid would run, half thinking it would be better if he did. He wasn't in any kind of shape emotionally to look after a kid. He knew that with a certainty that bothered him. The term 'kid' wasn't accurate in a way that it would have been three months ago. He could only imagine what Pro had been through since the die off.

He watched Pro inhale his Chicken a la King with an enthusiasm that made him smile. How hungry did someone have to be to eat baby shit with that kind of gusto? He saw Pro dispense with the spork and use a finger to wipe the contents of his bag clean. Jason looked down at the remaining contents of his own bag and turned up his nose.

"Hey," he handed over his entrée. "You need this a lot more than I do."

Pro ate that too. He could remember what it was like to be a growing teenager, always hungry, never full. He also knew the kid had nearly marched himself to death during his run from Tysons.

He saw Pro eyeing him and the cookie he was eating.

"Oh, sorry," he remembered the dessert that had come in the kid's MRE, and fished the fig newton-like fruit chew out of his cargo pants and tossed it across the space between the recliner he occupied and where the kid sat on the couch facing him.

They both laughed as Loki, thinking the thrown food was meant for him left his side and darted to the end of the couch. The dog rested its massive head on the arm rest of the couch, staring plaintively up at the kid as he opened the wrapper.

"Feed him and you've got a friend for life," he caught himself smiling as he watched the two hungry teenagers stare at the cookie for a moment before Pro broke off a piece and offered it up.

"He's greedy," Pro said with a laugh. "How old is he?"

How long had it been since he'd heard another's voice that wasn't coming through the tinny speaker of a Motorola radio?

"Almost a year or so, I think. He belonged to one of our neighbors."

"Oh," Pro said. It was never very far away. Dead neighbors, like dead family and a dead world that was always just outside. It was the background music that you could tune out at times. Every time you stopped doing something, it was there waiting for you. Weather that wouldn't change.

"Makes him a teenager like you, in dog years, I mean."

"Does he know any tricks?"

"I don't know." He should know that.

He was watching Pro and the dog share the last of the cookie wondering what the next step was, when Pro looked up at him.

"What?"

"I just realized; that was the last of the food I brought with me. You up for a little foraging tonight? It's a lot warmer than the last time you were outside."

"I think so. Sorry, I've been lazy, and eating your food."

He waved it away. "You almost died, Pro. You're entitled to all the rest you think you need."

"I'm good to go," Pro said.

It was such a Northern Virginia thing to say, 'good to go.'

The first house had been a bust, somebody there had survived a while and eaten through the house's dry goods before getting sick and dying on the living room couch. Jason had figured the night time exercise would give him a chance to observe the kid in action and make sure he was up for the eight-mile hike back to the house. True to his word, Pro seemed fine. Jason watched him move with stealth between the yards of the houses, moving from shadow to shadow in the moonlight.

He'd figured he'd be able to teach the kid something about how to go through a house, but he found himself taking notes and laughing at his assumptions as he had watched Pro slip a scavenged dress sock over the end of the flashlight. The resulting light was just bright enough to read labels and inspect the interior of kitchen cabinets.

"Going to be stiffs inside," Pro whispered as he stood outside the door of the next house, tying a t-shirt around his face, "front door is locked."

"Maybe they tried walking out," Jason offered, looking at the two cars sitting in the driveway. Pro seemed more at ease with the idea of finding the dead than he did.

"Betcha the next MRE cookie."

Jason nodded, "OK." Why not? The kid seemed very sure of himself.

The dark interior of the house, in the heart of winter had that sweet sickly smell that had replaced the stench of active rot they'd all lived with through the fall months. It would no doubt be back with a vengeance as it warmed up in the spring.

Pro stopped and faced him; he figured the little smartass was smiling behind his t-shirt mask.

"How'd you know?"

"There was a shovel outside, leaning against the garage, always means a deader inside."

Right... "Come on let's check the kitchen," he said trying to remember if he'd put the shovel back after burying Sam. Apparently, even a world inhabited by the dead had its clichés.

Jason found a small jar of instant coffee on the kitchen counter and he pocketed it. He had bags of vacuum sealed beans back at the house, but he'd used the last of the instant stuff he'd brought with him that morning.

"This place is a goldmine," Pro pulled out a pair of cardboard barrels of oatmeal still wrapped together in its cellophane. "They shopped at Costco, always good, and there will be guns and bullets here too."

"How do you know?"

Pro looked at him over the open cabinet door, from where he knelt on the floor. "There was a National Rifle Association bumper sticker on the car in the driveway, almost always means guns, especially if it's on a car, not a truck. Houses with a truck and that sticker have guns a lot too, but I've always found guns at houses when the sticker is on a car. Weird, huh? I think some guys with trucks just have the stickers. But if their wives have the sticker, they really have guns."

"Yeah, that's weird." Jason mentally shook his head. He knew the reason behind the stickers, but that didn't mean he would have ever been able to figure it out on his own like the kid had. *From the mouths of babes.* Pro was probably better equipped to live on his own that he was.

"They're usually in the bedrooms, along with... you know."

"Don't worry about weapons and ammo, I've got plenty. Just find something to eat that will get you through tomorrow. We'll walk back to my place tomorrow night, get a real meal."

"Do I have to go with you?" The kid's voice and demeanor changed in an instant, he was suddenly standing.

"No," Jason said calmly, "you don't." The kid seemed so easy going at times, it was easy to forget that he'd just spent that last three weeks as a prisoner. "In fact, I'll help you get back to Herndon if you want, or wherever you want to go."

"Oh," Pro relaxed a little.

"But you're welcome to come with, if you want. I just want you safe. I do think you'll be safer with me and Loki. I've got supplies... quiet neighbors."

He was relieved to hear the kid laugh. "Quiet neighbors! I get it."

"You're not a prisoner," Jason said laughing a little at his own joke. "You can leave anytime."

"Will you teach me to fight? I can help you fight the sheriff."

Jason leaned back against the counter of kitchen, and regarded the slim shadow of darkness in what little moonlight came through the sliding glass door behind them in the next room. The desperation in the kid's voice had surprised him.

"I'll teach you to fight, so you can survive." He shook his head, wondering if the kid could see it in the darkness. "But you're not going anywhere close to those clowns again. I did, just to help get you free and clear. That's done."

"It's not done for Michelle or Sleepy... or all the others. They need help."

"Friends of yours?" He was certain 'Sleepy' was one of the names circled on his whiteboard back at the house, next to the radio scanner. One of the captains, one of the names he'd been hoping to run into the night he'd grabbed the kid.

Pro went back to the cupboards and poked around a little, setting a few cans on the counter next to the oatmeal.

"I guess they're friends," Pro said after a moment. "Not like my own age, old like you. But they were nice. They warned me about Lonny and a few of the others. Michelle helps run the cafeteria, and Sleepy... is her boyfriend, I guess. He's one of the soldiers that caught me that first night, but I'm pretty sure he didn't want to."

Jason watched Pro move to next cabinet, "That's enough food. Trust me, I've got a lot food at home."

"Just looking for Pop-Tarts." The kid moved along the opposite kitchen counter, checking the contents with the flashlight.

"What do you mean he didn't want to catch you?"

"Sleepy doesn't like the way the people who aren't soldiers are treated. At least that's what Michelle said. He can't do anything about it, because the sheriff would find out and beat him to death, and send Michelle back to the ballroom."

"The ballroom? What's that?" Jason thought he knew, but he had to ask.

"It's where all the ladies sleep, the ones who don't have somebody like Sleepy looking out for them."

"And the soldiers?" Jason asked. "They...?"

"Yea," Pro nodded. "Michelle had her own room, cuz she was...

"With Sleepy?"

"Yeah," he could see Pro nod in the darkness. From the sound of the kid's voice, he knew the kid's face was probably three shades of red right now.

"And all the soldiers have a lady?"

The kid took his time answering. Jason could tell the whole subject made him uncomfortable.

"Some do, like Sleepy," the kid paused. Jason could see the shadow looking at his feet. "Most just... have the women in the ballroom, but only the soldiers. Michelle says that why a lot of them sign up to be a soldier."

"I'll bet..." The cold anger in the pit of his stomach grew. It wasn't any different than what any warlord did; subjugate the people, reward the soldiers. He'd seen the same set up all over the Middle East and Africa and now it was happening here, amidst the sliver of humanity that still lived in America. It was happening eight miles from where he slept every night. He could see Sam's face, traces of dark blood running under her skin, beneath her eyes, across her neck. *'People are going to need your help, promise me.'*

"I never... you know, went there. I swear... they said I wouldn't be able to until I was a soldier, in about a year."

He realized he was scaring the kid. "It's not you I'm mad at. They were going to make you a soldier?"

"I just wanted to leave, but they said they were going to make me one. Everybody does what the soldiers tell them to, if they don't..."

"The sheriff beats them to death?"

"Yeah, or the soldiers do it for him."

"They aren't soldiers, Pro. They're just thugs." Jason heard the hardness creep back into his own voice. In his mind, he'd slotted the thugs as subhuman since his first foray back into the changed world when he'd found that gut shot woman in her lawn chair. It made things easier. Simpler. He needed to be able to sleep. Was he right to be hunting these people when there were so few left anywhere? Sam's voice in his head assured him, it was.

"I'm going to have to try and stop what's going on there," Jason said after a moment. He knew he was talking more to himself than the kid at the moment.

"I thought you said, you were done with that?" he could tell the kid was looking at him again in the darkness.

'*Done*' was a concept that made him want to laugh. He doubted it would ever be done. He'd promised Sam... he tried to tell himself that she couldn't have known what she'd been asking. Then again, maybe she had.

"I promised somebody I'd try to help."

"Who?" It was an innocent question. Pro waved his flashlight's beam at two cans of Chili he'd just sat on the counter.

Somebody I couldn't. He hopped off the counter, "That's plenty for tomorrow, Loki loves chili too."

"Who'd you promise?" the kid asked as he dropped the cans into his bag, "Will they help us?"

"My wife," he faced the kid. "She didn't make it."

"Oh... sorry."

"It's ok," he said as they moved towards the door.

"We all lost people. Most of the time, I'm glad she didn't have to see any of this."

Pro may have nodded agreement as he led the way through the dark house back to the front door. There, he paused, staring out into the street for threats, standing still as he slowly swung the door inward.

The kid had the habits of situational awareness that he'd seen among his men in Iraq, the veterans.

"Looks clear," Pro said in front of him. He thought the kid was about to go but he held his position and finally turned back to face him looking up over his shoulder.

"Thank you, for helping me," the kid said.

"Don't worry about it, you're welcome."

"I'll come with you, if you promise you'll teach me to fight." Pro turned to look at him, "I'm going to help them."

"Sleepy and Michelle?"

Pro nodded back at him, meeting his eyes and looking a lot older than his fifteen years. "There's lots of good people trapped there, most of them aren't soldiers... or thugs, but there's a bunch of bad guys too."

"There always are, kid."

"If you don't let me help you, I'll do it on my own."

He was about to respond, tell him that he wasn't going to drag a kid off into a fight, but Pro smiled at him, and held up a hand,

"You wouldn't want to leave a kid out here alone, on his own, at risk from random psychos or the next pack of wild dogs? Would you?"

"Where the hell did that come from? You been practicing that?"

"It's what the sheriff said to me, when I asked him if he'd let me go. But you're a lot nicer than he is."

"Come on," he said shaking his head and pushing open the screen door.

They were almost back to the darkened house that had served as their refuge for the last four days.

"You're a bit of a smartass, aren't you?"

He saw the kid smile and laugh a little to himself. He was surprised at how good that made him feel.

"Maybe, kinda... a little bit."

*

Chapter 13

"This is the neighborhood," Jason said.

Jason was letting him use the night vision goggles, 'NODS' he called them. They were beyond awesome, but he didn't like having to wear the helmet they were strapped to.

He followed Jason as he turned off the main road into a neighborhood. Loki padded along with them, content to run off and investigate whatever caught his fancy but he always returned. Every house he could see from the entrance to the neighborhood was a charred ruin surrounded by dark sentinels of what used to be the trees of the neighborhood. While the NODS didn't provide any color, he could see houses stretching out on either side of the road before them. Some were burned down to the foundation, others looked like hollowed out shells of brick or stone with half burned trees fallen across the road.

"You live in there?"

"About half a mile farther in."

"What happened here? Pro asked as he followed Jason, detouring off road, over a shallow ditch into a yard. The burnt remains of a several large trees had fallen across the road.

"You remember all the fires? From early on? All the smoke?"

Pro nodded and then remembered he was following Jason in the pitch-black night.

"Yeah."

"Once I figured out where I was going to hole up, I dropped a few trees and set fire to these houses myself. I was hoping that your people at the mall weren't going to spend a lot of time checking to see what's left of this neighborhood further in? You've foraged with them, does that make sense."

Pro wanted to answer that they weren't his people, but he knew that wasn't what Jason had meant. "I guess so. The soldiers go through a neighborhood before the foraging teams. They want to find all the guns, and booze. They decide where we go house to house."

"Smart of them," Jason answered.

He knew Jason was trying to get information from him, just like the sheriff had, and then later, Ben. The difference was, Jason was honest about it, and he usually explained why he was asking something.

This was a nice neighborhood, or had been, he thought. With the night vision, he could recognize the massive yards, private pools, and sport courts. He'd gone to a teammate's birthday party in a neighborhood like this one once. He'd had a tough time imagining that people needed houses this big. He struggled to remember whose party it had been. Mark something, he'd been a decent third baseman. He couldn't remember what the former ten-year-old teammate looked like, and didn't want to imagine what had happened to him.

They walked on in silence. Pro threw the occasional stick for Loki to fetch. It gave him something to watch through the NODS. The strange device turned Loki's pitch-black coat into a dark green bullet hugging the ground. Ahead of him, Jason was a man shaped blob of light green. They made it to a section of the neighborhood that wasn't all burned up. Some of the houses were huge like those that they'd already passed, and some were smaller houses, clearly older, sitting on yards that were absolutely enormous. Jason seemed to be looking up at one in particular on the left side of the road as they were walking, staring off up the hill in total darkness.

"Is that where you lived?"

Jason glanced over at him. "Yeah."

He could tell it wasn't something Jason was going to talk about. Backyard, he thought. He couldn't see any signs of a grave from the road. Survivors always buried their dead when they could. Except when they'd been scared to leave their apartment, or when they'd waited too long. He wondered if Jason would be willing to help him; take him to Herndon and help him bury his mom and sister.

A couple of houses further into the neighborhood Jason stopped and pointed up through the trees bordering the yard. "This is it."

"It's big," was all he could say.

"Has power too. I'll show you how to use the lights, we still need to be careful with that, even here."

"I know," he agreed. "That's how they catch a lot of people. Usually, it's candles or a flashlight, though."

"Loki! Go home! Go boy!" Jason called out to the dog who shot up the driveway and disappeared around the side of the house. "He's got his own door in the back. He'll let us know if there's anybody inside."

"This is amazing." Pro stood in the kitchen behind Jason's back as the man rooted around in the fridge and came up with a beer for himself and handed Pro a Coke. The power was on, there was water from a well that came out of the faucet, and the refrigerator worked. There was even a separate ice machine under the counter churning out ice cubes.

Pro watched the soda bubble and fizz amidst ice cubes for the first time in over four months. Not even the Ritz had ice, except for the ice trays in the kitchen's big freezer but he'd never been allowed to use them. He knew it was stupid that he should care about something so silly as ice for a Coke, though at the moment it seemed like a miracle.

"While it lasts," Jason saluted him with his bottle of beer. "And it won't. Nobody left to repair anything, no spare parts to order online." Jason waved his empty hand at the house around him. "I have to keep in mind that this, as nice as it is, isn't a long-term solution. Prepackaged, canned, freeze-dried food will run out. We need to be thinking down the road to that day."

Pro nodded, he'd heard much the same from Sleepy and others from the mall he'd foraged with. "The Sheriff wants to start farming in the spring. He says they are going to have farms."

Jason nodded at him. "Come on, I'll show you around. You got your pick of bedrooms upstairs with your own bathroom. You can throw your stuff in any of them."

He laughed a little. "My stuff?" He thumbed his sweat shirt; the same one he'd been wearing the day he ran.

Jason just looked at him a moment and then rubbed his face. Pro thought he was angry for a moment.

"I'm such an asshole," Jason shook his head. "I'll loan you some of my clean clothes, you can wear them. We'll make a road trip tomorrow night and you can get some stuff that fits."

"Road trip? As in drive?" he asked.

Jason nodded, and then grinned at him. "We'll take the tank. I'll even let you drive if you want. I know a store in Sterling that I'd like to check out."

"I don't know how; I mean I know how... I've just never, wait... a tank?"

Dagman's refurbished and modified Land Cruiser was close to fifty years old. He knew it was from the early 70's, but he doubted there any part of it beyond the chassis that was older than the kid. He couldn't fathom the amount of time and money Howard had put into the vehicle. The black 'Antique Vehicle' license plate was the only thing about it that hadn't been modernized. He'd moved it out of the garage before he'd torched the houses around the neighborhood's entrance. A five-minute walk from the house, its parking spot was well hidden behind the burned-out shell of a house.

He could tell Pro was less than impressed. "Figured me for a Cadillac with rolling rims?"

Pro just looked at the legendary SUV and then at him. "No, it's cool, I mean in an old-fashioned way."

Jason shook his head. "Well it's older than I am, and will probably outlast the both of us. These things are indestructible."

Jason swung the spare tire and gas tank out of the way, and then opened up the rear door.

"Loki! Come on! Hop in boy!"

Loki came running out of the woods and leapt into the back in an arc that started a good eight feet behind the boxy looking vehicle. Oh, to have that much energy he thought. The dog was basically an overactive, spring loaded, four-legged athlete. While he was a depressed, 33-year-old widower, now responsible for a teenager at the end of the world.

"I'll drive out. You can try driving back if you want. Deal?"

He saw the nervousness in Pro's eyes, and had to laugh as the kid just nodded without hesitation. "Sounds good."

He had a lot to teach the kid and they'd been at it all day. Driving was only one of a hundred things he needed to get Pro up to speed on. They'd spent some time in the back yard after breakfast, plinking with a suppressed .22 and M4 from the back deck until he was certain Pro wouldn't accidently shoot himself or Loki. He'd been impressed with the kid's marksmanship. Pro possessed a lot of raw talent to work with and didn't have any bad habits to break. He said they'd worry about hitting the target later, and explained that shooting was just like shooting free throws. You needed to get to the point where you were surprised when you *missed*.

That had started Pro in on how much he liked sports, and that he'd played basketball and baseball and was going to play football when he got to high school. Jason had remained silent as Pro caught himself with a cringe; remembering that there would be no high school. No football, no homecoming dances, no SATs... the list got depressingly long every time Jason thought of how different Pro's childhood was going to be than his own. That wasn't quite right, he realized. Pro's childhood had died four months past.

Jason had dug a football out of the garage and they'd played catch for a while in the yard, with Loki a very frustrated man in the middle. Jason had shaken his head in disgust when Pro had said he was a Vikings fan. He couldn't help himself, and explained that if any team was capable of surviving the end of the world, it would have been the Packers. Pro's look of confusion hadn't lasted long.

"They still have a team in Green Bay?" Pro had been pretty happy with himself for the comeback and Jason had caught himself laughing out loud.

He looked through the open front doors of the vehicle, across the front seats. He'd put a kit together for Pro. In the dark, the kid looked like any other tactically suited operator.

"Ok, you got the list of everything you need?"

Pro slapped a cargo pocket in his leg, "Got it."

"Radio? Knife?""

"Got em."

"Ammo?"

"Two extra clips for the 9mm, two for the M-4."

He just glared back at the teenager in disapproving silence. He was amazed how much Pro thought he knew about firearms, all of it learned from video games and television, most of it, wrong.

"Sorry, magazines."

Jason nodded. "Ok, MREs for two days, water in your pack?"

Pro nodded, "Yep."

"A bag to put your new clothes in?"

Pro slapped his other leg. "Two garbage bags."

"OK, NODS on." Jason crawled in behind the wheel and flipped his night vision googles down from his helmet. "No flashlights until we are inside, and then use the red light."

"Got it, umm you're going to drive without lights?"

"NODS..."

"Oh right." Pro flipped his own goggles down. "Won't somebody still hear us? We should be driving one of those electric cars that can almost sneak up on you in a parking lot. My mom hated those. She almost got hit by one in the parking lot at the grocery store. She never even knew it was there."

Because *Land Cruiser*! he almost answered and then thought about what the kid was saying. It was worth looking into. He should find a Prius or one of those Tesla wagons and see if the house's power system was robust enough to charge one.

"That's a damn good idea, actually."

Pro nodded to himself. "I could always hear the Humvees, way before I saw them."

"We'll work on that."

The last thing he wanted was to get the kid into a situation he couldn't handle, but at times he caught himself thinking Pro was better suited for the new world than he was. He was going to do his best to prepare the teenager to be able to survive a changed world, but he was going to do his share of listening too.

There was no doubt in his mind the kid was helping him. It hurt to admit it, but spending time with the boy seemed to make him feel better, accelerating a process that Loki had started. Giving him a reason other than a promise to Sam to wake up each morning.

They were out on Rt. 7 headed west in near total darkness. The moon was a barest sliver of a crescent standing low on the horizon. Stalled cars, empty buildings and dead neighborhoods flowed past them in the eerie ghost green stillness produced by the night vision.

"Where we going?"

"Sterling," Jason answered. "There's a department store out there that I had a brief look at. Looters seemed to have missed it and I've never seen the mall's gang out that far."

Pro shook his head. "It's night too. They usually don't go anywhere at night except for the ones on guard duty, but they just patrol around Tysons."

"There's survivors out here though," Jason explained. "I've seen them a couple of times. It wasn't anybody that looked as organized or as dangerous as the Sheriff's thugs but we need to keep a close eye out."

"Always." Pro's reply made him wonder if he was smothering the kid. He scanned the surroundings as they rolled down the highway, reminding himself that the young man had managed to live on his own for months.

They pulled into a parking lot of a Babies R Us, and Jason killed the engine.

"I don't think this is the right store," Pro was leaning forward looking at the building through the windshield.

"There's a Kohl's behind it, smartass."

Pro laughed, "I know. I've been here. You know … before."

"Ok," Jason pointed out Pro's window. "We'll go quiet, through the tree line at the edge of the parking lot, all the way around to the back, through the loading dock. No unnecessary talking or noise. Hand signals when we can, but…" Jason tapped his ear bud, "radio check?"

Pro reached into the front of his vest and turned his tactical radio on.

Jason tried it again and Pro gave him a thumbs up, and then said "Radio check."

Jason flashed him a thumb, the sound activated mics were working. "Use the radio only when you need to, but don't hesitate to use it either. That's why we have them, make sense?"

Pro laughed and waffled his hand back and forth.

"You keep Loki with you, but keep him quiet. He does a good job on picking up on my stress level, usually. Don't hesitate slapping his nose if he gets out of line or noisy, he's a teenager."

"Was that a joke?"

"If it makes you feel better to think so, then yeah, sure."

"Ok" Pro said.

Jason could see well enough with the NODs to catch the kid's smile.

The large box department store was pitch-black inside and the NODs effectiveness dropped off considerably. Jason stood just inside the back wall of the store without moving for nearly five minutes. He did it without explanation wanting to watch Pro. At the same he wanted to give Loki the idea that they weren't playing. Jason moved out slowly, the stock of his MK18, an M4 variant designed around close quarters battle requirements, snuggled tight against his shoulder.

The store was dark as a tomb. There was a slight glow from the small amount of moonlight highlighting the glass doors at the front of the store. What stood out most was the smell, a mixture of new textiles and lingering perfume, and the complete lack of dead bodies.

"You with me?" he whispered as he moved forward.

"Yeah," Pro whispered back.

Jason realized he was in the middle of an aisle, bins of underwear, t-shirts and socks around him. He halted and pointed at Pro and then in a wide circle around him.

"Go to work, get what you need. I'm going to check out the front."

He watched as Pro moved off pulling out a garbage bag. He was about to tell Loki to go with the Pro when he saw the dog had already made that decision, padding calmly behind the kid's heels.

Traitor; he smiled to himself and moved off towards the front doors in a tactical crouch, his lower back reminding him he wasn't 25. He was quickly getting back into shape though. Two months ago, this would have truly hurt. He been out this way, west on Rt. 7 towards Ashburn and Leesburg twice since the dying time; 'The Suck,' as Pro insisted on calling it.

During both of those trips, he'd seen survivors around the neighborhood that backed up against the community college which sat across the street from the department store. They'd seen him too, something he let happen from a distance. They'd been armed, but they'd run. Which was an understandable reaction. The problem was, he knew it was a natural instinct for somebody who was dangerous every bit as much as it was for somebody who was scared.

He moved across the front of the store, just inside of the row of checkout lanes. He slowly climbed up on the counter opposite a register and looked back into the store from a better vantage point. Able to see down the few aisles he was lined up with, he took his time until he went to one knee started the wall to wall check again. He was careful to not look at anything; relying on human evolution for his eyes to be drawn to something. He was about to decide he was being paranoid when he thought he saw a dim glimmer of something flash against the ceiling tiles towards the back corner of the store.

It was probably just the NODs resetting to a darker area he told himself. These were solid Gen III's; the goggles were expensive yet commercially available. They were at least a generation, maybe two behind what he'd used in the Rangers, years earlier. But they worked, and he was already swinging back down to the floor.

"You still good?" he whispered.

"Yeah, about halfway on the list." Pro whispered back.

Jason moved to the far edge of the store opposite from Pro and moved up through women's shoes, into the dresses, working his way towards the back. He was crouched down below the racks of clothes moving as quietly as he could. Something at the limit of his hearing pulled him to a stop. His instinct was to remove the ear bud, and listen with both ears but he knew that for a rookie mistake. It would take him out of communication with Pro and a hand off the gun. He waited for a few moments before he heard it again.

He moved forward and peaked around a display case piled high with clothes and froze in shock. Forty feet away, there were two women, girls, zip tied together, their mouths duct taped. The NODs gave him an image that he recognized immediately. They were sitting back-to-back, unnaturally hunched over. They were hogtied, one's hands bound to the other's ankles. He'd used the same technique himself, they all had, rounding up insurgents. Shit...it was common practice across the army, when detaining prisoners that you couldn't afford to watch... when you were busy doing something else.

"Pro, hide. Right now." He tried and failed to whisper.

There wasn't an immediate answer as he turned on his heels and started back across the store towards where he'd left Pro.

"Whaa... Hey there. I'm just getting some clothes." Pro wasn't whispering, clearly talking to somebody else.

Fuck. Jason sped up, trying to move as fast as he could without his boots squeaking on the floor. He cut as straight a line as possible through the store, but it was impossible. These places were designed to prevent people from moving in straight lines.

"How many are there?" he asked.

"You're scaring me mister; can you point that gun away?" Pro sounded scared.

"This stuff? ... I found an Army jeep, with a bunch of stuff inside it, over by Reston."

"I'm fifteen."

"Really, I am. I would have had a birthday in November. It's past that, isn't it?"

"Keep him talking," he whispered as he moved closer, seeing the glare of a flashlight an instant before he slammed his eyes shut in defense against the light amplification of the NODs. It almost worked. He was left with seeing dots and a moving banner across the inside of eyes that that he tried to blink away.

"Have you seen those guys from Tysons?"

Jason listened to Pro answer the twenty questions someone was subjecting him to. He was doing well but he could hear the fear in the disembodied voice as he crept closer. Whoever it was, seemed to be pumping Pro for information. He had no illusions what was going to happen when the questions all got answered. What he'd seen in the back of the store had been all the evidence he needed, to know whoever it was, needed to be put down.

"Honest, I just hid. They don't like to get out of their jeeps."

Jason pulled up, he could see the profile of the man, towering over Pro, standing directly between them.

Damn. Jason, pulled his head back slightly from the aimpoint site and moved to the side angling for a safer shot. It was then Loki decided that he'd seen enough. There was a growl, then a fierce bark that he didn't need the radio to hear and didn't sound anything like the playful Loki.

The armed silhouette towering over Pro lurched to the side, as his gun fired. Jason was already moving, sprinting, he rounded the corner of a display just in time to see Pro fire his Glock twice into the mass of moving shadow.

He pulled up, ready to fire himself as the pile of dog and man collapsed to the ground. Loki disengaged and separated himself from the pile. Jason was about to stop Pro, but he was too slow. Pro took quick step forward and fired once more into the man.

Jason came up on Pro's side, grabbing the arm that held the gun.

"You're good, you're ok," he said as he took the handgun. "It's me, let it go, Pro."

Pro released the 9mm and turned to look at him. "I'm all right."

"I know, I know." He said, already fearing what he was going to find in the back of the store. Pro didn't seem fazed in the least.

"You sure? You're ok?"

"Yeah, I'm good." Pro knelt and gave Loki a solid two-handed ear rub. "There was something seriously wrong with that guy. Loki here didn't like him either, did you boy?"

Jason stared at the dead man on the floor. He was dressed in tree bark patterned hunting gear and had an old AK strapped to his chest. He wondered how long this piece of shit had held his two hostages in the back. What the hell was wrong with people?

"You ok?"

Jason started, when he realized Pro was talking to him.

"Uh, yeah," he handed the 9mm back to Pro, pleased that the young man pulled the slide back and checked the gun, before dropping the mag and replacing it with a fresh one.

"You about done here?"

"Almost," Pro pointed at the two large bags of clothes, "just need some socks and I'm good. What's wrong?"

Jason rubbed at his own face. I just saw a teenager kill a guy with as little concern as he would have had over scraping dog shit off his shoe. Nothing wrong with that... Shit! This world was so wrong.

He dropped his NODs back down over his eyes. "Thought I'd lost you," he said. "Again."

Pro just shrugged. "Nah, I'm good."

"Look, I need you to finish up here, and get your bags to the back door where we came in."

"Ok," the kid answered, "you think there's more?"

Jason shook his head. "Guy like this isn't going to make a lot of friends. He's got... prisoners. They're tied up in the back." Christ, he thought, prisoners? That wasn't what he'd seen. Wishing he could get the image of the trussed-up girls out of his head.

"I'm going to take Loki, ok? I need you to stay away until I call you. Can you do that?"

"Who are they? I can help," Pro gave up on rubbing the dog, stood and re-holstered his sidearm.

"They're women... girls, I don't know, I couldn't tell. In rough shape..." He looked at the kid, "I think it might go easier if there's just one of us."

He glanced back at the dead man on the floor before kneeling and taking the AK. He found a snub nosed, wheel gun as well. He draped the AK over his shoulder and pocketed the wheel gun.

He looked up at Pro who just stood there watching him.

"Go, I'll meet you at the back."

Jason had collected two blankets from the store and draped them over the girls before he'd carefully pulled off the duct tape from the older girl's face; it was impossible to tell how old she was, definitely more of a young woman, than teenager though. Her lips were puffy, her face scratched, one eye socket looked like it had been blackened but the old bruise was fading to green.

"He's dead," he said simply. As the woman pulled back from him in fright. "Was there just the one?"

The young woman, squinted from his flashlight and just jerked her head up and down twice as she cringed away. The young girl, who was younger than Pro by a few years, gasped in pain as the woman's movement pulled on the zip ties.

He reversed the flashlight and oriented it away from them onto his face.

"You're safe now. I'm not going to hurt you."

He cut their bindings, cursing to himself when he saw how the zip ties had sliced open the skin at their ankles and the wrists. He watched as the young woman grabbed the younger one and held her close under the blanket, as she pulled them both back into the corner atop the pile of blankets they'd been laying on.

"He's dead," he said again. Seeing the younger girl more clearly, she couldn't have been more than twelve. "I'm going to try and help you, if you'll let me."

He switched his flashlight to its lantern setting and propped the base of it on the floor in front of him. The girls winced at the light and he slowly removed his helmet and dug a bottle of water from his fanny pack and handed it over. He could see from the way they looked at the bottle that they were desperate. He dug around and found a protein bar and held it out as well.

They both eyed him, the younger girl looking to the older one for guidance. He sat them both on the floor between them and backed up a few feet.

"It's all I have with me, but I've got a lot more outside."

He could see the older girl's eyes pull back in fear.

He held up his hands. "I'm not like that... other man," he shook his head.

"My name is Jason."

Loki slinked around the corner from where Jason had told him to stay. "That's my friend, Loki."

"Did you kill him?" The younger girl asked.

Jason shook his head. "No, my young friend did. He's watching our stuff by the loading dock. We just came here to get him some clothes. He's not much older than you are."

He averted his eyes as the woman's arms came out of the blanket and grabbed the offered food and water. He just rubbed Loki. He looked back at them once he was sure they were back under their blankets.

"What's your name?" he asked the young woman.

"Rachel," the girl said with her mouth full of the sawdust tasting protein bar. "Elsa," she nodded at the youngster who was pulling on the water bottle.

"Well, Rachel, Elsa," he rubbed at his face. "I don't know what to do here, other than to make sure it's exactly what you're comfortable with." He pointed at the flashlight, "I'm going to leave you the flashlight. You girls find yourself some clothes, you're in the right place for it. Come back to the loading dock when you're ready. If you want."

The young woman, Rachel, just stared back at him like he was crazy. He saw nothing in her face that led him to believe she'd do anything but run.

"If you want to head out the front door, and run, you can. I'm not interested in taking prisoners. If you don't want our help, I'd still like to be sure you're all right. I'll leave you a gun and some supplies, outside, after we leave. I don't want Loki here, my young friend... or, well me, to get shot."

"You'll give us a gun?" the older girl Rachel spoke with what he guessed was an English accent. He ignored his surprise.

"You know how to use one?"

"We lived in S. Africa. My dad showed me how."

"Alright, I'll leave you a gun and some ammo. You aren't going to be safe without them."

"Can we go with you?" The younger girl asked.

Jason just smiled and turned his head back towards the young woman.

"I think that would be a good idea, at least for the short term. It's something you two will need to decide."

"Can we, Rachel?" The young girl asked without an accent. They weren't sisters he realized. He wondered what the odds would be for two people out of any family to have survived.

Jason stood slowly. "If you don't run," he looked directly at Rachel. "We'll be outside in the back. I can wait a couple of hours, but then we need to roll. You can tell us what you want then, ok?"

Rachel just nodded once. From the look on her face, he doubted he'd ever see her again. He wasn't about to force her to do anything.

He paused at the edge of the horseshoe shaped display case that had been their personal hell for how long he didn't want to think about.

"If you do run; before I go, I'll leave a bag with some supplies, and a gun, behind the dumpster on the loading dock of the baby store next door, you know where that is?"

The older girl just stared at him, and nodded once. "Thanks."

The way it came out, he knew it was forced. He couldn't imagine how hard it was for the young woman to say.

"Come on, boy." Loki whined once in complaint but followed him out the back of the store.

*

"I don't think they're coming?" Pro said, from where he sat on the curb next to the Land Cruiser.

Jason had brought the vehicle around to behind the Kohl's and stood at the open tailgate arranging a drop bag for the girls out of the supplies that he and Pro had brought along. He couldn't disagree with Pro's assessment. After what they'd been through, he couldn't fault the girl's lack of trust, in anyone. He looked down at the bag and wished he had brought more food with him. Then again, this trip had begun with the intention of finding Pro some fresh underwear.

"Doesn't look like it."

"We can't just leave them out here!"

He looked over at Pro, the moon was higher now and there was enough light that they could see each other's faces without the NODs.

"That's the same thing the sheriff said to you," Jason finished separating the supplies and zipped the drop bag shut. "They've... had a real bad time, Pro. I'm not about to force them to do anything."

"Can we leave them a note?" Pro asked. "In the bag? Maybe come back for them in a couple of days? Maybe they'll change their minds."

Jason just looked at his young ward. The kid was right.

"You still have your clothes list?"

Pro dug in his pocket and came up with his list of clothes. "I saw a pen in the truck."

Jason smoothed out the kid's list as Pro reappeared. "What are you going to say?"

Jason wrote quickly. "Just what you said, we'll be back here tomorrow night if they change their minds."

"You sure they'll come get the bag?"

"I'm sure," Jason nodded. "They're hungry."

"Who would do that to somebody?"

Jason closed his eyes against the image of the girls trussed up. The oldest one, Rachel, had been beat on, and from the looks of her, she'd fought back.

"I don't know kid, come on."

It was a quick drive around the parking lot to back side of the baby store's loading dock. Jason pulled up, and motioned to the bag at Pro's feet. "Put it behind one of the dumpsters."

Pro hopped out with the heavy bag, and Loki barreled forward between the front seats and followed Pro out before he could stop him. Jason just shook his head. "Stay, Loki."

He glanced at the old-fashioned analog clock and compass combo affixed to the dashboard, realizing that Howard had probably been preparing for an EMP or something else he could have protected himself from. He wondered if his neighbor would have cared what time it was, if he'd been the one to survive. If he was sitting here now.

Loki's barking startled him back into the moment, and he glanced out the door at Pro who was standing there in front of two figures, wearing heavy coats. He leaned forward to get a better look, his hand going to his sidearm when he realized it was the two girls. He watched as the smaller girl bent down to dig through the dropped bag.

Damn, now he might be faced with an armed and very pissed off young woman who had absolutely no reason to trust another man. Just the situation he'd been looking to avoid. For the second time that night, it was Pro he found himself worrying about.

He popped his door and slowly walked around to the back of the Land Cruiser, giving him a better angle at the older girl who was just taking the gun from the bag. Their eyes met as she casually pulled the slide back on the Glock let it snap forward with a familiarity that surprised him. He could see her thinking about her next move, her eyes going from him, to Pro, the Land Cruiser, and even Loki. She might have smiled a little bit at the dog. With what might have been a nod to herself, she stuffed the gun into her pocket along with her hand.

"I had to know," she said as if that explained everything. "Does your offer still stand? Now that I have a gun?"

He caught the English accent again. He looked over at Pro who looked at him, pleading with his eyes. Elsa, the younger girl, was on one knee, rubbing Loki's ears.

"That depends." He jerked his chin back towards the department store, "on whether you blame us for…".

The young woman looked to be in her early 20's, it was hard to tell, she'd clearly seen better times. She shook her head once, as if trying to convince herself…

"I don't."

She looked like she was going to break down in tears. He had absolutely no idea what to do.

"You're welcome to come with us, but I have to warn you. Loki is going to be really upset if you shoot me."

"So, would I," Pro spoke up. "He's not lying to you. He found me."

Jason watched as Rachel's eyes drifted over Pro, and the M4 hanging from his chest, trying to decide. He couldn't blame her, but he didn't want to get shot either.

"Can we go with them? Please…" Elsa, the little girl pleaded.

He could see the war of emotions playing across the young woman's face, wanting to protect herself, and the young girl at the same time.

"Ok," Rachel nodded after a long moment. "But I'm keeping the gun."

Christ, *Jason's Armed Orphanage.* He should put out a sign.

"I think that would be best," he answered. He knew he was trying to convince himself as much as her.

Jason sat alone at the small kitchen table, a bottle of rye whiskey in front of him, and a glass that he'd just refilled for the second time. He'd left the girls with a first aid kit, and they'd disappeared behind the master bedroom door with a very loud click of the lock being thrown. Pro was asleep in his own room, or playing Xbox. Loki was curled up on his dog bag in the corner of the kitchen, chasing rabbits in his dreams. What the hell was he thinking? What the hell was he supposed to do now?

He was holding a picture of him and Sam, from right after they'd first met. He thumbed the cheesy photo booth picture they'd taken at some street fair in DC, when he saw the glare of a flashlight coming down the stairs reflect off the wall of the living room. He watched as the beam of the flashlight flashed over to the couch, where he'd said he'd be.

"I'm in the kitchen," he called out, consciously running a hand across the .45 holstered to his hip, and hating himself for doing it.

Rachel came out of the darkened living room, wearing sweatpants and a hoodie, her hair still looked wet from the showers he'd heard them taking. He'd sent them back into the store with Pro and Loki to grab some extra clothes before bringing them back.

He noted the heavy sagging weight of the 9mm he'd gifted her in the front pocket of the sweatshirt.

"You two need anything?" he asked.

She just shook her head. "No, Elsa's asleep."

"How long have you two been together?"

"Since the beginning," Rachel answered, not moving. "We were in the same group trying to walk west. Everyone else got sick."

The girl's accent seemed thicker than it had, more refined. She was well educated, he guessed, wondering if she'd been on vacation when the virus hit.

Rachel looked around the kitchen, taking in the light on the kitchen desk that was burning behind him. "I cleaned up and bandaged Elsa. I did my ankles, but I... can't." She held out her wrists, that looked like they'd been wrapped in barbwire.

"Right..." he sat up straight. He'd offered to help earlier, when they'd first got back home, but had been met with an angry stare.

"Let me get some wrappings."

She backed up quickly into the dining room to let him out of the kitchen. Jason held both hands up, instantly sorry he'd moved so quickly.

"I have another medical bag in the living room."

She just nodded at him, but the hand in her sweatshirt pocket, with the gun, hadn't moved.

When he came back to the kitchen, bag in hand, Rachel was sitting at the table. She held the picture of him and Sam.

"Your wife?"

"Yeah," he sat down across from her. "Her name was Sam, Samantha."

"She's very pretty."

He just nodded, willing away the lump in his throat and held his hand out for the picture.

He took the offered photo and put it back in his shirt pocket.

"Let's have a look at those wrists," he said.

Rachel held one hand out and laid it on the table, her other hand stayed under the tabletop next to her gun.

He didn't say anything about it, just went to cleaning the cuts on her wrist, dabbing at them with hydrogen peroxide, and covering them in Neosporin, before wrapping it tightly.

"Were Elsa's cuts this deep?" he asked not looking up from his own hands.

"No," Rachel said after a long moment.

He just nodded, as he tied off the wrapping. "Ok, let's see the other one."

Rachel slowly switched her hands, her right hand not coming out from under the table until the freshly bandaged hand had disappeared beneath.

"I've got to ask, your accent…"

"My father was posted to the British Embassy in Washington."

"Ahh," he examined the torn flesh, the girl wasn't far from needing stitches. "I get it. You mentioned South Africa. He'd been posted there too? Foreign Service?"

Rachel nodded. "We lived in an armed compound there. It was pretty rough outside the gates. He made sure my sister and I knew how to use a gun. He headed up the consulate here, considered a posh job. A reward for doing six years in South Africa. That sounds like a joke now."

"Everything sounds like a joke now," he grimaced. "Except these cuts. I need to see if I can find some real antibiotics around here. Otherwise, tomorrow, I'll make a run to the pharmacy."

He stayed focused on her wrists. "And you? What were you doing before?"

"Taking a gap year. I had just graduated from American University last spring."

"Wish I'd done that," he shook his head, and glanced up at her. "A gap year, not American. No way I'd have gotten in there."

"Sorry," he felt her flinch at his ministrations. "This is going to hurt little." He tied off the bandage and let her hand go.

He looked up and there were tears rolling down her cheeks in a torrent of emotion. The 9mm was in her hand, now resting up on the table.

"I can't do this!" she sobbed, breaking down. Her shoulders heaving up and down as she struggled to breathe. "I'm so tired, I don't care... I just want to be able to sleep!"

The girl almost screamed the last. The gun slid across the table as she pushed it over to him.

"Take it! Do what you're going to do, just leave Elsa alone. Same deal as before..."

She pointed at the gun. "You can stop pretending you're just going to help us, keep us safe... there's a price. I... I know that now. Just leave Elsa alone."

Oh, dear God, Jason swallowed. Sam ... Sam should be here, anybody but him.

He picked up the gun and slowly reached back across the table and laid it in front of her.

"This is yours. You and Elsa are safe. Do you hear me?" He raised his own voice until she nodded.

"There's not a price. Not ever..." He leaned forward until he was sure she was looking at him. "Don't hesitate to put a bullet in anybody who says otherwise."

She just stared at him for a long moment and then nodded, and sucked in a lung full of air with a huge effort in between sobs.

"Thank... you." She managed between gulps of air.

Jason was torn between wanting to comfort the girl and suspecting that a hug might get him shot. He was not what the young woman needed right now.

"Rachel, you need to sleep, and you can. I'll leave something outside your door, for in the morning. You and Elsa can have room service, that is if Loki doesn't find it first." He tried to joke, and was relieved when Rachel managed a smile as she wiped the tears from her face and glanced over at Loki who was now awake watching them both.

"Sleep as long as you want. I'll hit the pharmacy as soon as I get some shut eye myself."

"I'll come with you," Rachel said, wiping her running nose with her sleeve.

He got up and came back to the table with a couple of paper towels, and handed them over.

"I'd rather you two just stay here, get some rest and food, I'll need to hike. I don't risk driving during the day."

"No, I need to come. Something I need to get." Rachel looked up at him with her red eyes, bruised cheek bone, cracked and swollen lips.

She'd fought, hard, he realized. More than once.

"I don't want... to be pregnant."

Oh,shit... "Right... I'll see what I can find, but you need to rest."

He poured more whisky into the glass and took a sip, and then held it out to her, "Help you sleep."

Rachel nodded hesitantly and accepted the finger of whiskey and drained it before she stood up slowly and with a very tired smile turned to go.

"Rachel."

She stopped and turned around.

"Your gun?"

"Do I need it?"

"No, not here. If you do, I'll leave on top of the refrigerator where Elsa won't see it."

The young woman just nodded and left him alone with his glass which he refilled quickly. Loki was looking at him in question and offering no advice. What the hell was he supposed to do now?

Chapter 14

"All I'm saying is, you need to talk to them." Michelle whispered next to him in bed. Bauman was turning him paranoid as well. He had a boom box playing a cd on the other side of the room. He hoped it masked anything they said, if anyone was listening. Bauman had been a cop, and he wouldn't put it past the guy to try and plant a bug in his room.

Sleepy knew Bauman had people watching him during the day, to see if he was somehow getting chummy with the new guys. Some of whom were on thin ice with Bauman and most of the other hard cases. They'd been able to hold on to their women, those that had been found with them. Except a couple of cases where the women wanted nothing to do with the men they'd been found with. Those same women were now down in the ballroom, and he wondered if any of them regretted their decision.

It was the same old story. The new foundlings as a group, were a mixture of people trying to hang on to some decency, and others who had given up all pretense of even trying. Some of the new people they'd found during the snow storm had taken to Bauman's power structure with enthusiasm, others not so much.

It was the latter group Michelle wanted him to talk to.

"How many you think there are?"

"Grant's whole team, the librarian looking guy, and Bobby, and that other guy, the stocky bald headed one that's friends with him."

"Jay?"

"Yeah, that's him. And he's gotten pretty tight with those two newbies that walked in a couple of days ago. Kirby and the other one..."

Sleepy did the math. That was eight, maybe nine, gun carriers; nowhere close to enough.

"Reed," he answered. "At least that's what he goes by." He didn't need to be reminded of Kirby and Reed. The two-armed men had been discovered doing their own foraging *inside* the mall. Somehow, they'd managed to walk right through the security patrols on the perimeter without having been seen. Bauman had verbally torn him a new asshole on that one. Not that he could have done anything about it. It was impossible to get soldiers to stay awake during the boredom of guard duty, when most of them had been up partying all night. Which is was what most of them did, every night.

But yes, he could definitely add Kirby and Reed to his list. Potential list, he corrected himself. Eight guns, and him, against Bauman and at least a couple, or three dozen that would fight hard to preserve their position and authority, maybe more. If it came to a fight, there were others that might come around if they thought Bauman was going to lose. Some of that same group would just as readily turn him in if they thought it would mean extra privileges.

"It's not enough, not even close." he whispered. "It's something that'll just get us all killed, you and their women thrown into the ballroom - if you're lucky. You have no idea how paranoid he is. It would take just one person deciding to rat us out, and we're dead," he snapped his fingers. "You do understand that? Right?"

She was scared and angry, he got that. They all were. It hurt him more than he cared to admit that he couldn't be the hero she wanted him to be. He couldn't make it all right. Sleepy held no illusions that Bauman's control over the tiger he was riding was anything other than a close-run proposition. That tiger was represented by the three dozen or so degenerates whose humanity had died with their families. A couple of the worst, were men that Bauman would have locked up before the Suck. Without a doubt, he knew the status-quo at the mall had an expiration date.

Most of those he had to worry about had been broken by what had occurred, who they'd lost or by what they'd had to do to survive since. The Suck itself had broken most of them. Wayne Patterson, was by far the worst, and he'd been a car salesman at a Mercedes dealership in Bethesda, married, with two kids. There was no way for him to know if Wayne had been someone with issues before. But he surely hadn't been the guy that now arranged caged knife fights between the elderly citizens they found.

Wayne was broken inside, and was as smart as he was dangerous. He was surrounded by his own circle of broken crazies. Sleepy wasn't about to make the mistake of thinking some of them weren't every bit as wily and intelligent as they had been before the world had died.

He lumped Bauman into that category as well. The man had been on the walls around the capital when the riots had raged. How many innocent people had he tried to protect, while his own family was at home dying without him? Flash forward four months, and seven billion dead later, the former sheriff's deputy was a changed man. He had inherited the FEMA refuge and managed to hang on to it through running the place on fear and reward.

The problem was; some people, like the woman lying next to him were tired of being afraid. Worse, many of those soldiers reaping the rewards, like Wayne and his circle, were beginning to realize they didn't need Bauman's pipe dream of rebuilding to reap anything they could manage to take.

"Maybe you could just leave them a note. Let them know they aren't alone..." The desperation in Michelle's voice worried him more than anything.

"And when they're caught with the note?" Sleepy shook his head. "Might as well just shoot them myself. It'd be cleaner."

"You're not going to do anything?"

He was going to keep her alive. That included not telling her anything about what he was doing with Bauman. His plan, such as it was, boiled down to an attempt to manipulate someone he secretly worried was a lot smarter than he was, and paranoid to boot.

"I didn't say that," he mumbled. He was tired and he had to make a road trip tomorrow with Rob Ward. Wayne may have been crazy; his buddy Rob was just plain mean. To Rob, the carcass of the world was his personal playground.

"I'm not going back to the ballroom, Daniel," Michelle whispered next to him. "Ever. I'm not afraid to die. You don't get to use me for an excuse not to do something."

He liked it when she used his real name, even when she was driving him nuts. 'Sleepy' was something post-Suck, it wasn't who he was or had been. In a way, Michelle was responsible for the name. He'd been new to the Ritz, one of the first to find the former FEMA center on his own. He'd kept his head down, watching, trying to decide whether or not he'd stay while helping out where he could. He was quiet by nature and like a lot of people, the shock of what had happened hadn't worn off.

It had happened in those first few days after they'd all stopped pretending the government had any role at the Ritz, just as Bauman was coming into his own. He'd seen another soldier, he couldn't even remember who it had been, rough up Michelle and drag her off right through the lobby on the way to the elevators. Something in him had snapped, and he'd crossed the lobby and beat the guy half to death before he'd realized what he'd done.

Bauman, Lonny, and a few others, had watched it happen, laughing, cheering him on.

When he was done, standing over a broken and bleeding body that Bauman would have shot a few hours later, somebody had made the joke; "Sleepy just woke up."

He hadn't realized they were talking about him until the name had stuck. Bauman had used him as a threat for a short while. *Careful, you don't want to wake up Sleepy.* It had lasted until Bauman had bigger and more dangerous dogs to call on. The name though, that had stuck.

Right now, he needed to figure out a way to get those same dogs to turn on each other.

"What if it's Wayne? Or Rob and one of the other goons that get caught passing notes?" He turned his head towards Michelle, "It might just send him over the edge."

"Bauman?" she asked. "Would he believe some of those guys can read or write?"

"He's insane," he said simply. "If it's a threat to his authority, he'll believe it." More and more, Bauman's role was a voice on the radio. He knew he couldn't be the only one who realized how weak Bauman's grip was.

"What do you need me to do?" Michelle was entirely too eager for his liking.

*

"I'm serious, Boss." Sleepy felt like Bauman was seeing right through him, and maybe he was. The sheriff seemed calmer than usual, sharper.

"I'm getting looks from these guys... I think they want me dead, and they know I'm your guy. Wayne, Rob, some of the other hard cases, I think they might be wondering why they're taking orders from anybody."

"Cause you're getting looks?" Bauman scrunched up his face, "Christ, Sleepy! You're my number two, deal with it."

"They aren't happy with some of the new guys."

"Neither am I," Bauman shook his head. "I took your advice on that, I eased up, let 'em keep their war brides. Now you're telling me the shit storm I was worried about is real?"

"We're riding a tiger here, is all I'm saying." Sleepy had heard Bauman use those words and threw them back at him now. "The men are either under control, or they aren't. What difference does the reason matter?"

"They're under control," Bauman smiled back at him. "Some of them may not like you, but that's a different issue. Maybe you need to enforce a little control yourself. Unless of course you're not able to, or scared." Bauman scratched his nose as he was looking at him. "Which begs the question whether Wayne might not make a better number two."

"You honestly believe Wayne would be satisfied with being number two?"

Bingo, he could see that scored in Bauman's psyche from the look that flashed across his face.

"And you are?"

"I've told you, I don't want anything other than to hold this place together. That means keeping nearly four hundred workers happy. Because Wayne, Rob, and his ilk, hell... you and I, aren't going to be farming when the food runs out and it will."

Bauman's jaw was working furiously. He'd cracked the surface calm, and could see the emotions playing across the man's face.

"All I'm saying, my head is on a swivel."

"So's mine," Bauman barked. "Don't you ever doubt that."

Sleepy nodded, he was counting on it.

Bauman, calmer after a moment, pointed at the door. "You guys need to get going, stay on the radio."

*

Michelle was scraping plates and pots in the hotel's kitchen along with half a dozen other women. Two men were watching them, or supposed to be. Jay was trying to make eyes at Lisa, one of the new women who'd been picked up during the snowstorm, along with some men who hadn't treated her very well. She was currently working herself out of the ballroom, through a revolving list of suitors. Although, you couldn't really call them suitors when they showed up at night and picked you out of the group and took you back to their room. The apocalypse had its own take on speed dating and it wasn't pretty.

Lisa looked like she was about to crack. Michelle had been there - not for long, but long enough until Daniel had acted out, for her protection. Early on, after she'd been chosen and thus protected by Daniel, she would think back and try to remember if Daniel had ever been one of those that prowled the ballroom at night taking what they wanted. He hadn't been. She knew Lisa was dealing with that same dynamic. Any of the guys with a half a decent heart weren't down there at night picking out their next lay. Most of the decent guys seemed to pretend they didn't know what was happening.

The woman had stopped crying when she'd realized the others weren't that sympathetic. They'd all lived through it, or were still living it. Besides, Lisa was new and a knockout. She was in demand which took some of the pressure off the rest of them.

Michelle glanced at Jay, who she knew was too stupid to be truly dangerous. Across the doorway from him, was one of the new guys she didn't know. Her gut was telling her that he was a future goon because of the way he was looking at her, but also because she hadn't seen him hanging out with any of the others that she felt were half decent.

Every day; for breakfast, lunch and dinner, she helped cook and serve the food. She'd listen to them talk as they ate, as she wandered from table to table making sure the Sheriff's soldiers got all the food they wanted. She felt she knew who Sleepy could trust and who he couldn't. The new guy looked bored, like he'd rather be out wrangling a foraging team than watching the post-lunch clean up.

She'd written the note, just like Daniel had suggested. Just two lists of names, in separate columns. The left side were scumbags in Wayne's camp. The right-side column were twelve relatively new soldiers whom she thought Daniel could trust. There were arrows drawn from the left to the right; left side names matching up with a newbie that was in their squad. From a certain way of looking at the note, it looked like soldiers were being tasked with a name on the right side. She'd plant the note; it would be up to Daniel to make certain it was seen in the right light.

She'd slipped the note in between trays that were being scraped clean into a bucket on the other side of the kitchen.

She watched as Olivia worked her way through the trays, the stack shrinking. She started to lose hope. Had the woman ignored it? Added it to the garbage bucket? She did her best to focus on the pan she was scrubbing when she glanced up and saw Olivia staring at the note, stuck to a tray. The woman didn't even hesitate, and pounded the tray against the side of the trash bin until the note fell free atop the rest of the used napkins and empty juice cartons.

Michelle cursed inwardly, and shook her head. She'd try again at lunch, and then dinner if she had to. Daniel had thought it important that the note was found today, but she hadn't been able to get him to say why. She knew he was scared of what would happen to her and she hated that she was the axe hanging over his head. She was scared too. Daniel had said to put his name in the right-side column, opposite of Rob's – and she'd done just what he said. Sleepy, in all caps, underlined twice was at the top of the right-hand column. Daniel had taken a team to scout east, inside the Beltway earlier in the morning, and Rob had gone with him.

*

"Here's good," Sleepy said.

Rob slowed the Humvee to a coasting stop, looked around and then pulled forward to park the vehicle behind a burned-out bank along Glebe Rd. in North Arlington. They were still a good two miles from Ballston, and the self-imposed DMZ that their group had established between Tysons' control and whoever was running things further to the east. As far as they knew, there were at least two sizeable groups out here in the territory between Ballston and Crystal City.

South of that, was a no-go land firmly controlled by a group that called themselves 'The Reapers.' Sleepy had seen them up close one time, and he'd be happy if he never had to again. He might be dealing with some run of the mill insanity with Bauman and fellow soldiers like the man behind the wheel, but no one in Tysons thought of fellow survivors as a food source. Slave labor, sure; but they weren't collecting survivors to sacrifice and eat.

"Why so far out?"

Sleepy had figured Rob would just bitch. He wasn't prepared for a question.

"Because we haven't had anybody this far in over a month. Who knows who controls what?"

If a man's face could shrug, Rob's did. "You two limp-dicks awake?" he yelled at the occupants in the back.

"Yeah," Kirby, one of the new guys perked up.

"We walking all the way to Ballston?" Jennings joined in.

"We are," Sleepy ordered. "You two are going to take the lead, going right up Glebe, on the left side of the road. Rob and I will be behind you on this side."

"So, we're the ones that get shot?" Jennings protested.

"Exactly," Rob smiled over at him in what might have been thanks. Sleepy just turned to stare at Jennings in the back.

"You have a problem with that?"

Jennings opened his door and hopped out. "This is bullshit."

Rob laughed and pointed up the street with his assault rifle once they were all on foot outside the vehicle. "Well it's your bullshit, Jennings - so start walking. You too, noob."

"We get separated for any reason," Sleepy called out from behind the pair that was already moving off, "meet back here by dark. Ride will be leaving with or without you."

Sleepy stood there next to Rob for a moment, aware that in a one on one fight, Rob would tear limbs from his body. In Rob's world, that was how things were ordered.

"Why the fuck are we doing this?" Rob sneered. "I get the sheriff wants to check on his neighbors and all. We should just send in some sheep and watch it go down. Then we'd know."

"Come time to start growing crops, we're going to need those sheep. Besides, if they were taken, they'd probably be smart enough to talk and we don't want that."

"And those two dickheads? They wouldn't talk?" Rob pointed with his chin up the street at the other pair of their team.

"They're carrying," Sleepy patted his own rifle. "Would you wait to see if they want to talk, or just light them up?"

Rob just looked at him a moment and then smiled. "I guess I should thank you for not sending me up ahead."

"Would you have gone?"

"No fucking way."

Sleepy waited until Jennings and Kirby were a good two hundred yards ahead of them on the opposite side of the road. "Come on, it's still going to be a long walk."

Rob was silent for about a hundred yards or so. "You know, Sleepy; every time I think you're an ass-kissing pussy, you surprise me. You're a cold one. You're all right."

"Imagine my relief," Sleepy answered, without even looking over at his partner. He wouldn't give the crazy SOB the pleasure of thinking he cared one way or another what he thought of him. To Rob, that would have been power, and if you gave someone like Rob Ward an inch, he'd take both arms and a leg and beat you to death.

Rob was tailor-made for this world. He had no conscience, no concerns beyond where his next meal or lay was coming from, and he was perfectly willing to go to any lengths to procure either. At some level, that described a lot of Bauman's soldiers.

He knew he wasn't special; he'd killed. But he didn't do it for kicks, and he'd never killed when he had an option. For Rob, and guys like him, there was no thought process, no conscious, no filter. The decision cycle was a straight line that went from zero to a hundred in a split second by default.

It was almost an hour later when Sleepy paused them, when he and Rob reached a gas station where Glebe turned into an overpass crossing over I-66. They'd almost caught up parallel to Jennings and Kirby who had slowed down considerably the closer they got to the high-rises in Ballston.

They were both looking back across the road to Sleepy, as if he had somehow changed his mind. He waved them forward in frustration, towards the urban forest of high-rise office buildings and condos.

"You want me to shoot the new guy? That'll speed Jennings up."

Sleepy just looked over at Rob as if he was mulling over the idea.

"Nah, we might need the gun," he responded. "Besides, not like we are on the clock here."

Rob hawked up something nasty from the depths of his lungs and spit to the side. "If somebody's there, they probably got a rifle scope on all of us right now."

Sleepy nodded. Just because he was an animal, didn't mean Rob was stupid. "It's what I'd do if I were them. Wait for us all to get out there in the open."

"You and I aren't going out there? Are we?"

Sleepy turned and grinned. "Let's see if those two make it across."

Rob had both hands on his M4, its muzzle pointed down at the cracked tarmac of the gas station's parking lot as they crouched behind an old ice freezer outside the convenience store. The fact that Rob was behind him was not lost on Sleepy. Sleepy had his rifle up, looking through the scope at the high-rise windows across Washington Ave., the next cross road to intersect Glebe. Kirby had made it across the I-66 overpass in a run and was half way across Washington Ave. Jennings was falling farther behind his partner, crouching down behind a windowed bus stop terminal as if its clear glass sides could somehow hide him from view, or stop a bullet.

Sleepy didn't see any movement within the high rises, but too many of the windows were missing for his taste, especially on the third and fourth floors, that would provide a great angle down to the streets below. He glanced to his left at Jennings who showed no sign of getting up and crossing Washington to join his partner.

"That piece of shit," Sleepy swore. "Radio Jennings, tell him you're going to shoot him if he doesn't move his ass."

Rob chuckled behind him, and fired off a three-round burst that didn't miss Jennings by much, shattering the bus stop's glass sides.

Sleepy's head pounded with the concussion of the shots, and his left ear ringing.

"Thanks, for the heads-up asshole," he yelled, aware that he could barely hear himself.

"He's moving now, ain't he?" Rob yelled back, then started laughing. "Sorry 'bout that."

Sleepy turned back around to see Jennings huddled next to Kirby, behind a Metro bus that had been abandoned in front of the first large office building that marked the beginnings of the Ballston Metro area.

"Now what are the fuck nuts waiting for?"

"Probably to see if you just woke anybody up. Which sounds like a good idea bout now." Sleepy said, keeping his eye glued to his scope, tracking against the office buildings that towered above their two colleagues across the wide thoroughfare.

"Least we'll know, and can get the hell out of here," Rob fired back.

Sleepy moved the view through his scope against a glass and steel office building, with more missing windows than whole. He was trying to concentrate on what he was doing, praying for somebody to be there. He didn't see anything.

"Wait! I got something," he lied.

"Fourth floor, there's a rifle..." Sleepy calmed his nerves and nestled in closer to the scope.

"Good," Rob whispered behind him. "Now we know, let's go."

"Radio Jennings, tell them to run back this way when I open up."

"Leave the shits, let's go."

"I wouldn't leave you out there either, Rob. Do it." Sleepy kept his sight focused on the empty window frame, and flicked the fire selector to full auto with his thumb.

"Shit," Rob spit out, but Sleepy heard him unzipping his jacket for the radio.

"You two run back this way when we fire, we'll cover you." He heard Rob's transmission.

"Ok, radio base, tell them we've confirmed armed defenses at Glebe and Washington and are preparing to beat feet under fire." Sleepy waited for a second and Rob still hadn't radioed in.

"Shit... I've got three barrels now," he lied again.

"Fuck!"

Sleepy listened to Rob's switch channels on the radio and contact the Ritz. He heard Deana's voice in the former FEMA center's radio room read back the message. He waited for Rob to push the transmit button and opened up against the side of the building, aiming at nothing, two stories above Jennings and Kirby.

"Fall back!" he screamed to Rob, between bursts.

"No shit!" He felt Rob leave his side, running.

Sleepy pulled back behind the freezer, pivoted on one knee and shot Rob in the back with a long burst that started in his ass and ended with a shot that took him in the back of the head. He pulled out his 9mm and fired shots back behind him at the Sunoco sign at the edge of the road, blowing the sign out and hopefully giving Jennings and Kirby something to see as they ran.

He holstered the sidearm, broke back around the corner of the building and delivered another long burst into the high rises across the street. Still on full auto, he waved the rifle in a wide arc until he ran dry. He let the empty magazine drop to the pavement, reloaded, and fired off more shots as first Kirby then Jennings crossed in front of him, going around to the other side of the gas station. When they appeared around the far side, they both ran up behind him. He pulled back and looked over at Rob's body by the gas pumps, and the dark stain spreading out beneath it on the pale concrete.

"You guys hit?"

"I... I don't think so," Jennings shouted, breathing like a freight train. Kirby just shook his head and moved forward to peek around the freezer.

"Which building are they in?"

"Above the bus you were behind," Sleepy put in a new magazine and looked back at Rob and the radio that lay a few feet from his body.

"Third and fourth floor," he jerked his head behind him at his imaginary targets. "Give me some cover, I'm going to get the radio. We'll fall back into the trees behind us, stay behind the building and out of the parking lot. Whoever they are, they have an angle on it," he pointed at Rob's body for emphasis.

He jerked Jennings to his feet from where he kneeled, "You run like hell for the trees when I go for the radio." He turned to Kirby who was waiting with his rifle, "You ready?"

"Go!" Sleepy waited until Kirby opened up with his M4 and then ran for the radio, more worried that a real enemy would decide to show up than maintaining his charade. He grabbed the radio and sprinted for the trees where Jennings had disappeared.

He swung to a stop behind a tree and brought his rifle around towards Kirby, "Ok, now move!"

He fired up at the buildings as Kirby fell back to join them.

Sleepy dropped the empty magazine and nudged Jennings, "give me a mag!" He had two more of his own but Jennings had yet to fire a shot and could spare them.

He got reloaded, and looked around him.

"They've stopped," Kirby shook his head, breathing from the adrenalin rush as he joined them.

Sleepy shook his head. "Because they can't see us, stay down behind this hill. We'll stay in the trees, fall back to the side streets and work our way back to the Hummer through the neighborhoods."

"Sounds good," Jennings flashed a thumbs up at him. "Thanks for not leaving us back there."

"Come on," he said waving the man off, "we aren't safe yet. You guys ready?"

He got excited nods from both of them. "Let's go."

The world erupted around them as they stood to go, the trees above them shook with the impact of what sounded like a jack hammer as a heavy machine gun opened up targeting the hill side they crouched behind from somewhere across Glebe. He couldn't even be sure if it was coming from the building he'd been firing at or the one next to it. Sleepy fell hard and rolled to the side coming up against Kirby. He was about to tell the man to get down the hill when he realized the top of the man's head was gone. He'd just gotten a decent man killed, traded for Rob Ward, and now he may not even live to regret it.

Whoever had shown up, they were no longer imaginary and they had brought heavy ordnance.

He glanced down at Jennings, further down the hill near his own boots. The soldier was just frozen in shock staring at Kirby's lifeless form.

"We need to scoot down the hill," he said and ended up kicking some mulch in the Jennings' face to get him to listen.

"Stay low. We get to the bottom, we go right and move fast, got it?"

Jennings just looked at him, his mouth hanging open.

"You understand me? Are you hit?"

Jennings shook his head and slid further down the hill after a thinking about it for a moment.

"Go!" he screamed at the man before he slid down the hill himself.

He let Jennings run ahead of him, setting a scared jackrabbit pace. They ran hard for three blocks through a residential area west of Glebe, moving back north. An occasional rifle shot boomed out of the high-rise area behind them, impossible to tell if it was aimed or not.

He whistled Jennings to a stop and waited until the man came back to him, to where he knelt by the side of a house, chest heaving with the exertion of having sprinted while imagining cross hairs in the middle of his back. No need to pretend anymore, it had been very real. Kirby proved that. Jennings left the cover of a tree with reluctance and duck walked back towards him.

He handed over the radio. "Call it in. Let 'em know about Kirby and Rob, I'm going to circle back a block and see if we are being followed. You wait here, and then we'll get to the rig."

"Don't be stupid!" Jennings spit. "Let's just go!"

"They'll just follow us back to the wheels, and hit us there. We need to know what they're doing."

Sleepy moved around the edge of the house, staying behind a shrub and scanned the intersecting residential roads in front of him as he heard Jennings behind him establish the radio link. He didn't see anything and suspected that since they'd been scared off, whoever was firing had little reason to follow them. He hated what he had already decided to do, but Jennings was as dangerous as Rob in his own way. What he lacked in initiative he more than made up for in cruelty and his willingness to do anything he was told. Rob had been a psychopath set loose by apocalypse; Jennings was just a natural born Nazi prison guard.

He listened as Jennings shouted his report between gasping breaths.

Sleepy edged back around to the front of the house to where Jennings's eyes went wide with shock at seeing him again so quickly.

Sleepy pointed at his own eyes. "We need to go, now."

"Bad guys, we're moving," Jennings said in to the radio.

Sleepy reached out and grabbed the radio back, and zipped it inside his vest under his coat.

"Come on, we're gonna do this fast."

*

"What just happened?" Gwynn Alexander pulled the binoculars away and glanced at Harold as she removed her ear plugs. The former Maryland National Guardsman still squatted behind the .50 caliber, its barrel smoking, looking at her in confusion.

"Yeah, that was a new one."

"Well, they're running for the hills now. Radio it in. Tamara won't believe this shit."

"They shot their own guy! What the hell?"

*

He and Jennings were two blocks from where they'd left the Humvee. Both of them were kneeling behind a poured concrete front stair of an old brick house, watching for any sign of pursuit.

"Looks clear to me," Jennings was more than ready to go home.

"Feel free to walk out there and check."

"Fuck you!"

"I think they dropped off," Sleepy said ignoring the man. "I say we wait till dark, just to be sure."

"We could just hoof it, screw the wheels."

"No, we need to know if they'll go to all the trouble of following us this far, this is our territory. Bauman will want to know."

It was getting dark fast, and Sleepy's conscience matched the darkening sky. Losing Kirby hadn't been part of this plan, and now that was on him too. It'd be dark in thirty minutes and then he could even the scales a little bit again.

"He ain't here," Jennings tried again, desperate to move.

"We wait."

Jennings looked like he wanted to say something. Sleepy just stared him down.

It was dark enough.

"Let's go." Sleepy sat off without waiting to see if he was going to be followed.

He was, at a distance. Jennings was making it clear, Sleepy was the one who was going to act as the trip wire. He paused at the corner of the burned-out bank that smelled like charcoal and rotting, water-logged carpeting. It felt safe. As opposed to what he'd told Jennings, he hadn't seen any pursuit at all since the heavy weapons fire at the hill behind the Sunoco station. For all Tysons knew from Jennings's radio reports, they were already dead or had been in a running gun fight all afternoon.

He stepped out from the brick wall of the bank and crossed over to the side of the Hummer. He could hear Jennings's feet pounding up behind him. The man fairly collapsed against the side of the rig.

"Made it!"

"Not really," Sleepy shook his head.

"What you mean?"

He fired his 9mm three times, point blank into Jennings chest.

Sleepy looked the man in the face as the blinks of surprise stopped with his heart. "I'm sorry," he mumbled; surprised a small part of him meant it.

*

Chapter 15

Jason felt a little sorry for Pro. They'd both been in the kitchen and overheard the radio communications between his friend Sleepy's group and the crew at the Ritz. But that had been hours ago and they hadn't heard anything since. It seemed to him that they had bitten off more than they could chew. Indications were, there was another group of survivors organized inside the capital beltway that didn't like trespassers. Then again, maybe it was the Tysons group in particular that they had a problem with. He would have paid a lot to know the answer to that particular question.

He knew Pro had other questions and they weren't being answered by the silence on the radio. The kid sat there playing Go Fish at the kitchen table with the young girl, Elsa, who seemed in remarkably good spirits considering what she'd been through and according to Rachel, seen. Each time he thought about it, he found himself wishing he could go back and kill the girl's captor slowly. Some people just didn't deserve to go quick.

"Fours," Elsa laughed. "I know you have a four."

He watched as Pro picked out his card and sheepishly handed it over to the eleven-year-old. "Three in a row," she crowed, "you suck at this."

Pro shrugged in defeat, "I guess I do."

He was pretty sure Pro was throwing the game, he'd heard him ask for jacks three times. He was making sloppy joe sandwiches, without the buns. All they had for bread was what he'd tried to come up using the Dagmans' bread machine. Either he was doing something very wrong or the recipe was flawed, because the result was just about inedible. Everyone had given him a hard time for screwing up the bread. In his opinion, it wasn't anything sloppy joe sauce from a can couldn't fix.

"Control, Sleepy. We were ambushed at the Humvee. They were waiting for us. They got Jennings. I'm moving west on OD, on foot. I think I've lost them. I'm going to find a place to hole up for the night. I'll call for a pickup tomorrow when I get to McLean."

"He's alive!" Pro pumped his fist in the air.

Jason could see the look of relief on Pro's face, but his mind was already two steps ahead.

"Grab our go bags," he said. "We're going to try to find him before he gets picked up."

Pro just looked at him in shock. Not the reaction he had expected.

"To just talk," he added in explanation. "I need to know if he's the guy you think he is."

"There's enough here to do whatever you want," he showed Rachel the basement from the bottom of the stairwell. "There's some more stuff in the open safes in the back room, as well as some directions to a place out west of here, near the West Virginia border."

"But you're coming back, right?"

He waved at the shelves of food and ordnance. "Just in case, we don't."

"Take us with you," Rachel looked scared. She'd looked scared when he'd asked her to follow him down into the basement as well. But she'd followed him down with her hand on her gun. The look of concern on her face was now coming from an entirely different direction.

"Not going to happen," he shook his head. "Stay with Elsa and Loki, you'll be safe. If everything goes all right, we'll be back sometime tomorrow night."

"Why are you doing this?"

"I promised I'd try to help." He didn't say who he'd promised. "If I don't figure a way around the crowd at Tysons, none of us are safe. This guy out there, he might be able to help."

"The guy that captured Pro? Seriously?"

"It's complicated..."

"Ready," Pro shouted from the top of the stairs.

"Keep Elsa out of here, unless you are with her, ok?"

Rachel nodded at him. "Just make sure you come back."

He'd driven like a madman down the winding Georgetown Pike, lights off, with his NODs down over his eyes. They had lucked out in that it was a pitch-black, moonless night. He almost hit a deer as he came out onto Dolly Madison and went east past the CIA Headquarters compound on his left. He went right on Kirby Road, and drove to where it crossed Old Dominion. That had to be the 'OD,' Pro's supposed friend Sleepy had mentioned on the radio. Sleepy's vehicle, as best as he'd been able to figure from the radio broadcasts hadn't been parked far from where Old Dominion intersected Glebe about three miles further east.

He parked the beast at the edge of the parking lot in front of a windowless Starbucks in the Chesterbrook shopping center. They had a good view up and down Old Dominion in both directions, towards Glebe and back towards Mclean.

"What now?" Pro asked adjusting his own NODS over his eyes.

"You watch your way, I'll watch mine. Your buddy said he'd be coming down 'OD' - this is Old Dominion. From where they parked on Glebe, he'll have to come this way, if he already hasn't."

"I hope we can find him."

"Me too, kid." He didn't like the idea of having to hide during the day tomorrow, away from the house; which they'd have to do, regardless. If this Sleepy character wasn't the squared away guy Pro thought he was, he'd have to take him out before could radio his asshole buddies. If he screwed up; he and Pro would be running for their lives.

He looked over at the back of the kid's head. "Pro, I'm going to be honest with you. I'm not going to take any chances with him. It's not just me and you anymore. You understand what I'm saying?"

Pro looked back at him, and nodded. "I understand."

"There's two very scared people that we have to think about, and I won't put them at risk. Even if it pisses you off."

"I know."

"Ok, then. You remember that, and do exactly what I say, when I say it and we just might make this work. Otherwise, next time, I'll leave *you* home with the dog."

"I get it, I do. But I'm right, he's a good guy."

Jason found himself hoping Pro was right, and thinking on what it could mean if he could gain an ally inside the mall.

An hour passed, the analog clock above the dash showed that it was a quarter past eight, and the thermostat read 37 degrees. If this Sleepy character hadn't gone to ground for the night, Jason imagined he soon would.

"Do you think the soldiers from the Ritz have safehouses scattered around?" he asked Pro. "You know, places they keep food and supplies, or will he looking for an empty house to sleep in?"

They both knew what empty meant. One that wasn't shared with rotting corpses. Someplace you could breathe without gagging.

"I know they sometimes took supplies from the mall to somewhere else, I don't know where, though."

"But Sleepy would know?"

"Yeah," Pro answered. "What if he's already walked past this point, we won't see him in the morning."

Jason adjusted his NODs and remained silent, he'd just seen something at the far edge of what the night vision device was capable of, way up the road, back towards Glebe. Movement that had drawn his eye. At this distance, it could be a deer, a dog, or hell a black bear. They'd seen a couple in the last month as the animals moved back into a habitat that had long been overrun with people. He supposed it still was, just that the people were now half frozen carrion attracting anything and everything that ate it.

He focused on the spot his eyes had been drawn to and waited, nothing. And then he saw it, a sole figure, coming back to the road down a drive way. House must have been 'occupied,' he imagined. He focused on the silhouette, at this range, just a vague lumpy figure in light green, a shade lighter than the dark green background produced by the night vision goggles. The figure, still a good three hundred yards off was moving closer, and then disappeared again as he moved into the foliage on their side of the road.

"Jason?"

"Yeah?"

"What if he's already gone past?"

"He hasn't, I think I just saw him." He didn't turn his head. he kept his vision focused on the spot the figure had disappeared from.

"Where'd you see him?" He felt the car shift as Pro wriggled around in his seat next to him.

Jason held a hand up between them, "Wait…"

After a solid five minutes, the figure hadn't reappeared.

"Ok, I think I see where he went into a house, general area at any rate. You are going to stay here. I'll bring him to you."

"No way! I'm coming too."

"Nope. You are going to stay right here, I'm serious. You are not going to move, not make a sound. If you see anybody coming, other than me coming back, you are going to let me know on the radio and then you're slowly going to get down on the floor board. Remember what I told you about quick movements, they'll get you seen."

"You're going to shoot him; I know you will."

"Not unless he makes me," he answered. He kept his head turned out the window, doing his best to mark the position where the figure had disappeared in the distorted night vision. The overhanging branches above the road formed a reference point, a recognizable pattern near where his quarry had disappeared, but he knew that pattern would change as he moved closer and the perspective altered. He mentally tried to gauge the distance that separated the Land Cruiser from the spot where the man had disappeared from the road.

"Ok," he turned back to face Pro, and withdrew his map book. There was a crossroad in the general vicinity of where the man had disappeared from sight. If he went up that way, they were screwed. He'd never find him inside those neighborhoods in the time they had.

"If I'm not back in two hours, move the truck behind the shopping center. You can do that right?" He taken the kid around the neighborhood a couple of times teaching him to drive.

"Yeah."

"Stay with the vehicle, I'll come to you. Hopefully with your buddy."

"He's not my buddy, he's just a good person. But, be careful."

"Oh, I will be."

"Jason," Pro called out as he had one leg out the door. "His real name is Daniel."

"Right," he managed with a nod as he shut the door. He wished Pro hadn't told him that. If this went sideways; taking out another thug, a target named Sleepy wouldn't bother him in the least. Daniel, though? Targets weren't supposed to have names.

He'd reached the spot where he believed his quarry had disappeared. It was impossible to be certain. The effective range of the NODs on a night like this, with so little ambient light, made everything here appear very different than it had from inside the Land Cruiser. To make matters worse, an intersection lay just ahead with a road breaking off to the left, the same direction as the figure had disappeared in. There were three houses to the left side of the road as well. Hoping he was right, he dismissed the home furthest from him, thinking it may have been the first house he'd seen the man check and reemerge from. Which would make the one he stood in front of, his best option.

He peeked out from behind the tree and looked closely at every window facing the street. Nothing. Not that he expected anything. Sleepy would be worried he was being followed by whoever had ambushed him. He wouldn't be doing anything so stupid as firing up a flashlight in the front room of a house.

Shit! Who was being stupid? Here I am, creeping into a house where someone who has been shot at all day might be holed up. Stupid.

He went up the bricked in concrete stairs and paused at the front door, listening for anything in the still of the night. Nothing...

The front door's handle was hanging on bent mounting screws, but the wood around it looked like that had happened a long time ago. He gently pushed the door open with the muzzle of his rifle. It opened with a scratch of wood on the broken door frame. He felt himself wince at the noise, knowing he shouldn't be taking risks like this. The stench of rotten dead meat hit him like a wall as he pushed further into the entry.

He backed away, holding his breath until he was back on the outside stoop. No one was going to spend a night holed up in there. He looked to his left, at the next house and immediately saw a slight glow from the small basement window on the side of the house. The window wasn't anything more than three feet wide, and maybe eighteen inches high, and it was half hidden by a shrub. The NODs though, had no issue picking up on the faint glow within.

*

Sleepy had heated up a can of chili with a stack of candles, and then laid down on the basement couch to sleep. He worried over how he'd spin his story tomorrow, hoping Michelle had been able to successfully plant their list.

Which Bauman he dealt with tomorrow, paranoid or full monkey tilt crazy, would depend on whether Michelle had been able to get the note planted, and then discovered. He didn't give Rob or even Jennings a second thought. Rob had been insane, probably even before the Suck. Jennings had a lot of innocent blood on his hands too, especially with the old folks that he'd visited Bauman's "mercy killing" upon. It was Kirby that he kept thinking of. He'd been a decent guy. Someone he could have liked, if he allowed himself to like anyone, which was just stupid these days. In that way lay madness.

What the hell was he going to do? Tysons was supposed to have been a refuge, not the hellish camp he was now fully a part of. If it wasn't for Michelle, he knew wouldn't even be going back.

Life had thrown Daniel Levine, former high school English teacher and freshman girls basketball coach, a serious curveball. He shook his head in dismay. He'd killed two evil SOBs today, and gotten a good man killed. Afterwards, he'd feasted on a can of chili warmed by candles held together with a rubber band in a stranger's basement.

He pulled the blanket he'd found on the nearby recliner, up close to his face. Strange scents, another man's aftershave, someone else's detergent, another life. He wondered where the homeowner was. Dead? Rotting on the side of a road? Or maybe asleep in another stranger's house, using a blanket that held echoes of yet another life lived and gone.

Sleep took him quickly; fitful and full of dark, stress driven dreams. Kirby was there, shot crossing the road rather than at the hillside where he'd died. He kept seeing it on replay in a dream that he somehow thought he should be

245

able to control. For some strange reason, his sleeping mind thought it important that the vision be accurate. Kirby died on that hill. He'd stuck his head above the hilltop, not in the road...

Kirby materialized in the recliner across from the couch where he slept, a rifle pointed at him. The dream shifted into another gear. Kirby's ghost had re-lit the candles on the short table between them. The ghost looked angry. He'd be angry too; he'd gotten the man killed.

Less and less like a dream, it felt like his eyes were open looking at Kirby's face. "I'm sorry."

Kirby looked different.

"I took your guns," the not-Kirby said. His mind started to spin up, enough that he realized he was no longer dreaming. This was definitely not Kirby, or even his ghost. He sat up and felt for his sidearm, it was gone.

The man seated in the recliner was all in black, wearing what looked like a smooth black bicycle helmet, a set of night vision goggles resting on top. The candles cast enough light to see the assault rifle with a suppressor pointed at him. It was him, the ninja. He supposed he deserved this, but all he could think about was what would happen to Michelle.

"It's you," he managed.

The man's eyes lacked any sign of concern, or mercy. They just stared back at him, a vision of calm that scared him.

"You're the ninja?"

"I hate that name," the man shook his head. "I'm just a guy that used to be a real soldier."

"You heard my radio call?"

"Been listening to your chatter all day." The soldier nodded in agreement. "Sleepy, I have to admit, I was rooting for you a little. For the longest time, you've just been just another name circled on my white board at home."

He felt his head shake from side to side. "It wasn't real, at least at first. I needed to take out a couple of assholes. Unfortunately, the real bad guys showed up too."

"You expect me to believe that?"

"I don't give a shit what you believe." It came out of his mouth before he'd realized he was saying it. Strangely, he found he didn't care. It wasn't what he'd done to Rob and Jennings. It was Kirby, his senseless death should mean something, even if this was the price to be paid.

"Who were the assholes?"

"Just crazies, if there was any justice in the world, people like them wouldn't have survived the Flu."

"What were their names?"

"Who?" Why the hell would this guy care? "You keeping track of us?"

"Something like that," the man may have actually smiled.

"Rob Ward and Jennings, I don't think I ever knew his first name."

The soldier's head shook a little, and the rifle barrel raised another couple of inches. "Don't start bullshitting me now, there were four of you."

"And Kirby, the others, whoever they were, did for him. I got him killed. He was a decent guy."

"Kirby." The soldier said. It hadn't been a question. It was like he was talking to someone. It was then he noticed the radio on the table between them, next to the candles. There was more than one of him...

The man just stared at him and nodded at something unseen. "Kirby was a recent arrival? Or abductee?"

"How'd you know that?"

"Pro didn't recognize the name."

"Pro..." The name threw him for half a second. "The kid? You found him?" He felt himself smile.

The soldier, pulled an earbud from his ear, and leaned forward to switch off the radio on the table. The barrel of the man's gun never wavered away from where it pointed at his chest.

"Pro convinced me that you were worth talking to. If he's wrong, this is going to be a short conversation."

"He's safe now? He's with you?"

"As safe as anybody can be, with assholes like you running around playing Mad Max."

"Look, we are trying to take down Bauman and his crew, but we are way out-numbered. Today was just me evening up the odds a little."

"Who's we?"

"Right now, just me and one other." He realized how crazy that sounded as soon as he'd said it.

"Michelle?"

"Pro would have told you that. She was sweet on the kid. She lost a couple of boys of her own."

"Just the two of you?" The look on the soldier's face looked almost disgusted.

"There's more, I think. But they don't..."

"They don't, what?"

"We haven't reached out to them yet. It's not that easy. I could kill Bauman right now. But there are others that are worse, way worse. Rob Ward was one of them. In his screwed-up way, Bauman keeps the lid on. I'm not defending him, please don't think that. It's just..."

The soldier rubbed his face, nodding knowingly. "The devil you know?"

"It's worse than that, I know both of them. Bauman is bent, but he's still managing to control some real nut jobs. Men and even a few women that were just broken by what happened. Now though, even that is starting to come apart. Me, Michelle and a lot of others wouldn't survive Bauman going down. Not unless I figure out a way to deal with his goons."

"His goons?" the soldier shook his head. "You're his freaking deputy!"

Sleepy shook his head and tried to smile. "Well, I have you to thank for that. You've been killing the other candidates."

"Fair point," the soldier said. "Does that mean you owe me one?"

"What is it you could want from me? You're safe! Take Pro and get away."

"Not sure I can share this world with slave-owning assholes."

Sleepy felt himself set up a little more. "What are you saying? You'll help us?"

"You willing to help yourselves?" The soldier's gun dropped away from his chest. Now it would be his knee caps that would get shot if he gave the man cause.

"From where I sit, you've got a couple of hundred of people that far outnumber the Sheriff's posse."

"It's not that simple," he tried to explain. "The... workers aren't allowed to touch a gun. Most are worked, morning to night, besides being watched. If they screw up, or give offense, they die slow... in front of everyone as examples. Bauman controls the soldiers, barely. And the soldiers have it real good."

"The guns are going to figure out they don't need Bauman." The man was nodding his head, like he knew how this scenario ended.

"It's already happening. It's why I could use your help. The Sheriff is a delusional sociopath, getting more and more paranoid every day. The thugs he's got control of, for the moment, are starting to wonder why they are sharing the compound with anyone. I don't have to explain to you what will happen to the innocents there, if the crazy gets worse. If I kill Bauman; and believe me, I want to. I wouldn't last an hour, neither would Michelle. I've got no idea what to do."

The soldier just stared at him for a long moment that seemed to stretch. The ninja, looked like he was listening to somebody again. But he'd seen the man take out his ear piece.

Sleepy could see that a decision had been made in the man' eyes. He wondered if he was now going to pay a price for not doing anything earlier, or pay a price for Kirby; either reason made sense to him. The soldier stood up and looked at him for a moment, and then waved at the stairs leading up out of the basement with the barrel of his gun.

"I've been thinking on it," the Ninja said. "I might have an idea or two."

"It's just you and the kid?"

The soldier just stared back at him for a moment, before pointing at his own weapon leaning against the wall. The sidearm was sitting on the TV stand.

"Grab your weapons. Pro wants to see you."

He just looked at the man in surprise.

"I've got your mags, Sleepy. If you play it straight, we'll make certain you can make your pick up in the morning. If you don't..."

"Yeah, I get it," he hopped up. "Is Pro ok? I figured the guys that caught him tuned him up pretty good."

"They did. They almost killed him. But I found them."

"I know you went back through Reston on foot, after the Hummer died on you." The ninja stopped and looked at him in what may have been surprise.

"I saw some tracks," Daniel explained. "Headed down into the creek off the road. I convinced Bauman you went towards Vienna. I swear, I was on the kid's side."

"You saw two sets of tracks?"

He shook his head, remembering back. "No, just one. I figured you had already dropped Pro somewhere safe and went back for him."

The soldier smiled then and may have relaxed a little. "I wasn't that smart; the kid was heavier than he looked."

"Huh...I hadn't considered that."

"Let's go, Daniel." The man waved him forward. "Stay in front of me, we've got a five-minute walk."

He paused the sound of his name. "Pro told you my name?" he asked, paused with one foot on the bottom step. "Why all the Sleepy routine?"

"He did." The soldier shrugged. "But Daniel, I need you to understand something. To me, until just a moment ago, regardless of what Pro thinks, you were just Sleepy. One more name on my to-do list. Don't make me think of you as Sleepy."

"Right..." Daniel had the feeling he was staring at a machine. His gut told him that there wasn't anything inherently evil about the soldier, in fact, the soldier was a good man to have done what he did for Pro. That said, this 'Ninja', clearly had no problem compartmentalizing what needed to be done.

"I won't," he answered. "For the record, I never asked for the name Sleepy, any more than I suspect you asked to be the Ninja."

"Fair enough." The soldier nodded, dropping a hand away from his rifle to hold it out to him. "I'm Jason."

He shook the hand, trying to remember the last time he'd done that. Maybe when he'd first met Bauman? When the Feds still controlled the Ritz. Hopefully this would turn out differently.

"Good to meet you, Jason."

The soldier remained quiet until they left the house and were standing in the front yard. Daniel could barely see the hand in front of his face. Jason stood a good ten feet away, and flipped his night vision down over one eye, and turned to check up the street towards Glebe.

"You weren't worried about being followed by the others from Ballston?"

"They never followed us at all. They just shot from the high rises in Ballston proper. That's where they got Kirby. I killed Jennings at our vehicle. That's why I had him making the reports on the radio. Bauman will be thinking we were pursued all day."

"That was smart." The Jason said as he stepped out into the road ahead of him and checked both ways, adjusting his ear piece for the radio. He waited a moment, listening to something before waving him forward.

"Ok, Daniel. The kid's excited to see you, let's go."

The use of his name meant more to him than this stranger could know, and the effect it had on him, mounted quickly. His father had always said that the concept of an epiphany was myth, best reserved for religious contexts. What people often described as having an epiphany was in reality, nothing more than a sudden acceptance of something long known, or suspected. He was, in an instant, willing to fight for a chance to live in this near-empty world as Daniel Singer Levine. He didn't have to be 'Sleepy.' Not anymore.

*

"You sure about this?" Pro looked at him, raising his eyebrows in a way that made the kid look a lot older than his 15 years.

Jason waggled his radio back and forth. "It might give Daniel's story some legs."

"I wish we could just rescue Michelle and him, they could come back with us."

He shook his head. Pro was young enough to still think 'wants' and 'wishes' had some power to dictate one's life. He was just learning what it was to be responsible for someone else, to accept that responsibility and the corners it painted you into. Helping Daniel and Michelle meant helping everyone at Tysons, everyone, that in Daniel's words, hadn't gone full Nazi prison guard.

"Maybe down the road," he answered. *If we live through this.*

Pro's chin jerked back down to the road, "there they are."

Jason raised the binoculars and could see two Humvees rolling to a stop where Old Dominion ran into Mclean proper. "Damn, to have young eyes."

Sleepy/Daniel could be seen jogging up the road away from them, towards the vehicles. Jason smiled and pressed the transmit button on his radio. Daniel had given him the new channel for the day.

"You Tysons assholes hear me? The ones sitting in the middle of the road in Mclean picking up your lost duckling?"

253

"Who is this?" A voice boomed back at him. He recognized Bauman immediately. Evidently the big man was monitoring the radio from the Ritz. Jason doubted if Bauman could have been bothered to make a road trip to retrieve his deputy. Daniel had mentioned the night before that the Sheriff rarely left the safety of the hotel.

Jason pressed the transmit button on his radio. "Somebody telling you the next time you send a team east of Glebe; you won't get a very lucky survivor back. I won't stop with delivering a warning message."

"Who am I talking to?"

"General John D. Simmons," Jason said clearly, and looked over at Pro and shrugged. The kid clapped a hand over his mouth and spun away stifling a howl of laughter. "82nd Airborne, out of Bragg," Jason continued. "Whom do I have the displeasure of speaking with? Anybody important?"

"You've delivered your message," the voice came back. "Get the hell out of our territory."

"I will. At the moment, you broke dicks don't have anything we want. If that changes, I won't be announcing myself first. Simmons out."

Jason clicked his radio off and looked at Pro. "Psychological warfare; we just backstopped Daniel's story and gave the Sheriff something bigger to worry about. Daniel showed us the cracks, we just add water and wait for it to freeze."

"What are you talking about?"

"Never mind," he smiled at the kid. "We need to find a place to hole up for the day before we drive back."

*

Corporal Tim Reece just stared at his radio scanner like it was speaking in tongues.

"General Simmons? Who the hell is this guy?" He had joined the Maryland National Guard a year before the virus had struck, and been called out to help enforce the quarantine around Washington before civilization went completely Tango Uniform. When it did, he was one of only two survivors out of his whole company that hadn't gotten sick and died, or gone AWOL, before they got sick and died. He'd been caught on the Virginia side of the river, for which he counted himself lucky. His home area of DC had been a quasi-warzone before the Suck. He'd fallen in with a group of survivors in the Clarendon area and they'd managed to fend off the Reapers with the weapons they'd raided from his old unit and foraged from a DHS warehouse.

They'd had an uneasy peace with the nut job in Tysons since early on. Glebe Ave. had been the demarcation point between the two territories. Until yesterday, when one of their observation posts had witnessed some whack job shooting one of his own people, and that was after unloading a magazine or two at an empty building. They'd sent a few warning bursts in their direction to scare them off with the .50 caliber emplaced in their OP, but the entire episode had just gotten stranger.

"Who the hell is General Simmons?" Tamara Cooper, the person they'd elected to lead them, scratched her head. Tim knew that Tamara had been an engineer of some sort, pre-suck, but prior to that, she had done four years as an Air Force Lt., in charge of a team that used to fly around in big planes intercepting signals. Tamara was smart, and she'd built their scanner and the antenna mounted atop the condo tower they called home.

"Beats me," Tim said. "We could use a general." He glanced up at Tamara, "No offense."

"None taken, I couldn't agree more."

"Note to self," Tim wrote in the air with an imaginary pencil. "Find a general for Ms. Cooper."

"Smart-ass."

*

"You smell that?" Pro asked as they walked up the driveway towards the house. "What is that?"

"That," Jason caught himself smiling, "is fresh bread."

It was delicious. He smeared another slice of the warm bread with reconstituted "butter like" spread and stuffed half of it into his mouth.

"Wha' you'd do iffernet?" he asked, still chewing.

"Pushed the button that said, 'Rise Cycle' on the bread machine, before I pushed start." Rachel sounded smug, but he was happy to see her smiling.

He was surrounded by smart-asses.

"Anybody can do it," Rachel said pointedly. "If you think we're going to stay here, cook and clean for you two, because we're girls, you are sorely mistaken."

He just looked at the young woman. He'd never intimated anything of the sort. Had he?

"I'll keep making the bread, because yours is bloody awful, but you are going to teach me to fight, and Elsa too." Rachel nodded at the younger girl who sat on a stool at the kitchen island.

He glanced down at Elsa mid-ambush and the twelve-year-old just nodded at him. "We decided."

"We did," Rachel added. "Different world, different rules. You aren't going to leave us here again, not knowing what to do with that armory you have down there, ok? We are never going to be defenseless again, and we are going to fight right alongside you. It's that, or I'll take Elsa and go."

"Just to be clear," Pro mumbled through a mouthful of bread. "You'll keep making the bread?"

Rachel didn't turn to answer Pro; her eyes were locked on his.

"All right," he managed. He didn't see any room for discussion in the young woman's face. "If we are throwing down rules, hear me when I say this; I told Pro the same thing - when we are out there, you do what I say, when I say it, how I say it. I am not going to live in whatever world we have left, if it means I'm sending freaking kids out to fight."

"It's the only world we have," Pro said quietly. "We have to fight too."

Jason looked over at Pro, weighing the hard truth in those words. Then down at the bread in his hands. Such a simple thing, a product and symbol of civilization for thousands of years. Once the canned food was eaten or went bad, it was again going to be something people killed one another over. He could see it coming, just as he knew Bauman, crazy as he was, could see it. How the food was going to be grown? Who would be doing the work? How they were going to be protected? Old questions, among the most basic humanity had ever faced. These kids would live with the answers, survivors like him left them with.

*

Chapter 16

"You really kicked over a hornet's nest out there, Sleepy."

He'd found Bauman in his darkened office. Everyone had warned him to give the man some space, stay away until later. He knew that would only have had Bauman wondering why he hadn't reported in.

"Couldn't be helped." He'd had enough time to get the story right in his head. He was surprised at how calm he was. It felt good to have some hope.

"We spotted rifles in the windows above Glebe at Washington Ave. Rob just went Rambo, opened up before we could pull back. They had a big ass machine gun overlooking the intersection. We didn't have an option but to run."

He covered the whole story he'd concocted; the running retreat, under fire, the ambush at the Humvee. The only thing true about any of it, was where and how Kirby had been killed. Bauman was leaning back in his office chair staring past him, focused on some repro print on the wall over his shoulders.

"Glad you got free," Bauman's eyes flicked over to him momentarily, and then away.

He knew Bauman had a built-in distrust of survivors, especially 'only survivors.' He'd known that going in. It was why he'd insisted Rob and then Jennings make the radio reports back to the Ritz themselves.

"Me too."

"You checked in with your lady yet?"

"No, she ok?" Shit, why was he bringing Michelle up? "I came straight here."

Bauman withdrew a key from the retractable zipline clipped to his belt and unlocked a desk drawer. He pulled out a piece of paper, stained with spilled coffee and pushed it across the desk at him.

"One of the guards in the kitchen found it, or rather a char staff scraped it off a tray, and he grabbed it up. You ever see it before? Or anything like it?" Bauman was now staring at him. "Your squeeze was in the kitchen, when it was found."

Sleepy looked at him in apology and reached behind him and turned on the office light. "What am I looking at?"

"Just names," Bauman shrugged. "See anything else?"

Sleepy, I'm Sleepy...all Sleepy. The mantra echoed in his head, Bauman would spot Daniel in his face, in his eyes, in seconds.

"I'm on it," Sleepy added with some surprise, his finger running down the two columns of names.

"Patrol schedule?... no these are different teams." He added, half to himself. "I'm sorry chief, what am I looking at?" He didn't have to fake being in serious need of some sleep. He'd been up all night, planning with Pro and his guardian angel.

Bauman nodded again at the sheet. "Give it sec, work it out... tell me I'm crazy."

Sleepy shrugged and looked again, knowing Michelle had written it left-handed, following his directions.

"Wait, these are all...shit!" he looked up at Bauman, "And these arrows?"

"I don't know," Bauman shrugged. "If I was a betting man, I'd say some of our more hardcore spear carriers have an issue with you and that list of soldiers in your column."

"Oh, shit," Sleepy rubbed at his face. "What are we going to do? What should I do?"

"Nothing," Bauman shook his head. "People on the right side of that page start dying, we'll know. I'm not going to gut my forces based on doubts. Especially after this so-called General Simmons, if he's even real. Who the fuck knows..."?

"Yeah, I get that." He waved the piece of paper between them. "I just don't want to be the one that proves there's anything to it. I'm the first name on that list."

"If that happens, rest assured, they'll pay."

And that's bullshit, he knew. His own death would actually solve some of Bauman's problems, at least for a time. He'd spent serious effort trying to remind Bauman that he had a conscience, of the big picture future they were supposedly working towards. Without him, Bauman would be free to follow his baser instincts right off the cliff. That is, until Wayne or one of the others stopped pretending that they needed Bauman or his greater vision.

"Not sure that makes me feel any better." Sleepy regarded the list. "Wayne's name has an arrow drawn to mine."

"I saw that, I'll make sure you two are never out there, without you having some back up from the names on your team."

He recognized the heavy-handed trap. "I didn't realize I had a team."

Bauman seemed to like that answer and nodded at him after a moment. Then, like a switch was thrown, he leaned forward, planting his forearms on his desk.

"You'll live," Bauman answered. "I'm wondering what the hell we make of this supposed General Simmons. You see anything yesterday to support that? One way or another?"

Sleepy shook his head after a moment. He hadn't heard the broadcast Jason had said he was going to make, but it had freaked out the team sent to pick him up.

"We never got a good idea of their numbers, beyond the half dozen or so chasing us. Then we lost them, or they dropped off to make us think we had. I really don't know. But we set up and watched the approach to the Humvee for almost an hour until it was dark, and didn't see anything. Either the same group chasing us dropped off and went to go set up on the Humvee before we got there, or they called in a separate team to set the ambush. But it was at least half a dozen guys there. If Jennings hadn't gotten excited and took off running ahead of me, I'd be dead too."

"Sounds like they were pretty well coordinated then?"

He nodded; "I'm guessing, but yeah, I'd say so. They were better at it than we are."

"How much better, you lost them didn't you?"

Sleepy felt himself shrug. "Like I said, only because Jennings took off running towards the Hummer. When they opened up on him, I just went to ground. They just seemed... I don't know, maybe they do have a real general. One thing is certain, they were close enough to us in McLean at the pickup this morning to see it going down, or to take shots at us if they'd wanted to."

"But they didn't," Bauman said. "I say it's bullshit, trying to get a bluff in, following the fuck up." He held up his hand; "Rob's mistake, not yours. You did well, getting you and Jennings as far as you did."

"How you think Wayne's going to take Rob getting killed?"

Bauman shrugged and pointed at the note on the desk between them. "Anything to that list, maybe it will make him stop and think before he does something stupid."

"Like killing me?"

"Don't start with the paranoia, Sleepy. That'll bring us down faster than anything."

It took every bit of self-control he had to keep a straight face. "Right."

Bauman rubbed at his face and then leaned back in his chair. "Go get some sleep, you look like shit."

*

When Sleepy whispered his story of seeing Pro and meeting Jason, Michelle's face lit up in surprise and a genuine smile broke out that made her look even more beautiful. If she looked this way more often, he knew without a doubt he'd already be dead. Either at Bauman's hands, Wayne's, or one of his crew. He knew the fact that Michelle was with him was a big part of the reason the hard cases wanted him gone. Just like the fact that there were relatively 'new' women that had come in or been found with some of the new soldiers and were similarly spoken for, or otherwise off limits to men who had grown used to having no limits.

Michelle was savvy enough to know the score. She generally went around pissed off, and ready to bite the head off of anyone that looked at her sideways. If he'd gone with Pro and Jason, she be in somebody else's bed right now, or dead. He didn't doubt she was serious about that not happening again.

"Ssshhhh," he rolled over to his side and held his finger over her lips. "He looked good, he asked about you."

"And he's with the ninja?"

He nodded, "since the night he disappeared."

"What was he like?"

"He's a real soldier, or was, I guess. He's... I don't know, pretty intense. A little broken, I think. Not like Bauman, just angry."

"Angry's good." Michelle whispered. "What now?"

"What do you mean?"

She just stared at him and raised an eyebrow in question.

"No, Michelle." He shook his head, "You are not involved, and it's going to stay that way."

"Not involved?" she managed to whisper and still spit the words at him as she pushed against him hard enough that she almost moved herself right out of the bed.

"Not what I meant," he started.

"Was I involved when that son of a bitch raped me on a mattress in the ballroom? His goons standing around, cheering him on? Was I involved then?"

She slid closer to him under the covers until her face was inches from his own. "You knew it might have happened before you got involved, maybe you guessed at it or just assumed it had. Daniel... it happened. I was there. I'm going to kill that sick bastard if it's the last thing I do."

"You do that?" Sleepy sat up on an elbow, "before we're ready - it *will* be the last thing you do. And all of this is a lost cause. If you act too soon, think about who will take over, it won't be me. I'll be disappeared right after Bauman goes down. Think what that will mean for everyone else here."

"Promise me, I get to kill him," she whispered.

"Michelle..."

"Promise me," she wiped away tears burning their way down her face.

"If we can figure out a way, I promise."

They lay there, for nearly an hour, in silence. Sleepy knew she was awake, he imagined he could see the waves of anger radiating off her shoulders.

"Who can we trust who works in the laundry?"

Michelle turned over to face him. "What?"

"Not just someone you have a good feeling about. Somebody who wants pay back as much as you."

"The laundry?" Suddenly interested, she nodded, smiling. "Why?"

*

Pro and Rachel were good. They'd been at it a week, and Jason had to admit, they were ready for what he had planned. They weren't close to the point he'd assault a position with them. In fact, he didn't care how good they got. That wasn't going to happen, ever. They could move well though, better than he did, he told himself. Their marksmanship though had been a real surprise.

In Pro's case, he was just a natural athlete, and very coachable. He picked up everything the first time and quickly got better with practice. Rachel was motivated in the extreme. Motivated... that was the word he'd chosen to call it. Anything else it might have been called, scared him. He'd actually seen her smile as she looked through the rifle scope as they practiced in the woods, miles away from the house. He didn't need to guess at what the young woman superimposed over the paper target. Whatever or whomever it was, it didn't affect her marksmanship.

He looked over at Rachel as the four of them walked up to the paper targets he'd stapled to a tree. They were all armed, except Elsa, who was satisfied with carrying a book bag full of ammo.

"Something you need to tell us, Rachel?"

The young woman grinned as she looked at the very tight group the suppressed M-4 had left in the paper at a hundred yards. Jason knew he couldn't have done any better.

"That's not exactly a competition grade trigger, but I'll get better."

He just stared at her.

"My high school in South Africa had a rifle team. My Da thought it was a good thing to know."

Jason pulled the target sheet off the tree and looked at it closely. "I see."

"I was team captain for three years, top marksman all four years."

Ok, right then. He gave his head a shake and walked over the next tree and looked at Pro's target. It was a decent performance. Pro had sent a couple of flyers but most of his shots were on target if not nearly as tight as Rachel's.

"I played baseball," Pro said in defense.

"Your turn?" Jason looked over at Elsa. The girl's blonde hair was matted inside the rain jacket hood she was wearing and she looked back at him with squared shoulders.

"I'll stick to the revolver," she said. "I don't like the big rifles."

The girl had done well enough with the .38-wheel gun he'd trained her on. She could hardly rack the slide back on the assortment of semi-automatic handguns they had access to and he wasn't about to give her something that she couldn't operate. She had a healthy distrust of guns, and that was something he played on. He converted it to respect, all the while trying to get her comfortable with the idea of using one should she have to. That part hadn't been a problem. Like Rachel, she knew firsthand how much one could be needed.

"Ok," he said folding up the targets and slipping them in his coat pocket, they'd already policed up their brass from where they'd been shooting. Dagman had invested in some fairly expensive reloading gear and feedstock. They didn't need the brass, but he didn't want to leave the stuff laying around for someone to find either.

"Let's flip a coin, to see which one of you goes with me tonight; someone is going to stay with Elsa."

"I'm going with you," Rachel said in a tone that offered no compromise. "We aren't going to toss a bloody coin." Rachel was looking at him, daring him to contradict her.

"That's not fair," Pro complained.

"I'm going," Rachel nodded at Elsa. "If you need us both, Elsa would be all right with Loki."

"What do *you* say, Elsa?" He asked the eleven-year-old, thinking her reaction would likely result in a coin toss to make certain one of the older kids stayed home with her.

"If I get Loki and the wheel gun, sure." The girl flashed him a thumbs up. "I can take care of myself."

He mentally shook his head in disgust, at himself. What an eff'd up world these kids lived in... The fact was, he could use Rachel and Pro both, and he considered taking Elsa up on her offer. In practical terms, for one night, he didn't think that she'd be in any more danger by herself than with Pro or Rachel. Not with the house sealed up tight and Loki guarding the place. That didn't lessen the guilt he felt in considering her offer.

He had to start somewhere, and tonight offered a good opportunity to begin. He had to end the threat, or none of them were safe long term. For the briefest of moments, he wondered if long term was even a valid concept at this point. Was there anything he could do, that would prevent Elsa growing up with a gun on her hip?

He watched the three of them walk ahead of him as they made their way along Difficult Run back towards the house. Pro was way out front, alone, head on a swivel. Rachel with her arm on Elsa's shoulder. Before the virus, they'd been in America. In one of the wealthiest areas of the richest, most powerful country the world had ever known. No one had ever worried about long-term shit then, either. Now, everyone was dead.

Rachel was laying close enough to him, with her head bent to the spotting scope, that he could hear the radio transmission from Pro buzz in her ear, if not the conversation itself. It was *that* quiet as they lay in the wet ground cover, a dripping shrub over their heads. At least the rain had stopped.

"Pro says, all's clear."

"Copy," he lifted his own head from the scope of the suppressed .338 Lapua, and turned his head to look over at his 'spotter.' Rachel seemed all too eager for him to start shooting, so did Pro. A month ago, he would have put their enthusiasm in a box labeled naive inexperience. He was no longer so sure. He knew them both better now, and they both just seemed to believe, without the slightest of doubts, that anybody who was subjugating other survivors in this fallen world didn't deserve to live.

He was sure it made things simple, black and white, in their heads. In his own, he couldn't help but wonder how many people he'd have to kill to get these kids something like security. He wondered if the Sheriff in Tysons, directing his thugs, used the same justification for what he did. To hell with intentions, the practical voice in his head yelled back. The only thing that mattered in the end, was what people did.

Rachel watched the target group from her scope, set up on a small tripod. The spotting scope had an IR setting and a built-in laser range finder. He'd given Sleepy a can of IR spray paint the night this plan had come together, and told him where he'd leave more. Dagman had a case of the stuff in his larder. Rachel had designated two of the three soldiers in his sights as having a single vertical line painted on their pants, one in front, one in back. He didn't know how Sleepy, or Daniel he corrected himself, had managed to get the right pants marked with the invisible paint. At this point, he had no choice but to accept the man's target selection. Daniel and the people he could trust in Tysons were seriously outgunned by those he couldn't. As his right hand took up the weight of the rifle's stock, he knew he was moments away from adjusting that score.

He tracked the group standing around the panel truck as a half dozen, unarmed 'civilians,' slaves, he corrected himself, carried box after box of medical supplies from the Emergency Aid clinic to the back of the truck. The radio message they'd intercepted the day before had led them to believe that the Reston Hospital had been the target. They'd had to hustle from where they'd already sat up there, to a position half a mile north. Their new 'hide' lay across Baron Cameron Ave from the emergency clinic, under a line of shrubs that separated the parking lot of a tile store from a Wendy's.

Memories were painful, some more so than others. It had taken him a few minutes to get the picture of a Wendy's double with bacon out of his head. Pro was a quarter of a mile away, to the east, hiding in the Home Depot parking lot where he could see down Reston Parkway and Baron Cameron. Either of those two roads would be used by the soldiers to drive out of here, or to bring reinforcements.

"Why are you waiting?"

Rachel's voice was a whisper as he opened his eyes. They had time and he wasn't going to go scope blind staring through one for an hour straight. That's why he had a spotter.

"There still there," he waffled his left hand back and forth. "It'll be dark in twenty minutes. Dark is always good for us, bad for them."

"What if they leave before then?"

"Then the wait will be over." He checked his sight picture through his Swarovski scope, as always, thankful for Howard Dagman's penchant for quality toys. The one guard in the group below *without* the IR paint was much taller and thinner than the other two. It made keeping him alive that much easier.

Rachel accepted that in silence. The girl wanted some payback, and he couldn't blame her.

"What does a .338 kick like?"

He knew where she was going with this. "Like an angry horse," he grinned. "Two hundred fifty grain bullet, just a hair under three thousand feet per second. And, no Rachel, not this time. You watch through the spotting scope, because those aren't paper targets." He pointed down range with his whole hand next to the trigger assembly.

"I know that," she hissed.

"I know you do. I just don't think you understand what that means. Both of those targets probably had families at some point, before... They may have new ones now, somebody might care about them, or they may care for somebody... or not. They could be irredeemable rapist assholes. Point is, we don't know, and never will. One thing *is* certain; once you pull the trigger, you end any future they might have had. No chance at redemption, no forgiveness, nothing."

She brushed her hair out of her eyes. "Yeah, I don't have a problem with that."

God help her, he thought. He absolutely believed her.

"Confirm the range," he leaned back into his scope, careful of body creep. Lying in wait, over time, his body would invariably get closer to the target, and his eye that much closer to the back ring of the scope. He'd seen more than one experienced soldier take a recoil in the eye socket. It usually resulted in a nasty cut, but he'd seen one guy who had shattered a cheek bone and nearly lost an eye.

"Five hundred forty yards, no wind."

"Copy, five four zero yards, no wind," he intoned. "Send ready, to Pro."

He waited as she pushed the pulse button on her radio three times in slow succession. Pro pulsed back once.

"He's ready," she said next to him.

"Gun's hot," he intoned, as he placed the scope's bullseye on the center of the chest of the gun thug facing him. No wind, and the target stood there talking to the man next to him; the skinny one without any IR paint marking his clothes, the one that would live. It was a shot he could make in his sleep, especially with this rig. The ammo calibrated scope had already compensated for the nearly 43 inches of bullet drop at this range. He took up the trigger on the pad of his finger and gently started applying pressure between breaths. The gun hammered back in to him and he jacked another round in, noting how far the bolt had to carry to eject the massive shell casing.

"Target down," Rachel breathed next to him. "Other side of the truck, second target looking around, not moving."

He acquired the target quickly, the man was just starting to move away from him, towards the back of the truck that hid the clinic's entrance from view. He sighted in slowly; the worst thing to do would be to rush the shot. It wasn't about what the target was doing, this was him and a tool that a short time ago he'd never have thought he'd pick up again.

This shot, he managed to follow in, and watched through the rocking sight picture as the bullet impacted between the man's shoulder blades, high up at the base of the neck. It almost decapitated the target, as his body was driven forward out of the parking lot, up on to the sidewalk where he landed like a broken marionette puppet that had its strings cut.

"Target down," Rachel whispered.

He looked over at her and felt a sense of relief on her behalf. Even in the dim light, her face seemed to have lost a little color.

He went back to the scope and saw the one remaining soldier had dove behind the truck and was out of sight. The workers had all managed to disappear into the building, or were hiding in the back of the truck unseen.

"Your turn," he whispered and rolled away from the gun. "Put one through the front of the truck's grill, engine block."

He accepted the spotting scope from her after rolling aside. She wriggled over the stock of the gun, reset its bipod and lay in behind it. She racked in another round, and settled in behind the scope. He was happy to see the proper distance between her eye socket and the scopes rear rings.

"Send it."

Rachel fired and he saw the impact point a half inch from the Ford plate in the middle of the panel truck's grill.

"That's a hit," he smiled. The young woman could shoot. "Were you aiming for the Ford plaque?"

"Yeah," Rachel grunted. "You weren't messing about, regarding the kick."

"Nope," he smiled. "I had an instructor that referred to it as sensory feedback. Next time, don't aim for an extra piece of metal the bullet has to go through to get to its target."

"Aaahhh, right... that makes sense."

"Ok," he said watching through the scope, "still hunkered down. They are probably on the radio calling it in, let's go."

He intentionally left the brass behind for someone to find, if they cared to look for it. He didn't want them to doubt the word of the survivors, not that the grizzly remains of his targets would have allowed much room for doubt.

They retreated off the formerly landscaped shoulder at the edge of the retail area they'd set up in, and moved at a fast jog, past a looted and burned out Trader Joe's and further into a residential area. Pro would already be on his way. They had three miles to go to where they'd hidden the Land Cruiser.

"Next time," Rachel looked up at him. "Can I shoot?"

"You still want to?"

She nodded her head firmly. "I see what you mean, but yeah, I'm sure."

"We'll see," he agreed, sort of. In his mind, it was a firm 'No.'

"They'll get smarter as they start losing people, then we'll have to change up tactics."

"Why didn't we wait for their help to arrive, and hit them too?"

"We're not ready for that." He knew that was a whole different ball of wax. Shooting the tiger was one thing, getting into in a cage with one was something different and not something he wanted to do. With or without Rachel and Pro along.

"When will we be ready?" Rachel's measured English accent would have sounded reasonable if he didn't know the intent behind it.

Hopefully never. "We'll see."

"I'm not a child, Jason," she said. "Not any more. I've got as much right to set things straight as you do! Or that Sleepy character. What the hell kind of name is that anyway?" What was it about a refined English accent that mutated 'pissed off' to something sounding more reasonable?

"His name is Daniel," he answered. "And it's not about you having the right to do what you want. It's me, Rachel. I am not going to be responsible for getting you and Elsa killed, or Pro for that matter. I didn't help you just to throw you into a meat grinder."

Her laughter startled him. "You think you're some bloody knight errant? We're the damsels in distress?"

"For fuck sake, Jason," she swung him to a stop by the arm. "We watched everyone we cared about die. At least those we had around us. Elsa's dad was on a business trip, like Pro's father, I gather. My mum was back in merry old England, died along with my older sister and all the rest. No bloody English determination, just bloody dead people, like here. We didn't even get to say goodbye as our world died.

273

You don't get to put your bullshit, macho chivalry on us. You!... You, don't get to decide that for us."

"No, I don't." He agreed with her to a point. "But you don't have the right to ask me to do something that I know is just wrong."

She smiled at him. "I'm sorry for you, Jason, I am. Because whether or not we have the right to do it, we're still asking..." The girl started to walk again and then stopped just as suddenly and turned back to him. "And if I don't get the answer I want, I'll do it on my bloody own. Pro will too, and you bloody know it. He had it right; this is the only life we have left. We have to make it better."

He was a little stunned by the outburst. Rachel had clearly given voice to thoughts she'd had for some time.

"You got quite the mouth on you, don't you?" He choked back a laugh. He had to laugh. If he didn't, he'd be yelling too.

"I'm serious," she stamped her foot, her voice cracking. "Train us to do this right or one morning we'll be gone, and your errant knight bullshit can go back to eating that shite you called bread."

"Oh, so now it's threats." He tried to smile; it was all he could do against the sick feeling in his gut that he no longer had a choice in this.

She started walking ahead of him, angry, mumbling something unintelligible to herself just ahead of him.

"What's a knight errant anyway? I never understood that term."

Rachel slowed a little until he caught up with her. She brushed the hair out of her eyes, and shrugged.

"He's a decent guy, with a good heart. Just stuck in a world that doesn't exist anymore."

He rolled his eyes at her. "Let's get back to the beast, come on."

"I heard the 'yes,' in there," she mumbled loud enough that he was meant to hear it.

They walked in silence for almost an hour before they spotted Pro waiting for them in the front lawn of a daycare, a block away from the Land Cruiser. He'd radioed ahead to let them know where he was. He fell in with them, all smiles until they reached the vehicle. He jumped into the back seat and leaned forward until his head stuck between them.

"Hey, how come we didn't hang around and ambush the relief squad too?"

It was all Jason could do not to explode in the kid's face. Rachel sat there cradling her backpack, her dark eyebrows arched in a "*yeah, how come?*" look.

"Put your seat belts on," he said managed between teeth that could barely open. "Both of you."   *

Chapter 17

Son of a bitch, Bauman thought, as he looked at the LCD screen on the back of the camera. It was hard to see the photos in the daylight outside the mall, but he could make out enough details to know what he was looking at. He'd wanted to talk to Sleepy before he got inside amongst the others, so he'd been waiting for them on the top level of the parking garage ever since Sleepy had radioed in. The pictures were of his latest dead soldier, just one this time, thankfully. Sleepy had recorded the scene well enough that it brought back memories of crime scenes he'd investigated.

Sleepy had handed the camera over to him with a hangdog look. He'd known what it was going to show. Same as the previous seven dead soldiers they'd lost over the last ten days. Somebody was hunting them with a big ass gun. Big enough that he told Sleepy and Wayne to quit bringing the bodies back. He had morale issues enough without dead bodies pouring out of body bags in the parking lot of the mall.

"Found this," Sleepy dug a brass shell out his pocket and handed it over.

He struggled to read the stamped caliber on the base of shell.

"Christ, .338 Lapua." One of the guys on the Fairfax County SWAT team had been a Marine sniper. The asshole had always been going on about how he was better with his .308 than some of the SOF guys were with their .338 Lapuas or .50 calibers. They'd all gotten tired of the endless debate, it was all a big piece of lead moving really fast.

"How far away?"

Sleepy shook his head, grimacing.

"How far, Sleepy?"

"A little shy of 700 hundred yards."

"It's him, it's got to be." That black suited bastard was back. He'd suspected it after the shooting at the clinic in Reston almost two weeks ago. Seven hundred yards! It had to be him. "You were there, you see anything?"

"Nothing," Sleepy shook his head at him. "We had two teams of sheep loading from that restaurant distributor warehouse. Two trucks full by the time the shot came. We had six shooters there and he fired just once. Just as it was getting dark, we were about to pull out."

"How'd he get there? I thought we were staying off the radios?"

"We are," Sleepy shook his head. "Far as I know, we never said a damn thing about the location to anyone. When we had to call for another truck, we met it three miles away and escorted it to the warehouse."

Bauman remembered that, he'd heard that communication himself from the radio in his office. So, he had to have been in the area already... he said as much to Sleepy.

"That would make three distinct areas, he just happened to be in when we were there." Sleepy seemed as suspicious as he felt.

"You thinking there's more than one?" Shit... this just gets better and better.

"Maybe," Sleepy scratched his chin, "but I don't think so. He, or maybe it is they, had us dead to rights." Sleepy pointed at the camera; "McKee was standing in a group. Hell, I was right next to him. From where he shot, we had no cover, none. If that shot wasn't a fluke, why not take out more of us when he could have. It's like he's maybe worried about getting away after. It would make sense if he's a loner. Doesn't want a stand-up fight."

"Possibly," he admitted. As much shit as he gave Sleepy for being too soft, the man was no dummy. In fact, this wasn't the first time he'd thought Sleepy would have made a great cop; back in the day when it was laws that needed enforcing rather than authority.

"Why don't we set an ambush?" Sleepy asked after a moment. "We could get a bunch of men out early, set up in a wide net – a big ass circle. Maybe a whole day before, then we schedule a pick up somewhere inside that ring. The usual forage crew and their guards. Nothing on the radio until then, all planned back here."

He liked the idea immediately, anything to get the guy reacting to them. He could tell Sleepy had been thinking about it awhile. "I like it, where?"

Sleepy held up a hand. "Not me, Boss. You decide the where and when. Throw a dart at the map on the wall in the dispatch office for all it matters. If he does show up, maybe we can figure out what direction he's coming from."

"How you figure?"

"Look, I'm no soldier," Sleepy shook his head and grimaced. "As you and everyone else keeps telling me. I just think if we have a net set up," Sleepy drew an imaginary circle around where he stood, "say he's moving to the bait we set up in the middle, wherever at the circle's edge he's spotted, logic says he's coming from that direction. At least if our net is far enough out, right?"

"Maybe," he was picturing a wagon train circle in his head. "The wider our circle, the thinner it is. We'd have to put out damn near everybody."

"I know, I know," Sleepy shrugged back at him, holding up his hands. "It's just an idea, but it's all I've thought of as way to maybe get ahead of him."

"Have to be some place logical, something that needs a couple of days to clean out," he was thinking out loud. "Who's to say the asshole shows up on the first day."

"Sounds about right," Sleepy said turning away from him as the two Humvees transporting the rest of his team arrived.

Bauman could tell there were a bunch of the guards emptying out of the vehicles that his deputy didn't like or trust. Welcome to my world, Sleepy. He didn't trust any of them. *Not even you, Sleepy.*

"Where do you plan to be, Sleepy? Part of the bait or the net?" His deputy seemed particularly proactive all of a sudden and he mistrusted change. Maybe Sleepy was finally stepping up the way he needed him to, maybe he was being played.

"You decide," Sleepy just shrugged and stared back at him.

"Why?"

Sleepy grinned a little. "Because of the way you're looking at me right now. You need to know there's somebody you can trust."

He couldn't help but laugh. He could do without Sleepy's amateur psychology bullshit, but that didn't mean he was wrong. "Sleepy, if I can't trust you? We're truly fucked."

Sleepy nodded firmly. "One more thing, Boss; Reed went missing while we were combing the area."

"Reed?" He didn't know the man. "One of the new guys?"

Sleepy nodded, "It's not what you think. He was behind us, he's not a runner. I found the cap he was wearing," he handed over the black watch cap. "There's blood on it. I think he might have been grabbed up."

Bauman glanced at the rest of Sleepy's team that was still unloading.

"How many people know?" Some of the guys, mostly Wayne's crew, were already rumbling that it was getting too dangerous out there. They'd rather stay back, drink and get laid than work. He couldn't give in to that and maintain control, any more than he could give in to Sleepy and solve the Wayne problem once and for all. He needed the guns. The camera he held proved that.

"Nobody, yet." Sleepy shook his head. "I found the hat where I'd sent him to check behind the strip mall." Sleepy nodded back towards the Humvees, "I told the guys we rolled out with that he pissed me off, and I was leaving him overnight... see if anyone came back around. That won't hold when we don't bring him back."

"We need to end this guy," he muttered, "I don't care if we lose a dozen guys doing it, this shit has got to end."

"I know, boss. He's just chipping away at us."

"What can this Reed tell him? Was he worth a shit? Or just another mouth to feed."

"That's where it hurts, he doesn't know any more than anybody else, but he was definitely one of the better guns, at least among the new guys. Some sort of Navy construction guy from before. He was one of the two that walked into the mall during the big snow storm."

Christ his head hurt, if he wasn't careful, he was going to stroke out. It was just one shit sandwich after another. "New guy, so he's been standing guard duty, right? He'd know about the observation posts, the patrol routes?"

Sleepy shook his head, "No on the new observation posts, he wasn't scheduled for that until next week. He's done the roving patrols a couple of times."

"Switch the routes up." He took a step away and rounded back on Sleepy, "Today."

"Will do, Boss."

God, he needed to hit something.

*

"What did Sleepy tell you?" Jason stood over their 'abductee'. They were in the basement of a townhouse that reeked of the two dead bodies on the top floor. For the first time, they'd acted in the middle of the day. If the Sheriff flipped his lid and sent men back out to look for them before nightfall, they would need every advantage he could think of. The overpowering stench of the bodies in the townhouse might keep them away.

"He just walked me out to a spot and pointed to the back of the mall and said to check out the area, and that if I was unhappy, it was my chance to get out."

"That it?"

"I swear," the man nodded. "I thought it was some sort of test or something. I figured he'd shoot me if I tried to run."

"Why'd Sleepy send *you*?"

"Send me?" The man looked genuinely confused, but Pro had whacked him a lot harder than he'd needed to. He'd been somewhat surprised the man was conscious when he'd gotten to him.

Jason took a knee and moved the man's head to the side; there was a hell of a bump on the back of the man's head, and a shallow cut in the middle of it. The man struggled a little with his wrists that were still tied.

281

"Relax, we aren't going to hurt you."

The black man, maybe mid to late twenties, looked up at him with a very dubious look in his eyes. Pro had swung the Maglite flashlight like a one-handed Louisville slugger.

"I mean, again. Sorry about your head."

"Who are you people?" The man struggled against his tied wrists, that were lashed to another zip tie daisy chain that ended in a loop around his ankles.

"Sleepy said you weren't in agreement with what's going down at the Ritz. He isn't either, neither are we. The question is; are you willing to do something about it?"

"Sleepy said?" Their prisoner just glared at him a moment before shaking his head. "Mister, Sleepy is the Sheriff's bitch. Try again."

Jason stood back up and went to his pack and dug around for an instant ice pack. He broke the inner bag, shook it up and tossed it at their prisoner. He slid down until he was seated against the opposite wall. Pro came down the stairs wearing a bandana around his face, laced with some perfume that Rachel had found.

"Still all clear, they don't look to be coming back." He watched as Pro glanced over at the man he'd clubbed. Their prisoner was staring daggers at the kid.

"Ok, go hunker down with your partner. Stay off the radio unless you don't have a choice. We'll wait for dark."

"That's the guy that whacked me? Isn't it?" The man asked, after Pro retreated up the stairs and they heard the back door open and close. Jason watched as their prisoner, struggled to get the ice pack to his head with his hands tied.

He sighed, got up and placed the ice pack between the man's head and the wall.

"He's just a kid, got a little carried away. Don't blame him, I told him to."

"Oh, I guess that make it better then. Who are you people?"

"Who are you? Reed Chase?" Jason did his best not to smile at the man's reaction to his own name.

"Look, Sleepy passed a message that he'd be sending us somebody that might be willing to help. That was you. He wasn't testing your loyalty; he was giving you an out."

The man just looked back at him.

"How many men have you guys lost over the last two weeks? Starting with the two at the med clinic in Reston?"

"What do you know about that?"

"How many?"

"Seven, I think," the man nodded. "That was you?"

"It was us. In fact, you were standing right next to that poor asshole we serviced last night."

The man, Reed, he corrected himself, shook his head and may have smiled a little. "He wasn't no poor asshole; he was just an asshole."

"So I gathered," Jason smiled. He looked at the man a little more closely, he looked a little pale, gray around the forehead. "You nauseous? If you have a concussion, we need to get you laying down. You thirsty?"

"Hell yes, I'm nauseous!" the man yelled. "Don't tell me you can't smell the easy outs upstairs."

"Easy outs?"

"They don't have to live through this shit, do they?"

Jason couldn't help but smile. He liked the name. It somehow seemed more respectful than the other names they used; 'stiffs,' 'deaders,' and lately as time had passed and it was getting warmer, Pro had taken to referring to the dead as 'puddles'.

"Sleepy gave me your name, Reed. He said you'd walked into the mall with a guy named Kirby, who was killed up on Glebe about a month ago. I know you aren't part of whatever Bauman's got going."

"Like I said, Mister. Sleepy works for Bauman."

"How many of the seven guys we've serviced in the last two weeks are part of Wayne's little gang?" Jason could tell the question threw him.

The man's head came up a little after a moment. "Sleepy's taking out his competition?"

"Sort of," Jason explained waggling a hand back and forth. "He's dead set against the Sheriff. But think about what would happen if Sleepy took Bauman out."

The man nodded once, real slow. "Sleepy wouldn't last the day. Wayne and his boys would go full party mode."

Jason nodded in agreement. "Which is why we've been thinning out Wayne's book club."

"And me?"

"You have a choice. You can run for real... I won't stop you. Or, you can stick with us and help free the four hundred slaves they've got under their guns."

Reed smiled and shook his head. "You think the black guy's going to help you, 'cause you called them slaves?"

Jason just grinned and nodded. "If I thought it would help, I'd try anything." He drew his knife and cut the zip ties around the man's ankles. He held the knife up between them where he kneeled.

"I don't give a rat's ass what color you are, but I could really use some help here. So could Bauman's sheep. That's what he calls 'em, isn't it?"

He cut the man's wrist ties and backed away re-sheathing his knife. "It'll be dark in an hour and we're out of here. If you want, I'll leave you that bag, a gun, and you can run."

Jason went back to his spot against the wall and sank back down with a slide against the wall watching the wheels turn in Reed's eyes.

"You'd let me just walk out of here?"

"After we're gone, yeah."

He watched as Reed adjusted the ice pack and stretched out on the floor. Within a few minutes, he thought the man was asleep. At the moment, sleep was quickly moving up on his own personal 'to do' list.

"You ain't going to be able to snipe all of 'em. You going to run when they start shooting back?"

Good question, Jason thought. If it was just him, he would have answered with a firm no. What was he going to do with Pro and the girls if the fight went bad? He wondered if they'd give him a choice in the matter, especially Pro. Rachel was angry at the world, a little like him, he had to admit. Pro was focused on ending the Sheriff and his soldiers. He'd heard from Pro how bad it was for the civilians at the Ritz. He might have tough time imagining how people could treat each other that way, Pro had lived it.

"They've been shooting at me for a while now, I'm still here."

Reed just grunted, and then rolled up on elbow. "You're the ninja they whisper about?"

"I didn't pick that name."

"What did you do in the military? I'm guessing sniper from the bodies of late, and you said 'serviced the targets,' that's sniper talk."

"Army," Jason replied. "Two tours, one in Iraq early on, last one was in Afghanistan." Sleepy had told him that Reed had served in the Navy.

"Navy Seabee," Reed said. "I helped build some firebases in Afghanistan, or re-build actually, I wasn't there for the fighting. We were at Norfolk, getting ready to ship out to Djibouti when everyone started getting sick. Maybe if we'd left port a few days earlier we'd be safe at sea. Probably be starving to death by now."

"You'd still be alive." Jason recalled what Sam had said about the incubation period. "You're immune. You might be starving, marooned at sea, surrounded by your easy outs. But you'd be alive if something else didn't get you. Being at sea wouldn't have saved your shipmates. People were carrying the virus a long time before they got sick. Ships at sea probably didn't fare any better, unless they never made a port call, or took on new personnel, supplies or mail. I remember seeing that on the news before everything went dark. Maybe some subs survived, but sooner or later they have to eat and make port."

Reed snorted to himself. "Navy didn't do shit. Told us it was a bad flu strain. Delayed our departure for a couple of days. By then, people were dropping like flies. I picked up a rifle from a guard shack and started walking north. Ran into Kirby outside of Williamsburg and came up 95. We managed to stay alive until we made the mistake of checking out the mall. We just wanted new boots..."

"How'd that work out for you?"

Reed glared back at him for a moment before giving his head a slow shake. "It's truly fucked up in there. The Sheriff's got some bad wiring, but he's not as bad as some of the others."

"I've heard," he answered and pointed at the staircase Pro had come down. "The kid that got the drop on you used to be an unwilling guest. One of Bauman's sheep."

"I guess that explains why my head hurts..."

"You going to be all right?"

"Long as I don't move my head, yeah."

"Wait a minute!... this kid? He the one that offed the pedophile in his hotel room?"

"Yep."

Reed chuckled to himself and stopped immediately. Jason saw the pain flash across his face. "That went down before we got there. The kid's a very quiet legend among the sheep. The one that killed a wolf, and got away – know what I mean? And you, you're the freaking boogeyman. Sheriff'll kill anybody he hears talking about the ninja. What could go wrong?"

"You'll help?"

"I'm no soldier," Reed shook his head. "Last job I had in the Navy was pulling Cat-5 cable through an old building on Fort Eustis."

"You're a step up from what I've got now. One teenage boy, and one recent college graduate, a woman. She'd just earned her BS in economics and probably has PTSD."

"Tell me you're joking?"

"She was behind the rifle last night."

"That's messed up."

Jason nodded in agreement. It was indeed. He wondered for the hundredth time; was he protecting them, or enabling them?

Reed was quiet again for few minutes. "I'll help," he said. "The people at the Ritz? They're slaves all right, and they know it. You can see it in their faces."

287

"Ok, then. And thank you." Jason closed his eyes briefly and said a prayer of thanks. He couldn't do this by himself. He pulled himself upright, thinking on how much he was looking forward to getting a good night's sleep. He glanced out the small basement window that showed the last glow of twilight as he repacked his small bag.

He walked over to Reed with the intention of helping the man up, but he was out cold, breathing regularly.

He nudged the man's leg with his boot. Nothing. He slapped Reed's face and held a finger against his neck, checking for a pulse. It was there, strong and steady and he seemed to be breathing deeply. In fact, he was starting to snore. A concussion... Dammit. He finally got some help, and they damn near kill him. He was getting tired of putting people back together.

*

Chapter 18

They were wrapping up the second day in downtown Oakton, five miles west of Tysons. Daniel didn't know whether to feel worried or relieved that Jason had yet to make a showing. The run-down, neighborhood strip mall was a genuine find; two small ethnic grocery stores, one Indian and one Korean, had somehow escaped the worst of the looting. A big chain drugstore, next door hadn't been as fortunate, but it still held a lot more than most of its kind did by this time. The hardware store and used book store sharing the common parking lot both held enough loot bait to make the trip worthwhile. They'd been there almost two full days sorting through the leftovers and loading trucks. Jason was almost out of time.

The two full foraging teams were down to loading up their fifth truck load of the day and they were nearing completion. Some were excited at the prospect of some ethnic food; others were pleased to be getting some new reading material.

Michelle was genuinely looking forward to cooking up some of the food they'd found. She spent a lot of her time cooking for everyone at the Ritz, guards and sheep alike. She was as tired of preparing the same stuff as he imagined they all were of eating the same staples every day. The fact that Michelle was here now, among the foragers, was the reason behind his relief that Jason hadn't shown up to spoil the trap he and Bauman had organized.

That the plan had been Jason's to begin with, didn't help. Michelle was oblivious to all of it, she wasn't even supposed to be there. Her inclusion had been Bauman's idea and it had come at the last minute before they had rolled out. He supposed it was the Sheriff's way of twisting the knife a little, just to let him know that he still wasn't totally trusted.

He watched as Michelle labeled a box coming out of the Deccan Deli-Mart. For the thousandth time in the last 48 hours he wished she wasn't here. He hadn't had a choice about that, any more than he'd 'decided' to be part of the bait rather than the nearly sixty plus guards encircling the strip mall throughout the residential area at a distance averaging a mile or more.

In fact, there were only twenty or so guards left back at the Ritz. If he'd been thinking better, he'd have directed Jason to the hotel, while they were all focused on killing him here. But he'd left his message, thrown out of a Humvee on a rolling patrol, the night after Bauman had let on where they were going to set up. Jason either got it, or he didn't. If he didn't show tonight, he had no doubt Bauman would try this set up again. The Sheriff had ended up buying into the plan with a gusto, and added some wrinkles of his own that he didn't like.

He only had to look at Michelle, and the dozen or so other 'sheep' carrying empty rifles, dressed out in reclaimed BDUs around the parking lot to recognize once again, that Bauman might be crazy, but he was still capable of rational thought. In fact, of all the guns in the parking lot, only four, including his, had ammunition. The other three truly armed guards in the lot were marked with the IR paint, but odds were, so were some of the sheep. Bauman had just raided the laundry and handed out the gear. For all he knew, Michelle was wearing a giant X on her back.

He still had the hollow feeling in his gut that had hit him hard with Bauman's curveball. "You're going to be bait, Sleepy. I need eyes on, and you can coordinate with the security cordon, and help me vector them in." Bauman had smiled that way he did when he thought he being particularly devious, "And your lady is going to be right there in the middle of it with you."

Well she was here, all right. Happy as hell to be outside the mall and clueless as to the risk she was running gathering groceries. He hadn't told her anything beyond what he had to, namely to get Ginny in the hotel's laundry room to help out. Ginny had had a rough time at the mall, especially after her man had been the one that had fallen asleep on guard duty. The same one Bauman had beat to death in the middle of the dining room. Ginny wouldn't talk.

"That's about it, boss man."

Earl's voice snapped him out of his funk.

"Right," he caught himself. Earl was nominally one of Wayne's guys, but not by natural disposition. Earl was a world class ass-kisser. He'd just happened to get assigned to Wayne early on.

"Grab some hands, and do one more check of the pharmacy," he said. "Make sure everyone has that list, antibiotics and pain killers. There's a shit load of stuff still on the floor in there, looters always miss shit we can use."

"Close to the witching hour, man." He doubted Earl had brushed his teeth since the Suck. The man's breath smelled like death itself. Earl's nervousness was justified. He'd been standing next to Cliff Jackson when the former real estate agent had taken a round to the head while the two of them were gassing up a Hummer on the back lot of the car dealership adjacent to the mall. Like all the other sniper attacks, it had come as it was getting dark.

"Better get started then."

"Ah-yup," Earl said nodding, with his hands on his hips. Sleepy was about to yell, but the man started off towards the drugstore shaking his head.

Sleepy toggled his radio. "We're about wrapped here, stay sharp."

A booming echo of a gun shot rang out of the distance, bouncing around between the buildings. His eyes went to Michelle, half expecting to her be laying on the ground bleeding but she was there kneeling at a box looking at him. It took him a moment to realize the shot had come from a long way off, to the south. In his mind's eye, he pictured Jason well to the south of his southern lookouts, outside the net, shooting in at the edges. Somewhere out there in that endless sea of residential neighborhoods, schools, parks and business centers.

"Anybody hit? Report in, people." He knew Bauman would be listening in from his office at the Ritz.

He waited for either an answer or another shot. Finally, his radio crackled.

"Say again," he spoke loud and clear, the same way Bauman had trained them all to.

"This is Vincent, at Parklawn and Dewey. Dallas is down, I repeat, they killed Dallas."

"Can you tell from which direction it came?"

"South of me, from the loo..."

Another shot echoed and rolled across the Vienna suburbs, cutting off Vincent's report. Same as before, from way off to the south.

"Vincent, come back!" He took a tone assuming the worst. It was theater, neither Vincent nor Dallas would be missed by anyone other than Wayne.

He pulled out the map that indicated where everyone was set up.

"Team four and six, proceed south on Vine and DeGallo respectively, do not move towards team five, proceed outward. Let me know you understand and are moving."

Silence greeted him...

"Get moving!" Bauman's voice cut in loudly over the radio. The transmitter back at the hotel had a lot more power than the handhelds. "Or don't bother coming back!"

"Team four, moving south on Vine."

"Yeah, we are on DeGallo, going south."

"Who is this? Stay in contact, update!" Sleepy shouted back, he knew who it was with a just a glance at his map. Martins, to hear him tell it, had been some big shot finance guy back when money mattered. He didn't like taking orders from anyone.

"Team six, on DeGallo."

He was more than a little surprised at Bauman cutting in. He knew the man would be looking at the big map in his office, moving pins around like he was some general in an old war movie. He was also surprised by the "or don't come back." Comments like that were dangerous when he knew there were a bunch of people out there who just might take this opportunity to run. Bauman had created the two and three-man teams himself, always a mixture of new guys and Wayne's people mixed together. It was a futile attempt at creating some esprit de corps among the men and away from the cult of personality that Wayne had built around himself. Sleepy knew that was impossible, the whole place was held together at the moment by Bauman's own paranoia and threats.

Sleepy checked his map again, "team three, get in your vehicle, proceed down Lake to Rt. 50, set up on 50 and Walney. Advise when you are there."

"Team three moving."

Sleepy waited for another shot. Jason had clearly spotted the outer net like he hoped the man would, of course he'd known about it in advance. Five minutes later there was still nothing.

*

"Ok, now it's our turn." Jason said, looking back across his rifle scope at Reed. "You up for this?"

Reed didn't need the blacked-out face from a burned cork that Jason had applied to his own face. Even without the face paint, fully kitted out, Reed looked like a soldier in the quickly fading light. Of course, compared to an angry, smart-assed, hormonal teenage boy, and a young woman suffering from what he was almost certain was PTSD, his bar for a brother-in-arms was decidedly low at the moment.

Rachel and Pro were almost four miles southeast of them, and they'd started the ball rolling. Daniel's guys were reacting pretty close to what they should be doing, at least the ones he'd directed by radio were. He and Reed had approached the security cordon from due west, and the duo they were watching through scopes were visibly relieved the action was elsewhere.

For two hours they'd watched them in silence, and now Jason had to use his night vision goggles to see them clearly outside his scope. One thing about the collapse of civilization, night and darkness were again synonymous. The targets were sitting in an old GMC pickup, curbside in a residential area. Both had been slid down in their seats, sitting up just high enough to see over the dash. Now though, with the action miles away they were more relaxed, sitting up higher. Jason could imagine the radio sitting on the seat between them as they listened in on the action as if it were a ball game in a different city. They had no idea they were up to bat.

"That's Griff behind the wheel, Griffin or Griffiths." Reed was looking through his scope. "I'm sure of it. None too bright, but he's a decent guy. The other guy is Jordan Davis, big SOB, likes to hurt people."

Jason's sight picture drifted from one to the other, Davis *was* big. The silhouette of his shoulders stretched half way across cab of the old pickup.

"You think this Griff would come with us? He have anybody waiting for him, back at the Ritz?"

"Don't know," Reed shrugged his shoulders in the darkness. "We didn't exactly sit around the lounge at night spilling our guts, you know."

Jason nodded. "Range?" He liked Reed. Against his better judgment, he'd taken the 'new guy' back to the house. He'd planned on dropping him elsewhere with supplies until he had a better feeling for him. As it was, they were lucky to have gotten him to a bed. The man had slept for nearly 36 hours and been delirious and nauseous for the next couple of days, as they all took turns looking after him. It was now a week later, and he couldn't help but notice the huge hug that Elsa had given the man when they'd left in the predawn darkness. Between the young girl and Loki having both given their stamp of approval, who was he to worry at this point.

"Three hundred twenty-one yards to the front of their truck. This thing works just like a surveyor's scope. Laser's a laser I suppose."

"Ok, when I turn Mr. Likes to Hurt People inside out, unless this Griff's an idiot, he's going to kiss the floorboard and get behind the engine block."

"What if he runs?"

"Then he's stupid, and we can't use him." Jason looked over at Reed who was glaring at him. "I won't shoot him."

The relief on Reed's face was evident. Jason took that as another coin on the right side of Reed's scale.

Jason settled back against the stock of his gun, noting the ebb and flow of his breathing. They'd been stationary for most of the day; at this point his breathing was almost tidal, no sharp peaks or valleys, a perfect shallow wave form. He knew the bullet would tumble as it blew through the glass wind shield. It wouldn't matter.

The recoil surprised him as it was supposed to. The bullet had already arrived by the time he regained his sight picture. The lack of visible light in the cab of the pickup was decidedly less than it had been. His target's torso had fairly exploded from the hydrostatic pressure and painted the inside of the truck.

"God forgive us," he heard Reed whisper next to him. He hadn't realized Reed was a religious sort, but then again, he hadn't been one for sitting around the kitchen table spilling his guts either since Sam died. For his own part, he had to believe God would understand that he was trying to help people. Sam understood, she told him so nearly every night.

"Amen," he replied, looking for a sign of movement in the cab. He didn't see any. The expected radio call broke in seconds later.

"Where was that, team ten through fifteen count off in order."

Jason had to give Sleepy credit; the man was selling it well.

They listened in on the reports coming back.

"Team ten, all clear, shot from our northwest."

"Eleven here, couldn't tell."

"Twelve, all clear, North of us I think."

"Thirteen here, shit... think it may have been fourteen."

There was a pause of at least ten seconds. "I guess they were fourteen," Reed dead-panned.

"Fourteen report in," Sleepy's voice shouted.

"This is fifteen, shot to our left and forward, definitely fourteen."

"Let's go," Jason settled the butt of his rifle on the ground and came up on his knees. Reed was already out from under the tarp hanging off a dead somebody's wood pile that they'd been hiding under, and two steps ahead of him.

"Teams fifteen and thirteen proceed forward, on your current facing, four blocks and hook in, fifteen to the left, thirteen to the right. Stay in contact, and count off the blocks."

Jason half listened to Sleepy's orders as he ran. The guy may have been a teacher, in the before, but he seemed to have his shit together. He got his M4 QBR slung back around off his back about the time he came up on Reed who was approaching the truck with his handgun out.

"Griff, you ok?" Reed yelled.

"Uhhh... somebody...uhhhh! Blew up Jordan!" The vehicle's occupant was screaming.

"You're ok, Griff. I'm going to get you out."

"Out! Get me outta here!"

Jason looked up and down the street as Reed pulled open the truck's door to a flood of body fluids that Reed managed to jump back from and avoid. He heard Reed retch and maintained cover as his comrade pulled Griff off the floor board and stood him up, leaning back against the bed of the truck.

"Reed...? You're dead. Oh my God, I'm dead! I knew it!!"

Reed slapped the man hard enough to get him to stop blubbering, "Shut up and listen," Reed yelled. "I'm going get you away from all this."

"I just want to go away..." the man mumbled, he was delirious, even at a glance Jason could tell the man's eyes were having trouble seeing Reed. Understandable, Griff was maybe five foot seven or so, a hundred fifty pounds soaking wet, and he was wet. The man looked to have been dipped in a vat of chunky tomato soup ala Jordan. Griff was still wearing chunks of his former seatmate.

"This way," Reed said and began to lead him back towards their hide.

"Stop! Get him out of his clothes, he's just going to leave a trail." Jason flicked open his knife and handed it to Reed. "Cut 'em off, hurry. We gotta go."

"Seriously?"

"Or I shoot him, you decide," Jason was listening to the two closing teams count off their blocks. Team fifteen, coming up on their right side, seemed a little too motivated for his taste.

"Going left on Glen Allen," he heard the team report. Jason looked down the road, back towards the hide they'd shot from. He'd noted the last road they'd run past, Glen Allen Ave.

"Reed, get him back to the house where we stashed our packs. Hole up there. Keep him quiet and do not leave that basement. I'll get back to you."

He was backpedaling as he finished speaking, Reed just looked at him with his mouth hanging open. He crossed the road into the lawns on the other side of the street and sprinted for the corner house at Glen Allen Ave. Hugging the edge of the house, he turned right and sprinted across the lawn to the next house.

"Report, goddammit!"

It was Bauman's voice blaring in his ear. He stopped under a carport and turned the volume on his radio down. Even wearing an ear bud, somebody screaming at the other the other end could be heard. He knew he had to intercept this team before Reed and his blubbering package crossed the road behind him, and he needed to do it far enough away that they wouldn't be seen. He dropped his NODs back down over his eyes. There was a quarter moon just barely visible above the horizon of roof tops to the east. If the team moving to intercept him had night vision of their own, he'd have to give them something else to think about.

"This is fifteen, all clear so far."

Jason ran for all he was worth about a block and a half, aware that team thirteen would at some point be coming at him from behind, but they were moving much slower. He used a hedge lining a drive way to make it out to the edge of the road and a small pickup. He climbed up into the bed of the truck and settled in against the back of the cab. Raising himself up, he was able to watch up the street through the back window. He wished he knew how many men made up these teams. It would be dangerous to assume they were all just two-man teams, like Griff and his exploding seat mate had been.

He didn't have to wait long and spotted one soldier turn the corner two blocks away, on his side of the street coming towards his position. The soldier looked bulky with body armor, but the man's silhouette didn't suggest that he was wearing any sort of night-vision. If the thug stayed on the sidewalk, he would pass within seven or eight feet of his own curbside position. Careful not to move his body in the slightest he shifted his vision, to the other side of the street seeking out the other part of team fifteen. He didn't see anything, and when he shifted his view back to his side of the street, there were now two of them.

The lead one walked like he didn't have a care in the world, the trailer had a radio up to his face.

"Fifteen on Glen Allen, just crossing Leland, all clear."

The IR binoculars were back with the sniper rig. Jason watched them come with no knowledge of who had been marked by Sleepy and who hadn't. He already knew he'd take them both if he had to, but he had a small back up IR illuminator, nothing more than a weak flashlight outside the visible spectrum attached to his rifle's lower rail. Turning it on, sitting up in the back of the truck, getting it on target, making the shoot -no shoot decision; all without getting shot was starting to look more difficult as he realized his two targets were separated by a good twenty yards. He'd have to hope he could remain hidden until they had both passed his position before acting. And if one of Daniel's 'good guys' was the one holding the radio... and tried to use it, it wouldn't matter if he was marked or not. He couldn't let it matter.

He slowly laid down in the bed of the pickup, on his back, feet pointed towards the tail gate with his rifle across his body and pointed towards the sidewalk. He willed himself to become part of the truck. The bed liner smelled of old mulch, and a sickly-sweet smell of old garbage, but that might have just been the neighborhood of 'easy outs.'

The first target passed by without slowing, his labored breathing sounding far too close for comfort. Jason's left hand was underneath the barrel, his thumb ready on the IR illuminator as the footsteps faded away. He didn't hear the second guy approach at all, he was quiet until he spoke into the radio standing right next to the pickup.

"This is 15, almost to the next cross road, still clear."

Jason struggled to hear something to indicate the man had moved away, but the blood was starting to pound in his own ears as adrenalin flooded his own system.

"Copy fifteen, take a left on Ash, fourteen should be there. Report when you get there."

The soldier wasn't wearing ear piece, and Jason could hear Sleepy's voice over the radio loud and clear. From the radio, he thought the soldier had moved past him and was closer to the tailgate.

Jason flipped the illuminator on and sat up in one, slow, fluid motion. The light passed over the nearest target giving him a clear look at the man's back; no IR paint marks. The soldier started to turn around at the noise. Jason did his best to ignore that and sought out the first target, now twenty yards up the sidewalk. That one had stopped and was facing back toward him as well. A large diagonal slash clearly visible across the front of his pants.

"What road?" The man turned and shouted back to his partner just before he spotted Jason.

Jason let go a long a burst from the suppressed assault rifle, and was already vaulting over the far side of the truck's bed to the road as his target collapsed. Shots hammered into the small pickup. He rolled and came to his feet closer to the middle of the road and fired a short burst into the air, anything to keep the man off balance. Keeping the truck between him and the remaining soldier, he backpedaled across the street. He put another short burst into the front of the truck, as he went behind a car parked along the opposite curb. He maneuvered quickly reaching the opposite sidewalk, and used two parked cars for cover as he ran forward in the same direction his targets had been headed.

His target fired again at the pickup truck, the guy was blind out here Jason realized, probably seeing glow spots from his muzzle flashes as well. He moved forward until he could peek around the bumper of the car that hid him. The remaining soldier was crouched down behind the pickup he'd been hiding in. He watched as the man fumbled a new magazine into his gun, and then reached for his radio.

Jason put a single round into the tailgate of the truck.

"Toss the radio out into the road, or the next one goes through your head!"

Jason was about to shoot in warning one last time, when the man fumbled with the radio.

"Contact..."

He heard the man whisper over the radio before he launched the Motorola over the side of the pickup where it landed in the middle of the road.

Shit... He couldn't fault the guy's guts and he almost tagged him right then. No IR paint though. That meant Daniel must have thought the guy was at least redeemable.

"Now your gun, throw it into the back of the truck, side arm too."

"Fuck you! You're just going to kill me."

"Dumbass, if I wanted to kill you, we wouldn't be talking."

"Say again," Sleepy's voice sounded half panicked over the radio. "Who was that?"

"This is thirteen, he said contact I think."

"I heard that, too," another voice he didn't recognize broke into the airwaves.

He lost his chance for a clean shot as the man moved further around the truck towards the front bumper, out of sight.

I should have shot him. Jason surged to his feet and sprinted across the street directly at the body of the man he'd already taken down.

There was a Prius, on flat tires, its windows broken out, parked at the curb well behind the truck. He crossed the back of the small car, moving up until he had a clean shot at the remaining soldier.

He kneeled and took his time. The target was peeking around the front bumper of the truck, back across the street. He put a round into the tire of the truck, a foot away from where the man knelt, and moved forward leading with his gun.

"Lose the gun, now!" he yelled. "Last chance."

The soldier stood slowly, and dropped his rifle on the grass between the road and the sidewalk.

"Sidearm too."

"I don't have it with me."

"You won't mind if I check that..."

Jason moved forward and patted the man down with one hand, the muzzle of his rifle staying in contact with the man's body as a reminder. It was a stupid way to do it, but he didn't have the time to stand off and have the guy strip.

"Put your hands through," he dangled a loop of heavy zip tie in front of him. "Now tighten it with your teeth."

"Tighter," he gave the man a jab, taking a close look at him for the first time. He was closer to his own age than Reed, mid to late 30's. Taller than him as well, though he was whipcord thin.

"Ok, we're going to run. That way," he pointed back up the street towards the position where he and Reed had set up. "You lead the way, run."

They reached the wood pile a few minutes later, breathing heavily. Jason pushed the man into the backyard, through a gate, across dead space from a buried pipeline of some sort until they were in another backyard on the far side. He guided the man towards the house and thrust him in through the back door. Reed was standing there in the stairwell that led out of the basement, gun leveled at him.

He had a brief moment of panic, and then a sudden relief washed over him; it could end now. Reed just had to pull the trigger.

"Oh... it's you," Reed let out a held breath and dropped the muzzle of the gun.

"It's me," he breathed, ignoring what he had just felt.

"Another guest, he stays tied until I get back."

"Got it," Reed grabbed the prisoner, as Jason turned and ran back across the yard towards the sniper nest.

"Reed?" The new 'prisoner' just looked at him, confused. "You're dead."

"Save your breath, dude. It's a long story, and I don't want to have to keep repeating it."

Jason was halfway back to their original sniping position when another large boom rolled across the night sky. It sounded just like the shots from Rachel, or maybe it had been Pro, that had started the evening's festivities. He cursed them both, because they both should have been well out of the area by now. He listened to the panicked shouts from Daniel and various dispersed teams as the fact that there was more than one of 'him' was again made obvious. Somebody named Chip had just been taken out well to the south.

"Team thirteen, what's your location?"

Jason didn't need to wait to hear the response. He peeked slowly around the edge of the wood pile and could see three figures approaching Griff's original pickup truck, coming at it in the middle of the street. He belly crawled back under the tarp and moved to the forward edge of it, crawling up to the sniper rig from the back, and nestled himself into position. He managed a quick left to right scan of team thirteen through the scope. Two of them, the one in the middle with the radio and the one to the left, carried the invisible paint line on the front of their pants.

Jason willed his breathing to slow as he bent down behind his gun and jacked in another round. The first shot blew the center man off his feet and back a good five feet, depositing him in a pile that didn't move. Jason slowly worked another round into battery and took aim at the man on the left who was just standing there in shock, looking at his buddy. Jason fired again, and the man went down hard. He jacked another round in and acquired the last of the trio, who was running away. He watched through the scope thinking it had to have been a teenager, no adult could have run that fast.

"Team thirteen, report, are you there yet?"

He smiled to himself, as he confirmed through the scope that the radio was laying in the road a few feet from the first man he'd shot. Team thirteen was going to remain quiet on the issue.

"Team thirteen? This is the Sheriff, report in."

Jason waited a few minutes as reports from the south were coming up empty as well.

"Sleepy, get them out of there!" Jason smiled to himself at the panic in Bauman's voice.

"Copy that. All units back to base."

Jason hoped Daniel could survive his bosses' anger. From Bauman's optic it had not been a good showing by team Sleepy.

*

Chapter 19

Michelle got out of bed and hugged him before he left the room. She'd never done that before, and the surprise must have shown on his face.

"I know you aren't going to tell me what it is you're doing," Michelle whispered into his ear as she kissed him on the cheek. "But I'm proud of you."

Was it that obvious? If it was, his meeting with Bauman and Wayne would be painfully short. He'd sent those men in to get killed. Not that they didn't deserve it. Maybe they all did. They'd done things since the Suck that turned his stomach. He still felt like he'd been pulling the trigger himself. Not something a Jewish kid from New Jersey had imagined he'd be doing at this point in his life.

"You should be proud, too." Michelle whispered and let him go.

Proud? She still thought he was something he wasn't. In her mind, he was the 'good guy' who'd rescued her. He knew different. He knew he was, and couldn't forget some of the things he'd done. Michelle didn't know or had chosen to forget.

He took the fire stairs down, something he'd always done unless he was pressed for time. The use of the elevator was just one item in a long list of privileges that Bauman used to enforce the divide between soldier and sheep. There was nothing temporary in this setup. He knew Bauman's vision of the future included the same chasm separating those with power and those who worked to support the former.

Taking the stairs didn't assuage the guilt he felt, had felt for a long time, but it helped him hide it. He'd done things he wasn't proud of, especially early on, when no one left alive thought they'd live to see the next day. The world dying had granted him a skewed moral compass along with the insanity that they'd all fallen prey to. He'd been seduced by the power and control that Bauman and the Ritz had offered early on. It was modern day feudalism on steroids, and he'd been entrusted with a gun that he'd been willing to use. Bauman had recognized his worth in a fallen world, and followed up by providing him a castle and serfs.

Only, they hadn't gotten sick and died like he had expected. For a short while, as that reality began to set in, but the insanity had yet to fade, Sleepy, along with the rest of them thought they were the lucky ones. They found themselves on top of the world's carcass and they were willing to do whatever it took to stay there. It was then he started having doubts. That had been about the time Michelle had walked into the Ritz, seeking FEMA assistance from a government that had been dead for two weeks.

He'd watched her for a week. He'd seen the relief and hope go out of her eyes as the reality of what Bauman's 'sanctuary' really was for the sheep, for the women, especially the attractive women. He'd always maintained, had always told her that he didn't know what had made him snap and come to her rescue. It wasn't true. He'd wanted her, and in the end, he'd decided to take her for his own because he could. Some asshole, just like him, had been in the way at the wrong time. And the Sleepy story had begun.

He could remember her first words to him, in an elevator, his head ringing, hands bleeding, pulse still pounding from the fight.

"Thank you, I didn't think there were any decent people left."

She might as well have stuck a gun to his forehead and pulled the trigger. He remembered who he'd been before. What he'd been before. Certainly nothing special, but a decent guy, with a fiancé, a future. Decent... suddenly the word had seemed to take on weight of its own; the absolute minimum a person, a human being *had* to be. Screw good, understanding, solid, nice, empathetic, or awesome. Those were concepts that had died along with civilization. But decent? The bare minimum? He wasn't even that.

He'd left her in his room. Told her she'd be safe there. On the roof of the mall, he'd broken down in gut-wrenching sobs, on his knees, trying to hide from what he'd become. Trying to forget that he'd thought of Michelle as his prize, as he'd led her to the elevator. His foe's blood still dripping from his hands, and she had thanked him. Underneath half a dozen acres of solar panels that were the foundation of Bauman's power, he wept, and for the first time in a decade, prayed.

That had been almost six months ago and a lot had changed since. A lot more hadn't. He exited the stairwell in the lobby of the hotel, and immediately saw the hangdog looks of a group of civilians carrying armloads of food from the mall to the hotel's kitchen. One of the older civilians, a guy he'd been introduced to a month ago, but whose name he had forgotten, dropped a box. One of the guards, one of the new ones discovered during the snowstorms a couple of months past, stopped and picked up the box for him... a decent guy.

DJ, one of Wayne's main guys, kicked the new recruit in the leg and forced him to drop the box. "We don't fetch and carry. Not ever."

He watched the anger on the recruit's face - Potts, if he remembered the name - and wondered if the incident was going to go south. DJ had backed off a step, smiling, daring the much bigger and younger Potts to argue. Gun or not, the recruit backed down as another civilian stooped down and added the box to what she was already carrying. Decency died piecemeal.

He passed Wayne in the hallway coming out of Bauman's office. The barrel-chested soldier, with his buzzcut hair, looked nothing like the Mercedes salesman he'd been pre-Suck. The asshole just grinned at him as they passed each other in the hallway.

Bauman looked up at him as entered. He didn't recognize the look on the Sheriff's face. It was hangdog angry, maybe a little scared.

Bauman pointed at the chairs. "Shut the door, would you?"

"Let me guess," he said as he closed the door. "Wayne just delivered an ultimatum. he's number two or he's out of here with his guys."

It was nice to know he could still surprise Bauman.

"How'd you know?"

"I've been telling you for a month it was just a matter of time. We lost nine men in that shitstorm, seven of them were his guys."

"They aren't his guys..." Bauman was clearly trying to convince himself.

"Yeah, they are... or were. He just proved it."

"Can't let this stand," Bauman shook his head, "I can't."

"Then call his bluff," Sleepy said. "It'll come down to a fight, but we could stop pretending."

"He has no vision, he'll be content to hang out here, eat, drink, and fuck." Bauman may not have even heard him.

Sounded a lot like what Bauman's role had been from the beginning, but he managed to bite back on his reply. There was an opening here, if he could get Bauman to take the next step.

"Yeah, I don't see Wayne too interested in rebuilding anything. He just wants to rule what's left. When that's gone..." Sleepy shook his head slowly side to side, "my guess is he'll take his show on the road. But the rest of us won't be part of that equation, no matter what he may be saying."

Bauman wouldn't meet his eyes. "If it comes to a fight, how many guns could you count on?"

"If it just happened? Half a dozen, tops. Most would just sit it out or join in on the winning side. He's got what? Twenty-five, maybe thirty or so hardcore nut jobs left?"

"This can't be happening."

"But," Sleepy continued, leaning forward, "with a little prep, if it happens on your authority, your schedule? We might be able to get close to him numbers-wise; he's lost a bunch recently."

"He'll be expecting that, watching for it."

"No doubt," Sleepy agreed. "I doubt we'd get very far."

"There's got to be something we could do."

"Boss, there's close to four hundred people here that would like nothing better than a little payback."

Bauman looked back at him like he had three heads. "You think they'd stop with Wayne? We'd be just as dead."

Yep, Sleepy thought. Nothing wrong with that either. Decency had a price.

"Those are our two choices." Sleepy stood up, "Something that *probably* won't work, and something that will, because he'd never think you'd be willing to consider it."

"Where you going?"

Sleepy stopped with a hand on the door. "I'm pretty sure Wayne is waiting out in the lobby to lay down the law to me."

"Fuck!" Bauman raised his voice, not quite a loud enough to be heard outside. He was not a man used to having things decided for him.

"Fine," the man said after a moment. "Start talking to guards you can trust, and maybe have a small group of sheep ready to go, out of the pool we've been thinking of moving up anyway."

"That won't work," he shook his head. "Those replacements? Who do you think's been holding out delusions of power and grandeur to them?"

"'Cause you haven't been doing your job!" Bauman's face was as red as the leather chair in front of his desk.

"I've been warning you for months that as long as you rely on Wayne and his thugs to instill fear, he is going to figure out that he has all the power. We play that game, we lose. You change the game or we lose - everything."

Bauman came out of his chair in a quick movement that slammed his chair against the back wall with a crash. Sleepy was looking down the barrel of a very large handgun.

He managed a smile, willing the man to shoot. There'd be some justice in that, not enough, but some.

"The only thing we have left is the mercy of others. You decide where the best chance of that comes from, Wayne or your sheep." He pulled the door open and looked back once before walking out. "Let me know."

*

Reed was tired in a way that only a day of sleep and solitude could fix. He could tell Jason was on his last legs as well. They'd stayed hidden in the basement of the house Jason had picked as their rally point for the entirety of the next day following their attacks on the Sheriff's men. There hadn't been much opportunity to sleep. Griff had been in shock; still was, Reed wagered. The man had snapped more than a little when his fellow guard had been killed, and hadn't stopped talking since. A continuous nervous prattle of questions and meaningless chatter.

He remembered Griff had been a nervous talker even before his seat-mate had exploded next him. The man hadn't shut up during their long walk back to the vehicle and the drive to Jason's neighborhood. Once there, he and Jason sat on a couch in front of a massive, dark flat screen in an abandoned house, struggling to stay awake. Griff could be heard through the walls, complaining that he was having to pee into a shower drain. A few minutes later, he was complaining there wasn't any power.

"You sure we shot the right one?" Jason asked him. Reed was almost certain it was a joke.

He was sure; or would be, once Griff snapped out of it. He'd spent enough time with the guy on patrols to know he was a decent sort. Cory, who'd been brought back, trussed up by Jason, was doing much better, nothing but relieved to be out from under the Ritz. Of course, the lanky former stage manager for some traveling ice show that had been cancelled due to the world ending, had been less than pleased that they were going to leave him in sole possession of Griff.

313

End of Summer - S.M. Anderson

"Where are you going to be?" Cory had asked Jason, with a panicked look towards Griff.

"Not far. One of us will be back to check on you tomorrow. The house has everything you need, food and water in the kitchen. No fires, it sucks, but it's temporary." Reed could see Jason's exhaustion in the man's face, hear it in his voice. He was tired of taking care of people.

"You're leaving too?" Cory had looked at him, and he had to admit to himself that he was surprised Jason wasn't going to leave him at the abandoned house as well. He said as much once they were back outside.

"I want to give them a chance to run," Jason had shrugged. "If they want to, they can. I don't want them knowing about Pro and the girls."

The house they'd left Griff and Cory in was at the opposite end of the neighborhood from Jason's house, and they had about a mile to walk in the dark.

"You hear that?" He asked, pulling Jason to a stop after a few minutes.

Jason tensed up, looking at him in the moonlight. "I don't hear anything."

"Nice, isn't it..."

Jason rolled his eyes and started walking again. It was nearly a minute later when Jason snorted in laughter. "Last time I ever ask you which one to shoot?"

Reed started laughing too. It felt good to be going somewhere he could put his head down and sleep with a clean conscience, not worried about what was happening in the rooms all around him. It was as close to a feeling of home as he'd had in a long while. He was with good people. He was certain of that, just as he knew it was important for him to be so. He'd been studying in the Navy, during off hours to get ordained and apply for the Navy Chaplain program.

It was about as far from being a Seabee as one could get. The way he had figured it, at least back then, was the world had enough men of faith who had been raised in good neighborhoods, and lived clean and righteous lives. What was needed, he'd thought then, was somebody who could talk to people who'd grown up and lived in the shit that the world had to offer. At this point, he figured he had a PhD in shit.

It had seemed like a calling. Now though, it was just that small part of his soul that he retreated to in quiet moments. As much as he felt God was needed, he didn't doubt it would be a hard sell. Would anybody accept that the Suck could have been part of God's plan? Could he?

He hadn't said anything to Jason about it. A week ago, the man had still been looking at him in suspicion, or with the same cold indifference that he looked at one of his guns. Part of him suspected that Jason talked or listened to somebody besides God. They had bigger worries right now than his need to share, he knew that. God wasn't going to help anybody that didn't help themselves. He knew that in his bones. He'd lived it before, was living it again.

The relief at seeing Rachel and Pro alive and well when they stepped through the back door to the kitchen was short-lived. They'd entered after yelling the password, "Open Sesame" from the back deck. Jason had let Elsa pick the password. They'd walked in to an excited tail wagging Loki and hugs and high fives all around.

Before they could even drop their gear, Rachel had asked how many they'd gotten and Pro had jumped in with a description of how he'd got the drop on a scumbag he remembered from his time at the Ritz and 'blew his head off' for his second 'kill of the night.' Rachel was on about how she'd dropped a guy at 500 yards, how they needed to do it again - take the fight to the mall itself. How the thugs were just a bunch of 'pikers.'

Reed felt the temperature of the room drop next to Jason, who stood there holding his backpack by the straps. Jason looked between Pro and Rachel as if he didn't recognize them. He turned and leaned the sniper rifle in its protective case against the wall, dropped his bag next to it, and continued right on back out the door, shutting it hard enough that it rattled some of the dishes in the nearby shelves.

They all looked at one another, Reed focused on Elsa whose happy smile had disappeared with Jason's exit.

"What just happened?" Rachel grabbed at Elsa and pulled her into a hug.

He went to the sink, and pulled the blackout curtain aside, he could just make out Jason's form walking back down the driveway before the darkness swallowed him up.

"You two don't get it, do you?"

"Get what?" Pro asked.

"You think this is a video game? We took people's lives out there, killed people. You could have been killed." He glanced at Elsa out of shame, "I'm sorry girl, you didn't need to hear that."

"It's ok," Elsa smiled. "I'm going to help Rachel when I get older. Right?"

Rachel tussled her hair, "We'll see, kiddo." The look on the young woman's face said otherwise.

Reed nodded to himself as he watched the two girls.

"You think this is fun for him?" Reed looked back down at them. "He's been a nervous wreck since our radio crapped out and he didn't know how it had gone for you. Me too, for that matter. He's responsible for you both."

He held up a hand to Rachel and stopped her from whatever she'd been about to say.

"Whether you think he is or not, he is. Nothing is going to change that. And... and he sees you, becoming something... something he doesn't like. He blames himself for that too." Reed crossed to the table and sat down in the seat next to where Rachel stood, motioning her to a chair.

"How'd you feel if somebody you cared about, was responsible for," his eyes glanced at Elsa, "went down this path with not a care in the world? How'd you feel if that person started enjoying it?"

Rachel looked away and nodded. "I get it, but it's not his fault, or his choice."

"Not his fault," she said again, with a glance towards Pro. "We don't have a choice."

"Sure, you do." He said it with a surety that he could tell she couldn't fathom.

"We all do." He reached forward and tussled the top of Elsa's head. "But we've made the choices we've made, he's made his. Part of him maybe knows he don't have no choice concerning you two. But don't either of you think, ever, that he's going to be ok with people he cares about turning into hardcore killers."

"We've talked to him about this," Rachel argued, and nodded at Pro, "we both have. He doesn't get to make that decision for us."

"I understand what you're saying, girl. But I think you're wrong about that. If you push him, he'll make that decision."

317

"I'm no girl," Rachel fired back. "And he, or you for that matter, don't have a monopoly on making the world right."

Jason had told him what had happened to Rachel, he could more than understand her anger. "There's no making it right, I think the best we can hope for, maybe for a long while, will be just making it a little safer."

"Same thing," Rachel said. "I'll settle for safer."

"Me, too," Pro added. "But I get it, I know it's not a video game."

"Ok," he put his hands up in surrender, "just try not to be so damn happy about it, can you do that for him? For my sanity?"

"Yes," Rachel agreed. Reed doubted there was a person alive capable of stopping this young woman from getting her payback.

He turned to face Pro.

"I get it." The teenager nodded with mock seriousness. "No more excitement at killing the bad guys, making the world a better place." Pro leaned back in his chair and shook his head. The teenager may toe the line, but he wasn't going to be happy about it. The kid really was a smartass.

Reed nodded after a long moment. "Ok, good talk. You guys have anything to eat?"

"We've been waiting for you," Elsa chirped up. "I made brownies; Rachel helped a little bit."

"A little bit?" Rachel sounded offended.

Elsa nodded in mock seriousness. "A very little bit."

"Where'd he go?" Reed asked.

"His old house probably," Pro piped in. "He goes there sometimes. His wife... he buried her there."

"Got it," Reed stood up, and pointed a finger at Elsa, "I'll go get him. You get those brownies ready."

Jason had been relieved, more than he'd dared to admit, to see Pro and Rachel had made it back in one piece. They'd started in on their stories, bragging on their kills, and the feeling of relief had dropped away with a sickening hole that seemed to open up beneath his feet. Guilt had rushed in to fill the void. He'd let his gear fall to the floor and walked back out.

He'd stood over Sam's grave for how long he didn't know. There was enough moonlight to see that there were fresh shoots of spring grass bleeding into the soil around the edges of the grave. He spilled his guts to her, asking for the hundredth time if he was doing right in dragging people into his promise to her. She didn't answer, but at some point, he realized what he had to do. Those kids, Elsa... couldn't grow up thinking hunting people was somehow normal. The civilians at the Ritz couldn't go on living as slaves, until they lost their humanity and were promoted to Nazi prison guards.

He wiped away the tears that were streaming down one side of his cheek.

"Just wait a little longer, I'll be seeing you soon." He didn't look back as he walked away. He was done talking to her grave.

Reed was laying on his back at the bottom of his old driveway. In the darkness, Jason almost stepped on him.

"What are you doing here?"

"You notice how much better we can see the stars since the lights went out?"

"What?"

"Elsa made you brownies. I said I'd bring you back." Reed stood and brushed himself off. "You looked like you needed some me time."

"I did, thanks."

It was a quieter reunion when they returned to the house for the second time that evening, but within a few minutes, Elsa had them smiling and Pro had them laughing. At one point, Jason poured himself and Reed a whiskey, and clicked glasses. Rachel went to the cupboard and came back with a glass of her own and held it out. He poured her one, which she raised in a smiling salute to him.

"Sorry about earlier," she looked as if she were surprised at her own admission.

"S'ok," he waved her off.

"Me, too," Pro said somewhat sheepishly.

"I'll get used to the fact that you two have your own reasons for doing... this," he said lifting a finger off his glass towards the sniper rifle leaning against the wall behind him. "In the meantime, I'll get over it."

"I won't," Reed shook his head. "End of the world... I just can't get over it."

"Ahem," Pro coughed. "I just meant, me too? - can I have some whiskey?"

The laughter was real and the brownies weren't bad given that the ingredients came out of can designed for long term storage. At one point, he just leaned back and watched them, knowing they had each other's backs. They'd look out for each other. They'd be all right. Reed was solid, and he knew in his heart, a lot better suited to play surrogate dad than he was. All he could do was give them the best chance he could.

Pro woke the next morning as he usually did; by having Loki's cold wet nose slam into his neck just under the jaw line. It was as near as he could tell the world's most effective alarm clock.

"All right, all right, I'm up," Pro sat up in bed. Loki bounded off to the floor and ran to his bedroom doorway, where he spun in an excited circle a couple of times and barked once.

Pro had never seen Loki like this, maybe his doggy door was stuck or something. He followed the dog down the stairs into the kitchen and Loki just barked a couple more times at the back door leading out onto the house's deck.

Pro toed the doggy door and it swung open and shut without an issue.

"What's wrong boy?"

He knelt down and rubbed the dog's ears, but Loki kept looking at the door.

Reed walked into the kitchen, holding a handgun, and just looked down at them. "What's his problem?"

"I don't know," Pro shrugged. "Never seen him like this."

"Oh, shit," Reed said slowly.

"What?" Pro spun around and followed Reed's gaze to the kitchen's island.

There was a note and a couple of handwritten pages underneath it. But even from where he stood, he could read the big letters on the top of the first page.

"DON'T FOLLOW ME"

*

Chapter 20

It had taken him a solid three hours to get everything he needed. He could have done it a lot faster if he hadn't needed to be quiet and not wake anyone. Loki clearly knew something was up but had been satisfied to follow him around, back and forth from the basement armory and the back deck where the two large duffle bags slowly grew heavier. It wasn't until he had finished and led Loki back in to the kitchen and told him to stay, that he wrote out a note for all of them, praying they'd listen. He bribed the mutt with a new rawhide bone to seal that particular deal.

Getting the bags through the neighborhood back to where he'd parked the beast had taken two round trips; ammo was heavy. A lot heavier at thirty-five than he remembered it being at twenty-five. He had no idea how many of the civilians at the Ritz had been contacted by Sleepy to be ready. He packed guns and ammo for fifteen. It would either be enough, or it wouldn't. All he had to go by was a week-old message from Sleepy, describing the Sheriff's grand plan to catch him in Vienna. The note had said he was working on confirming the support of others, as was Michelle. He knew from Pro that Michelle was more likely to start some shit than Sleepy was. A hothead, was how Pro had described her.

He also had a smart phone photo of Michelle, so he could recognize her. Phones hadn't worked since the first two weeks into the Suck, but their cameras still did; just as long as you could keep them powered. Sleepy's last dead-dropped note had been rubber-banded around a smart phone. He had photos of the Sheriff, the Wayne character, and half a dozen different men who Sleepy, or maybe it had

322

been Michelle, had placed in a file titled *'shitbags.'* In the realm of target selection, it would have been a lot more useful to have photos of the few people Sleepy could trust. For his part, and for the sake of ease in taking the fight to them, with very few exceptions, they were all shitbags.

Driving with his NODS down over just one eye, he approached the Tysons area via Springvale and left the beast in the rear parking lot of a retirement home adjacent to the toll road. The multi-story condo-style building was a little over a mile from the mall. He made his way inside just as the first glow of the sunrise was visible across the eastern horizon. He found a bed in an empty room on the ground floor where the smell of the abandoned dead seemed less overpowering.

By the time he had his own gear and the two duffel bags inside, he was dead on his feet. Laying back on the bed which had a lingering mothball scent, the last two days caught up to him with a vengeance. He was asleep before he knew it, and managed to sleep through most of the day without a care. He ate the best part of two MREs going through his planned approach and contingencies in his head as he waited for the sun to go back down.

If he'd been smart, he would have taken another night to surveil the mall, and confirm what had changed in the months since he'd been this close. That had been when he was watching the place in the hopes of spotting Pro after he'd been caught. During that time, watching the Ritz's operations from a high-rise across the road from the mall's parking deck, he'd run countless scenarios through his head. He'd always come to the conclusion that regardless of how incompetent most of the supposed soldiers seemed to be, there were just too many for him to assault on his own.

So, how has any of that changed, dumbass? He knew the guard locations, patterns and habits had no doubt changed since then, but taking the time to be sure would only give Pro and Rachel more time to follow him. Which was his whole reason for doing this now. If he could, he needed to keep them out of this. Emotionally, he wasn't suited to watch either of them go down this road. Part of him worried he'd already failed on that score. That didn't mean he had to make it worse. Didn't have to be around to see it or get them killed.

He'd given them the skills to survive, but that was a far different thing than using them as soldiers. The best he could do was give them a chance, a clean slate to make their own way. A way that wouldn't leave them feeling as empty as he did.

"All I can think of;" he was apologizing to Sam, out loud. To a wife who wasn't there, who wouldn't answer. He was lying to her and knew it. It was the only way he could think of, that would assuage the guilt he felt from knowing he had no intention of surviving. This was his best way, maybe the only way of getting to Sam that wouldn't break his promise to her. If he took the Ritz down in the process, so much the better. Reed was a good man and would look out for Pro and Elsa. Rachel... Rachel was a long way from being a kid. He figured that part of her had been well and truly destroyed. At this point, Rachel was more than capable of taking care of all of them.

He listened in on the occasional radio chatter coming out of the Ritz. It sounded different; the conversations were subdued. No one was flicking anybody crap, no one was complaining like they usually did. Of course, they'd just had their asses handed to them, courtesy of himself and team ninja. He hadn't heard the Sheriff on the radio since the sociopath had ordered Sleepy to recall his goons three nights ago. He didn't know if that was good or bad, and as he set off, personally weighed down with twelve magazines of .556, he realized it didn't matter. He was going to kill as many of them as he could. If Daniel's sheep weren't willing to fight for a chance to be free, it wouldn't matter.

He'd driven a risky half a mile closer to the mall once he felt he had a decent idea of where the rolling patrols were based on their radio chatter. He pulled the beast into a nearby apartment complex and spent the next hour and a half ferrying his gear and duffel bags into the lowest level of the mall's garage. He was at ground level, and there were entrances to exploit, but the primary commercial entrances to the mall, and most of the guards, were up above him on the top of the two-level garage which shared a common elevation with the surface roads.

With the two heavy bags of guns and ammo he was carrying, beyond his personal loadout, he wasn't able to make more than a hundred yards or so before needing to take a breather. He'd had to wait for two rolling patrols to pass by. He knew the men in those vehicles would roll back here as reinforcements the second the balloon went up. With the passage of the second Hummer blowing by the car he hid behind, he waited for a minute more and moved as quickly as he could across the street into the darkened interior of the garage's lowest level. He found a good hide behind a thick rectangular concrete support column, dropped the bags and scanned into the cavernous darkness.

This bottom level of the garage was as empty as it was dark. He turned towards the mall, and saw a guard on foot walking the perimeter sidewalk, away from him, towards two more soldiers standing guard at the ground floor entrance of the Macy's, some hundred yards further down the mall's exterior. The roving guard seemed to hang around and shoot the shit with the other two, before he turned and headed slowly back towards him. He followed the man's progress, getting closer and breathed a sigh of relief when he looked closer.

The guard was roughly the same size he was, and was wearing what looked like a baggy lightweight jacket. It was as good an opportunity as he was likely to get. He waited until the guard turned the corner, out of the line of sight with the department store entrance and the other two soldiers. He moved slowly, deeper into the darkness of the garage. The few lights they had on didn't extend past the guarded entrance. Once he was certain he wouldn't be seen, he ran back to the outside perimeter of the garage and circled around until he was behind the receding figure of the man patrolling on foot. He made it to the side of the mall and went to ground between the brick wall and a large evergreen shrub, waiting for the guard to retrace his steps.

A possum moved out from under a bush with a hiss that just about made him jump out of his skin. It stared at him a moment, its glassy eyes looking like small lightbulbs when he brought his rifle and its mounted IR illuminator up. The creature gave another squeak as a parting argument, before scurrying across the road into the parking lot. Jason could feel the pounding of his heart in his face and ears. *Shit!* He forced himself to breathe again.

He only had to wait for a few minutes before the one-man patrol was on his way back towards him, staying to the sidewalk ringing the mall. The man was smoking. The idiot had no idea how that little red glow at the end of the cancer stick destroyed night vision. Not that it would have mattered. He waited until the guard was half a step past him before moving. The weight of his gear and ammo was entirely cancelled out by adrenalin. One hand went up against the man's mouth twisting sharply, pulling the guard's head back hard, the other hand sunk six inches of blued steel into the man's neck.

Jason ignored the twitching feet and smell of shit as he quickly stripped the jacket off the man and zipped it up over his vest. He dragged the body back into the mulch bed and hid it behind the same shrub he had used. He found the pack of cigarettes and a lighter in the jacket and lit one, tossing the pack into the bushes.

He walked quickly to the corner of the mall and forced himself to slow down. He rounded the corner and could see the glow surrounding the guarded entrance ahead. Only one guard was visible at the moment, and he was slowly walking back into the recessed entrance. The man had glanced at him, noting his presence, but apparently wasn't alerted by anything he'd seen. Jason pulled on the cigarette to keep it lit, without inhaling and blew the smoke out a moment later. It tasted like dirt as far as he was concerned but he would use it.

He swung out to the edge of the sidewalk when he was within forty yards of the door. From his angle, he could see one guard leaning against the brick wall of the entryway and he looked to be talking to his fellow guard on the hidden opposite wall. The guard glanced up at him again and he quickly took another faux drag off the cigarette and kept walking. He angled back to the mall side of the sidewalk, losing sight of the guard. When he was within fifteen yards of the entrance, he stepped into the mulch bed, keeping a large shrub between him and the entrance. He stood facing the brick, inches away, head tilted back in his best approximation of taking a leak.

When he didn't come into view, in the next few seconds, the guard that had seen him, walked out into the circle of light covering the sidewalk and spotted him.

"Seriously, Mills? You got the whole damn building to piss against, and you wait to till you get here?"

"Bite me," Jason grunted.

"What'd you just say?"

The man took another step closer. His partner must have been hoping to see a beat down or anything to break the monotony of guard duty and stepped out away from the heavy glass doors to join his partner on the sidewalk.

Jason pulled heavily on the cigarette, exhaled and flicked it at them over the top of the shrub. He was already bringing up his suppressed 9mm and had fired four times, just as the cancer stick landed on the sidewalk with a tiny explosion of red ash.

He checked their bodies as he dragged them behind the bushes. They weren't wearing any body armor. One guy had an M4, with no extra magazines, probably hadn't wanted to be weighed down, standing guard. The other one had a beat to shit AK, but at least he had an extra mag in his thigh pocket. He could hope the luck of dealing with incompetents continued. He smiled to himself, remembering his Dad saying countless times throughout his youth; "Hope in one hand, shit in the other, see which one amounts to anything."

He checked behind him and scanned out into the parking lot one more time. There was nothing to see, no reason to wait. He knew there were guards up above him, on the upper level of the garage, but they were on the outside perimeter of the parking lot facing the road. Except for those at the main entrance on the top level, but that was two hundred yards further along the front of the mall. This was as close to a back entrance as he was going to get. The Macy's anchored one end of the mall.

He pushed through the heavy glass doors like he owned the place. Inside, it was only slightly better lit than the garage itself. All the interior lights were off, save the occasional red glow over the exits and the widely spaced emergency lighting shining weakly from the ceiling every hundred feet or so. He quickly moved off down a side aisle getting away from the door. He noticed the amount of food and gear that was stored here. Industrial shelving had displaced racks designed to display clothes. Twelve feet high, with cut out cardboard placards tied to each shelf listing what was stored on it. The Sheriff might be paranoid sociopath, but he clearly had a little OCD mixed in as well.

He went down an aisle storing motor oil, new tires and car parts, until he reached the interior wall and went left towards the store's inside entrance to the mall proper. He walked past rack after rack of boots and heavy jackets, then gardening equipment. He stopped and stared at two mid-size Kubota tractors parked next to half a dozen, toppled, naked mannequins. The Suck strikes again, he thought to himself with a smile as he reached the wide-open mall entrance.

He peeked through a display case that acted as part of the interior wall, and noticed the mall's cathedral-like gallery was lit with the same occasional, dim spot lights at wide intervals. He knew from previous visits to the mall, usually around Christmas time, trying to find a gift for Sam who never seemed to want anything, that there were two levels above him. If he was remembering right, the entrance to the Ritz was roughly in the middle of the mall, on the second floor. He could see one of the glass-lined skybridges crossing the gulf of the space within, stretching from one side of the mall to the other above him. The closest emergency light to him was directly over it. Outside the Macy's wide entrance, the mall's main promenade was in dark shadow.

Old training and lessons flooded back. He straightened up and walked casually out of the store headed for the bank of still escalators located about thirty yards in front of him. He didn't see any activity on the ground floor, but with just a cursory glance into the stores, he could see most had been converted to house society's leftovers collected by the Sheriff's foraging teams over the last six months. The Sheriff had the beginnings of the right idea here. If one could get past the fact that the asshole was insane and thought society should be modeled on some sort of feudalistic serfdom, this was a good way to start. For his part, he couldn't past the insane part.

Music and voices reached him before he located the source as he was halfway up the escalator. A high-end culinary supply store, with cast iron and copper pots and pans mounted to the outer wall, spilled light out onto the second floor of the mall. He paused long enough to note half a dozen people moving items from boxes to shelving. A solitary guard, looking bored, stood watch over them in the doorway, looking inward and away from him. The sawed-off shotgun the man held at the elbow by one bent arm, made it clear who was guarding whom. He made a split-second decision, and the brass knuckles were in his hand as he stepped off the metal staircase and reversed course towards the store.

He made it within ten feet of the guard before one of the workers spotted him. The guard noticed and turned around.

"How's it going?" Jason said.

The guard grunted, noticing the rifle, but making nothing of it. "It's goin'..."

"We haven't met," Jason walked right up to him. "I'm kinda new."

"Yeah, I don't..."

That was enough. Jason slammed the knuckles into the man's jaw rather than shooting him. The guard went back and down and didn't move.

Jason brought up his rifle one-handed to cover the work crew, as he put a finger against his lips.

"Is there another guard?" He asked quietly, noting one of the women workers looked like she was about to lose her shit. She looked a year or two younger than Rachel. One side of the woman's face was swollen with days-old bruising. They all just stood there, hands up.

"Just that pig..." The battered woman pointed at the unconscious form on the floor.

"Find something to tie him up with. Gag him."

They just stared back at him like they couldn't understand him.

"Now." He said with a little more force.

One of the men bent down over the fallen soldier and just shook his head. He drew a folding knife from his sock, and opened it.

"Just tie him up," he repeated, when the man hesitated doing what he had been setting out to do.

"Fuck you, mister." The woman with the beat-up face said, as she stepped forward, kneeled down and held out her hand for the knife.

Jason stepped forward over the body, brushing them both back. He withdrew his 9mm and put a single suppressed round into the man's chest. It was cleaner. This lady might have cause, but if he could, he'd save her from the nightmares later.

"This ends here tonight. You people willing to fight?"

"With what?" the man who still held the knife said from his knees, holding it out.

"I brought guns, enough for a bunch of you."

"It's you," a voice said from the back of the group. There was a middle-aged man wearing an old baseball cap with the Miami Dolphins logo.

"Who?" several voices piped up.

"He said you'd come to help."

Jason waved the man closer. When he was close, he grabbed him by the front of his shirt and pulled him away from the others. He made sure the man's back was to the group.

"Who said I'd come?"

The man hesitated for a moment, shook his head once. "Sleepy."

Jason winked at him. "Right answer, Miami. You'll help?"

"Hell, yes, I'll help."

"These others, you trust them all?" Jason whispered.

The man shook his head slowly.

"How many do I have to worry about?"

Miami held up a hand against his chest, and flashed a single finger.

"Ok, go stand next to him."

Jason spun the man around and pushed him back to the middle of the store.

"Here's what we are going to do," he said loudly, "and I'm only going to say this once, and I'm not asking." He pointed a hand at a short skinny guy with glasses, holding a clip board. Miami had walked over to stand next to him.

"You, what's your name?"

"James." The man said squinting at him in question as he said it.

"The rest of you... tie James up. Gag him."

The man dropped the clip board and started a mad dash towards the door but was clotheslined by Miami. Several others fell on the man in an instant. Within minutes they had him trussed up in the back of the store with half a roll of duct tape.

He stood over the man. "If I see you again tonight, I won't hesitate to end you. You escape? You'd best run, and keep running."

"Miami," he signaled the man over. The die was cast. These people wanted to be free of the insanity running the place or they didn't.

"Who here can get to Sleepy or Michelle? She works in the kitchen."

"Sleepy'll be up in his room most likely. None of us can get up to those floors," Miami answered.

"Which floor?" he asked.

"Sixth floor, I know Michelle," a woman his own age spoke up. "Room 602, that's where she stays with Sleepy. But she'll still be cleaning up after dinner."

"Ok," he pointed at the woman who had spoken, and then to the girl with the two black eyes; she looked motivated. "You two get Michelle, do whatever you need to. Just tell her that I'm here, and to let Sleepy know to get his people to the Neiman Marcus, this level. Can you do that?"

The older women hesitated and then nodded. "I think so, but... who are you?"

"He's the ninja," Miami said, looking at him. "Aren't you?"

He saw the look of recognition on all their faces.

Use it. "Not a name I chose."

"We got a chance," one of the men who had been silent, spoke up. "Finally."

Jason bent over and picked up the dropped clip board and handed it to his messengers. "Take this, it always helps."

She nodded in thanks, and the women took off running.

"Walk!" he yelled at them. "There's nothing wrong."

Satisfied as they disappeared into the darkness of the mall's central corridor, he turned back the others.

"Ok, listen up, you're going to have to move fast." ..*

Chapter 21

"You'd think he'd have brought a bloody radio with him." Rachel was whispering as she lay prone on the third floor of an office building overlooking the Galleria Mall. She was bent over the scope of her rifle, watching the guards at the mall's main entrance adjacent to the top deck of the parking garage.

Pro was seated next her in a swivel office chair looking out the window with a pair of NODS over his eyes. Rachel's rifle was aligned with an empty space in the window where a shard had been knocked out, but the rest of the window was whole and hid them both. The thugs below on the parking deck were oblivious to the angel of death watching them from above.

"He has one," he said. "He'll be listening to them, not us."

"We could..." Rachel started.

"No," Pro pulled his off his night vision goggles and looked down at her shadowed form, laid out on the floor. "He'd know we're here and so would the Sheriff."

"I know, I know..." He heard Rachel half mumble.

"You don't know him as well I do. If he figures out we're here, he'll flip. Be worried more about us than what he's doing. Probably call it off and go home." Or just disappear, Pro thought.

"Would that be such a bad thing?"

"This... needs doing." Pro sounded like an old man to himself.

Their radio squelched once. Pro grabbed it off his vest. "Go."

"Found a dead guard, fresh." Reed whispered back over the radio. "North parking lot, bottom level, up against the building, hidden in the bushes."

"That's him," Pro said. "He's going in through the Macy's."

"Well there's piss all we can do for him here," Rachel cursed. "If he's on the lower level, the garage is in the bloody way, isn't it?"

"Check the bottom entrance to the store," Pro said into the radio. Jason had said their radios were safe, they frequency hopped or something. They'd all agreed before setting out that afternoon that they weren't going to take any chances and would try to speak around things in case they were overheard. Reed had been at the Ritz far longer than he had; he'd know the door he was talking about.

"He's already inside." Rachel was panicking. Pro knew she had feelings for Jason. He didn't think Jason knew. Sometimes he wondered if Jason was capable of those kinds of feelings for anyone. He knew Jason still talked to his dead wife.

"We can't do anything until we know where he is. Their radios will go nuts when they figure out he's inside, then we'll know. Trust me."

Rachel's radio was tuned to the Ritz's current channel, and there had been hardly any chatter at all since they'd set up here. Just the occasional normal updates from the two roving patrols, one driving circuits on the Beltway, the other out in Oakton on Dolly Madison. Pro figured the Sheriff still thought Jason, aka 'the Ninja,' was based out in that direction. The only thing that struck him as weird was that it was Wayne's voice, he kept hearing, giving the occasional direction. It was usually the Sheriff, sometimes Sleepy on the radio this time of night.

"What are we going to do when they start going off their kettle?"

Pro smiled at Rachel's funny English; he knew what she meant without having a clue what the saying meant.

"It depends," he said as firmly as he could. "We don't commit until we are sure."

Rachel barked a laugh. "Are you *trying* to sound like him?"

Pro shrugged to himself in defense. It was all he had.

*

It took Jason the better part of half an hour, dashing from one shadow to the next, waiting on people to pass by before he was set up behind a counter in a small, high-end women's shoe store directly across from the elevator entrance to the hotel. This store must have been too small to have been converted into storage. He was looking at shoe boxes that had fancy brand names that he felt like he had known at one time. But like most of what was left of the old world, if you couldn't eat it or shoot it, it was worthless. He shook his head in disgust; a box in front of his face read $799.99. The society that made shoes for eight hundred dollars was dead, yet the shoes were still here.

He focused on the foot traffic streaming by. It seemed to be coming from the mall's main entrance and was headed, in a strung-out group, to the entrance to the hotel. The large group of sheep and their armed guards were returning from somewhere. They looked tired, especially the civilians. He found it harder to think of them as sheep after what he'd seen the woman in the kitchen store almost do with a pocket knife.

They were cowed, no question about that, but they were also pissed off. The soldiers among the group had bunched up by the time the elevator doors opened. He watched as they disappeared inside. The civilians were admitted to a stairwell adjacent to the elevator by a single asshole with an electronic badge he'd swipe to access the door. He watched the single guard take his time groping some of the younger women before letting them pass. They were the only ones he bothered to frisk. The women stood there, heads down and just endured it. The other soldiers, anyone carrying a gun, had just been waved to the elevator without a second look. Once the strung-out gaggle had disappeared into the hotel, he was left staring at the bored guard who wasted no time in starting to pick his nose.

This guy didn't deserve to breed. He hoped he wasn't too late in that regard. He stood up slowly making sure to keep the shoe store's walls between him and the guard and moved from shadow to shadow within the store. Once he was near the entrance, he checked both ways for any foot traffic. Satisfied, he stepped out and rounded the corner of the main hallway and found himself walking straight towards the elevator. Still wearing the wind breaker over his MOLLE vest, he let his rifle swing free against his chest.

"What up?" The guard jerked his chin at him in greeting when we he was fifteen yards away. He wanted desperately to pull the 9mm that he'd shifted to his ammo bag hanging from a shoulder strap. Internally he took a deep breath, knowing the longer he delayed the alarm the better.

Jason pointed at the stairwell door. "Going to get me some."

"You ain't gonna ride?" The man tilted his head towards the elevator directly behind him.

"Nah, been sitting in the Hummer for the last few hours."

"Cool man, whatever."

The guard stepped to the stairwell door and swiped his badge. Jason pulled it open with a nod, "Thanks." He felt the steel door start to swing shut, until it stopped. The guard held it open with one hand peering in at him.

"You new? I haven't seen you before." The guard suddenly looked interested in Jason's rifle.

"Yeah, I'm Pete." It was the first name that came to him. He held out his hand, as friendly like as he could manage.

The guard was eyeing him with a look that danced between suspicion and envy. "That's a nice rig. How's a new guy rate that?" The guard turned a little closer and extended his hand.

"I'd tell you, but then I'd have to kill you."

"Funny, but seriously?"

Jason pumped the hand one more time.

"I just walked in with it," he said. His left hand came in underhand. The knife went in at the bottom of the man's jaw, up through the roof of his mouth, and into his brain. The guard was on his tip toes, eyes bulging in those last few seconds of coherent thought that couldn't have been anything more than surprise.

Jason switched his grip to the man's belt and armpit and waltzed him into the stairwell. Letting the body drop at his feet as soon as the heavy door slammed shut, he pulled the heavy knife out with a sharp tug, wiped it and his hands off as best he could on the guard's clothing. The still face, and dead eyes stared back at him even as the body's feet were still twitching. Pulling the knife out, had left the guard looking like he was frozen in mid-yawn.

He shook his head and pushed down the bile he could feel building at the bottom of his throat. He knew he'd do far worse before this was over. Philosophically, emotionally, hell... even morally, he was fine with what he had just done and would continue to do. The momentary nausea was there just to remind him that he was human and there would be a price to be paid later. If there was a later.

"I was serious," he said to the corpse, closing the man's jaw with the toe of his boot. It fell back open in laughter the second he moved his foot away. It was now only a matter of time before somebody found this guy or one of the others he'd already serviced. Moving fast, he stepped over the body, went down the stairs knowing the hotel's lobby was beneath them on the street level at the back side of mall. He had no plan beyond his intention to hit hard and fast. Passing another steel door at the next landing, past the sign that read *"Mezzanine Level – Ballroom,"* he found himself wishing he'd been here before and had some idea of the layout; but neither he or Sam had been Ritz types. He continued down to the next landing, slowing down, making certain he had full magazines in the rifle and the 9mm.

The deep breath he took on the safe side of the heavy wood door did nothing to calm his nerves. Mounted directly in front of his eyes was a brass plaque that read 'Lobby.' He pushed the bar and stepped through into a richly carpeted and dark wood paneled hallway lit by frosted globe lighting fixtures. He ignored the overdone opulence of the place and looked down the long hall, out into the small corner of the lobby that was visible from the alcove. There were a few soldiers with guns moving around, but they weren't looking in his direction. *Now or never.*

He'd taken three steps when two women swung around the corner from the lobby into the hallway, walking straight at him. Neither was armed, and he stilled the impulse that had almost brought his rifle up and around. One of the women had stopped, her hands covering her mouth, staring at him. It took him a second to process, and then he saw the bruises. It was the woman from the kitchen store. The other woman's head went from the woman to him. She nodded as if she were making a decision and started walking to him.

He realized then it was Michelle. She was even wearing the same red and blue Washington Capitals hooded sweat shirt-shirt she'd had on when Sleepy had taken her picture.

"Where's the Sheriff?" he asked.

"In his room, under guard. Wayne's in charge now. He's in his office," she jerked her head back toward the way the women had just come from. "Follow the signs for the business office, past the front desk. I'm going to go get Sleepy."

"Right, she tell you?"

He shifted his focus to the other woman, "you remember where I told them to go?"

"Yeah," the woman nodded weakly towards Michelle. "I told her."

"There's maybe a dozen soldiers in there, at least one, maybe two with Wayne in the back offices." Michelle was very cool, but he couldn't help but pick up on the excitement on her face, in her eyes.

He nodded in thanks, more for her brevity than the info. She was focused, with a calm smile playing at the corners of her mouth that struck him as almost strange. Pro had it right; this woman was a hothead. But her anger was ice cold, focused.

"You have a gun?"

She nodded in the affirmative. "Don't worry about the Sheriff," she said. "He's done." Michelle turned and signaled the other woman closer and grabbed her by the elbow. "Remember what I said, now go!"

Michelle turned back to him. "You too," she said, before making a shooing motion at him, with both hands.

Turning to watch them go for a half a second, he shook his head. "Yes, Ma'am," he whispered to himself.

Turning the corner into the lobby, he walked past a mixed group of civilians who looked like they were waiting to be told what to do. There were half a dozen soldiers with guns coming and going from different directions. As he approached the main desk, he could see a Humvee through the glass doors of the entrance, sitting in the pull through, unloading its occupants, all soldiers. So far, so good.

"Who the hell are you?" A shrill voice screeched from behind the main desk. He could barely see the top of a woman's head seated behind a chest-high arrivals desk.

"I'm Pete." He waved a hand and continued around to the back side of the heavy dark wood of the counter. She looked like an overweight version of the 'Church Lady'; mean in a way reserved for people who knew they were right and he was clearly invading space that she considered hers.

"The new guy." He kept moving towards her once he was behind the counter.

"I don't know you Mister, and I know everybody."

She started to sit up and look over the high counter for someone to call to. Jason slammed the Sig into her head just above the ear. Her head whiplashed to the side and she started to slide out of her chair. He pulled her back into the seat and laid her head on her computer keyboard.

"Yeah, that's me," he said loud enough to be heard and smiled down at the back of her head. He glanced up at the guard standing between the double set of glass doors. The man was looking at him, probably attracted to the movement.

Jason smiled, looking down at the unconscious church lady and jerked a thumb over his shoulder towards the business office. "He wants to see me?"

He nodded as if the head he was looking at was conscious and speaking. He turned to go, eyes sliding across the lobby looking for anyone moving his direction. He forced himself to move slow. No one here would be excited to have to go see the boss in crazy town. It would take just one person glancing over the counter, or to walk behind the desk to figure out the Church Lady wasn't sleeping for the game to be up. He walked through a set of double swinging doors into a hallway with no exits doing his best not to think of the number of guns behind him. He'd stopped counting at ten and knew he'd missed some.

A quick glance ahead and he took in the four office doors, two to a side and what looked like a set of bathrooms at the end of the hall. He supposed it was due to the evening hours, but all the offices were dark save a single one at the end of the hall on the left. He glanced into each of the darkened doorways as he went past on the thick plush carpet but didn't stop on his way to the lit office. Holding the suppressed Sig against his outside leg as he swung in through the door way. There was a soldier sitting in a leather arm chair in front of the desk, a new M4 leaning against the wall next to him.

343

It wasn't Wayne, or anybody he had a picture of.

"Where's the bossman?" he asked casually just as the occupant of the chair looked up.

"Shitter," the man waved down the hall, before his eyes scrunched up in confusion.

"Who the hell are you?"

"New guy," he smiled, "Sleepy sent me."

The man's eyebrows went up further as his head pulled back in question.

"Never mind," Jason said before bringing the gun out and putting two quick shots into the man's chest. Suppressed or not, the gun's escaping gases and the sound of its action working sounded loud in the office. He didn't hesitate slipping the gun back into his ammo bag and dragging the man out of his chair around to the floor behind the big desk.

Jason heard the muted sound of a toilet flushing through the wall. It was amazing how the sounds of civilization stood out in a dead world. He did his best to push the body halfway under the desk. Certain it couldn't be seen from the door, he moved to the couch underneath the window that would have looked out into the hallway if it weren't for the venetian blinds hanging closed.

"Been thinking, Bob," he heard a loud voice from the hallway. A second later Wayne stepped through. Jason noted the massive desert eagle .50 caliber hand cannon strapped to the man's thigh immediately. It was all he could do not to laugh. He'd been wearing it in the surreptitious photo Sleepy had taken of him. Typical thug; no different than the Iraqi warlords he'd operated against all those years ago. The man in charge needed to carry the biggest or shiniest gun.

"Dammit," the man muttered as he realized 'Bob' wasn't where he had left him, wasn't hanging on his every word. His target stepped through the door and started to turn towards him. Jason waited just long enough for a look of surprise to register on the man's face, before shooting him in the stomach. As much as he wanted to just end the guy, he needed him to talk. He was up from the couch and moving as the sound from the shot was still reverberating. Wayne was a big guy, going soft, but still solid under the accumulated layers of lazy. He wavered on his feet, a look of surprise frozen on his face, head down, trying to come to terms with the leaking hole an inch above his belt buckle.

Jason snapped out a quick punch at the man's throat, not hard enough to crush anything, but he didn't want him yelling out either. He used a forearm under the shit bag's chin to keep him upright and pulled out the desert eagle that Wayne was trying to paw at, and tossed it onto the desk. He frisked the man quickly, finding a .38 wheel gun in an ankle holster, a tiny belt knife, and a big Bowie-looking pig sticker. He tossed all of it onto the desk, grabbed a handful of the man's shirt, and spun, throwing him onto the couch.

There was a cry of pain when he landed. Jason knelt with one knee on the couch next to him and slapped him on the cheek to get his attention. Jason held a finger to his lips. "Sssshhh..."

"Who... who are you?" The man wheezed, struggling with a throat that wasn't working right, not to mention the hole in his gut.

Jason ignored him and placed the muzzle of the suppressor against the man's knee.

"I'm going to ask you a few questions, and if you want to live and not lose your kneecaps, you're going to answer me."

He tapped the man's knee cap with the end of suppressor. "Nod if you understand me."

A whimper accompanied the head jerking up and down.

"What room is the Sheriff in?"

"Penthouse, top floor," Wayne's voice sounded raspy.

"Where's the main radio control room?"

"I'll give you the Sheriff," Wayne swallowed and grimaced in pain. "Anything you want..." Jason knew the shock of being shot was wearing off, the pain would be building in the man's gut. He suddenly thought of that first night he had learned of the gang operating out of the Ritz. The image of the old woman in the back of the truck popped in to his head. She'd taken a day to die with a gut wound far worse than Wayne had, courtesy of these assholes.

"Anything you want." He could appreciate the desperation in the man's voice. Maybe he truly did appreciate the situation he was in.

"You didn't answer my question." Jason felt himself smiling as he said it. Something in his face clearly scared Wayne.

Jason lowered the muzzle a little. "If you scream, I'm just going to throat punch you again. Nod if you understand."

Wayne's eyes went huge, suddenly he couldn't nod fast enough.

Jason squeezed his trigger and put a round through the top of Wayne's foot.

Wayne's head shook back and forth, jaws clenched, face turning purple.

"Wayne," he slapped the man's face. "Where is the main radio terminal?"

"Top floor," Wayne grimaced in pain. "Next to the stairs... to the roof."

346

Jason nodded and was about to say something nice, in thanks for the straight answer. It wasn't like he couldn't be civilized.

The half-muted sound of an air horn, somewhere in the distance cut that thought off.

"Control, guard team at Macy's bottom level is dead. Somebody shot them." A panicked voice crackled over the radio set on the shelves behind the desk.

Wayne turned to look at him and he shrugged as if to say, *'yeah, that was me.'*

A second later, somebody hit the alarm and the relative quiet of the Ritz was shattered by the hotel's fire alarm.

A look of relief blossomed on Wayne's face, maybe even the beginning of a smile. Jason just shook his head slowly and the hope in Wayne's eyes died abruptly. He brought the gun up and shot the man in the forehead. He heard the swinging doors at the end of the hallway slam open and feet running toward him down the hall way. He came off the couch and took a step deeper into the office, lining himself up with the doorway.

"Wayne?!" A soldier yelled just as he slid into view, going bug eyed as he noticed the barrel of the gun lined up with his head.

It wasn't Sleepy. Jason pulled the trigger twice, catching the man in the chest and head before he collapsed. He stepped out into the hallway to pull the body inside and looked up, towards the swinging doors, just in time to see a soldier in the lobby bringing his gun up. The swinging doors were stuck open.

Shit! He rolled back into the office as the carpet, overhead lights and drywall gypsum exploded around him. He felt a tug on his calf as he pulled up inside the doorway.

His lower leg was on fire - just a grazing shot on the back of his leg, a couple of inches below his knee, but it hurt like hell. Karma, he thought immediately, he shouldn't have played with Wayne. He got to his feet and collected the Desert Eagle from Wayne's desk.

He ran through half a magazine with his M4, aimed indiscriminately down the hall out into the lobby to get their heads down, he even thought he might have hit some unlucky SOB that had been standing at the head of the hallway. He shifted his aim to the ceiling, taking out the hallway's lights including the strobing alarm spotlight over the swinging doors.

He tossed Wayne's Desert Eagle through the doorway into the dark office directly across the hallway.

He wanted to be able to shoot down the hallway off his right shoulder, and that meant he needed to be in the office across the hall. He quickly unscrewed the suppressor from his M-4 and dropped it into his ammo bag. The bag was heavy as hell, but he figured he'd have a remedy for that very soon. One way or another, he was done packing it around. He dove through the doorway, across the hallway into the office across the hall. He rolled as he landed, and his lower back – below the back plate of his body armor - landed directly across the top of what had to be Wayne's hand cannon. It felt like a jagged rock.

"Dumbass," he grunted, shaking his head to clear the pain as he rolled to his feet. In the near pitch-black darkness, he felt for the Desert Eagle next to his foot. He grabbed it up and made sure there was a round chambered with finger check. Reaching around the door frame, he didn't bother to aim as he fired two quick, booming shots down the hall into the lobby. The shock wave from the massive pistol drowned out the alarm for a moment. The ringing was there all along but seemed to return and build slowly as his aural nerves fought back against the .50 caliber's pressure wave.

"There's two of them!" A voice yelled out from the lobby.

He pulled back into the darkened office and smiled to himself. Their stupidity wouldn't last, but he'd take it while it lasted.

"Lay down your weapons!" he yelled. "And we won't kill you all when we come out there."

The was a slight pause, and he could hear furniture being pushed around.

"Who are you? Where's Wayne?"

"Which one's Wayne?" he yelled. "Big fat guy? With a buzz cut?"

"Yeah, Wayne you there? Wayne?"

"I'd be careful if I were you," he yelled back. "You already hit him once." He shook his head. He was dealing with scared idiots. That particular blade cut both ways. '*Scared*' always produced stupid shit you could never guess at.

Guns opened up in the lobby and a storm of lead flew down the hallway, shredding the walls. He hugged the floor, noting that several rounds came through the interior walls passing through the walls of the first office between him and the swinging doors. Drywall wasn't any sort of protection. He did his best to become part of the floor, thinking that they must not have believed Wayne was still alive. That, or they didn't care.

He switched out magazines as their fire dropped away. Squirming to the edge of the door on his belly, he had a great view of the backlit lobby down the long dark hallway. The top of one soldier's head stuck out around the edge of the front check-in counter. He took his time, and sent one round. The upper half of the man's body lying on the floor twitching was far more visible than the side of his head had been.

He squirmed backwards to where he was fully inside the doorway, using the open door's thick wood as some added protection as they opened up on him again. He couldn't do anything besides wait for the barrage to pass. They all seemed to run dry at the same time. He recognized the typical spray and pray, though when that many rounds were coming in his direction it was going to be effective sooner or later.

He waited, mentally imagining them reloading. They seemed to pause themselves until someone fired, kicking off another shit storm. This fusillade chewed up the walls above him. Pieces of carpet and gypsum dust were hanging thick, the former floating down around him in the darkness, the latter choking the air with its fine dust. The sound of broken glass, falling from the windows of all the offices was still in the air when the shooting stopped.

Forcing his breathing to slow, he didn't react, didn't move. Focusing on the word 'patience' in his head, he wondered how much ammo these clowns carried with them. There was another long pause, and he moved slowly into position, waiting. One gun from the lobby fired. He could tell from the passage of the bullet, as it screamed by over his head, it had been aimed right down the middle of the hallway. He lay prone in the dark. Only his rifle, right shoulder and the right side of his head projecting out beyond the door jamb. One good flashlight from the idiots in the lobby and this would go from bad to worse.

"We got him, go!" he could hear somebody yelling orders at the end of an argument whose details were beyond his hearing.

"Fuck you! You're so sure, you go!"

A single shot rang out. It hadn't been aimed at him.

"You two, go!" The voice in charge yelled after a moment. Jason could picture an aimed barrel accompanying the order.

Not the A-team by any stretch, shooting their own people. Someone out there had just elected themselves head honcho.

He waited, did his best to relax, ready to roll away into the partial protection the office offered. The heavy swinging doors were still stuck open, which from the pitch-black darkness of the corridor, he had no problem seeing out into the lit-up lobby.

He waited as the two unlucky selectees crept down the hallway, hugging the same wall that included the doorway of the office he was in. Their rifles were up on their shoulders and angled at the opposite wall, towards Wayne's office. He waited in the dark, tracking their back lit forms as they crept closer.

"I think we got him," the one in front turned his head back towards his partner as he stopped his forward movement. Jason could hear the strength of hope in the statement.

"Go." The one in the back nudged him with his own gun.

"We need a flashlight..."

He fired two, quick, three round bursts, dropping both of them and moved as fast as he was able, half rolling, half inch-worming backwards on his elbows.

Another barrage let loose just as he reached the desk and crawled underneath it. This time, all the fire was targeted on his side of the hallway. The office came apart above him as leaned into a set of desk drawers between his body and the lobby. Rounds passed easily through the drywall, kept going and went through the far wall chewing up everything in between. A bouncer or a piece of exploding furniture hit the heel of his of one of his boots jerking it to the side. He breathed in relief when there wasn't that blast of pain that followed being shot. Not counting the current crease in his calf, he'd been shot twice before. In those previous instances, it had felt like somebody tugging at his shirt or pants leg in one case until his brain had caught up with delayed responses from traumatized nerves.

He let out a held breath in relief, he already had one leak he doing his best to ignore.

The assaulting fire seemed to go on forever. The part of his brain that was still functioning noted it was still spray and pray, they couldn't be sending anybody else up the hall way in the middle of that fire. They all were firing on full auto until the actions of their rifles tried to pull a round from the magazine that wasn't there. They all stopped firing within seconds of each other. If he was any judge of enemy fire, he guessed there were at least ten or fifteen guns arrayed against him in the lobby.

He waited for a full ten count before he slowly belly-crawled back to the doorway through a new carpet of broken glass, picture frames, pieces of computer monitor, a printer and God knew what else. This time, they only sent one poor bastard down the hall. But a smarter one. There was a flashlight attached to the tactical shotgun he glimpsed before pulling his head back.

Going up on his elbows, he let his assault rifle hang from its sling as he slowly cinched its harness up tight against his chest. He pulled his knife, and came to his feet, as he watched the beam of light dance erratically on the walls of the corridor. Maybe he could get them to think he was out of ammo. He could tell the soldier was close and checking out the first set of offices, opposite each other. Then the light fell back into the hall way and started working its way towards the rearmost offices. The man paused just out of sight, wary, listening for any indication someone was alive. Jason thought he could hear the man's quick shallow breaths.

The barrel of the shotgun broke into his line of sight within the doorway, a split second after the weak beam of light illuminated the desk and began working its way across the office to his corner against the door. He lunged and grabbed the barrel of the shotgun with his left hand, forcing it up and away through a counterclockwise turn. The gun went off with a massive blast that showered them in pulverized ceiling tile. Jason's knife hand was already swinging, following the turn of his shoulders.

The shitbag holding the shotgun was stronger than he looked and tried to block the swing with the barrel of the gun. It almost worked, but he was too slow. The knife sank into the man's neck to the hilt. Jason pulled the thug into the room by the grip on his knife and the barrel of the gun. The blade popped free with a grizzly resistance he did his best to ignore. He grabbed the shotgun away from the soldier, and ignored the bubbling noise blowing out of the space where the man's throat had been. He moved to the door and pointed the shotgun and its light down the hall towards the lobby.

"I got him, I got him." He yelled. He tossed the shotgun to the floor of the office, making sure the light wasn't pointed out into the dark hallway and moved back into the hallway, crossing at a diagonal towards the lobby to the first office on the other side.

His voice must not have sounded anything like the last sacrificial lamb. They opened up again before he got there. It was worth a try, he thought. He dove behind the desk, breathing in relief as most of the gunfire was directed at the other side of the hall and his last position. He was curled up in a near fetal position, under the desk. More than a few rounds came his way as it seemed there were even more guns out there now.

His hand felt for one of the two grenades in his bag. The hall way was too long to throw into the lobby, and covered in heavy carpet. Bowling the grenade out to where it would do some good wasn't an option either. He waited through the fire, thinking that he would now be shooting off his left shoulder at the doorway or exposing a lot more of himself to shoot normally.

The hallway lit up just as the fire slowed and then died away with a shout from somebody out in the lobby. The bright light moved against the walls. Someone had gotten smart and set up a spot light. Any worry about his shot angle went by the wayside, they'd be coming. He peeked around the desk and was startled to see the swiss cheese of the walls around him backlit by the powerful search light. Raising his head slowly, he located a couple of larger holes that gave him a view out into the hall way. He grinned knowing his rounds would go through the walls as well.

*

"No way he lived through that shit."

Jeff Lacey was crouched down behind the heavy wood of the front desk. Martinez's body lay a few feet to his left, the top of the man's head was spread across the lobby's floor. He looked up at the voice that had spoken. He almost ordered Junior to put his theory to the test. He'd already shot one asshole that wasn't listening to him and as much as he'd enjoyed that, he needed these guys not to turn on him, or run. The growing pile of bodies in the hall, was making either option more likely.

He caught Junior's eye and nodded in agreement. He frog-walked down the length of the check-in counter towards the outside wall of the lobby. Standing by the glass door was Brady and the rest his rolling crew, who had raced back to the hotel. It was their spotlight that had lit up the office hallway. He didn't recognize the new guy holding it, but he was hidden behind an overturned couch with the megaphone shaped spotlight held over the top edge.

"There's nowhere for him to go," Brady shook his head at him as he walked up. He knew what Brady was *not* saying; *'don't even try to order my ass down that hall.'* With the Sheriff out of the picture, Wayne probably dead, this place would fall to him, or Brady. If it was him, he'd need Brady to help keep everyone under control.

He gave his head a slight shake. "Let's light it up again, and then wait for a bit. He's in the logs office across the hall from Wayne's office."

"You sure about that?" Brady asked.

The Brady way asked, there was more than a hint of question of how things had been handled so far.

"Let's try it, and then you pick a team to send after we wait a bit."

"Why me?" Brady wasn't trying to hide his suspicion.

"'Cause I've already picked everybody to send, and shot one asshole who wouldn't go." He pulled the man farther to the side as he whispered. "We in this together?"

Brady regarded him for a moment in silence and then nodded in decision. "Where the fuck is Sleepy?"

Lacy just shook his head. He'd been wondering the same thing.

"Good question. We finish this asshole and then we do for Sleepy."

Brady popped a grin, and spun around directing his team to take up positions with snapping fingers and pointed hands.

Lacey watched everyone in the lobby swap out their magazines, half of them coming up empty and asking for a handout. He did the same, noting that he only had one more in his cargo pocket. He wasn't about to waste it on some asshole that was probably already dead. When this was over, he and Brady would clean house. If his new partner didn't play along, he'd need to fix that too.

*

Chapter 22

'*Miami's*' real name was Gene and earlier in the evening, he'd expected to have to work until midnight emptying out the kitchen store. After that, he'd hoped to find a quiet place to sleep because he knew his team was slated for an early morning departure on a foraging run meant to fill up the same store. The former insurance adjuster hadn't expected to have seven other people looking at him in question for answers he didn't have. They'd just found the two large duffle bags with assault rifles, right where the ninja guy said they'd be.

"Anybody familiar with this stuff?" he asked with a lot more hope than he felt.

"You bet your ass." Johnny kneeled next to him and pulled out an M4.

Johnny would no doubt be a soldier right now, if he hadn't put up so much of a fight when they'd first caught him. He was just recently healed enough from his introductory beating to have been added to their work team.

"Well, I'd say you're in charge then."

"Not so fast." A voice reached them out of the darkness.

They all looked up as three black suited soldiers with guns leveled, walked out of the dark recesses of the bottom level garage.

"Drop the gun, friend."

*

Michelle had nearly bowled him over as he waited for an elevator to take him down to the lobby. She had popped out of the stairwell door moving fast. Sleepy had been on his way downstairs; the sentries at Macy's hadn't reported in at the top of the hour. He personally didn't give a shit. It was nothing that didn't happen all of the time, but he was on thin ice with Wayne. The guy was actively looking for a reason not to keep him around. He'd seen the man staring at Michelle. By Wayne's thinking, Michelle was probably more than enough justification to off him. He needed to stay alive long enough to recruit some people willing to fight back.

Michelle was wearing a smile that he didn't think he'd ever seen before; she was almost vibrating in excitement. He did a double take wondering what was going on. Michelle grabbed a handful of his shirt as she glanced past him down the hallway, making sure she wouldn't be overheard.

"Your Ninja friend is here." She was beaming with joy. "I just ran into him in the main lobby."

"What!?"

"He wants you to get your team together, and meet up with Gene and his work group at the Neiman Marcus, on the hotel entrance level. He had guns for all of them."

He was having trouble catching up, "Who did?"

"Jason," she almost yelled. "He brought a bunch of guns for them, but you need to hurry. He was on his way to find Wayne in his office."

"He's crazy, he can't just..."

Michelle's slap rocked his head back.

"It's happening, Sleepy! Now! We have to deal with it."

His face stung, and looking at her, she seemed far too excited considering how this was likely to end. One glance at her, and he knew she wasn't in the mood to hear any of that. His mind caught up; she was right, it was happening.

"All right," he caught his breath. "Lock yourself in the room. You still have the gun?"

She patted her back under the heavy sweatshirt. "Of course."

"Don't open the door for anybody, but me. You understand?"

She nodded, leaning forward and kissed him. "Take care of yourself, Daniel. But do what you have to do. This has to end."

"You're right," he said as he held the elevator doors open with his hand. They were buzzing in protest. He stepped in and turned to face Michelle. "Stay in the room."

"Go!" She said back to him as the doors closed on her face.

*

Michelle made certain Sleepy's elevator was on its way before turning back to the stairwell door. It was a long climb up to the 14th floor but it was all she could do to force herself to take one stair at a time. The last time she'd been up there was during her first week at the Ritz. Then, she'd ridden the elevator, with Bauman. She'd known what was going to happen at the top of that elevator ride. By then, she'd spent two nights in the ballroom and suffered far worse. She could remember her secret wish that Bauman would lose his temper, kill her.

The Sheriff, new at the time to his position and power hadn't lost his temper. His sick smile, threatening laughter and what had come after, had been worse. He'd made certain she knew she was selling herself for food and a safe roof. That was how he'd thought of it, just part of the natural order of things. She'd been a prisoner, and couldn't have left if she'd tried. That she hadn't tried, was her greatest shame. More than what he'd made her do, Bauman, before he'd tired of her, had killed any hope she had.

She'd come to the Ritz with the long since dead radio broadcasts having sold it as a bastion of safety. She'd driven in from Ashburn to the mall in her dead husband's Jeep Cherokee following signs promising sanctuary. Aside from the countless dead on the road, the husk of civilization seen through every broken shop window, the empty streets and soot filled sky, it was a drive she'd made a couple of times a year. She could remember that feeling of relief when she'd first rolled into the parking lot amidst a mixed crowd of forty or fifty people. She could remember the sense of hope she had felt that they weren't shooting, fighting or rioting. She couldn't have known the calm she had seen was fear.

She'd been out of her car for just a moment before she noticed the women, and their bruises. A few caught her eye, shaking their heads, willing her back into the car, most numb beyond caring. Men with guns surrounded her and she was escorted inside the mall as the people outside were herded into the backs of trucks. The next two weeks had been a hell that she couldn't have conceived of before. Her time forced servicing the Sheriff, more degrading, if less painful than those two days in the ballroom. It had come to an end when someone fresh was found. Someone whose hope and dignity were still intact.

She couldn't remember the woman's name. She could remember not wanting to know, even as she'd been relieved that Bauman had a new diversion. The newcomer had swallowed a bottle of aspirin a few days later. If not for Daniel's intervention, Michelle knew she'd probably have been sent back upstairs to the Penthouse. Bauman had wanted her back.

She stopped, realizing that she'd run out of stairs. She was standing at the stairwell landing for the 14th floor. She was back.

She couldn't remember most of the climb. The barest echo of gunfire danced at the edges of her awareness coming up the stairwell. She pinched her arm hard, attempting to get out of her own head. Bauman was a broken man according to Daniel. Wayne and his thugs had grown tired of pretending they listened to him. By himself, Bauman could probably kill Wayne. But he'd spent too much time holding himself up, separating himself from the men he relied on, with the bullshit story of rebuilding for a future. Wayne had known the world was dead and was going to spend his days eating its carcass. In the end, and to the strong, anarchy was an easier sell than the hard work civilization required. Bauman's dreams of the future were just images in his own head to justify what he had done.

The Sheriff had been sulking for days. Daniel was half convinced the man would off himself. If he had, she was going to kick him in the balls so hard he'd come back so she could kill him again. The blast of the fire alarm shocked her out of her funk and she was running down the hall for his room. She pounded on his door until Bauman's face appeared within the open crack. The fact that he had the safety bar engaged on the door demonstrated how far he'd fallen.

"Sleepy killed Wayne. He's got a bunch of them trapped in your office. He sent me to get you."

"Sleepy killed him?" The man's distrust was always there, and his wariness caught her by surprise.

She nodded, not having to feign her heavy breathing. Her heart was suddenly pounding in her chest. "Hurry, he needs you! I could hear gun fire."

The door slammed in her face and was wrenched back open. He had grabbed her by the arm, pulled her inside and slammed her up against the wall before she knew it. A beefy hand went around her throat, tightening.

"Bullshit."

She tried to talk, breathe, but just gagged until the pressure relented.

She dropped to her knees sucking in air, willing her vision to clear.

"He needs your help," she gasped. "We all do."

"I don't need his whore to tell me that," he fired back. "How many men does Sleepy have?"

"All of them." She nodded. "Except for six or seven of Wayne's guys trapped in the admin hallway, in Wayne's... I mean your office."

"Why should I believe you?"

She didn't need to force the fear she felt.

"Sleepy said I was the only one you'd believe!" She looked down and away. "I didn't want to come here."

Bauman seemed to take too long considering her words. The asshole was so paranoid, it took a moment for his ego to catch up.

"Come on," he relented finally in a softer voice. "I know you've missed me." He reached down leering at her, and dragged her to her feet slowly. He smoothed out the sleeves of her sweatshirt in a comforting gesture that made her skin crawl.

"So, Sleepy sent his woman to come and get me?"

"We need you. Everybody is wondering what's going on – who's who."

Bauman liked hearing that. He was needed; but his paranoia hadn't let go.

"Did you bring a radio?"

She shook her head. "Sleepy waited until a lot of Wayne's guys were out on patrol. If he uses a radio. They'll hear and rush back."

"Sleepy's being smart." Wayne jerked his head once with his hands back on his hips. She could see his ego puffing up in front of her. "Wait here."

He moved off into his bedroom she could hear something being moved around. Bauman came back a moment later with a hand gun, waving it proudly at her for a second before slipping it inside his belt.

"Wayne thought he got all of them. Let's go, sweet cheeks."

She held her ground, still in the process of catching her breath. "The alarm... the elevators are locked down. I can't do those stairs again."

"Suit yourself," he said, surging past her and slapping her on the ass on the way. "Your talents lay elsewhere, anyway."

She listened to his laughter for just a moment before pulling out the handgun hidden at her lower back. It was a Glock. Sleepy had shown her how to use it and she had spent hours dry firing it in her room and the dark the picture of her mind until she was certain she wouldn't hesitate.

She stepped into the hallway and aimed for his legs and fired, following him down the hall screaming. Bauman went down in a tumble and rolled, a bright red blossom of justice sprouting in the middle of his back. She fired three more times, only hitting him once in the thigh.

He was on his back, unmoving. His fingers were spasming as if he were plugged into a wall socket. The front of his stomach was red where the bullet must have exited. She stood over him and smiled as she kicked his gun farther down the hallway.

"Almost thought you were back on top, didn't you?" she said.

"We need you Sheriff, help us, please," she sang to his face and then laughed enjoying the look of shock on his face. "You... pathetic piece of shit!"

She backed off half a step and launched herself forward, her size seven Timberlands trying to drive his balls into his head.

He gave a muted grunt, eyes rolling up into his head.

"So, you can still feel that... I was worried, I was..." She grinned.

"Bi..tch" It came out as a sad moan.

"You can do better than that," she smiled.

He still hadn't moved. She'd seen enough gunshot wounds in the last eight months to realize his spine was hit or at least damaged.

"You just have to convince me," she whispered, kneeling down close to him. "Convince me you really care. You remember that game, don't you?"

She tilted her ear towards his face, she could see the struggle on his lips. "Come on, you can do it."

"I... I... sor"

She pulled her head back and looked at him. "You know, I'm just not feeling it."

She stood back up, watching the blood continue to pool beneath him.

"I've always wondered what your wife and kids would have thought of you, if they could have seen what dear old dad had become." She left him with that and walked off slowly towards the stairwell, stopping to pick up his gun as she went.

She made it to the stairwell door before she turned to look back. He still hadn't moved, couldn't. The top his head faced her.

What would Frank and her own children think of her?

She was walking back towards him before she realized what she was doing. She didn't say a word, didn't gloat. She just raised her gun and fired once into the top of his head.

*

Daniel stepped out of the elevator into the mall and noted the absence of the guard posted to the elevator. He swiped his card on the stairwell door and pulled it open. Simmons lay there dead, looking as if he were laughing at something. No loss there, Simmons was a certified mouth-breathing degenerate and one of Wayne's lackeys.

He stepped back out into the mall and pushed the heavy steel door shut against the slow closing hydraulic arm. Before it latched, he placed Simmons' diamond encrusted Rolex in the jamb. A testament to an era when things like time and money had value. The idiot had no doubt taken it from one of the several high-end jewelry stores in the mall.

He jogged across the mezzanine sky walk into the Neiman Marcus cul-de-sac and pulled up short as the fire alarm in the hotel went active. The mall itself had a different system, but the loud ringing could still be heard clearly. So close to the hotel's mall entrance, the massive, three-tiered department store had been the first to be emptied and then restocked with scavenged supplies. Food mostly, stacked in labeled boxes, stretched well over his head on shelves they'd looted from warehouses, restaurants and homes. This was the real prize, he thought. Not for the first time, he considered trying to set fire to the mall. There wasn't anything in it worth the cost of what these people had inflicted on other survivors.

No, he stopped in mid-thought; the food and supplies weren't evil. They meant survival for somebody, for a lot of mouths. For whoever survived this evening, regardless of who was in control, those people could be fed from here, at least for a while. He continued toward the bank of escalators in the middle of the store, half expecting to get shot by one of the sheep that Jason had supposedly armed.

This wasn't at all what he and Jason had planned. He was at least a good month away from pulling enough people together to take on Wayne and he'd fucking told Jason that in the last message he'd sent. A message he knew had been picked up. It had been the same one outlining the plan to trap him in Vienna. Something must have happened to force Jason's hand. Whatever it was, it wasn't as if he had a choice at this point to do anything other than throw in.

Wayne, dead or not, had a lot of friends. The type of friends that wouldn't spend a single second mourning the asshole before they tried to take over. They all knew what a good thing they had going. It was their very own post-apocalyptic playland. They wouldn't run, and they'd probably welcome the opportunity to thin the herd of people needing to be watched.

"Stop right there," a cold voice from behind brought him up short. A woman, something strange about her voice.

He stopped and held his hands up.

"Sleepy?" He turned around at the second voice, a familiar face, blackened with face paint stepped out from behind a pallet of rice.

It took him a second to recognize Pro. The face behind the war paint had smiled, and that had done it. The kid seemed to have grown but that might have been the body armor and assault rifle.

"Pro?"

The kid stepped around and walked up to him giving him a big hug. "Is Michelle ok?"

"She's locked in my room."

"Sleepy! I was hoping you'd have more guys with you." Reed approached him, Cory and Griff in tow, all decked out in gear like Pro. Behind them stood Gene and his work crew or what was left of it. They were all similarly armed but lacked the body armor, helmets and boots.

"I could say the same," he shook Reed's hand. "We need to hurry, but there's at least three more guys I can count on, out at the parking deck, but they aren't close to alone."

"How many?" It was the woman who had got the drop on him. It seemed like she was in charge. "And I thought your name was Daniel."

"Probably ten or fifteen guards on the top deck," he answered. "I've stayed off the radio, but the entire mall team and one of the rolling patrols are supposed to enforce that main entrance if the alarm goes off." He tapped his radio hanging from his belt. "Lacey's in the hotel lobby, he'll be calling the shots if Wayne is dead."

He nodded at the young woman, who glared at him because he hadn't answered her question. "Jason knows me as Daniel, to everyone here, I'm Sleepy."

"Rachel, he's cool." Pro added his judgement to the debate.

"Wayne's dead?" One of the women from Gene's group stepped forward, holding the clearly unfamiliar M4 awkwardly at her waist.

"Hopefully," he nodded, worried that she might have a problem with that. People were strange, some of them positively adopted their guards.

The woman grinned, "It's a start."

His radio barked with static, followed by the distinct sound of gunfire. "We've got armed rats trapped in the admin hallway. They ain't going anywhere."

"That's Lacey." Daniel explained to them.

"Wayne's trapped in there too," the voice on the radio broke out again. "I need Brady's rolling unit here now. West rollers, get back here and watch the mall entrances on the parking deck. Deck crew get some extra eyes on the elevator entrance. Whoever this is, they are already inside. Guards at Macy's are down. Lock the sheep down!"

"Shit..." Daniel did the mental math in his head and pointed back the way he'd just come from. "Some will be headed to the elevator from outside, they'll set up directly across from us."

"Not a problem, Sleepy." It was Pro this time that spoke up.

He had a moment reconciling this version of Pro with the kid that had been captured by him and the Sheriff's men those months ago, or even the enthusiastic version that he'd spoken to with Jason two months ago in the middle of the night. Pro just seemed older; and had more of an edge.

"Right," he waved back towards the entrance of the department store. "Let's go, we can see who they are they are from inside here. They won't have any cover standing at the elevator."

They moved as a group, Gene's work team bringing up the rear at the young woman's direction. Shouts of alarm reached them from the next cul-de-sac over to their right which led out to the parking deck. They'd just settled in behind the shelves surrounding the store's entrance, by the time four figures ran by with their backs to them headed to the elevator.

"Don't shoot!" He hissed as loud as he dared. "The guy in the brown coat is with us."

"Which one?" Pro and the woman asked simultaneously on either side of him, their heads already down against their scopes on their M4s.

"Uhh, the one on the far left... our left!" He corrected quickly.

"Race you to the middle guy," the young woman said.

"You're on," Pro countered.

Their suppressed rifles barked twice each in close succession, knocking down the three soldiers standing next to Mitchell who just stood there in confusion, looking down at the figures on the floor. One of them was struggling to get back up.

Pro fired again and the soldier collapsed.

"I won," Pro said.

"You had to shoot your first guy twice," the woman countered. "You lose points for that."

"Whatever..."

Daniel tried to put the crazy next him out of his mind. Pro and this young woman had a strange idea of entertainment. Mitch, the sole remaining upright soldier had figured out where the shots were coming from and he had both hands stretched up over his head as he tried crouching down making himself smaller. There was nowhere for him to go, nothing for him to hide behind.

He stood and walked out from behind the counter that hid him. "Mitch, It's me! Get over here."

The surviving soldier just stood there for a moment before realizing he was alive for a reason. He sprinted over as best he could.

"Sleepy! What's going on?" The man's eyes got big as he realized how many people were hidden in the shelves and pallets lining the front of the store.

"Where's Parker and Naks?" Sleepy stepped up to him, close, aware that the young woman with Pro still had her gun leveled at Mitch.

Mitch pointed through the store at an angle. "Outside on the parking deck, with Joey T and the rest of his team."

"How many does he have?" Sleepy asked.

"Uhh... six I think, maybe seven, plus Parker and Naks."

Sleepy turned around and snapped his fingers at Reed. "You remember Parker and Naks?"

"Oh yeah," Reed replied.

"Ok," Sleepy nodded to himself as he looked around at the group. *This could work... if the sheep will actually fight. Better to find out now than later.* He knew there was no way Gene and his group could walk out there armed as they were, without immediately getting lit up. "How many handguns do we have here?"

Turned out they had more than enough. Pro, and he learned the young woman's name was Rachel, had been carrying two each. Neither had been happy about turning them over to 'the civilians,' as Rachel had referred to them.

A second round of heavy gunfire was heard from beneath them in the adjoining hotel and it ended any complaint she had.

Daniel walked casually out the main entrance of the mall onto the top parking deck leading Gene and his work group. The guard force was spread out in front of him, facing outward behind a semicircle of parked vehicles. Just like they'd practiced doing. Daniel was struck by irony of the situation. He'd had to beg, cajole, and in the end, threaten the soldiers to take security seriously. Now, when he could have wished they didn't care, they were ready for trouble.

"What the hell, Sleepy!" Joey T. turned as he pushed the heavy glass doors open. "What's going on in there?"

Joey T. looked and sounded like he had come from the streets of Newark. The short, olive skinned man had sideburns from the 70's, and enough gold chain around his neck to be an extra in an MTV rap video. Sleepy doubted if the protection racket being run out of the hotel was the first the man had been involved in.

"We're staying off the radio," Sleepy explained still walking up. "Whoever this is, they're already inside, trapped in the admin offices. Lacey wants some more guns down there."

Joey swung his assault rifle up on a shoulder, and grinned. "That's what I'm talking about."

Sleepy looked around and spotted Parker and Nako, or "Naks", side by side behind a lemon yellow civilian H3 Hummer.

He pointed at them both. "Leave me those two assclowns, take the rest with you and get down to lobby." Joey just looked at him for a moment and was about to say something.

"The rest of you," Sleepy shouted. "Go with Joey T, do whatever he says, he's in charge." He waved at the rest of the crew. The fact they looked to Joey for confirmation instead of jumping at his order went a long way to show Sleepy how thin the ice was under his feet with Wayne's crowd.

Sleepy watched Joey puff up a little. Whatever Joey was going to ask died on his lips.

"Right! Let's go," the self-styled wise guy yelled.

"What you want with these sheep?" Mike Rogers, one of Lacey's friends walked up to him and pointed at Gene and his work crew. Joey was still there and suddenly interested in the answer.

"Just 'cause they don't have guns," he replied. "Don't mean they can't stand here looking like they do."

Sleepy clapped Rogers on the shoulder. "Go already, elevators are down with the alarm, you need to hurry."

Sleepy turned to Gene and the rest of his work crew. "You all spread out, look important."

"What are we supposed to do without guns?" Gene asked, but he was moving forward.

"Catch a bullet meant for me," Sleepy said.

Joey and Mike had a good laugh at that. It seemed to convince them that he wasn't trying to pull something. Sleepy let out a breath of relief as they turned for the entrance and led their team back into the mall. He watched them go through the first set of glass doors, then the second, before disappearing from view into the dark pit of the mall.

A few seconds later, both sides of the mall's entrance hall opened up in an explosion of muzzle flashes and the sound of gunfire. It didn't last long. Sleepy wondered if Pro and Rachel had had a bet going on that round as well.

"Ok," Sleepy yelled. "Gene, send somebody back in for your rifles, and get them back to your people here. Anybody rolls up here, you know what to do." He pointed at Parker and Naks; the diminutive black guy and the tall burly Korean seemed like an odd Mutt and Jeff tandem to him. A couple of months on the road from Pittsburgh before being rounded up by the Sheriff had formed a strong bond between the two.

"You two are with me and our friends inside. You ready?"

"We're ready," Naks said. "Been ready." Parker who never said much, just nodded in agreement.

"Let's go, then."

*

Chapter 23

The assclowns in the lobby were using the spot light to good effect, Jason thought. This barrage of automatic weapons fire was far better aimed. Most of it was still directed across the hall, but there were clearly a couple of guns out there with an angle on his side of the hall and they were using it. The couch against the hallway's wall slowed down the rounds a lot before they slammed into the wooden desk he was hiding behind. But it didn't stop all of them. The desk was full of holes, and it vibrated like a giant guitar every time a round impacted. The only thing that kept him alive was the rolling stack of drawers under one end of the desk. He huddled behind it, doing the best he could to weather the storm of lead as each successive round coming through the office walls let more light into the room.

He almost giggled in panic as the set of drawers vibrating against him took rounds and started to come apart. The fire started to slow and he let out a breath of relief just before a round tugged at the back of his left shoulder. He tensed for a split second, knowing what was coming. His nervous system must have taken that as permission because the pain that flooded outward, cascading down his arm was scream-worthy. He bit down on it, riding the wave with his mouth clamped shut. It resulted in a guttural keening he had no problem hearing within his head.

The fire let up completely and he didn't dare move, beyond his right hand which he reached up with to feel the three-inch-long furrow the bullet had dug through the outside of his shoulder. *That's going to leave a mark.* He struggled not to laugh as the initial tidal wave of pain settled in to stay with a heavy ache. There was enough of the spot light flooding into the room through the torn-up walls, that he didn't have to peek over the desk to see how much cover he had left.

He did anyway. It looked like the remains of the shredded couch was all that was holding up the remaining dry wall. Whole chunks of the wall were missing. There were holes with shredded edges, big enough for him to dive through, had he wanted to. He most definitely didn't. He moved slowly, praying the desk would hide his movement and dug his two grenades out of his bag. They might wait, they might not. One thing was for certain; after this last shitstorm, they'd be coming. He ignored the tearing sensation in his shoulder as he moved, converting the pain to anger. Anger he could harness, channel. He was about done with these assholes, one way or another.

They did wait. He did the same, ignoring the blood that he could feel running down his arm, soaking his sleeve. The blood made the grip on the grenade in his left hand sticky and slick at the same time. He mentally shook his head in disgust. Were they expecting that he was somehow going to go Leroy Jenkins on them? Charge down the hallway with guns blazing?

What they clearly didn't think of, was the fact that the spotlight cast long shadows of anything moving in the hallway. Or, maybe there were enough of them out there, they just didn't care. That particular thought didn't help his mood. He spotted the moving shadow; a nondescript mass of heads and limbs, a slow-moving stain on the walls and on the floor of the hallway outside his office door creeping closer. The mass of shadows grew shorter as it came closer. He laid out extra magazines on the floor, loosening his rifle's sling in the process. Once he was ready, he pulled the pins on the grenades, holding the spoons down. The tight grip on the grenade in his left hand sent waves of pain up his arm and across his back.

"Gotta be toast, man," he heard one of the shadows in the hall whisper.

Somebody told him to shut up and the shadow blob inched closer.

He waited as long as he could but with a suddenness that surprised him, actual figures were in view through the holes in the walls above the couch. Bullet holes, to be sure, they hadn't yet made it to the pillow-sized gap in the drywall that was his target. He knew they were backlit and he had a better view of them than the reverse. That would change the moment he moved. On his knees behind the desk, he gauged the distance to his target hole, noting the condition of the lower wall behind what remained office's couch, and the now sieve-like front of the desk.

There wasn't enough cover to mitigate the blast of a grenade, let alone two. He was fine with that math. The assholes in the hallway wouldn't have any cover. The leading edge of a shoulder eclipsed the edge of the biggest hole. He popped the spoons, and waited a second. It felt like a two-handed shotput, or a chest pass with a heavy basketball. Despite the pain in his shoulder and arm that made him want to scream, he couldn't miss, the grenades only had to fly about six feet. He knew that particular fact was going to go from advantage to disadvantage in exactly two and a half seconds.

He was pulling himself back under the desk as quick as he could amidst a couple of grunts of surprise from the hall way. Ignoring them, he grabbed the shot-up set of wobbly desk drawers and pulled it down to next to him for extra protection. It collapsed in on itself, reduced to a four-inch high stack of wood the moment it impacted the floor.

He almost laughed out loud. So much for that... if that wasn't a sign, not sure what would be. He pulled himself into a fetal position, tucked his chin and plugged his ears as he heard the first shots. They sounded like they were coming from the lobby, but he knew that couldn't be right. The world moved towards him. In a flash, the wall, couch, desk, and all the air in between, compressed to lethal density hammered into him in a series of impacts that drove him into the back wall. He felt something give in his back and was spared the lancing pain of the grenade's shrapnel riding within the shockwave.

*

Daniel counted off the people he had before they reached the stairwell door at the elevator. There were nine of them. Pro and Rachel flanked him, pushing him to hurry. He was glad Reed was there, he could handle himself. Cory was levelheaded but probably worth less in a fight than Griff, who would be next to worthless. Griff was a decent human being, but Daniel was fairly certain the man had to remind himself to breathe. He was motivated though; he'd not been treated well by Wayne or any of the other soldiers for that matter. Mitch, Parker and Naks were solid, they'd all been as vocal in their complaints as they could have been and survived. It was why they'd been among the first he'd reached out to.

And then there was him. Who was he kidding? Motivation was all he had.

"This looks like the right way," Pro said as he pulled the stairwell door open. They all stepped over a body they did their level best to ignore and went down the stairway taking the steps two at time.

"Wait there!" Sleepy yelled as Pro and Rachel leading the way reached the door to the lobby.

"Give me some grenades," he wheezed as they all piled up behind the heavy steel door.

Rachel scowled at him. "I'm going to need mine."

"Listen!" he almost yelled back at her. "Parker, Naks, Mitch and I should be able to just walk in. Give me some grenades."

She looked at Pro for an answer and unclipped one from the front of her vest when he nodded in agreement. Pro handed one to Parker and Reed gave up one to Naks.

"Ok, this door lets out into the elevator hallway that leads to the lobby, and lays perpendicular to the admin offices hallway. If we clear out the back of the lobby, we should have some cover, but we are going to be outnumbered big time."

"Let's go!" Rachel said nodding furiously. This girl wasn't going to wait for further planning.

"Ready?" He looked over at Gene, Parker and Naks.

They both just nodded as Rachel opened the door. "Go," she hissed.

Daniel led the way with his three compatriots following close behind. "I'll start it off," he said. "Be cool. Until then, remember, we belong here." He knew he was talking to reassure himself more than anything.

He rounded the corner to see close to fifteen or twenty people hiding behind overturned tables and couches, guns all leveled to the left of them down the hall way to the admin offices. Someone had one of the rechargeable spotlights up and over the edge of a couch, shining down the hallway.

Lacey spotted them the moment they rounded the corner. The man turned towards him, so did the end of his rifle.

"Where you been?"

Daniel pointed down the admin hallway. "He's not alone, we took out a bunch of them on the parking deck."

"Shit!" Lacey spit on the floor but managed to turn his rifle away as he reached for his radio.

"Don't!" He yelled. "They're listening in. There might be more."

Sleepy maneuvered himself next to a wide, dark wood encased support pillar in the middle of the lobby and directed the rest of his erstwhile team to find some cover in the back.

"How many in there?"

Lacey just grinned back at him and held up one finger and then placed it against his lips. Then he pointed down the long hallway. Sleepy edged around the pillar and saw five figures moving slowly away from him down the admin corridor. They were adjacent to the swinging doors, one of which was gone, of the other, only a sliver of it remained hanging from single hinge.

He swallowed and moved back around the pillar, he pulled the pin on the grenade and let it fly. It was far heavier than he'd imagined. He'd been a decent baseball player in his youth, and he aimed at a spot about halfway between Lacey and where Brady was standing with a couple of his party pals. Lacey was sadistic, Brady he thought was much smarter and probably more dangerous. The grenade bounced on the wooden floor far better than he imagined it would. It slammed into the glass wall fronting the lobby and went right through it.

Shit... He stared at the hole in the glass dumbfounded until he realized Lacey was swinging his gun around. He stepped behind the pillar just as the man and several others fired. A split second later the grenade went off. The wall of glass fronting the hotel lobby had a line of chest high sandbags on the outside. There was nothing stopping the heavy window from being turned into a shotgun blast of pebbled safety glass. Riding the edge of a shockwave, there wasn't anything safe about it. Sleepy heard the clatter of the glass shrapnel slam into the pillar behind him, aware of the deadly projectiles flying past mere inches from his face.

He managed to open his eyes in time to be assaulted by a shockwave and fireball roiling out from the admin hallway. The force of the blast, channeled by the hallway slammed into him and almost knocked him out from behind the pillar he was hiding behind. Something slammed into his arm, and he was spun around, going down hard, dimly aware that his world was being torn apart by gun fire.

"No!" Rachel screamed as the second, larger explosion rocked the lobby. They were stacked up behind one another against the inside wall of the elevator lobby, listening to Sleepy yell at one of the soldiers that had Jason trapped. There was the shortest of pauses in the conversation, when an explosion sent a wave front of glass spraying through the space of the lobby. Pieces of glass embedded themselves in the heavy paneling across from them.

Someone started firing, and she'd taken two steps, her rifle coming up onto a target when the fireball and shockwave shot out of the admin hallway off to her left. She was still screaming when the shockwave passed. Pro was beside her, and the others followed as they came in at a right angle against an enemy that was for the most part still kissing the floor out of instinct or screaming in pain at the horrific wounds from the glass shrapnel. She tried to control her shots as Jason had taught her, making sure those same figures didn't get up.

She spotted Sleepy, laid out on the floor, dead or unconscious behind a pillar. She ignored the man and stepped up behind the same pillar. She spun and came very close to shooting Griff, but realized he was shooting at other soldiers hunkered down behind a table. He was bleeding from a cut in his head, and screaming as he fired. She brought her gun up and stepped out from behind the pillar moving toward the receptions desk. She shot two more figures that were still moving on the floor.

A figure popped up over the counter, gun leveled at her, she was going to be too slow. The man's head snapped back at the recoil of Pro's rifle to her side.

"You're welcome," Pro laughed to himself for a moment before several soldiers opened on them from behind a couch. They had just levered the guns over the back of the couch were firing blindly. She heard the heavy, wet impact of something, and turned to see Pro spinning to the floor. She dove towards him, half catching him as they both hit the floor. She managed to get her gun around and fire into the couch even as she saw Reed and the Cory in the back of the room lay waste to the bastards from behind. A split-second later Cory was blown backward by a shotgun blast from somewhere unseen on the floor.

She watched as Griff spun in place, hit by something, but he kept firing as he just went down to one knee. She thought she saw Reed shoot somebody else in Griff's direction. Rachel stayed prone on the floor and log rolled at an angle.

She put rounds into every body she saw on the floor, too many of these bastards didn't know they were dead. The only figures she could see at the moment whom she didn't shoot were Pro and Sleepy.

A massive barrage of automatic weapons fire opened up at the rear of the lobby where the rest of their group was. Amidst the screams, the booming of a shotgun she turned her head in time to see Mitch, the brown coated soldier go down even as he held his trigger and sprayed the area in front of him. Several rounds pinged off the floor next to her head, gouging chunks of wood from the floor. She looked for something to shoot but all the action was at the back of the lobby, behind the walls of overturned furniture.

As quickly as it started the fire died down. She looked up to see Reed on his feet shooting at someone on the floor. Even with the ringing in her ears, she could tell it had gone quiet.

"Clear!" Reed yelled.

"I think so." Griff said after a moment sounding as if it were a struggle to breathe.

A figure stepped out from behind another pillar and Rachel's barrel came up in time. The man held both hands out, "It's me."

It was the Asian guy, Nako, Naks or something. She nodded and let her barrel fall.

"Did we win?" Pro said from next to her, she could see the blood pooling under his legs.

"You ok?"

"I got shot," Pro said. "What do you think?"

"Parker?" Reed yelled to the room that hung heavy with the smell of cordite and the coppery scent of blood.

"No," Naks shook his head. "He was next me."

"They got Mitch," Reed said.

"Cory is down," Rachel managed as she rolled over to where she could check on Pro.

"It went through the meaty part of your thigh," she said to him, stripping him of his belt and wrapping it tight. "I think you'll live."

"Of course, I will." Pro grimaced as she wrenched it tight. "I'm going to marry Elsa."

"You're in shock, you stupid twit."

"I'm not," Pro shook his head. He reached out to grab her hand. "Jason?"

Somehow the spotlight had stayed on, laying on the floor, still pointed down the former hallway. She followed its beam; the carnage and destruction down the hall was something out of a nightmare. There were body parts laying at the edge of the lobby that belonged to other larger pieces farther in.

She shook her head, "I don't think so. But, we'll…"

The sound of gunfire exploded from the stairwell they had come down. A lot of gunfire. Rachel got to her feet and dragged Pro behind a table and went back for Sleepy who still hadn't moved. Pro would never forgive her if she left him out there not knowing. His eyes were open and blinking. His arm was bleeding and so was his scalp.

She cinched up her rifle and grabbed him under the arm pits and dragged him over to next to Pro. There were three more shots in quick succession from the elevator alcove and then voices.

"Sleepy?!" a woman was yelling from behind the walls that separated the elevators from the lobby.

"That's Michelle," Pro said, from next to her where she huddled. She'd just slapped a fresh magazine into her rifle.

"Sleepy!" A woman's face appeared from around the corner and pulled back after a glance.

"He's over here," Rachel yelled back into space. "He's alive."

"Who are you?" The voice demanded.

"She's cool," Pro whispered to her. She glanced down at him as his eyelids slammed shut.

"She better be..." Rachel whispered. No one else in earshot was conscious.

Three women carrying rifles appeared hesitantly around the corner and paused taking in the destruction. Rachel watched as another two women, followed by a couple of guys, joined them. They were all carrying rifles or handguns but none of them, except one of the guys, was dressed in fatigues and they didn't seem worried about him.

Rachel slowly raised her hand and waved at them. "We're with Jason and Sleepy," she yelled.

"So are we," the woman said back.

Rachel paused looking at Sleepy and Pro, they both needed help. So did Griff, if he was still alive.

She stuck her head up above the edge of the table; they had been joined by dozens of others, most of them armed. Civilians... she smiled. They'd fought back.

"Sleepy and Pro are hurt bad," she said. "Do you have a doctor?"

The woman, Michelle, reached her in a run and kneeled down over Sleepy. She shook her head once. "Sort of."

Rachel stood as people gathered around and begin carrying Sleepy, Pro, and Griff away to their doctor. She watched as Reed took control of the people with the guns. She listened long enough to figure out there were still two groups of soldiers out there somewhere on patrol and one of them was on its way back to the Ritz. They'd be waiting. They could handle it, she thought. The dead's weapons were passed out until nearly everyone was armed.

Rachel nearly came out of her skin at the sound of a gunshot behind her. She spun to see a woman emptying a revolver into one of the dead soldiers near what remained of the revolving door. She fired three times until the gun clicked on empty, another three times before somebody went to her and walked her away. Rachel relaxed. *That* made sense to her.

What didn't, was the fact that these people were now free and Jason was dead. It wasn't fair, and she hated them for it. They'd used him up. Gotten what they wanted and had already forgotten him. She had to see him, she had to know. She picked up the spotlight and started down the hallway.

"Rachel," Reed barked at her to get her attention. Had he been calling her name?

"You don't have to do that," he said much more softly when she had stopped.

"I do." She said and stepped over a lower leg, blown off just below the knee. She noted some strange tattoo and instantly thought that Jason didn't seem the type to have had a tattoo. As irrational as it was, the wayward body part belonging to someone else gave her hope.

Past the remaining frame of a doorway in the hall, the narrow passageway opened up where the walls had been blown outward. She noted the door frames, one hanging on the wall at an angle, the other still attached to its adjoining wall but laying against the far wall of what must have been an office. She let the massive flashlight loiter for too long in one spot and she could feel the gorge of bile rising in her stomach. Body parts were recognizable, one man was strangely all in one piece, if still very dead. The rest of them... she'd gone deep sea fishing for sharks with her dad once off the coast of Cape Town, the stuff they'd thrown in the water for bait...

Chum was what they had called it. It was attached to most of the perimeter. Wherever her light fell, there it was, sometimes a stain or a smear, sometimes the piece of flesh that had left the mark. She had no idea where to look, or if she'd be able to identify Jason if she found him. These assclowns, as Jason would have called them, had thrown everything at him. Killed themselves in the process. She resisted the urge to kick the one whole body she could see.

She felt herself drop to one knee in the middle of what had been the hallway. It was relatively clear there. Everything had been scoured clean here by the explosion. She wiped away the tears that were filling her eyes before they could leave tracks down her face. He didn't deserve to die like this. The spotlight dangled from one hand and she could see where the explosion had happened. There was a large section of the hallway's carpet missing. In the middle of the bare concrete were two small craters; the edges looked whitish-green, like burned metal. As if the concrete had actually caught fire.

She stood up as she realized what she was looking at. The soldiers hadn't done this, Jason had *attacked them*. Her flashlight swatted back and forth from one former office to another, to either side. The straight edges and walls were gone, the space was roughly ovoid. She went left, towards where most of the bodies were; this was Jason she was looking for, after all.

*

Reed was still in the process of directing people and counting up the fallen soldiers, trying to figure out how many of Wayne's goons they could still be facing. Someone had managed to get to the armory and hand out guns to everyone when a firefight erupted. The popping sound of distant gunfire impossible to locate came through the walls of the hotel and adjoining mall. The echoes of the shots were fast and furious at first, but died down just as quickly.

"This is Gene," his radio belched at him after just a moment. "Tanner and his team are down, we ambushed them as they rolled up."

Reed breathed a sigh of relief. That left just four or five of the hardcore unaccounted for and they were all presumably in the one remaining patrol that was still out there somewhere. That same group was no doubt listening to Gene brag over the radio. He wasn't too worried. They had the numbers and weapons now; they could deal with them if they were stupid enough to show up. Bauman's former sheep were feeling their oats and spoiling for a fight. Many of them had come to him, to ask for permission to leave. He was at a loss for words. Why were they asking him?

He asked them to stay, for no other reason than they had no idea where the remaining patrol was at the moment and it could be unsafe.

He realized after a moment that he sounded just like the Sheriff had early on. *You have to stay, it's too dangerous out there.*

"If you really want to leave, take whatever you need and go with God," he said to one couple. "Come back if you need anything, I'd say this place is definitely under new management."

387

The man he didn't know, the woman standing next to him he knew, sort of, she'd worked in the kitchen with Michelle. He shook hands with both of them and was about to suggest that they stay close until things shook themselves out, when Rachel's scream nearly caused him to jump out of his shoes.

"Reed, he's alive. Help me!"

Chapter 24

Jason was going to live. Rachel didn't give a toss what the stoner alchemist who called himself a doctor said. He was going to wake up. She wasn't going to lose him again. She hadn't moved from the chair that they had moved into the hotel room for her. Some meals, a few walks and bathroom breaks were all she allowed herself. She had to be there when he woke or snapped back from wherever sleep had taken him. A part of her was convinced he wouldn't wake up if she wasn't there. She didn't know where the thought came from, but it was always there, hanging in the middle of the hope that kept her going.

Sleepy or Daniel, she couldn't decide which name suited him best, was healing fast. His left arm would take a while to get back to normal, according to their "doctor." But he was on the mend, having suffered a nasty concussion from the bullet or piece of shrapnel that had scored the side of his skull. He was asleep now, and Michelle was in a similar chair watching over him at the foot of the hotel room's other bed.

"Does he know?"

It took Rachel a moment to realize Michelle was talking to her.

"Sorry?"

"Does he know you're in love with him?"

It was said, or asked so point of fact that any thought she had of denying it, died on her tongue even as she shook her head.

"No," she whispered. It made her want to cry and she had promised herself so many times that she was done crying. She'd never admitted it to anyone else. It wasn't like there was anyone else around to talk to. Pro thought he knew, and teased her about it. But that was Pro, he was the little brother who teased her about everything. Jason didn't know. As far as Rachel knew, to him, she was just the crazy young woman whom he felt responsible for; another foundling, damaged goods.

"It doesn't matter," she looked hard at the other woman who was calmly staring back at her. "It's not about that. I'm... we're all he has left. We have to be here for him. I'm just a silly girl, he's still in love with his wife and she's..."

"Dead." Michelle finished the sentence for her. Standing up and dragging her chair over next to Rachel's, she sat back down, reached out and took her hand. The physical contact seemed almost alien to her. When was the last time someone besides Elsa had held her hand? Her dad, just before he had stopped breathing, choking on lungs full of his own blood.

"Like the rest of the world, she's dead. As dead as my husband." Michelle spoke slowly, her eyes filled and she wiped them with her sleeve. "As dead as my children and I'm not going to get them back, not ever."

Rachel squeezed the woman's hand in sympathy that could only be inadequate.

"The thing is," Michelle wiped at her own cheeks. "Sooner or later you have to live the life they would have wanted for you." Michelle nodded at Jason's unconscious form.

"He'll figure that out at some point, in his own time. I did, Daniel helped. Doesn't mean I feel any different, or have forgotten them, my life... before."

"He talks to her," Rachel sighed. "In his sleep." She noticed the glint of surprise on Michelle's face.

"It's not what you're thinking, he sleeps at the bottom of the stairs on the couch, like a guard dog." She felt herself smiling. "In fact, he sleeps *with* the dog. We've all heard him in his sleep."

Michelle took on a faraway look for a moment and shook her head. "Somedays I wake up on the back edge of a dream, I get out of bed thinking that today, I'll drive the kids to school so I can spend some more time with them before I have to go to work. Then I wake up." Michelle let out a low cough and shook her head.

"I don't know if it's habit, or our heart's way of weaning us off people we lose. I think a part of me will always live in the before. But it's a part that gets farther away, every day. Farther away, not weaker, not less." Michelle tossed her head. "Crazy, right?"

"It's not crazy," she knew exactly what the older woman was talking about. The loss wasn't any less. She couldn't think of her parents, her sister without reliving the ache that had come with losing everyone. Time had passed and the pain wasn't as accessible, as ever-present as it had been.

Michelle snorted a short laugh. "Hell, the first thing you do is forget all the annoying shit that used to drive you crazy. I used to watch my husband in his sleep, snoring like you can't imagine. I'd fantasize about smothering him with a pillow. I'd be so angry in the morning, I couldn't speak. When I think of stuff like that now, I smile."

Rachel was quiet, listening to the woman, wondering at Michelle's pain, at her strength. Wishing she could be that strong, that matter of fact. Wishing that Jason didn't see her as... broken, dirty and used up, not to mention crazy. She wasn't crazy... broken? Maybe. She squeezed Michelle's hand and did her best to smile.

"I'm happy for you and Sleepy. I mean... Daniel. I think Pro kind of adopted both of you in his head."

Michelle smiled. "He's a good kid, I think I kind of adopted him too. He's not what I lost," Michelle glanced over at Daniel, and then back to her. "But as painful as it is, Pro helped me remember. So does Daniel."

"I don't think I can ever be that to him," Rachel felt her own eyes fill. "I'm... not, I'm... I was..."

Michelle's grip tightened on her hand. "You were a victim, Rachel. We all were. You can be that for the rest of your life, let it define you or not. I don't think anyone who has met you since, thinks that of you." Michelle looked down at Jason. "I doubt he does either."

"No, I'm the abused princess he rescued." Rachel's anger surprised even her. "The asshole thinks I'm his little sister who needs to be protected. It's why I think he came here like he did. Didn't want Pro and I to have to sully ourselves."

Michelle smiled; the girl was in love. If Jason woke up and lived, he wouldn't stand a chance in the face of this young woman. A part of her was saddened by that thought. She didn't think this world would offer a man like Jason much peace, and Rachel deserved some peace. They all had that problem, she guessed.

"I'm guessing he feels a little differently about you than he does Pro. Maybe he hasn't admitted that to himself, but he's a guy. They're slow and can be, oh so very stupid. He wakes up, you tell him how you feel. He'll come around."

*

Antarctica
Dr. Yefrem Ilyaevich Mandel, lately of the Russian Academy of Science, tried to not let the cold bother him.

This was hard to do; he'd shed twenty kilos of body weight in the last six months. Still, he was Russian. They had a reputation to think of. The scientist in him knew there was very little insulation left in his body for his internal organs. The layers of clothing didn't seem to help, nor did the heater in the cab of the ancient Ugaz snow crawler. That said, it was something; a source of heat he didn't want to leave.

It was the end of autumn in the Antarctic, and the temperature inside the dilapidated, originally Soviet, snow crawler was a relative balmy two degrees Celsius. Outside the cab's interior, amidst the blowing snow, it was negative twenty if the thermometer on the dash was to be believed.

"Sir...? We've arrived."

He jerked himself upright in the seat. Had he fallen asleep again? His body was starving. They all existed in that gray muted world between life and death, their bodies striving to conserve enough energy to keep them alive, even as the process cannibalized the host.

"Pavel Eduardovich," he looked over at his driver, amazed at the strength the man exuded. Pavel had lost as much weight as any of them, more perhaps, as his body had started with more muscle mass. "Whatever occurs here, I wish to thank you. We would not have survived this long without you."

Pavel's gray eyes just stared out the window looking for some sign of the Americans they'd come to meet. What had nearly killed them all seemed to have given Pavel some source of inner strength. As if with the loss of everything, everyone they had known, Pavel had somehow been granted something extra.

Pavel just nodded once, slowly in recognition that he heard the words. The soldier pulled out the sidearm from his holster and shoved it into his pocket.

"Surely, they wouldn't come for us if they meant us harm, Pavel." He carried his own gun, at the younger man's insistence in his own holster. "They could have just ignored our radio broadcast, same result."

"The gun is not for them, Doctor."

Ahh, of course. If the American's plan to leave this frozen tomb had fallen through, he'd probably do the same or ask Pavel to do it. The soldier had been up to that particular task several times already.

"Quite right," he agreed. That was just good planning. "We Russians are nothing if not planners."

Almost an hour later, lights cut through the blowing snow. People always assumed it snowed a lot in the Antarctic. In fact, it was the driest of all the continents. The wind though, was a near constant. Picking up and blowing snow and ice crystals that had fallen last year, a century ago, or a thousand years ago. The Antarctic preserved everything. The bodies they'd buried behind their complex were in graves Pavel had blasted out of the ice. If the Americans couldn't get them away from this place, their bodies would be here for all time.

He glanced at Pavel, and internally swelled with pride as he saw the man's eyelids shut in peace. Even Pavel, it seemed, had his limits.

"Surprised that thing got them here, Sir." Antwan Sikes, drawled. They could see the ancient tiny snow crawler and pulled around next to it. The treads of their massive, RV sized-crawler were level with the windows of the Russian museum piece.

"Vodka, kerosene, and steel," he answered. The Russians had survived Hitler and communism. They'd have found a way.

Colonel Andrew 'Drew' Skirjanek unzipped his parka and pulled off his gloves and full-face mask once they had the two Russians inside their vehicle. The exertion had tasked him. Chief Petty Officer Cruz had fallen between the tracks of the two machines in exhaustion. They were weak and hungry. Looking at the two Russians, though, at their skeletal features, he felt guilty. Why the hell had they waited so long to contact him?

"You said there were eleven of you," he asked them both. He split the wrapping open on a survival bar, otherwise known as what would have served him tomorrow for breakfast, lunch and dinner. He snapped it in half and held the two pieces out.

The Russian scientist had been a big man, he could tell. Too much spare, almost translucent skin hung loosely on the man's cheek bones. He reached for the bar with a nod of his head.

"Spasibo."

Shit, it had been a long time since his college Russian classes at West Point.

He pointed at both them, noting the other Russian, clearly a soldier, just staring at his half of the survival bar.

"Vso?"

"We may speak English," the scientist said with a voice he recognized immediately from the radio. "The others are several miles back. Awaiting... our word."

"Of course," he accepted that. If there was anything as prominent as Russian strength, it was their crazy as a shit-house rat paranoia.

"I'm Colonel Skirjanek," he held out his hand. "I was the one on the radio. Our submarine is on its way in to pick us up. The rest of my people are already at the extraction point."

He slowly, very slowly withdrew his sidearm, holding it by the barrel and handed it over to the other Russian who had yet to say a word.

"We either trust each other, or you shoot me now."

The Russian soldier just eyed the gun without reaching for it. The soldier nodded to himself and pulled a hand out of his parka, patting his own pocket.

"Trust," the man said.

Cruz walked back into the passenger deck of the crawler from the cab, stopping when he saw the gun being held out by his Colonel.

"We copacetic, Sir?"

"We are," he holstered the gun.

"Bunch of Russian on the radio," Cruz held out the headset to him.

He took it and passed it to the Russian soldier.

The man listened for a moment. What color remained in his face seemed to fade away.

The soldier handed the headset back and turned to the scientist. He gathered the scientist was in charge. Someone at their base had maintained some semblance of command. That spoke volumes in his book. It hadn't been easy at McMurdo; he doubted if the story at the Russian's Vostok base had been any better.

He listened in on the conversation and was able to pick up on something about the 'mashina.' The vehicle holding the other Russians was dead, or out of fuel.

"Our other people, their snow machine has stopped functioning. Bad fuel they think."

He knew that story, they'd lost two of their three generators for the same reason.

"Ok, we go to them." He nodded at Cruz, who turned and walked back into the cab. He stopped at the narrow passageway.

"Where we headed?"

"I will," the Russian soldier struggled to stand. "I will lead you."

He watched his petty officer wave the man forward. When both men were out of earshot, the scientist leaned forward.

"Pavel Eduardovich has kept us alive; he is nearly used up."

Aren't we all?

*

They were gathered in the officers' ward room of the United States Navy's SSN *Boise*. The LA Class nuclear powered attack submarine was the only one remaining of the three that had been handed this mission. Captain Shelby Naylor had a full beard, as did most of his men, what was left of them. Gathered tightly around the table was the Russian scientist Dr. Yefrem Ilyaevich Mandel, the Spetsnaz Sergeant Pavel Eduarovich, Captain Naylor, and his XO. His third one. The first had shot himself. The second one had disappeared off the deck of the sub during a fishing evolution; no one assumed it had been an accident. The current XO, was Hoyt Sweet, he'd started the cruise as Chief of the Boat.

"Colonel, I know the plan was three boats, but the Missouri suffered some sort of accident." Captain Naylor addressed him directly. Dr. Mandel translated some of the harder to grasp briefing to his colleague Pavel.

"We were three miles astern of her, we could hear gunfire before their pump plant went tits up. I think they had some of the same issues we've had. They just lost control. You take the end of the world as you know it, add in hunger, and the fact you're trapped in a titanium cigar with the only other people you know who... who are left alive?"

"I understand," he glanced at the Russians. "We've both had similar... incidents. At least we had fresh air."

"I started with a hundred and four people, Captain." Skirjanek relayed with zero pride. "Volunteers, who knew what they were signing up for. I've got 37 left. The Russians have eleven people left, out of fifty-something. I'd say you're to be commended for still being operational."

Captain Naylor just stared at the table before looking up at Dr. Mandel.

"Doctor, I realize the promise our President made to you and your people, to get you back to your homeland. We won't make it. Our fresh water system, systems rather, are shot. We're picking up salt water inside our coolant loops."

"Corrosion?" the doctor asked.

"Yes, you understand, then?"

"I was not always a researcher, Captain. My first degree was in mechanical engineering. I served on our Kirov cruiser in my youth... in the reactor plant."

"I don't understand." Skirjanek, had been listening to the Captain, wondering how the Russians were going to react to this news.

"It's a matter of time, Colonel," Dr. Mandel said, turning to him. "The reactor's coolant is a closed system, or should be. If there is salt water making its way into the loop, the ship will lose its ability to cool the reactor."

Captain Naylor just nodded in sullen agreement at the Russian's explanation.

"So how long do we have?" He looked down at his plate, the remnants of a fish and boiled seaweed meal. The sub crew had been living off it for months. To him and the rest of their new passengers it was a smorgasbord of caloric delight.

"We've been underway since your retrieval. Beelining north, we're about a hundred fifty miles south east of Buenos Ares. If she holds together, at this reduced speed, ten days should put us in US waters. You have to understand; this boat wasn't close to new when this shit storm started. We were on our way to Bremerton for a major refit, when the Suck hit."

"The Suck?" Pavel puzzled at the word.

"We monitored radio and Sat TV as everyone succumbed to the virus," the XO Hoyt sweet explained. "The Suck... somehow it was the name that stuck."

"We'll get in close to the seaboard around Cuba," Captain Naylor continued after a moment. "The Florida straits. We'll know whether or not it's burned itself out before you go ashore."

"Before *we* go ashore, Captain," he said it as firmly as he could. The Captain just stared back at him.

Naylor scratched his beard for a moment. "We can't just pull up and turn the reactor off, Colonel. Doesn't work that way. I'll stay aboard, scram the reactor and scuttle the boat in deep water. It's the right thing to do."

He didn't see any doubt in the Captain's face. The man had clearly given this a lot of thought.

"Fine, that sounds like a plan. But you won't do that until we can secure a ship to follow you out, and retrieve you and any crew you'll need to scuttle her. Am I understood?"

"If the virus doesn't kill us." Captain Naylor answered with a nod, after a long moment wherein he may or may not have accepted the order. The Captain stood up slowly and nodded again. "Yes, sir."

They all watched the man walk out into the corridor and gently pull the accordion curtain back in to place.

"That man deserves to be saved," the XO whispered. "We owe him everything."

"As do we." Dr. Mandel nodded in agreement.

He turned to the XO. "Can we make Norfolk?"

The man just shrugged, used to dealing with things he had no control over. "Those are the orders." Sweet tapped the table with his knuckles. "If she starts coming unglued before then, we'll run to the nearest harbor and procure a ship. We'll get you to Virginia if we have to sail there."

"If we don't become ill," Pavel added the obvious.

With each passing day, he got a little stronger. They all did, even Dr. Mandel was looking healthier. The time on the deck of the submarine, in the increasing sunshine as they moved farther north, had as much to do with the improvement in their health as did the actual food. The submarine would pulse its powerful active sonar when the lookouts spotted a school of fish. The crew only had to land the floating fish with jury rigged nets mounted to the end of long sections of PVC pipe. The steady diet of fish and seaweed was already getting old. Compared to the ever-decreasing squares of survival bars he and his people had been surviving on, he didn't dare complain, even to himself. The sub's crew had been on this diet for close to five months, and it was just one of the things driving the submariners squirrely.

Captain Naylor had a crew of 122 when they'd got word of this literal last-ditch mission. They'd already been at sea for three weeks, with another two months of stores on board. By the time they'd rescued them off the ice shelf, the sub crew was down to fifty-one people, and they'd been on a fish diet for months. Supplemented by a small herb garden they managed to grow in the forward torpedo room, they were as fat and carb starved as the people they'd rescued.

With the addition of his 37 people, and the eleven Russians, both groups roughly half female, there was another growing problem that so far Captain Naylor had kept a lid on. He enforced a strict non-fraternization policy, for the newcomers as well as maintaining the policy for his existing female contingent which had survived the suicide epidemic much better than the male portion of his original crew.

He'd seen the same thing at McMurdo. It was clear the women dealt with the changing reality of an empty world better than the men did. He couldn't guess at the reason, and knew they didn't matter. No doubt, some sociologist or psychology wonk could have had a field day with the data. There wasn't anyone alive that would have given half a shit at what the report said.

All told, they had - *he had;* he corrected himself, 99 people as of this morning. Thirty-seven women, most of them scientists, climatologists or part of the original sub crew. Outside the Boise's crew, the military contingent of the joint US-Russian force had twenty-five personnel he had some confidence in as trigger pullers. He had no doubt they'd be needed, no matter how many survivors were out there. If they lived, he reminded himself. They all knew they could already be in the process of dying.

He was on the deck of the submarine, which was riding high in relatively calm waters. He stood next to the boat's sail, his bare chest and face soaking up the heat and rays of a Caribbean sun. He was looking off to starboard at the green, going to brown southwest coast of Cuba. Gentle rolling hills climbed up behind the rocky beach and dropped off to an unseen valley beyond. They were about a hundred miles south of the northwestern tip of Cuba and Havana Bay. They'd seen a solitary old man, alone in a boat the evening before, fishing. In one of those strange post-apocalyptic events, the fisherman had just waved at them and continued working his outrigged poles. Just a submarine going by at the end of the world, nothing to see here.

The excited shouts from the lookouts surprised him. Nothing seemed to get a rise out of the crew. It was as if any of the crew who were prone to emotion, any emotion - excitement, worry, or depression - were gone. That was wrong, he knew. They were all depressed. How could they not be? We've been getting closer and closer to the shore. People are waiting to get sick. With the incubation period as long as two weeks, we could all be dead right now, and just not know it.

There were several competing shouts but one word seared itself into his awareness.

Cows!

His mouth watered immediately at the thought of red, fatty meat. It was a toss-up, what his body craved more. Red meat or some carbs; he figured he'd kill for a potato just as quickly as he would a steak. The plan was to use Cuba to expose themselves to what may be still out there. They'd originally planned to pull into Havana and sit for a few days, and forage if the security environment allowed for it. Right now, he was looking at the area the lookouts were pointing at and he saw a small cove that looked like they could put the inflatables into. It was less than a mile from where a small herd of cattle grazed.

They'd spent three nights above the beach. With a watch crew in the reactor room, Captain Naylor had made certain everyone got time ashore. It had done wonders for everyone. He'd even seen Naylor crack a smile that morning, before the Captain seemed to remember something, the pain they *all* felt, or maybe something more private; it had disappeared just as quickly.

It was during the third night, when Pavel Eduardovich came to him. He'd been waiting for this, knew it had to happen sooner or later. He was sitting alone on a rock near a small fire, when he noticed the faceless form of the Russian Spetsnaz soldier approach, backlit by another larger fire farther down the beach.

"Not sick yet?"

The Russian laughed in response. "Maybe not, maybe yes. Do any of us know?"

No, they didn't. Not yet. But they would soon. A significant part of him wondered if it would be easier if the virus was still active. One of their foraging parties had come in contact with the rotting dead, you couldn't pick over the remains of civilization and avoid it. If the virus was still out there and live, they had it now.

"Not yet," he shook his head.

"The Capitan," the Russian pointed off shore, at the navigation lights of the *Boise*. "Still plans to sink ship, yes?"

"He does." *And I hope he's not planning on going down with it.*

"I worry, he will..." the Russian made a motion with his hands of the ship sinking, "go with his ship."

"Me too." He understood his own worry, he needed Naylor desperately. The man was a leader, if more than a little run down. What surprised him, was the fact the Russian seemed concerned.

Pavel just stared into the fire in silence for a long moment before shifting his balance atop his own rock.

"My mission in Antarctica was to destroy your base in the event of big war." Pavel shaped a mushroom cloud with his hands and grinned.

He hadn't figured the Spetsnaz soldier moonlighted as a climatologist – any more than he had.

"Now, I have no country." Pavel shrugged before looking up at him. "Neither of us do. Yet you still have mission, yes?"

"I do." He paused not out of concern over national security but because he knew it was as insane on the surface as it was in the details.

"I'm supposed to help people, the survivors, rebuild. There are supplies I can access." *If the vault's power system was still working, if his authentication code functioned, if the top-secret larder hadn't been found and raided by another survivor who knew about it, and if the virus didn't kill them first.*

"The plan was to rebuild after a nuclear exchange with you guys or the Chinese. For the people that survived, to start over. But this? There may not be enough people left to even try."

"This plan? Was it for survivors? Or for only Americans?" Pavel asked.

"It was our plan," he said as straight forward as he could. "It's a left over from the cold-war, based on the chance of war between the US and the old Soviet Union. There has been someone like me at McMurdo since the Cuban Missile Crisis. The plan hadn't been updated to reflect this." He waved his hands around him taking in the fire on the beaches and the quiet of a dead world.

"You guys," he pointed a knuckle at the Russian, "had something similar."

"Da," Pavel nodded in agreement. "I had satellite communication with our... how do you say? Emergency facility, buried deep in Ural mountain as virus was active. They reported that they had infected inside, and then within days... nothing more."

He thought back to his last official communication with somebody in the Strategic Air Command, living underground somewhere in the Midwest. The Airforce General had been sick, most of his people already dead. Two days later, there had been no answer.

"I'm updating the plan. I'm going to try and help everyone, all survivors. I meant what I said before we got on the sub. We'll find a way to get you home, if we can."

"Our people are home," Pavel said shrugging, laughing a little to himself.

"There is no Russia," the Russian continued after a moment. "There is no China, no United States. There is only this planet." Pavel shaped a globe in the air with his hands. "Our people not concerned about returning home to empty Russia. They have spoken to me, they more worry about treated well here, equal, yes?"

"Somehow, I'm in charge of this goat rodeo, at least as soon as we get off the damned submarine. I can guarantee you'll be treated equally. I agree, there are no more flags, just people." Precious few at that.

He reached across the fire, holding out his hand. "I could very much use your help. It would be most welcome." He held out his hand.

Pavel nodded once to himself and shook it in a strong grip. "Vso Poryadki"

"What's that?"

"It means, all is well." Pavel looked at him with a grin. "What means... goat rodeo?"

He did his best to explain and at some point, the Russian nodded with a smile.

"We have this saying as well, we say "Eta bardok.""

"Bardok?"

"Something that is... big mess, confusing. It is organized like Turkish whorehouse, a Bardok."

He had to laugh at that. "Yeah, that works. This isn't going to be easy."

"Do not worry," Pavel got up and stretched, sporting a rare smile. "Dr. Mandel thinks there is even chance we will all be dead in a week."

*

Jason was dreaming and he knew it. He knew it was Sam on the other side of eyelids that wouldn't open. She was holding his hand, squeezing it, in response to his own grip that seemed so weak and tired. He could hear her, but the echo of her voice reached him through a long tunnel. He just had to reach the voice, then everything would be ok.

"You can't quit, we all need you... I need you."

He focused on that voice like it was a lifeline. Sam would bring him home.

They need you, Jason. You and Rachel need each other. Sam's voice, rang clear in his head, standing out in contrast to the other. *I'm gone Jason, you need to live. I want you to live.*

You're not gone, he thought. I can hear you.

Not anymore, Jason. You saved them. They still need you. I'm in a better place.

Sam? Sam! Don't go! You can't leave me. He was screaming without a mouth. It scared him to the point he panicked and coughed. He felt pain flash through his body in more places than he imagined he had.

The hand holding his, squeezed harder and something slapped him. His eyes snapped open, a movement he heard, rather than felt. Like the seals of a long-shut freezer door cracking open. Light blinded him and he could see the shape of a face, Sam's face, hovering over him. Except it was changing. The face smiled down at him.

You need her, Sam's voice again, farther away.

The face blurred as his brain filtered out the bright light and it resolved into Rachel's. She had tears rolling down both cheeks.

407

"You ever do something like that again, I'll kill you myself."

He realized it was Rachel holding his hand. He looked at her, for perhaps the first time. Sam's words still echoing in his head. He did his best to nod and found he needed to settle for what felt like a smile and giving her hand a gentle squeeze.

He wasn't going anywhere.

***

I hope you've enjoyed the first book of this series. There is more to come...

I hope you hang in there with me. As always, you can sign up for my newsletter (not a newsletter - yet) on my website; www.smanderson-author.com. Sign – up and drop me a line, I enjoy corresponding with my readers. Several of you have had some input into this story, and for that I thank you. At any rate, you can stay up to date on my progress and get alerted when there is a new book out in this series or the *"The Eden Chronicles."*

Your review on Amazon, or on whichever portal you utilized to purchase the book would be very much appreciated. You can also review it on Goodreads, and follow me on Facebook at www.facebook.com/SMAndersonauthor/ .

I sat out writing this book with the idea that an event like the virus, a pandemic that kills almost everyone, would leave the survivors scarred. All of them. The good people would be just small matters of degree "better" than the bad people. No one would be afforded the luxury of ideals, and some attempts of hanging on to civilization would get very dark, very quickly. I know where this story is going from here, and I think it's safe to say Jason, Rachel, Pro and now Colonel Skirjanek and his contingent have no idea just how dark humanity can get – nor how much they are needed.

To all those readers that have been patiently waiting for Book III of the Eden Chronicle, please understand I had this story done, around the time I put out "A Bright Shore." I'm currently working to finish off Book III of the Eden Chronicles.

Best regards, S.M. Anderson

Made in United States
Orlando, FL
03 November 2023

38564722R00245